PRAISE FOR
VERNON F. GLENN'S BOOKS

"Glenn provides readers with a story filled with twists and changes, always powered by candid, revealing characters who interact in surprising ways."
—MIDWEST BOOK REVIEW

"Fans of crime and legal thrillers will savor this novel's eccentric Southern flavor and an enticing big-score plot."
—BOOKLIFE

"A lyrical Southern tale of rippling effects."
—KIRKUS REVIEWS

"Glenn writes real lawyers, courtrooms and secret settlement conferences better than anyone in the business."
—LAURIE HUTCHINS, NORTH CAROLINA DISTRICT COURT JUDGE

"Who knew plaintiff law could be so much fun? Watch Eddie Terrell and his merry team win cases with characteristically jaw-dropping methods. An insider's view of a most unorthodox law practice, Slim and None delivers adventure, laughter and tears."
—MORETON NEAL, AUTHOR OF
Remembering Bill Neal: Favorite Recipes from a Life in Cooking

SLIM

AND

NONE

Book Three in the Eddie Terrell Trilogy

E. VERNON F. GLENN

Slim and None
Copyright © 2023 by E. Vernon F. Glenn

All rights reserved. No part of this book may be reproduced or transmitted in any form or by any means without written permission of the author.

ISBN: 978-1-7329066-4-8 (paperback)
ISBN: 978-1-7329066-5-5 (hardback)
ISBN: 978-1-7329066-6-2 (large print)

Published by:

COOPER
RIVER
BOOKS

ALSO BY E. VERNON F. GLENN

Friday Calls:
Book One in the Eddie Terrell Trilogy

You Have Your Way:
Book Two in the Eddie Terrell Trilogy

You Never Know Who Your Angels Are
(children's book, illustrated by Cheryl Ann Lipstreau)

Where Did Everyone Go?
(poetry)

To my wonderful children—
C.C, Doug, and Rory and their wonderful mother, Andrea.

Also to my dear and good friends, Heather and Megan,
who have helped me so much along the way and
in doing so, have allowed me to help them.

CONTENTS

"Lawyers, I suppose,
were children once."

*(Inscription upon the statue of a child
in the Inner Temple Garden in London)*

—Jane Gardam,
author of *Old Filth (Old Filth Trilogy)* First Volume

PREFACE

EDDIE WAS VISITING with his ninety-six year-old mother and his brother had joined them for the Q&A gabfest. They sat in her bedroom, her eyes riveted to yet another all-silvered and glammed-up Turner Classic Movie as she flung yet another random, "Now, let me ask you this..." and another "Why did you do that..." at them. The gigantic flat screen flickered behind her boys with its closed captioning partially reflected on the lenses of her glasses.

Momma called for her helper wanting her eye medicine from the CVS drug store down the street. She always did so in the tone of a Parris Island marine drill sergeant. She told the patient-as-Job lady to hurry as she didn't want to go blind any faster than was necessary. Always a bit more drama was tossed into the pot.

They were used to all the distraction. It had been going on forever since beyond forever.

Momma was and always had been the poster child for adult ADHD though she had no idea what that was and even if she did, would have denied any semblance of such as pertinent to her person. To her, such must surely be a form of mental weakness or illness and there was to be none of that in her family.

After her composite review of who was recently dead, who was on the verge of the big dirt nap, who was traveling where, who had seen who and a flash around the globe inquiry and comment as to national and world affairs and all the trashy politicians and celebrities thrown in for good measure, her soliloquy cum sermonette wrapped up with her stern admonition as to "save your money" and "watch out for your drinking."

Her boys agreed as always to follow her precepts as they mentally demurred. They stood to go.

"You know, I've got a Zoom meeting at 4:00 p.m. I need to go to the bank before that happens." Eddie mindlessly stuck his hands in his pockets.

"Bank? Bank! Eddie, what are you going to do at the bank?!" There was a detached urgency to her question.

The brothers looked curiously at one another. Eddie paused and then replied, "Well, Momma, I want to get a sandwich and a milkshake before my meeting."

She peered at him.

"Well, then, I just don't get out enough anymore. I had no idea they offered such things as that these days. It's all marketing, I suppose. Let me ask you this. Is the milkshake any good?"

"I dunno. Just heard about it. Want me to bring you one?"

The brothers winked at one another.

"No, my stomach's been a little upset lately. Gassy, well, you know but really you don't...you go on and try it out and tell me about it tomorrow. Maybe tomorrow..."

The volume was turned back up to crescendo, the signal that they were dismissed and the audience was concluded. Her boys hustled down the hall, laughing quietly as they went.

"Wheels coming off?"

"Naw, not yet. She just fires away with whatever is rolling around in that scattered noggin of hers. Same as always. Same as always."

As their daddy used to say, "Don't worry. You too, like the cheese, will one day be old."

CHAPTER ONE

THINGS THAT GO BUMP IN THE NIGHT

Late March, Saturday Morning

EDDIE WAS DRENCHED in a cold sweat, not sure where he was. It was completely dead black dark. He lay stone still in his wet sheets as a paralytic might. He surmised he was in a spacious bed, the contours of which he dared not reach for. He felt he must not move. His mind was frozen in a great, overwhelming fear. He was very frightened and he did not know why.

Slowly, over what period of time he really could not tell, his mind engaged in a loosening of the unseen terror that had seized him. His spectral companion lingered near but seemed to permit him to loosen his limbs and mind enough to gingerly begin a broader consideration of consciousness. He still stayed virtually motionless.

Here he was, sixty-three-years old, a powerful, effective and feared litigator, and scared to death like a little child in a nightmare with unseen monsters.

All was quiet until a muffled, lurching hum began and cold air blew over him.

He now knew where he was. He was a guest at the wonderful Willcox Hotel in Aiken lodging in the luxurious Churchill Suite thanks to his fine friend, the gorgeous Tina McGillivray, long striding and long-time general manager of the elegant, comfortable nineteenth-century dowager queen. She had been looking after him for years and the flash of that memory brought comfort to him. Cases and trials had brought him here over the years and that was still the heart of the matter.

Carefully he sought the thick down comforter that he recalled being high-folded at the foot of the bed. Slowly he grasped it and drew it up to his neck.

He settled and leveled his breathing. He could feel his heart pulsing but slowing and he began to warm. He could open his eyes now which had been closed, squeezed tight in the face of this sudden trepidation. He was calmer now. He began an ordering of the past days when his travels had begun. Eddie assumed by mind marching backwards and then forward he could examine his fear and come to some understanding of it. What in the hell was going on?

Eddie had had a dream, a very vivid one. It came back to him now and he worked hard to remember its particulars. It was deep into summertime and it was hot in the Sandhills. In his nocturnal subconscious he had long strolled over to the lovely tree-draped Boundary Lane and then swung onto a dirt road that took him to the training track where a great amount of equine history had been made. There were a couple of horses getting in some work across the way. It truly was a bucolic setting.

The skies were darkening, gray and then charcoal black. Blooming cumulonimbus clouds towered up faster and faster, spiraling and twist-ing, an aerial Rorschach test. Thunder rumbled. Lightning cracked. Eddie could feel the electricity in the air. He shivered, felt the hair on his neck and arms rise. The wind came up, the air cooled quickly, and big drops of rain spattered down.

Eddie looked for shelter. The storm was getting stronger. It would be a quick but intense one.

He had already passed a large red boarding stable which he knew to be owned by a friend of Tina's, a gal named Gina, that seemed to be empty. He doubled back and began to jog to it. He allowed himself through the gate and looked around and saw no one. He walked down the stalls and saw a bicycle leaning against the boards.

He looked over the slightly open half door. The stall had been well mucked and was clean with fresh hay spread thick.

Nested in the hay was a long-legged beautiful blond girl, all in white, short shorts and tight top and tennis shoes. She was tall and well-sculpted.

It was as though she had just fallen into the barn from a country club tennis match. For a moment, ridiculously, Eddie looked about for her tennis racquet. Seeing none, he studied her. And then he leaned down and gently touched her shoulder.

She rustled, rolled over and faced him, reached out and pulled him close to her.

He did not resist. He quietly asked, "Are you okay?"

"I will be in just a minute. I've been waiting for you. Come here. I'm Blaze. Take your pants off. Oh, by the way, what's your name?" She giggled.

"Oh, okay. My name is Eddie."

"Come to me, Eddie, come into me."

Eddie inhaled deeply. The storm was hard hailing the tin roof and the wind was whipping. He did and she wriggled expertly out of her shorts. There was no thong, no nothing, just her. He was tumescent, swollen as the storm. He knew what was going to happen. She tugged her top off and pulled him down on top of her and the slow grind of fine, surging coupling began.

There was an explosion of crackling, ripping thunder just overhead.

And she disappeared. It all disappeared. And the great fear and confusion came over him. He tried to go back, with all his strength and concentration tried to go back but she and all of it were but a dispersing vapor.

And Eddie lay in his sweat and disappointment, tented in the comforter, and began to awaken, began to be frightened, began to try and figure it all out.

The telephone at his bedside began to ring. The bedside clock said it was 7:30. A bright sun slatted in uniform slices through the shutters.

He cleared his throat and picked up the receiver.

"Hello?"

"Hey, stranger. Zero dark thirty here. Coffee? Did I misapprehend our klatch I know we talked about last night? I didn't keep you up too late last night, did I?" He could hear the soft smirk in her voice.

He reoriented quickly. He did not want to let her down.

"Tina. Hey. No. No. Just a little on the slow side this morning. Sure, give me five. Brush teeth, that pants thing too, you know."

She laughed. She knew he was on the waking up dummy train. His voice was thick, dry and husky.

"Absolutely. I'll be back down at the end of the hall waiting for you. Now go get ungroggy. Bye."

Her voice cheered him. He turned on a light, sat up on the edge of the big bed, wobbly stood and went to attend to his ablutions.

They met in the breakfast room. Good coffee, juice, a little fruit. He loved the Willcox. It was handsome, traditional and comfortably appointed with a lobby full of comfortable chairs and couches and wonderful fireplaces. A throwback, he had stayed there many times over the years. The Willy had great food and a bar where he loved to perch and survey. He would drink it in and too, drink it in. He had worked many cases in Aiken and its environs and had made a lot of money with them, and it was fair to say that he felt the Willcox was his serious good luck charm.

The exterior of the place was an architectural mess that worked perfectly. Painted uniformly blazing white, it was more than three stories high and soared over intimate parking and trees everywhere. The whole place was intimate.

Eddie recalled many, many years ago when he'd read the hotel's historical sheet on the place that its style was a combination of Colonial and Second Empire, the latter once being pungently described by the great French novelist, playwright and journalist Emile Zola (also of "*J'Accuse!*" fame during the nasty, ugly Dreyfus affair) as "...the opulent bastard child of all the styles..."

They had gone for dinner and drinks the night before at a cozy steakhouse a few blocks away. Sometimes it was good to get out of the view of inquisitive eyes. After all, good employees did pay attention.

Eddie had had a cranky, grumpy, disappointing stretch over the last three months and he was glad to visit with Tina about it.

They leaned in and talked about work and family and recent frustrations, problems and complaints and solutions and the ever-uncertain future of it all. Over the years she had become a dear friend and they trusted one another with just about every secret.

Tina was a very good-looking girl. Soft raven hair, always pulled back tight into a back ponytail, great bones, a commanding elegance to her. She was very smart, had an expansive sense of humor, was self-effacing, and when she came down those lovely halls, you knew she was coming.

She was a fine horsewoman with a nimble mind and she was very discreet. In that business, you had to be or you wouldn't last long, especially in one of the best destinations in the South. Eddie liked her a lot and admired her so very much too. A pro's pro.

Eddie was on the last leg of his travels that week. He had come in that afternoon from Sylvester, Georgia, to have a visit with some very special clients from a few years back. Eddie had grown close to them, was very fond of them and had fought like the devil for them.

The husband and father had been stupidly mismanaged by some very poorly trained employees—interpretation: really not trained at all. The fine, in good shape, handsome man, a brilliant nuclear engineer had collapsed while playing racquetball and the health club folks had called 911 and brought an AED to his side but then astonishingly never used it. Four of them just stood there and gaped at him while his brain's oxygen depleted. EMS arrived. They instantly applied the AED but the clock was fast running down and they got no response. Adrenaline was injected into his heart and they applied the AED again. They got a mild pulse back up and rushed him to the hospital.

It was too late. He was brain dead. On the third day his family had him unplugged.

During the course of the case, experts from Emory testified that it was the delay that killed the gentleman. Ultimately the case settled. And over the course of almost two years, Eddie had gotten to know the family. They were fine people and had been good to work with. They mourned and they moved ahead. They were realists. They were interesting people. He had spent a couple of hours with them the day before in the comfortable lobby of the Willcox, having drinks and just visiting. Over the years, Eddie had stayed in touch with a lot of his folks.

Eddie padded down the back stairs and found Tina sitting, reading her newspaper with a large cup of coffee. He bussed her cheek and she got up to face him.

She scanned him quickly. "Eddie, what's wrong? What in the world...? Your face is not your face. You are so drawn in. What's going on? Sit down. Let me get your coffee."

He lamely, randomly tried to wave her off but without hesitation sat heavily down at the table.

"Tina, I have just had a very strange dream and then a scare after it, a big scare that is still with me. I'll tell you about it. I want to tell you about it."

She watched him carefully as the Keurig dribbled out his cup.

"You like it black, right?"

He nodded. She saw that his eyes were more blank than not and were darting.

She set the cup before him and sat facing him.

"Now, my friend, you look absolutely addled. I know we talked about lots of things last night—things that were troubling you but you didn't have this kind of paint on. Uhm. Tell me about this dream, the after, whatever... how can I help you? I'm so sorry you are in this obviously very beyond unhappy way."

And, slowly, he pieced it out for her. She was truly attentive, never questioning or interrupting.

Once he had described the looming fear and then full stopped, she quietly said, "Eddie, the dream means little, I think. Guys are guys and you surely are a guy and your libido is surely healthy. But, to me, the following fright and fear seems very intense, certainly real to you and I can feel it coming off of you too."

Eddie nodded and said, "Go on. Please, go on, Tina."

She could see he was hoping for the solace of some sort of solution or explanation.

"Yes, well, Eddie, I have known you for a long time now and never before seen or sensed anything like this, not from you, not from anyone. This seems almost mystical to me. Certainly mysterious. I have no words of wisdom to offer other than I want you safe. I hope this sensation passes soon. I know from our visit last night, you are wrapping up a many-day roundabout. Where are you heading next?"

"Headed back to Winston-Salem in just a little bit."

"Good. I expect that will help whatever this is. I hope and trust your friend Mikey will be waiting for you."

He whispered out a firm, "Yes, yes."

She stood up, pursed her lips, looked him over and bent down and kissed him on the cheek. He stood up and she hugged him tight.

"Please be careful. I mean it. I hate to say it but I'm worrying about you. You are one our most faithful and enjoyable. We want you safe and not just for mercenary reasons—though I note as you well know, you are a fun guest and a helluva fine tipper and, well, a profit center too!"

They smiled at one another. It lifted some of the gloom.

"Do you need help with your bags? I can have someone sent up whenever you say."

"No, no thank you. I'm fine. Traveling light. Will you please have someone email my bill?"

Tina shook her head and smiled again. "No, sir, not this this time around. This one's on the house. No protesting!"

Eddie hugged her again and said a quiet, "Thank you, Tina. You're as good as they come. Your company means a lot to me. The place is such a special place for me. It's been and you've been good to me and good for me too."

She could see his mood brighten.

"Now go on and get on home safely. And I can't recall when I've said this to any other guest over the past eighteen years, but how about call me when you are back in Winston to let me know you have gotten back alright?"

"I'm honored. I will. Thank you, dear. You are a dear girl, a dear friend. I am so grateful for you..." His voice tailed off and he quickly, almost abruptly, took his leave.

As Eddie went back down the hall to the stairs, she called to him.

"And don't be a stranger!"

He waved over his shoulder and called back. "Don't worry. I won't!"

He was in his car, moving along on the interstate. The sensation was still with him, just not so pronounced.

Eddie would in just a little while try to think back. His fear was still palpable and premonitory. It wasn't a vague wonder—something was definitely bad out there. He knew he had to get home as soon as he could.

CHAPTER TWO

BACK ON THE ROAD AGAIN
Late March, Monday Morning, the Week Before

HIS TRAVELS WERE designed to be a lazy loop to here or there. He did this from time to time. It was good for him to get out of the office and he did this regularly, at least once or twice a year, but after the struggles of the last months, it seemed to be a necessary and mandatory prescription to address what ailed him, what was ailing them all.

The previous quarter of the year had been aggravating, frustrating, and depressing for all of them, Mikey and Patty and Alph. Their sails felt becalmed and their minds were collectively in cages of lassitude. They did not know exactly when it started or who or what was the first infected, but they all had come down with it.

The travel was supposed to be a sort of relaxation, some time to be without all the work that had, most of the time, continued to grow unto them and to their benefit. They had become ridiculously successful, making money, and claiming victory after victory which also brought respect and a careful wariness from their oppositions. But, of course, there were bumps and dust-ups along the way. But this...this seemed to be different and had a pressing weight to it that had the sensation of long-term difficulty; this was not something to be just thrown off; it was going to have to be hard-wrestled away. Eddie got ready to go. It was now a necessary, hopefully mind-clearing effort.

He had explained his path and plan and its particulars to Mikey and Patty and Alph, told them he would be leaving on Monday and would return on Saturday.

Monday morning, first thing he chased Mikey happily about their house, and after some nice fireworks, gave her a big hug and a kiss.

Mikey chided him. "Why do you have to just up and go off for almost the whole week? I'll be lonely and bored. I know I can't go with you, dammit. Patty and Alph and I have so much to do. Can't you just go for a few days and then come right on back?" She made a grumpy face.

"Honey, that all sounds very nice and all and I really appreciate the sentiment, but I've set this schedule up to check out some case possibilities and there are some folks I need to catch up and visit with. I'll be back by Saturday afternoon and I promise we'll go out for a nice time, dinner, maybe a movie or something. Does that help? I hope it does."

She shrugged and made another face. "Eddie, sometimes I think you love the law more than me."

She put her hands on her hips and faced him with more than a little defiance.

He was amused by her casting couch appeal but played it straight in order to not annoy her. Eddie did not want to knock the edge off of the excellent fun of but only fifteen minutes before.

"Honey, let me tell you a quick story. It's a baseball story. It's about the great, Hall of Fame manager, Tommy Lasorda."

"This better be good." Mikey rolled her eyes but paid attention.

"Tommy's Dodgers had won a big game, had swept a series from their arch-rivals, the San Francisco Giants. Tommy took a bunch of his Dodger coaches and some sports writer buddies out on the town in LA to regale and celebrate after the game. It'd be fair to say that Tommy got home late where his wife, patient Jo, was sitting in the living room waiting for his return. Jo was, just by the way, from down the road in Greenville, South Carolina. And also just by the way, they were married for, get this, for seventy years!"

"Eddie, how about get to the point or you're gonna have seventy smacks on your head pretty soon!?"

"Yes, dear. Anyway, Tommy rolled in thick-tongued and wobbly and sat down on the couch next to her. Tommy loved telling this story. He was a legend and a damn fine baseball manager."

"Eddie!" Her voice flared.

"Okay. I'm getting there. I promise. Anyway, Jo looked at Tommy in silence for a few seconds. Tommy was watchfully waiting, tongue tied. 'Tommy, I'm glad you got the sweep and I know you needed to burn off some steam, but I swear, sometimes I think you love baseball more than me.' Tommy thought on that for a moment and then carefully replied, 'Well, Jo honey, sometimes that may be true, but I swear I always love you more than football or basketball.'"

"Jesus!" She laughed. "What am I gonna do with you? Hell, let's get on to bed."

"And Jo led dizzy Tommy up the stairs. End of parable, end of lesson." Eddie held his arms out, slightly genuflected and said, "Sometimes, as you well know, I am required to love the law and accept her difficult embrace no matter at what heights my love for you lies."

Mikey smiled, then laughed and shook her head. "Yeah, yeah, yeah, I remember. I get it. The law is a jealous mistress. Let's go on and get to the office, boy wonder. Sometimes I do wonder how in the hell I got into this one clown car parade and then again, I remember. Oh, brother." She winked at him and kissed his neck.

They headed off in separate cars, then met with everyone at the office, made sure work and case priorities were in order as they, all together and nicely focused, ran quickly through the black book of all cases. There were close to two hundred now, some difficult, some not so much, much value in one way or another to all of them. Some would have to be tried, but the great majority would settle, by way of mediation or at the court. As their reputation for success grew, they got lots of calls from citizens and often from other lawyers. They excelled at identifying winners, culling the herd.

Of course, there were some dogs, some losers in the accepted mix, but such designation was never apparent at the point of their initial retention and when that sort of negative evolution began on one or another, losses were cut, compromises sought and even sometimes they were able to turn dross into some gold. Their earned reputation was a helpful assist on this sort of matter too. There was no sense in poking the stick of claimed upper hand at a cunning veteran who had shown long ago how lethal he could be if matters got serious.

The great majority of them were going to end just fine with a good lick of sugar always forthcoming. It was just the way it was.

After a quick, early lunch of sandwiches and Coca-Colas, Eddie ordered the contents of his brief bags for the correct documents and materials and checked his overnight (this was a clothing comfortable run, just jeans and collared shirts, track shorts and T-shirts, no suits, ties or shiny lace-up lawyer kicks).

As is the wont of many courtroom lawyers, an obsessive component of the trial profession, he made sure he had at least eight (he was anal about this) legal pads and plenty of pens and markers. There was always a weird worry that he would run out of them. It just came with the territory.

It always made Eddie silently chuckle when he thought upon his ultimately finding the big dirt nap in the sky, the thought of those coming behind him to clean it all out, all the drawers and cabinets and closets and desks and bankers boxes and files...God knows how many pads and pencils and pens they would find. The number would surely be at least in the hundreds and few thousand. Ridiculous, wasteful, and essential.

And so he began his move to hit the road. First stop Charleston. He loved the city, its culture and history and food and music. He had enjoyed much success there and planned on replicating that sort of thing again. He figured, God willing and the creek don't rise, he was midway in his subjective third quarter and had plenty of space and time left yet to work with. He was thoughtful and contemplative.

As he was going out the door, Patty came up beside him and quietly spoke. "You're back Saturday, right?" Eddie nodded. "Good, rest up and be ready to think effectively on Monday. Mikey and I been putting our minds on something and we all need to kick it around and work on it. Okay?"

Eddie frowned. "Hmmmm...what is it? Is it bad? Alph know?"

"No, it's good, real good and we want to keep it that way before it starts heading to bad. Trust me. Please. Like you always have...and yes, Alph's been given the same request and instruction."

"Okay. Fair enough. I promise to come in the door on Monday with my head screwed on right."

"Good. Now go on and be safe."

He had been a general practice lawyer the first few years, always courtroom centric, and did everything—civil, criminal, wills and estates, domestic, bankruptcy, small claims, contract and real estate litigation and just about anything else that came along. If it could quickly be turned into some papers in a file, he would jump on it as would a duck on a June bug. Just getting into a courtroom, any courtroom enticed and excited him. They were true arenas of contest and pushed his adrenaline and mind up. So few people had such task-specific places to go, where the mind and the voice and the body language were the weapons of contest.

Then one day when he was just still a baby lawyer, he received in the mail a green paper stapled trifold solicitation to attend "The John Allen Appleman Trial School" at the University of Tennessee in Knoxville. It was a two-week course being taught by well-credentialed lawyers and judges at the empty law school there over spring break. The attendees would stay at the Holiday Inn on the river next door. It proclaimed an intensive and thorough immersion in tort practice. It was named for Mr. Appleman, now long gone but still a scion of tort and insurance practice. His multi-volume treatise on the same was still in broad use and grainy, long-aged recordings of his lectures were part of each day's teachings.

Eddie had no idea how he had gotten on the mailing list. It was another of those chance things, he supposed. He instantly wanted to attend and so he did and loved it. It was like drinking from a fire hose.

And when he returned to Winston-Salem, he was asked by a friend while they sat in the bleachers at Hanes Park at dusk, drinking cold beers, watching tennis matches. "Okay. You really liked it. So, what's next?"

"I want to become a big-time trial lawyer."

And that is when his quest truly began.

He loved to drive, enjoyed it so much. When alone, he could listen to audiobooks and music. It allowed him to think, to contemplate and he could and did make little notes along the way, tasks to get done, ideas for cases, appointments to be made. Sometimes a one-word exaggeratedly large jot or scribble on a pad, a signal reminder (over the years his handwriting, never good to begin with, had rotted to the scrawl of a punchy child). Sometimes a more lengthy ramble dictated into his phone, sometimes a cell call back to the office or to clients or opposing counsel or to expert witnesses or family and friends.

His car, a powerful BMW X5 could be punched up nicely, had plenty of room for hauling the tools of case work and in essence, was one of his adult playpens, a fine cocoon.

Winter had melted into a lovely, mild spring and the oncoming summer was on the horizon. Everything along the way was greening up brightly from the grays and browns of the cold, dreary months.

After a quick five-hour run, he had checked into the Planter's Inn right on the Market. He had cleaned up and then called his old lawyer friend, Truck Tinker. It was 5:30.

"Truck, me boy, it's your devoted agent and servant Eddie. I need to see you. Are you still at the office? I hope. Buy you a drink? Staying at the Planter's. We could slide over to the bar at Peninsula."

"Eddie, what brings you to town? Excellent news! I'll save my curiosity for when we visit. Will surely meet you there for a pop, maybe two..." He laughed and added, "Well, hell, it's Monday. Two would do it. Don't want to wander home under the influence of spirituous liquors. The missus would get cranky..."

"Hell, Truck, I promise if need be I'll give you a hall pass for Horty. I expect she'll be pleased that we've had a chance to gather at the river. How about in an hour, about 6:15? I'll be at the bar and will save you a seat at that shelf of fine liquors. That work?"

"Deal," said Truck. "See you in a bit."

They clicked off. Eddie kicked off his shoes, hopped on the bed and shuffled through some shiny magazines that adorned the room. At six, he was up and on his way downstairs. He made sure he had the envelope he had brought with him. This was always the fun part.

He found two seats at the long bar, mirrored, flanked by large urns of dazzling flowers, ordered a bourbon for himself and one for Truck and placed the envelope and the glass of brown in front of the stool next to him to secure it for Truck's arrival. He relaxed and in a few minutes Tinker pulled up next to him and hopped onto his seat and slapped him jovially on the back.

"Hey, you old dog! Good to see you! You got another case down this way? What's going on?"

"Not yet, but how about find me something along those lines, a good, messy bloody tort, maybe two somethings? You know how much I like coming this way."

Truck allowed that was a fine idea.

"You know, last time was pretty edgy and fun, don't you think?"

They were both grinning.

"Not only that but nicely lucrative too." Eddie took a long swallow from his short glass, nodded to the barkeep for another and tapped the envelope he had laid in front of Truck.

"Please take a look and accept with my great gratitude."

Truck looked sideways at Eddie, his head cocked.

"Go on. See what it is."

"Hmmmm…"

Truck picked up a nearby bar knife and edged the paper open and pulled its contents out and studied it. He looked at Eddie and then looked at his holding again.

He low-whistled. "Eddie! Damn! Eddie!" His voice was low and urgent. "I'm pretty sure I know what this is about but, Jesus! A hundred grand! Good God! This is nuts! Eddie, I can't…I just can't…"

Eddie waved him off with low laugh, "Oh, yes you can and you damn sure will. You were of enormous help to me in that case. You went along with me on my adventure to Thee Doll House. You became my shade and innocent cover at that dressed up titty bar, you became my key witness to expose their methodology of reeling the stupid fish in—you know, that old hymn about "liquor and women"—what a delicious combo platter of pay-off sin that was and of course, still is. You wrote it all down verbatim and as such allowed me to ram it up their asses at mediation.

"You were with me at the Patricia Manor having dinner, again making us look like two golfing rubes when that precocious young hustler, what was his name…yeah, Tommy Davis, like the old Dodger baseball player came over to us and with his coat and tie, Little Lord Fauntleroy, well-rehearsed marketing patter, handed us the keys to the kingdom against the Block House. You would have been the witness to all that, to the bullshit 'private club, my ass, come on.

"If I had just said all by my lonesome, 'Hey, y'all, here's what I got, A,B, C, X, Y, Z and so forth,' they'd just said, 'Where's your witness?'

"But I didn't have to suffer all the extra hoop-jumping because you were there and willing to be deposed, to give your sworn testimony which I know the thought of which made you nervous and I'm glad you didn't have to but, Jesus H. Christ, you were an enormous bomb down both their pants! Don't you see? You are serious value-added! Hell, you even came with us to the mediation and son, you do have credibility because you a nice guy, an attractive guy, an honorable guy and this kind of case is nowhere near what your practice sandbox looks like."

Truck had begun to pleasantly nod. "Well, I appreciate that and it was fun and interesting, but a hundred grand? I'm doubtful..."

Eddie could see that he wasn't protesting any longer; Truck's good manners were only kicking in. Eddie moved in to seal the deal.

"Truck, you will recall that after I made my presentations to opposing counsel and our mediator, I asked if you could be excused as we were getting down to the nitty-gritty of our negotiations and you had no active role there and Tom Wills said that would be fine and the others quickly assented and off you went. And after that, they all, individually and collectively, became my personal piñata and you were my whipping stick! It was, as they say, delicioso!

"So, have a big, stiff swallow. Here's a pen, endorse the check for deposit into your account, let's have a good visit and another rip and catch me up on Horty and your boys."

And he did and another page turned.

CHAPTER THREE

SOME DAYS ARE DIAMONDS, SOME DAYS ARE DUST

Late March, Tuesday

THE NEXT MORNING Eddie drove to Savannah. Its twenty-two squares, all with different plantings and monuments, were always nice to wander about in and wonderful architecture surrounded them all. Eddie had been asked by a battle fatigued and pleasantly lazy Charleston lawyer to check out a potential death case for a sad and bewildered family from up in Hanahan. It sounded maybe promising but the fact situation was, to put it mildly, out of the ordinary.

It was often said that Charleston was the dignified doyenne and Savannah was the racy younger sister who drank too much, partied too well, and was willing to take her pants off too easily. Too many shadowy corners and dark alleys, good places to misbehave or to put it another way, behave as one wished. It was a sybaritic town.

Eddie plugged down 95 and then swung east. He came up over the Tinkertoy Talmadge Bridge which was, at best, pretty dinky. Named for the blatantly racist Eugene Talmadge, daddy of Squirmin' Herman Talmadge, a political crook if there ever was one, it spanned the Savannah River and gave a nice, high south view of Charleston's bad girl little sister's layout.

Off and down to the slight north, just below the bridge sprawled a large set of public housing apartments. And that was the subject of Eddie's interest. It was where the story ended and it was a gruesome end indeed.

Eddie pulled down the off-ramp and swung over the center of the shabby complex.

In places like this it was always the same. Peeling, faded paint, scuffed out dirt paths, lonely clotheslines dressed with worn out garments and scruffy, fragile shrubs and bushes tilting or wilting randomly. There were no trees. Three or four large dumpsters squatted about here and there.

Earlier that year, Saint Patrick's Day weekend blossomed into a perfect spring bacchanal. The temperature was mild with breezes balmy and copious sunshine warmed all celebratory cockles.

The "Hostess City" flung her doors and her legs wide open for the revelry. Big city New York and Chicago led the way for the holiday celebrations, but Savannah's was the third largest in the country and her beautiful squares and riverfront were totally swarmed with a few hundred thousand, most of whom knew nothing about Saint Patrick and more of whom could give a damn about the, in truth, potentially (maybe?) creepy old saint. The greatest interest was green beer and shots of Jameson and the giant party that flowed from her inebriations and discarding of inhibitions.

The deceased was a young man, early twenties, who had randomly wrestled with drugs and alcohol but not yet to a destructive degree. His name was Bobby "BoBo" McGee. He had dropped out of high school when he was sixteen and became quite a good groom out at the stables at Middleton Place outside Charleston.

He then joined the seasonal circuit and got good, similar work up in Saratoga and down in Ocala and would go back and forth from each locale, always stopping in the middle along the way to visit his family.

He was said to be skilled and an affable fellow. He was a natural with horses.

Piecing the last chapter together was not difficult.

BoBo had gone to Savannah to meet with friends and join in the three days of festivities. He had visited with his folks before hitchhiking down to Georgia. He, it was said by many who were interviewed by a private detective before Eddie arrived to survey, partied hard and hearty but had no trouble with any authorities.

In the late afternoon and early evening on into night of the weekend's Saturday, the weather made a dramatic shift from glorious spring to bitter, brutal cold winter. Temperatures suddenly plunged from the low eighties to the low thirties. The winds picked up to a steady blow of twenty-five to thirty miles per hour with gusts up into the forties and fifties. A hard, cold rain with sleet mixed in slashed down from time to time. Weird thunderstorms broke out. Electrical transformers all over the city began to freeze up and sizzle and then explode. The skies went from sunny to bleak, dark gray. Doors and windows rattled and shook and the wind was a menacing howl. Lesser buildings and structures trembled. Garbage cans and yard ornaments and furniture were flung away. Flags and banners were quickly shredded.

Businesses shuttered. All took to the indoors. Doors were locked and window shades and curtains drawn. What only hours before had been a happy, outdoor throng had evaporated into a bound up, shut down tight ghost town.

BoBo had been on a serious three-day bender and was asleep (or more likely passed out) on a friend's floor in a three story, sagging walk up just off Forsyth Park. It appeared that when he came to, he realized that the weather had gone veritably south on him and he needed to get out of there quickly.

He gathered his meager belongings, said to have been but enough for a paper grocery bag, and made his way, surely fighting and leaning hard into the wind, to the foot of the Talmadge Bridge where he hung his thumb out and hoped for a ride. But there was very little traffic moving and what there was, was not stopping for the poor guy. After a few minutes more of being hard pushed and blown by the weather, he retreated into the public housing area.

He banged on one door after another, called out for help, for shelter. No response. Witnesses who peeked from behind their closed windows said he was dirty, disheveled and very unsteady on his feet. He looked like a crazy person and those that saw him in his last hour were not about to give him comfort, or let him into their secure homes.

He looked about and then made his move. He was seen to have climbed into a dumpster. Maybe thirty minutes later, the big garbage truck rumbled into the yard, extended its steel arms and lifted the big bin up and over and dumped its contents in the haul back where the compressing steel wall crushed and compacted the refuse to make room for more. The weather was bad, but the big heavy truck was up to the challenge and rounds had to be made.

Bobo's mangled body was discovered later that afternoon as the truck's load was dropped and raked out at the landfill outside town.

Some early research indicated that it was a known habit and practice around the country of many trash companies to have their drivers get out of their vehicles and look into the side doors of same. The homeless were often known to sleep in dumpsters. But the weather on this occasion was so awful, it would be fanciful to imagine that a jury would fault a driver not to get out for a look-see even if Eddie could find an expert witness to set a standard of care.

Eddie parked, got out of his car, and walked over to the nearest one for a closer look.

There was no warning signage on it. That was weakly hopeful, but there was a sign on it that said the dumpster was the property of the City of Savannah Housing Authority. The others checked out the same. That was not promising. Being there in the center of where Bobo's end had begun gave Eddie pause and his internal tort signal was trending to the negative. And any suit would have to be against the governmental entity, the municipality, they being usually far more insulated from liability than a private entity.

Georgia was a modified comparative negligence state. If he took the case, he would have to convince the jury that poor old Bobo was less than fifty percent responsible for what happened that brutal day in order to recover damages.

Since Eddie was not licensed in the Peach State, he would have to convince a respected local counsel to get him admitted to try the case and sit with him as second chair and also would have to share any fee with that lawyer. Damn little enticement there.

And obviously BoBo was drunk. There was an autopsy and his blood alcohol levels were well in excess of what was considered legally allowable. But before the first draws and laboratory analysis were undertaken, the steps of historical recitation told that story all too well.

Standing there at the scene, thinking about it all in combination, in reality, not in theory, summed it up. It was a loser. As the wise old bird noted long ago, you can put pearls on a pig but no matter what, it's still a pig.

Eddie still vividly recalled something the late great Norwood Robinson taught him at the very beginning of his practice. Norwood, bigger than life itself, boomed forth with, "Remember, the most important cases you have are the ones you don't take!"

It was true. He had done, as was always his practice, the necessary due diligence. Time to move on.

To report and opine as was his responsibility, he called the referring Charleston lawyer from his car, a funny fellow with the goofy name of Bumpus who had had the moniker Rumpus appended to him long ago. Roger "Rumpus" Bumpus was a nice fellow, often amusing, but no one was ever going to stretch his reputation for effort and intellect into significance. He just wandered along and if there was even the whiff of potential money, all such things were pushed up the line to the likes of Eddie. If some people made coffee nervous, Rumpus's activity level made speed sleepy.

Rumpus listened to Eddie's straightforward summation and then sighed and released with a soft, "Oh, what the hell...kinda figured that...oh well...Eddie, I appreciate your checking it out for me. Hey, you didn't just make a trip down that way just for this one, did you? That was mighty nice of you and I appreciate it."

"Rumpus, thank you and, no, I didn't. I'm making a swing down this way on a bunch of things and your matter just ended up geographically being stop two on the travels. Wish I could be of help here but I just don't see it. I hope you understand. And, when you talk to the family, if they'd like to speak with me, I am happy to make myself available."

"Thanks, Eddie. Don't think that will be necessary but will pass it along to them. I'll sign off now. And you know I'll be back in touch about something else, hopefully soon. Take care of yourself. As you know, go-getters like me need you."

Rumpus and Eddie both light chuckled. "Bye, Eddie," and then the click.

Eddie paused, thought of nothing for a few seconds, then turned the ignition and headed out of the sad squalor and over onto East Oglethorpe where in but a few minutes, he was canopied by old oaks. He found a parking space near the cobbled curb, grabbed his things and checked into the ornate and fascinating Ballastone Inn, which in keeping with the marvelous history of the place, was located just around the corner from the Juliette Gordon Low House, the founder of the Girl Scouts.

Down the way was the Green-Meldrim House where Sherman had rested after his effectively vengeful March to the Sea, culminated by the city fathers of Savannah riding out to meet him, throwing their hands up in affable defeat, pleading that their fair city not be put to the torch, that it was all his. And it was left intact and was indeed all his.

Being bracketed by the beneficent Girl Scouts and the Mars-like efficient Sherman appealed to Eddie; he often, vaguely felt that same way as was the yin and yang of the masks of comedy and tragedy; his lawyer psyche so readily and simultaneously pulsed.

Each one of Ballastone's sixteen rooms was themed differently; many on the Southern belle-fairy-outlandish side, but all were luxe and comfortable.

He had made a reservation on the way down to Charleston and the desk clerk lady eyed him just for a moment, sized him up quickly when he came to the front desk parlor and smiled and said, "No doubt. No doubt at all. Rhett's Retreat for you, Mr. Terrell."

"Why, thank you, miss. Still third floor?"

"Yessir. I take it you know where the elevator is?" She handed him the tasseled key.

"Yes, ma'am. Thank you."

He went to his room which was handsome and quietly wood-paneled. He had stayed in it before. It exuded masculinity in the way of an old London gentleman's club and it pleased him that the gal at the desk had matched him thusly. He surely wasn't getting any younger. His brown mop had long ago given way to close-shaved silver and gray and he had surely lost a half inch in height and had gained more than a couple in his belly.

Eddie laughed when he thought that when he was eighteen, he was six feet, one inch, weighed two-hundred-seventeen, and had a thirty-four inch waist. Nowadays, things were about the same. He was still six and almost one inch, still weighed two-hundred seventeen, but his waist was now a blossoming thirty-eight. Gravity had gotten him. The decade plus that had passed assisted him in standing up straighter in order to pull his abdomen in, but the damn slump of age had inevitably come to him.

But he was still and always strictly a male and when people saw him coming, they paid attention. It was smart he had not yet been consigned to pastels and pinks and buttons and bows. He still had a pulse.

He did some reading and thinking and then went back downstairs to the street, hailed a pedicab and clattered over to Elizabeth's on 37th for some drinks and early dinner. Always good food, the place was an institution and worthy of being so.

Eddie recalled the night many years before when the fine and distinctively voiced actor Morgan Freeman was seated at a table next to him.

Freeman was in town filming the memorable movie, *Glory*. It was hard not to stare, at least just a little bit.

He indeed had a striking mien and was accompanied by a curvy, café au lait Eastern Airlines' stewardess (the flat, boring and one too many words "flight attendant" came into common usage about the same time that Frank Borman's grossly mismanaged Eastern Airlines was unceremoniously shoved into the junkyard). A lovely, very young gal who giggled and cooed over his every word as he stroked her sky-blue uniformed back and shoulders.

As various water boys and bartenders and wine stewards and bar backs and waiters and waitresses hovered and scurried near them to be in that realm of celebrity, Freeman assiduously made sure that all and all within earshot knew this was his niece Celestine who had come in on a flight from Miami.

Eddie recalled thinking amusedly to himself that he was certain that "Auntie," aka Mrs. Freeman, was not around this time in this loving familial loop. The gleam in old Morgan's eye was far more than avuncular. It was understandable.

Eddie had a fine meal of softshell crab and creamed corn and three good, ice cold pops and gratefully paid his ticket, leaving a generous thirty percent tip. On his way back, he called Mikey for quick "good night, sleep tight" rendition. She was yawning and he was close to same. Once back at the Ballastone, night was falling. He got in bed with one of the grand John Mortimer's *Rumpole of the Bailey* series and settled down to be entertained.

Eddie could never quite find the ties that were supposed to bind with John Grisham's books. After the first couple of them, it all felt like the eating the same formulaic dish and he quickly gave them up. Grisham surely had the gift and while it flattened out for Eddie after a while, it was nonetheless admirable.

He fell asleep with the book on his chest. Rumpole was declaiming about his wife, the formidable, "She who must be obeyed!" as he bolted down his next flagon of Thames River plonk. Eddie's eyelids were flickering and rolling downhill as a small set of ocular avalanches moving in slow motion tandem. He was tired. And there was more potential death case roadwork to come, which of course, he would think about tomorrow. But just not now.

CHAPTER FOUR

A MOVING INTERLUDE
Late March, Wednesday

EDDIE SLEPT LATER that morning. It was a nice and welcomed luxury and as he had gotten a little older (just a "little," mind you), his ability to awaken, mildly orient, and then roll back over and sleep again soundly was a gift.

He always slept with his cell at his side and a little after nine, he started the process of coming to and stretching and looking about. He checked his messages and his emails and his Twitter feed and last night's scores and these simple acts of focus brought his mind up to a good, clear point.

He showered and dressed, again informally and went downstairs for coffee and a piece of toast and a newspaper, bringing his bags with him. He sat quietly in the front room of the place and ordered his mind and watched others come and mostly go.

He went to the desk clerk and asked to settle his account and for a copy of his bill. She asked, "Was everything satisfactory, Mr. Terrell?"

"Indeed it was just as it has always been. Would you please do me a favor or at least try to do me a favor?" He grinned at her.

She was not immune to his kind attention.

"Of course. What may I at least try to do for you?"

"Thank you. Would you please call The King and Prince over down on the coast and see if they have a nice room I might have for the night? Last time I looked, it's just Wednesday and I'm thinking…well, I'm hoping they can put me up. Shouldn't be all booked up in mid-week. Please ask them for an early check in, say around noon. I'd like to get out on the beach or at the pool for an hour or two and grab some lunch before I go checking on some case work I might end up having down there."

"I would be happy to make that call right now." They had his credit card on file.

"Great. Thank you. While you give that a try, I'll go put my things in the car and come back to see if that might work. I really appreciate it."

"My pleasure. See you in a minute."

When he came back up the stairs and opened the door, he saw her give the thumbs up sign accompanied by, "You are good to go, Mr. Terrell. Come back and see us soon now."

He waved his thanks and now a bit more energized with his next destination secured, scooted down the steps and started the next leg of his ride.

He slid down West Bay Street and then to Interstate 16 and then soon was back on I-95 heading south. It was only at best a two-hour ride. He took it easy. He listened to music. It was a very pretty day and he temporarily sank his mood into it. But the mellow didn't last long.

His cell beeped. It was his chief legal assistant and Sheena, Queen of the Jungle, Ms. Patty Cherry who could out-talk, out-bitch, out-smoke, out-type and outdo all the rest. Voluptuous unto any painting by Rubens, she was way better than all the rest and knew it. Eddie looked after her but good and she appreciated it. She was one of those people with the natural skill set that replicated those performers one used to see on *The Ed Sullivan Show.*

Patty reminded Eddie of a sailor-suited Frenchman who could spin first one, then two, then twelve plates on spindly sticks while riding a unicycle and playing a harmonica buried within his lips. She was the ultimate multi-tasker and was very good at it.

"Hey, boss lady, what's up?"

"Just checking on you. Where are you? Today?"

"On the way to St. Simons to check on that rock fall case that Lennie Mac sent me to look at, then over to Sylvester to see an old friend I haven't seen in years, then back up to Aiken to visit with our nice racquetball/AED case clients and maybe some other friends, then on home."

"How did Charleston and Savannah go?"

"The Holy City was a holy shit hit. Truck was surprised and then pleased and then, really thrilled. I'm glad we could be generous. We had plenty in that bucket so no pain to it. There will be referrals from him in the future. Hell, we might be getting into some interesting real estate and contract litigation—go fight with some tight-ass suits!"

"That's good. I like it. What about Savannah?" He could hear her blowing out the fantastic smoke rings she was always able to conjure up. They looked like thick doughnuts floating along a train.

"Savannah was a bust. The case is and always will be a loser, a dog. No way we're messing with that. Too many ways to get whipped and too many ways to throw good money after bad. I've already talked to Rumpus. He understood."

"Well, better to wipe it off quick." She paused. "Uhm...who you going to see in...where?...Sylvester. Sylvester, Georgia? Where in the hell is that? And who is your old friend?"

Patty was never one to hang back.

"Okay, let's see. It's about three hours due west of St. Simons, dinky little place, Hell, no more than five, maybe six thousand folks at best."

"Uh huh."

"It's sorta in the center of a triangle. Albany to the west where Ray Charles and Paula Deen were born, Tifton is the grass, not dope, but Turf Capital of the world so they say and Valdosta, also known as Title Town because they have more total wins in high school football than any other high school in the country."

"Uh, Eddie, all this south Georgia history is just fas-ci-na-ting—" she drew the word's syllables out slowly, caustically, "but who, check that, what girl are you going to see?"

"How do you know it's a girl?" Eddie smirked at his phone.

"Jesus! Do you think I just fell off the turnip truck yesterday? I know your ass! Does Mikey know this stop is on your TripTik?"

"First, no she doesn't and there's nothing to it. Not a thing. So how about keep this part to yourself. No sharing, please. Just want to say hey to her. She's a legendary bar keep at the Southern Woods, a big plantation and hunting lodge just outside of Sylvester. Got to know her many years ago when I spent about ten days down there with a bunch of guys hunting quail and shooting skeet, not that I was ever worth a damn at that sort of thing.

"No touching allowed, strictly enforced, but she was great to visit with. We were in there every night for drinks and she was a force and I'm just curious to see if she still is. So quietly harmless, thank you very much, Miss Joe Friday!" Eddie stuck his tongue out at the phone and Patty sighed and then laughed.

"Okay, I got it, but you better damn well make sure you keep the lessons of the Georgia Satellites in mind."

"What might that be?"

"Don't hand me no lines and keep your hands to yourself. And I don't think I'm gonna be asking you about any of your Aiken friends..." Drolly, she left it hanging.

"Good. Roger that. I copy. Now where do things stand on Red Neck Romeo and that crazy bitch?"

"I'll let you talk to Alph about that one. Then when all are done on that, tell Alph to get me back on the line. I want to talk about Cameron."

She hollered. "Alph, pick up line one. It's Eddie. He wants an update on Red Neck Romeo. And once you all are done, please give him back to me."

Alph picked up and in his always melodious voice, opened with, "Halloo, Eddie. How are you? And where are you?" Alph Baron had as sunny a disposition as could be found which well matched his rosy cheeks and silver hair. He had been the biggest dog in one of the biggest insurance defense and corporate firms in the state, had been president of the North Carolina State Bar, was respected from Manteo to Murphy and was a crackerjack fine trial lawyer. He and Eddie had been adversaries many times and not so long ago, Alph had represented a law firm that had really screwed the pooch in a nasty and expensive legal malpractice case.

Eddie had wrestled a huge settlement out of Alph's clients which was to be paid from the firm's and partner's personal funds, secured by everyone's personal guarantees. The matter was fraught with problems and the old goats who had fucked up almost spit the bit and the settlement was on the verge of implosion, but Alph saved the day, gathered his entire group of lawyer clients, went to their office, gave them soup to nuts reasoning as to why settlement was the only thing that would save their firm from total dissolution and hollowed-out wreckage. And in doing so, Alph put his career and license hard on the line. It was in the words of Lord Wellington, "a damn close run thing," but Alph pulled it through, earning Eddie's deep and grateful appreciation and admiration.

In essence and for sure, Alph made a spectacular, running diving catch in deep center field and saved the day and their asses.

During all of the high wire zigs and zags, Eddie got to know Alph much better, admired so very much how he creatively and steadily brought his angry and embarrassed clients around to the finally agreed-upon peace in the valley. Eddie enjoyed Alph's goofy humor and his fine legal mind. And he was an eminently and fine, very sweet mind and could lawyer and deal with the best and the worst of them. They became friends and then good friends.

So, after just a little while, Eddie asked Alph to join him and Patty and Mikey on a quick private jet ride to Charleston to sit in with them on what turned out to be a very successful resolution in a dram shop and auto tort matter out of South Carolina's tacky version of Atlantic City, aka Myrtle Beach, with multiple victims, all of whom had been badly injured.

It was there in Charleston that Eddie, after private and due consideration with himself, popped the question (not on bended knee but with bending elbows) and asked Alph to join his practice as "Of Counsel" with every bell and whistle benefit that suited Alph. Patty and Mikey, at Eddie's urgings, got all over Alph as they were flying home and implored and giggled him to come along with them. And he did and it has been a good and happy match.

"Hey, Alph. How you doin'?"

"Well, great, just great. We're getting things done and awaiting your return. How are your travels going?"

"Not too bad. Had a nice visit with Truck Tinker. The dumpster dive case in Savannah is a no-go. Now, I'm on the way to St. Simons to check on another death case. Fellow was crushed to death. We'll see. You know what they say: 'You gotta kiss a lot of frogs before you get to a princess' and, hell, as you well know, if you don't go scouting a little bit, you'll never know."

Eddie thought for a moment and then laughed. "And then again, Alph, you were an insurance defense whiz kid. You didn't have to do much scouting. The fish just jumped in your boat."

Alph returned the good humor. "Of course. I know what you mean and you are right. And when do think you'll be back?"

"I'm thinking Saturday. Gonna stop in Aiken for a bit. Visit with some old clients and some friends and then head back on up to the Twin City. Now, tell me about our boy, the Red Neck Romeo and his femme fatale squeeze, Floretta. Any further word or all quiet on the Western Front?"

Alph laughed. "Eddie, I think we've just about got it all tightened up. That one was a damn big mess in a small box, but it was fun to see it get worked out. Just paperwork now and I'm on it and keeping Nestor Broadway tubed in and in the loop."

Eddie laughed back. "Excellent. Thank you. You got that right. One big damn mess. Everything else going okay?"

"Yes, we're fighting back from that blues stretch we had a few weeks back. Don't you worry. Me and Patty and Mikey are running a tight ship."

"Glad to hear it and I'll see y'all soon. Please tell Patty we'll all get caught up on everything including Cameron once I'm back next week. No reason to kick at that big boy now while I'm cruising about down this way."

"Got it and will do. Be safe."

"Roger that."

CHAPTER FIVE

EVERY FRESH DECK HAS A COUPLE OF JOKERS

Winter, a Few Months Before

NOW OFF HIS cell, rolling along, Red Neck Romeo (RNR) was a case impossible to not intently recall. He bent and caressed RNR's case across his mind's eye as a Vegas dealer would arc a newly opened deck of crisp bicycles from hand to outstretched hand in perfect numerical and suite order before shuffling and repeating and shuffling again. Its memories, like the stiff cards, snapped to the fore.

It had been a helluva fast ride, compressed in short intense time and amusing, enjoyable, quickly profitable and exhausting. It was a red flashing light as to why Eddie was not fond of matters of the "fucking and fighting and family" variety. He reminded himself to remember that in the future. Domestic discord was always a certainty in this life and its excitable spawn were generally repugnant to Eddie. Everything was always an emergency.

The Red Neck Romeo's real name was Boyard Bustings. He said he went by "Yard" as in hitting a homerun out of the ball yard. "Y'all get it?" He grinned. He featured himself, they quickly came to learn, as a real jokester, going to be, no matter what, a funny-in-your-face type of fellow. He also, upon introduction, added in seriously humorous instruction, "No Chef Boyardee for me! Please."

He was distinctly attractive, well over six feet, clean shaven with a smooth, alabaster complexion, short, brown "Just For Men" hair, alert blue eyes with a voice-over voice and decidedly always manly and rugged but with welcoming gestures. He appeared to be, on so many levels, the love child of Tom Cruise and Gary Cooper. His voice was clearly that of a country Southerner, probably from western Virginia or maybe West Virginia, from out in the climbing hills and the rocky, difficult and tilting fields.

He was by self-description some sort of a "financial advisor" to an ever-growing number of blue hairs and olders from a place outside Burlington called Graham, some forty miles east of Winston-Salem on the road to Chapel Hill. There was some good elder money out that way.

He told them he was successful. "No brag, just fact."

The RNR had a very nice way with people, was uxorious and oleaginous, and it could easily be understood how he could charge his clients substantive management fees for their anchored and often previously sagging assets. "But all was always going to be just fine real soon," he would croon to them over turkey and ham and giblet gravy and bingo and spelling bees and Wurlitzer singsong fests while he smoothed them along with picnic table, red and white checked decor as he moved money and studied and massaged their accounts. There was a local reputation of magic to his work and most everyone got to be happy from time to time and they brought him more money to "invest." He was sort of a Warren Buffett of the Piedmont. That's what they said.

Aside from his office meets and being ever-ready to meet at their homes, he sent flowers and cakes and gimcracks and cards and threw big parties for all of them a couple of times a year out at the Holiday Inn on the interstate, one a Christmas dinner buffet and the other, a summertime ice cream social. He had a UPS driver buddy who did a limited, thrusting imitation of Tom Jones who always made an appearance and a couple of others who could play a little stand-up organ and plink at a banjo.

He had a dutiful wife and two dutiful daughters who ran the office and made sure the accounts were in some sort of discernible order. The daughters took their orders from their mother and their mother took orders from her revered husband.

Mrs. Bustings placed her Sun King husband as more infallible than the Lord Jesus as she had long ago found a typo in the Bible which signaled to her that the Son of God indeed did make mistakes. In her eyes, her husband did not and never had.

Yard had the special affinity to keep it all in his head and his administrators and helpers paid close and precise attention to his instructions and directives.

By the way and along the way of the matter, Eddie and Alph learned that their boy regularly went big game shooting down in South America and up in Canada, had what he called a couple of "safe houses" over on Lake Norman and had a significant interest in a large marijuana farm up the deep woods near the Great Dismal Swamp. He, with the help of some likable country boys who helped tend to the dope farm which included guarding it with plenty of firepower to run off snoopers and thieves, also ran a nice loan office operation for a lot of the rurals out that way. He also had a couple of Harleys he kept down at the lake. He was a man of many interests. He appeared at their offices one afternoon some months before, introduced himself and was quite courtly about it. He was nicely dressed and well-mannered.

Yard said he had been directed to Eddie by a lawyer in Salisbury whose name he could not recall, not that that mattered, said that he needed help, that he had a big problem and that he had, in good faith, brought a retainer check payable to Eddie Terrell in the amount of ten thousand dollars. He handed Eddie a letter he had received a few days earlier. It was from a law firm in Burlington, signed by a fellow named Nestor Broadway.

Eddie and Alph took him into the conference room and he told them his story.

Many months before, he had again run into a younger school classmate, Floretta Shinings, whom everyone knew as Flottie, out at the mall from some years before, a pretty girl who had gotten prettier and slinkier over time and she taught yoga and lifestyle at a local gym. She was married to a nice enough guy, a carpenter or electrician he thought he recalled. They had no children. She had always been real nice to him when they crossed paths from time to time, but this last time around, it was like a bomb went off and she became instantly taken with him.

Flottie immediately got his cell number and over the next few days began calling and texting him constantly. Yard loved the sudden, newfound attention, especially from this gray-eyed hottie. He could not figure it all out but in truth, made very little effort toward any such analysis. If Sparkle Pony wants to take you on a nice ride, then just hop on and hang on.

Within but a few days, they went down to Charlotte, danced in a honky-tonk dive out off of Providence Road and then she told him to take them to the South Park Marriott where she had booked them a room.

Yard obeyed with alacrity and within the hour had gotten very busy trysting while Flottie was draped over him in many pipe cleaner contortions, angles and positions. Thus began regular assignations. She was creative, acrobatic and always in the lead. He was just in awe. They would meet in motels, her place, his hideout houses over on the lake, other cities miles away. She was prolific is so many ways. She would write him sheaths of poems such as one ditty entitled "Cammo Love." The poetry always had "love" in the title. She was hotter for him than a five-dollar pistol on Friday night. And every time out, she ran him over like the 806 Express to Cleveland. She consumed him and left him wide-eyed and spent. Every time.

It went on for months and months and stretched beyond a year and some more.

Of course, one day the shit hit the fan when Flottie in frustrated spite told her cranky and suspicious husband that she wanted out and that she had a brand new special lover whom she would crawl over glass for. Furthermore, she recklessly told her husband that it was none other than the little town's high profile money manager Boyard Bustings and she loved him to the heavens and beyond.

The husband, having just been big time sucker-punched, walked out of the house without saying a word, drove to their little downtown and hired a law firm. He selected them because they seemed to have a nice office and high polished brass signage.

They explained to him that he could proceed with divorce proceedings immediately because of the wife's admission of adultery.

Additionally, they told him that he had more than enough information about his wife's carrying on with Big Money Bustings to file a lawsuit against him for alienation of affections, a cause of action that had been long ago put to rest by many courts and legislatures across the country. In North Carolina that was not the case and A of A was an excellent bludgeon, especially when there was long green as the target. That indeed was the subject and claim in the letter Bustings handed to the lawyers.

Alph read it over and handed it to Eddie who did the same.

"Alph, why don't you explain what we've got here to Mr. Bustings?"

"Of course. Mr. Bustings, we do have a significant problem here and we think you recognize that you do as well."

"Yard, please, gentlemen. Okay, I do. How bad is it and how does it work and what do we need to do to fix it, to make it go away?"

"Here is how it works and I'd say, because you have more than a little bit of money, they're going to come after you, shall we say, with high energy. Now, first, they have asked in the letter if, before they file suit, if we don't want to have a sit-down and see if we all can work this thing out."

"Well, hang on here. I don't want no lawsuit filed. What would it say?"

"It would be filed by Floretta's husband. It would say that the two of them, hubby and Floretta were happily married until you came along and charmed and seduced her away from him and into your bed and that your misconduct has forever alienated Floretta's affections from her husband. The lawsuit will ask for serious and heavy money damages to be paid by you to him, the injured party."

"Hellfire, boys, she's the one that came after me so hard and heavy. I couldn't resist. I was helpless. She was all over me like a duck on a June bug. She was the one alienating while we were recreating." Boyard Bustings chuckled, amused with himself. "Now that was a pretty good one, don't y'all think?"

Both lawyers grinned, shook their heads as they looked at each other.

Eddie said, "Not bad, not bad at all, but I don't think that tag line will play well in court."

"No, no, no, don't want to be in court with dirty laundry and such getting aired out in public. No," Yard said.

"Well, then, if you are adamant about that and you sure seem to be, then our options are limited. I personally would like to try this thing based upon the story you have told us, but you are the client and you will instruct us as to your wishes and if we can accommodate those wishes, we will surely do so. And I admit right off the bat that if the case is tried, every sordid and racy detail will get loose and fair to say, your reputation and business and maybe even your marriage and family could be badly damaged if not downright ruined. And that's even if we win. I know you will keep in mind yours is a very small county, all things considered. I think you get my drift.

Now, a question to you. Does your wife, do your daughters know anything about this?"

"No, sir, and they sure as hell ain't gonna know about it either."

"Does Floretta know anything about her husband getting a lawyer for this problem?"

"I don't know. I can call her."

Alph shook his head. "No, you mustn't do that. You must have no contact with her. It could be seen as attempted witness tampering. No contact at all. Do you understand that?"

"I guess so but she's the one that calls me all the time. You ought to see some of the texts she sends me. I save them. They're wild sexy hot. Want to see a few? They'll make you think she wrote for the Penthouse Advisor. Now, what do I do about that?"

"No, we don't need to see them right now, but make sure you hang onto them. Erase nothing. They may prove to be useful on down the line. Tell her to stop calling you. Tell her that her husband is trying to get you to pay him a lot of money because he says you busted up their happy marriage."

"I done no such thing. If anything, she busted up their marriage while she was busting me up! That's a pretty good one too, doncha think?" He obviously enjoyed amusing himself. It was an ongoing warning flare to Alph and Eddie that Yard might be a hard one to get to pay attention when he really needed to. He seemed to enjoy jumping the rails.

"The problem there is it would be great to get her to say that under oath, but to get that done, she'd have to be sworn, testifying in court and once we get to formal litigation, the cat is out of the bag for all the world to see."

Alph mused aloud. "Maybe we could approach her and get a private, sworn statement or affidavit that might calm things a bit, take some of the sting out of it?"

"I like the idea." Eddie called for Patty. Eddie introduced Bustings to her and explained the situation.

"Mr. Bustings, Yard, I presume you have Mrs. Floretta's cell number." He nodded.

"Please read it out to Ms. Cherry here. Patty, please call her, explain that we represent Mr. Bustings whom we know that you know. Tell her that her husband is accusing Mr. Bustings of destroying her marriage and luring her away from him. Tell her that Mr. Bustings says that's not exactly the way things went and he would like to find peaceful way to address these matters. Alph, I want you to go—you're older, have that gravitas, that look of seniority and maturity. Patty, tell Flottie that you and Mr. Baron, who is a senior lawyer in our office, would like to meet with her at any public place of her choosing and visit with her about this unfortunate situation. Now hang on. Don't make the call just yet. Let's check ourselves here. Patty, I want you to go to transcribe what we can, maybe even get an affidavit out of her right there on the spot, so take your notary seal just in case. And of course, we need you there as a witness if she ever tries to say we were strong arming or misleading her. Now, go make that call. Thank you."

Bustings gave Patty the number.

Bustings asked, "Y'all think this can fix it?"

Alph replied, "I doubt this can totally fix it, but it's worth a try to take some of the air out of their balloon."

"Eddie, don't you want to go instead of me? If this young lady is so attractive, what if I take a shine to her?" He giggled.

"Oh, God, Alph, don't go south on me that quick!" Eddie rolled his eyes. "Fat chance on that. Mikey wouldn't approve and I need you to go do that avuncular thing."

"I got it. Let's see what we can get done."

Bustings sighed. "Hell, it's always about the money, isn't it? They always want money. Whatever happened to honesty and honor?"

Eddie and Alph also shook their heads in dismay, a convergence of dismays headed in different ways.

They met at the Hardees, just off of the main drag. Flottie was tentative. Alph was gentle. Patty tried to stay in the background and take an inconspicuous note here and there. Alph explained the matter. Flottie relaxed and spoke candidly, it did appear, to the situation.

Flottie was surprised that her husband had done such a thing. He was still living at home and they were still sleeping in the same bed. She had only told him all that so boldly in order to try to get a rise and some fire out of him; he had been pretty much a limp noodle for a good while now and she wanted to juice him up. And, yes, it was true that she and Bustings had been having a lot of fun, but she still loved her husband and hoped that once he calmed down, he would forgive her and that they could stay married. She asked what could be done to put this particular fire out.

She had lovely, piercing gray eyes and intensity of purpose that radiated from them. She was a good-looking girl, one who would be hard to turn down. She had the hidden look of an enthusiastic predator if she put her mind to it, all that faraway yoga focus.

Alph thought for a moment. The idea of King Solomon crossed his mind. Don't get too pushy either way. Let's just see if he could deflate the balloon a bit.

"Miss Flottie. May I call you Flottie? Yes, thank you and please do call us Patty and Alph. After all, that's who we are." He smiled benignly. "Here are our cards."

Flottie took them and held them with both hands under her chin as she leaned forward.

"Here's what I think would be helpful. Let's prepare a little statement, just a little one. We will keep it simple and truthful. We can share it with your husband's lawyer and, hopefully, it will help turn down the heat. Is that alright by you?"

"Yes, I think so. What do I say? What should I say? Truthful, that is."

"How about I talk it out with you and if it is totally truthful, Patty here will write it down and you can sign it and we will get a copy to you immediately and present it to the other side. How's that?"

"Okay, fine, yeah, you say it out and if it's so, then let's get it written out."

"Alright, here we go...

Alph closed his eyes and began the slow-paced incantation.

"My name is Floretta Shinings. I am married to my husband of many years, Steve. I am happily married to Steve but have been dissatisfied with him lately. He has not been paying attention to me and has been keeping away from me starting some months ago. This has hurt my feelings.

"Frustrated, about six weeks ago I did take up with a nice man named Boyard who I used to know back in school. I really don't understand it, but I took a serious shine to him just right away. I called him a lot right from the beginning and texted him a lot too. I still do though I know now I'm going to have to stop that. We did some things together. He was also nice to me, paid attention to me as I wanted him to, paid attention to me the way I wish Steve would. Steve and I still live in the same house and sleep in the same bed.

"Mr. Bustings has not broken up my marriage and I want to stay married to Steve. I love my husband and I know he loves me. I hope he will forgive my foolishness."

Patty did a full read back to Flottie as Alph watched her carefully. She showed no sign of spitting the bit.

Alph asked quietly, "Miss Flottie, is that accurate? And if it is, would you please sign it there at the bottom where Patty has drawn a line for your signature?"

Patty had not been wasteful with her time as she had waited and had prepared the paper with all the necessary bells and whistles which made it—Prest-O Change-O—into a formal, sworn affidavit.

"Yes, it is. Yes, I'll sign it. Do you think it's going to help?"

"Yes, yes I do, but to what degree I'm not sure yet. Of course, we will let you know. We will keep you posted. We really appreciate your meeting with us and Patty will get a copy of this to you within the next day. Thank you. If you need to talk with me or you would prefer to speak with Patty, there's our number. Well, we better be off. Lots of work to do, you know."

She nodded her head uncertainly at them as they went into the parking lot to get back to the office.

"What do you think, Alph?"

"Well, we ain't out of the woods yet, but we have gutted the center of the mess—she swears under oath, "signed, sealed, delivered, I'm yours"—that her marriage has not been destroyed by this and if he wants to go public with this, he ain't gonna look so five-star hubby either. So I think it would behoove all of us to talk."

When they got back to the office, Mikey asked, "What y'all been up to? Where you been?"

Patty laughed. "Playing 'Can This Marriage Be Saved?'"

"What's that?"

"Used to be a column in some old ladies magazine, *Good Housekeeping* or something like that. They'd lay out a situation where the couple is on the rocks for whatever and then discuss in what I recall was a lot of lady chat whether or not there were ways to avoid the crackup.

"We're trying help a fellow out who just walked in here off the street, handed Eddie a big, fat retainer check. Guy's name is Bustings, from just down the road here. He's a good-looking man, who could be on the cover of *People* magazine. He's smart, organized and kinda goofy too. He's an entrepreneur, got a lot of stuff going on, some of it outside the lines."

"Interesting...and please go on," Mikey said.

"Basically," Patty said, "this is North Carolina's way of still allowing Domestic Court Extortion. Whatever happened to an 'enlightened' and 'equitable' system of laws? Such bullshit but if you've got the right side of the case, then you've got the whip hand. And most of these cases end up with blood, teeth and hair all over the dashboard and the zipper down daddy dog hunting for a barrel and a new set of cojones."

"Okay," Mikey said, "sounds like we don't have the whip hand. What are we gonna do? Cave and pay? Who is the lawyer on the other side, the one representing the jilted husband?"

"Let's get Eddie in here. Eddie! Come visit will you, please? We want to get you up to date on Bustings."

Eddie wandered in. "How did your little visit go with the gal?"

"Here, read this." Eddie reviewed the paper, now nicely formed, massaged and filled-in as a sworn affidavit.

"Damn. Nicely done. But they can still file, you know…"

Alph nodded. "We're thinking a sit-down with all hands on deck and let's get a good mediator to help nudge us all along. What do you think?"

"Sounds good to me. Let's get Bob Collier to mediate who's a retired Superior Court Judge. Smart, good guy, even-handed. Alph, you surely know one another well from over the years. Why don't you call him and see if he's amenable and also get us his take on Nestor Broadway? Hopefully, kill two birds with one stone. Alph, do you happen to know Broadway, by the way?"

"I don't, but I do know Bob Collier, know him very well. Will make the call now."

Alph went back to his office. They waited. Alph returned shortly.

"Bob would be happy to assist."

"What did he say about Nestor?"

"Well, it was a reading between the lines sort of thing. Let me see if I can noodle it out for us. Bob said that Nestor was a good enough lawyer, went to Duke, played it straight, said clearly his family had the *Iliad* and *Odyssey* in mind when they named him. Said he was always full of advice, kind of boastful, always spoke to his many successes, none of which anyone could remember just like old King Nestor of the Homerian epics. Ten-thousand-dollar car wrecks just don't count these days, last time I looked. Bob said he could not recall the last time Nestor Broadway tried a case before a jury in his courtroom and as you know, Bob was around for a long time on the big boy bench."

Patty and Mikey looked at each other with questioning, scrunched eyes. "*Iliad*, *Odyssey*, Homerian? What the hell is that all about?"

Eddie laughing, held up his hand. "I promise we will fill you in on some classical edification later. Now, may I interject a working opinion here?"

"Sure."

"What we have here I do believe is known down in Texas as 'All hat and no cattle.' I believe Judge Collier is telling us that Broadway likes to talk big but would much rather cash a check. He'd never admit it but I expect his M.O. is to sell the top end of a client's case and seize the sure money, you know, always harvest the easy, low-hanging fruit, all the while telling the client what a superb job he's doing. He's got his hands on what he thinks is a fat one, but I think, based on Ms. Flottie's affidavit, that we can put the case on a big diet. I think we need to set this one up quick for a face-to-face."

"Fine by me."

"Patty, please set it up for as soon as possible. We want everyone present. Please tell Mr. Broadway that we would like all parties present, that we want to make a hard effort at getting the matter resolved quickly and quietly. Tell him both Mr. Baron and I are prepared to negotiate seriously and in good faith. Please get Mr. Bustings on the phone for me now."

Eddie went back to his office and waited for Patty.

"On one."

Eddie picked up.

"Mr. Bustings, how are you doing?"

"I'm good. Remember now, Yard, please. Thank you for asking. Have you sorted this little hottie mess out for me yet? I want to go on down to Argentina for some shooting and I want to go without this mess walking around with me. You understand that, don't you?"

"Of course I do and we are working on it and trying to set up a meeting with all parties present and also have the services of a good, effective mediator there to assist us."

"What's that? What's a mediator?"

"Simply put, he's a smart guy who will help both sides come to an understanding, an agreement to compromise some and put the matter to rest. We want to try and do this quickly and quietly. We are trying to get a very well-respected judge to help us. The longer it lingers, the greater the chances that some word of it will slip out and we don't want that to happen, now do we?"

"Oh, good Lord, no boss! No, no on any slip outs!"

Eddie's office door opened and she mouthed, "It's on for next week." The door closed.

"Uh, Yard, we've got to get some work done around here. The meeting will be next week at Steve's lawyer's office and we'll want to meet with you the day before here at our office. Please bring that poem you say she wrote you and your phone with all her text messages to you on it. We'll be in touch with you with times, addresses, etc. Do you understand all that?"

"Yeah, I think I do. Hey, who's Steve?"

Eddie rolled his eyes. "Uh, Yard, that's Flottie's husband."

"How about that? Knew she was married but never knew the poor schmuck's name. She acted like he was basically a dead man walking, you know, when it came to the manly arts."

Eddie sighed, quietly grimaced.

"Alright. Yes. Figures. Now, you understand, don't you, Yard, that we are all going to be there, Steve, you, maybe even Flottie? You can handle that, can't you? Stay cool. You know what I mean, right?"

"Yes, sir. I got it."

"Okay, we'll be in touch. In the meantime, you are to make no contact with her, no contact at all. You understand that too?"

"Yes, sir."

Eddie hung up and went out to see Patty.

"What day we gonna do this?"

"Wednesday starting at 10 a.m. at Nestor's office."

"You tell him about Judge Collier?"

"Yup. He said that was great."

"How about call Flottie and set up when and where you can get a copy of her statement to her? And when you hand deliver it to her, make sure she knows about the meeting on Wednesday. Really need her there, I think. Suggest to her that she might want to bring a lawyer along, you know, to help protect her rights."

"Okay. But what rights does she have to be protected here? Seems to me, she ain't got none. This is just between her husband and our boy, The Yardman, right? She doesn't have a claim for any moolah, does she?"

"That's right I'm sure, unless there's new law to be made out there and I ain't heard about it. So let's keep it, shall we say, formal and with lawyer propriety. If we can get this done, don't want her hollering she was misled. It's a 'Let's cover our asses a little bit' thing."

"Gotcha. I'm on it."

Later that afternoon, Patty returned after the delivery and told Eddie that she had suggested to Flottie that she bring a lawyer with her to the Wednesday meeting.

"Good. What did she say to that?"

"Said she'd think about it but she probably wouldn't. She felt like she could do okay on her own."

"Interesting. Hmmmm...wonder what those words, 'do okay on her own' mean?"

He paused to give it some thought but there was but a blank. There was something but it was fuzzy to the point of being indecipherable. "If there's anything to it, I suppose all will be revealed somewhere down the line. Well anyway, we tried. She say anything about her statement, her affidavit?"

"No. She glanced it over, folded it up and stuffed it in the back pocket of her jeans."

"Was she nice?"

"Nice enough. Seemed a little distant."

"Makes sense. Suppose she's got plenty on her mind. Thanks, Patty. Now, let's get back to whatever creatures here in our weird world that are currently screaming for our attention."

CHAPTER SIX

LUST AND MONEY-OLD AS THE AGES

Winter, a Few Months Before

EDDIE AND ALPH met with Bustings the Tuesday afternoon before the next day's gathering. And they explained the process to him. They then asked to see the "Cammo Love" poem they had asked him to bring. He handed it to them. Eddie read it aloud.

You could say our love is camouflaged or somewhat in disguise...

I guess that is why it took us a few mistakes and twelve years to recognize.

The lesson is, you can't see the forest for the trees...

Holds very true...Que Sera, Sera...whatever will be, will be...

The Prince appeared on a clear summer night in a big cammo truck...

He swept me away to a soybean field...where then we did begin to fuck.

There were eight or nine more stanzas, all in the same vein. Iambic pentameter it surely was not but it did appear to help get the job done.

Eddie handed it to Alph who continue to read it down. It was luridly fascinating.

Eddie asked, "When did she give you this and have you known her for about a dozen years?"

"Oh, like I'd said, we were in school together but that was a long time ago. We'd run into each other at the store and such from time to time. She was always real friendly-like, always wanted to chat and visit. I didn't think nothing of it. We'd just go on our separate ways. Didn't think nothing about it, really. Just a pretty girl who liked to gab. Until the last time…"

His voice trailed off as he looked dreamily into the distance.

They then reviewed hundreds of text messages, all steamy, many incendiary, a few as graphically close to the other side of the dark web as could be allowed. She was en fuego and he obviously enjoyed carrying the gasoline and matches.

This was a case that had Alph and Eddie shaking their heads for so many reasons. Amazement, incredulity, disbelief, amusement, even sometimes embarrassment—some of this text messaging even made them turn their cynical lawyer heads away. Some of it was just Triple XXX porn. And too, it was clearly evident who had lit the fuse. It seemed that at the very least a blow torch had been used to ignite the bonfire of lust. There was no build-up or subtlety, just an initial explosion followed by more and more and more.

Bustings asked as they reviewed the threads. "Whattya'll think of all that? That girl's got a V-12 engine in her. Pretty hot stuff I'd say. She sure can do a low ridin' wheelie with that chassis!" He grinned like a chimp, all lips and teeth.

"Just offhand, Mr. Yard, I'd say this is all pretty interesting. Don't you think, Alph?"

"Yes, Eddie, I agree."

And they went back to their studies. Bustings just sat there, humming pleasantly, looking out the window, flipping through magazines. He appeared to be a man without a care in the world. Finally, they handed his cell back to him and cautioned him again to keep his phone completely secure unto himself and to make no effort to have contact with Flottie.

"Okay, and I won't call or text her. But I asked y'all about this before."

Eddie's ears pricked up. It appeared there was a glimmer that from time to time Mr. Bustings had been paying some attention. "What from before?"

"I asked y'all what to do about her calling me."

"And we told you to tell her what was going on and that she must not be calling you anymore."

"That's all well and good, but sometimes with her, that's like telling the rooster not to crow when the sun comes up."

Alph cocked his head. "Mr. Yard, what are you telling us? Are your conversations just about fun and your relationship? Or is there something more going on here?"

"Well, never in texts, she kept it between the lines there, just fun and games, always did…but from time to time, she's been known to ask for some money." Eddie thought, *Well, there it is. No wonder she feels no need for a lawyer at our meeting tomorrow.*

"Yard, have you given her money in the past?"

"Yeah, sure, I wanted to give her presents. Greatest pussy in the world. Only a fool would not give a minx like that some tribute. There was no blackmail. No, nothing like that."

"How much?"

"Oh, twenty-five here and there, maybe three times all told. From time to time she'd get a little pushy, sorta grabby and I'd push back some. I told her a few times that she just had to understand that I couldn't crap a twenty-five or fifty out whenever she just upped and snapped her fingers whenever she got the hankerin' to."

The lawyers rolled their eyes and swallowed.

"A fifty sometimes as well…"

Alph and Eddie involuntarily glanced at each other.

"Do you understand you were, you are under no obligation to give her anything?"

"Never thought about it, but okay if you say so."

"Do you understand that her husband Steve is seeking to have you pay him a lot of money because he says you wrecked his marriage and that we are trying to keep that from happening or at least slow it down and minimize it by showing that she started all this?"

"Yeah, I get that."

Eddie looked at Alph. "What do you think?"

Alph said, "I think that a) this is about as strange as it gets, b) even with what we've assembled as a pretty good shield, I cannot imagine that they'll be willing to walk away with an empty-handed cuckhold and c) if Steve gets money, Flottie's gonna want some too."

Yard, suddenly very present, inquired, "So let me see if I get this straight. Y'all have gotten together some pretty good stuff to help me out, but you still think I'm going to have to go into my pocket for more to lay it to rest. Is that right?"

"That's a pretty good sum-up."

"Damn, I love to give that sweet young thing presents, you know, money... that's coming from me." He was differentiating the poon from his pride. He patted his chest. "But, damn, when my arm gets twisted, I don't like that so much. You know what I mean? It doesn't feel so right. I mean, it's the principle of the thing."

"Yes, we understand, but business is business and this surely is business. It's a money problem, right. So you need to be prepared to be flexible, right. Okay? Let's just see how it plays out and play it as it goes."

"I get your drift. Alright, I'll see y'all at that fellow's office tomorrow morning at what, 9:45? And yeah, I'll bring my phone. What else?"

"Just stay calm and let's see what we can get accomplished."

Yard got up and as he went out the door, he turned and with an impish grin on his face, asked, "Yeah, you said just a minute ago, 'What are we going to do?' Not exactly right. The question is: 'What are y'all gonna do?' Remember, that's why you get the big bucks!"

He winked and the door closed with a soft click.

Eddie muttered a soft "fuck." Alph just closed his eyes for a moment and shook his head.

"Welcome to the big time, Alph, my man, welcome to the big time."

They all gathered at Nestor Broadway's office the next morning at the appointed time.

Eddie and Alph and Patty had ridden over together. Mikey had stayed behind at the office. Someone needed to answer the phones and keep a face on the place.

Along the short ride, Patty, sitting in the back seat had asked, "Well, have y'all come up with anything, a plan, an approach?"

There was silence save for the tires humming on the interstate.

Alph cleared his throat. "Well, um, er...well, no, Patty, I surely have not. I'm pretty much unsure as to what to say or do so my plan is to keep my mouth shut and just watch and wait unless Eddie's got something." He looked at Eddie.

"In truth, I haven't got shit either." He wryly smiled. "You know, this is one of those classic deals they did not teach us about in law school. If you haven't got the facts, argue the law. If you haven't got the law, argue the facts. And if you haven't got either, throw sand!" They all laughed.

Alph noted, "Well, we do have some helpful facts. Don't you think?"

"Oh, I agree, but I don't think it's enough to keep them from pressing Bustings with exposure unless he gags up some significant bucks. So how do we keep the number within reason? Hell, I suppose we have to drive a wedge between King Nestor and his boy Steve, make sure he is well aware that a bird in the hand is worth a helluva lot more than two in the bush. Sorry, bad choice of words but sort of fits. If it weren't for 'bush,' we wouldn't be here…"

Patty said, "Sometimes you are such a kid!"

They laughed again and then fell silent.

All were pleasant as they milled about in the reception area but uncertainty hung in the air. Everyone was nicely dressed and polite, mostly well-mannered though Steve's face featured a combination of reticent hang-dog and surly. Broadway offered coffee and doughnuts. He was clearly pleased to get such a fulsome assembly to address the problem at hand.

Flottie, unaccompanied by counsel, was demure and still very pretty. She looked relaxed and well rested.

Bayard Bustings was all blue suited up with a garish, kaleidoscope of swirling colors necktie and a red rose bud in his lapel. He was all smiles and handshakes, very gregarious in a barely muted way. He even pumped Steve's dead fish hand and said with empathy, "I'm glad to meet you. Sorry it's under these circumstances. I hope we can get this all worked out. Flottie, well Flottie, she sure is a nice gal."

He just needed to sell and sell some more and with a filter that was all too often non-existent.

Steve's eyes got big, then narrowed and he simply said, "Well, we'll see about that."

Eddie and Alph and Patty were internally aghast but they poker-faced it and kept watching.

Judge Bob Collier, a big bear of a man, handsome, silver-haired, great sense of humor, beloved by the bar for his savvy, his smarts and his bearing came into the room. Now retired, his family had been prominent and wealthy with land and the development of land in these parts for years. Though no longer on the bench, he was constantly sought after as a mediator. He was a "get it done" kind of man. He was no pushover and no martinet either. He was helpful and thoughtful as a superior court judge and he was the same as a neutral party now.

"Good morning, everyone. I'm looking forward to see if we can't get this situation resolved. Some of you I know. Hey, Alph. How are you doing? I expect you're enjoying being on the other side of the wall these days." He winked.

Alph replied in exchanged good humor, "I think you are onto something, Sir Robert."

The bonhomie was so unforced. They, of course, went a long ways back.

"Eddie. Glad to see you have improved your artillery. Been a while." Eddie smiled and bowed, "Yes, indeed, Your Honor."

"Nestor, I've been looking out for you. Where you been keeping yourself these days? I've missed you."

Nestor managed a slight, forced, cheerful croak and a, "I'm around, Judge. I really am."

It was but a little message and whether it registered with all remained to be seen.

All were introduced in the reception area and after very brief opening statements that all consisted of 'I think we all know why we are here and we are here in good faith and hope we can work matters out,' they broke off into their various groups into their assigned rooms of waiting and evaluation and algorithmic calculating. Flottie had nothing to say; she just watched.

Since Flottie had no counsel and no vested legal interest in the proceedings, as the small herds began to shuffle about, it was decided by all counsel with the oversight of Bob Collier ("Okay, what is her skin in the game? Oh? none but well…maybe?…well, let's see…okay.") that she should be stationed in the center of the flow of back and forth, in the reception area and kept abreast of what was going on.

After all, she was the pivot to all the lust and ardor to begin with; she had brought this all to this point and she surely appeared to think that she indeed did have a vested interest.

There was no reason to rile her up or dismiss or ignore her. She was to be treated as a participant and all would just have to see how that worked out. She was a wildcard. She and her husband Steve barely, remotely glanced at each other.

Judge Collier, as was standard operative procedure in a mediation, went to visit with Broadway and his client first to get their take on the matter and look them over, do a little temperature taking.

While Alph and Eddie and Patty and Yard waited in their holding pen, Yard, who until then, seemed totally detached, suddenly lifted up his head and pointedly inquired, "What do y'all think their number is? Bet it's stupid big. And have y'all figured out what y'all gonna do about it?"

Eddie steepled his fingers and spoke slowly, "First thing we are going to do Yard is to see if we can't whittle away at what you call, and we think you're right, their stupid number. I expect we are going to hear something like a bit north of one million."

Alph nodded in agreement. Patty sat still.

"Okay, what you gonna fire back with first?"

"You'll see." Eddie winked. "Now, hope you aren't gonna play nickel and dime here. We are going to need to move some. You ain't no dope. This is like life. You're going to have to pay to play. You understand that, right?"

"Oh, yeah, I played some. Now I've got to pay some. I understand. Damn, pussy is expensive everywhere, ain't it?"

Patty looked down at her pad and covered her mouth with her hand.

He was in an almost expansive mood in keeping with his persistent display of his Cheshire Cat, now you see me, now you don't.

After a quarter of an hour, Collier knocked and came on into the room. There was some brief, pleasant small talk about sports and local gossip and rumor and who had recently gotten their ticket punched to the big finish and then Collier looked straight at Yard and noted, "Mr. Bustings. I'm sure it comes as no surprise to you that Mr. Broadway in there wants a nice big chunk of your hide to the tune of $1.2 million."

Yard amusedly replied, "No surprise at all and no offense taken."

Alph asked, "Bob, did the aggrieved husband have anything to say?"

"No, Nestor did all the talking. Expect Nestor has told him to let his lawyer work."

"What was Nestor's tone, if we might ask?"

"Sure, fair question. No table banging. Straightforward, sort of hopeful, no puffing. He says they've got your man here by the short hairs and that if he doesn't settle today, suit will be filed tomorrow for all the world to see. Says they've got some motel hotel receipts and of course, his wife's confession of misadventures with your client here."

"Uh huh. Now Nestor...he wants to count some money too, doesn't he?"

"Seems that way. We all know if they push too hard and this little conclave we're having today blows up, then he can get the satisfaction of destroying Mr. Bustings here, which does not necessarily mean that the cashing of a check is in the near offing. Appeals always take time, as you know, often years. And Alph and Eddie, on the other hand, if y'all want to play cheap and coy, that'll cause trouble here as well."

"Have you told them that?"

"Just like I'm telling y'all and in no uncertain terms. This case needs to be put down before it turns into a case. Do you understand that, Mr. Bustings?"

"Please, Judge, call me Yard. It truly does make me easier to work with. The nickname pleases me. Something that came to me years ago and it suits me. Bay Yard...like the tail end of it. And, yessir, I do."

"Good. Whatever makes you happier and more flexible and shall I hope a bit more generous, I am happy to seek out and use to your and all of our benefit."

Eddie reached into his briefcase and pulled out a sheet of paper.

"Judge, as you well know, we rarely play a lot of 'gotcha' in these sorts of proceedings, but all this has been put together on such short notice, we are just defending on the fly so apologies to them and to the Court. But it is what it is. I'd ask you to take a look at this. It's a poem, a love poem if you will. It's titled, 'Cammo Love.'"

Collier looked at Eddie. "Poetry? Well, alright." He pulled some readers out of his breast pocket and slid them over his nose.

"Please give it a good read." They settled and waited.

The judge read without expression, then began to silently mouth a word or a phrase here and there. He looked up, obviously not yet through it all.

"Who wrote this?"

Alph and Eddie spoke in unison. "She did."

"No kidding?!" He paused, slowly waggling his head in a slow figure eight loop. You could hear his bull neck creak. "Well, of course, no kidding. The gal in the lobby? And they haven't seen this?" He pulled his glasses by the bridge down his nose and looked over the half moons. "Interesting. Do I even need to ask who she wrote it for?"

Yard grinned with pride. "No, sir, I don't think you really do."

"Did you ever write her anything like this? Letters? Love notes? Poems?"

"No, sir. Well, maybe a few texts here and there, but she started this whole thing off and I just went along for a nice ride. Hell, I'm a man of action, not words."

Bob Collier nodded as counsel winced again.

Alph added, "No, they haven't seen it yet. We were thinking you could take it to them. They can keep it. It's a copy for them. And tell them we've got some other things for them that we think everyone will find, shall we say, interesting…"

"Well, alright then…they've opened at $1.2 million. What's your response?"

Eddie looked at Yard, "Twenty-five, fifty?"

"Go fifty."

"I appreciate that. I'm off to do the shuffle shuttle."

As Bob Collier left the defendant team, he walked through the reception area where Flottie was sitting.

She asked, "May I ask you what's going on?"

"Of course. Your husband's counsel has made a first demand of $1.2 million."

"Oh, that's just ridiculous. When pigs fly…maybe."

"Well, don't shoot me. I'm just the messenger."

"What did the fellows in there say to that?"

"I have been told to counter that at fifty thousand so the bidding has started. Now, may I ask you something?"

"Sure."

He handed her the poem. "Did you really write this?"

She looked it over. "Sure did and lots more like that too. Pretty good stuff, huh?" She was obviously proud of her work. "Yard just loves them."

"Yes, I can see that. I've got to see if I can keep this thing moving along. I'll keep you posted."

He went into the plaintiff's room and cut to the money chase with no preamble.

"They've countered with an initial fifty thousand." He handed the poem to Nestor. "I think y'all ought to take a good look at this and then, Nestor, just you come see me. Bring me your next, shall we say, more well-adjusted demand. I'll be out in the front room waiting or on the porch grabbing some fresh air." He left them and went out on the porch and sat down on a bench.

In time, Nestor Broadway walked out on the porch and sat down next to Collier.

"Offhand, Nestor, I'd say that little ditty is of no help to your side of it."

"Hell, Judge, that just shows what a trampy slut she is and how he stirred her up and knocked her off the rails."

"She says she has written him lots and lots of these things. She just told me that. She seems very proud and pleased about that."

Nestor was quiet, looking off across the hedge toward the road.

"Nestor, does it occur to you that maybe, just maybe that pretty gal sitting in there is the aggressor, the initiator in this thing? And you know, your demand is way too high. You know the old saying. A pig gets fat and a hog gets slaughtered. They're obviously willing to pay you some decent money, but y'all got to get within range. I presume you took this one on a contingent fee. That fellow with you seems nice enough but he's mild and I don't expect he can pay you by the hour. And by the way, I have a strong feeling they ain't just hauling a poetry book around. They've indicated they have some more stuff that they think all of us will find 'interesting.' Go back in there and talk to your client. Give him the uncertain preview and then please come back and see me out here again."

Nestor returned in due time, sat down again and said resignedly, "Okay, nine hundred thousand."

"Thank you. That's a good move. It's still an unreasonable demand but it's a good signal to them to keep moving. I'll be back. Go be with your client."

Collier thought, *I wonder how much stomach for an Armageddon fight both sides have? I'm thinking the husband not so much. Plaintiff's next move will, I expect, speak to that.*

Flottie asked as he passed. "Where are things?"

"Hang on. Let me see what the defendant has to say next and then I'll get you up to speed."

He quick-knocked and as he entered, Patty was sitting next to Yard and audibly whispering to him, the gist of which went along the lines of, "Don't be foolish. Keep the numbers moving. You've got the resources. Remember, this thing could be the ruination of you."

Yard showed no resistance and clearly was thinking and nodding.

Collier thought, *Good sign. She and her thinking are welcome in his head.*

He spoke to the group. "I like this move of theirs. They've moved to nine hundred thousand. Now I need a good move from y'all to sustain momentum. What do you say?"

Before anyone else could speak, Yard Bustings flatly said, "I agree. I understand. Let's go to one fifty, no two hundred. Now, Mr. Alph and Mr. Eddie, what will you show them next?"

Eddie stood up and stretched. "Please get your phone out and set it and lock it on the thread that begins within hours of your initial encounter of some many months ago. Please come over here and show Judge Collier how it starts from the beginning."

Yard did so and holding the phone so the judge could see, began the slow scroll through of hundreds of messages.

Eddie pointed out, "As you can see, from the very beginning, it was the wife who was aggressive, who initiated and sustained the first contacts."

Collier read along, a low whistle accompanying his darting eyes. "Yes, I can see that. And they haven't seen these materials either, have they?"

"No, sir. Again, it's a serious 'gotcha' thing, but as there is no lawsuit pending and thus no discovery responses pending, the 'surprise' factor is only that and not violative of any rule. Here's what I'd request. I am not about to just hand this cell phone to them. As we all know, 'accidents' can and do happen. I would like to accompany you, Judge Collier, into their meeting area. You can explain our position. I can hold and scroll the phone while they look and read. I promise to not say a word. Once they say they have seen enough, I will depart and you will further confer with them as you like. Does that suit?"

Collier thought and then said, "Yes, I think that's reasonable."

Yard cheerfully noted, "Damn, I'd like to be a fly on the wall for that one. I know y'all ain't going to let me go with you, but Judge, do you think those things help us pretty good?"

Collier was standing up and when he was all the way up, he was imposing. He loomed over Yard, not threatening but was simply large and very present.

"Look, Mr. Yard, Yard, whatever...let me make this clear. I'm not for anyone winning. The only thing I want to win is the resolution of the case. To have it be over. I am not for your side. I am not for their side. I'm all about and I do mean all about the case ending and that's the win. So, anything,

anything that helps roll the two sides closer and closer to a clean, neat finish line—that's what I'm invested in. Do I make myself clear?"

Yard was now very small. He gestured palms down, a patting motion. "Yes, sir, Your Honor. Yes, sir."

Eddie and Patty and Alph just slowly nodded. Client expectations and client control finally achieved. Praise Jesus!

Collier continued. "So I hope this next round of texts, these texts are part of that. I don't think your lawyers here, and by the way they are top notch, would offer them in these proceedings if they did not think so. So, now, let me ask you a question."

"Yes, sir, yes, sir, whatever."

"Do you really want to get sued and have your reputation and your business kicked to the curb just so you get to be 'right?' So you can stick out your chest and say I told you so while you're wearing a barrel and having to find a crummy apartment?"

"Oh, no, sir. Oh no."

"Then, keep some money flowing and stop goofing off and pay attention to your lawyers and let's keep closing this gap. Okay? Let's try hard and pay attention now. By the way, and I'm no tax expert or accountant, but I think it's worth exploring with smart people...as this entire matter truly threatens your very successful business enterprises, I would think a goodly amount of whatever you pay, if we can get it done here today, would be a tax deductible business expense and loss to butt up against your profits. Something to consider and explore, I think."

"Hey, thanks for the thought." He looked at his threesome of reps. "How come y'all didn't tell me that?" He was grinning. The three looked at each other and shrugged sheepishly.

Alph drolly noted, "I suppose it would have come up on our radar in just a little while, but fair to say we've been busy just trying to keep the baby from being thrown out with the bathwater."

Yard nodded graciously. "Fair enough. Understand. I'm not grudging or judging."

Collier ordered, "Now, y'all sit tight in here, I need to go tune Miss Flottie up and then I'll be back to get you, Eddie."

Out he went.

Alph looked at Eddie and asked, "Where do you think this is all going with her?"

In near unison, Yard and Patty said but one word, "Money."

Eddie continued, "It's the old New York taxi cab driver rule—When they say it's not about the money, go ahead and bet all you can on 'Oh, yeah, it's all about the money.' We are just going to have to play this one out and as we get to the short end of the stick, then we will see, I think."

More nodding and then silence fell over them.

In the meantime, Collier sat out across from Flottie.

"Here's where we are. Your husband, and by the way, are y'all still sleeping in the same house, living together?

"Yes."

"Good. Your husband is at nine hundred thousand and your soon-to-be-former friend, I know it's been fun but really is going to have to end, is at two hundred thousand. I'm now going to go in to visit with Nestor and your husband and I'm going to take one of those lawyers in with me so he can show them some texting that you and Mr. Yard have shared over the last many months. We hope that will continue to help move the needle. But remember, if we can't keep moving, they can ruin Bustings and you both with the stroke of a pen. Do you understand? I think you do and might I ask. What's your stake in this anyway? The law of North Carolina says you have none. You understand that, don't you? Are you just interested, sympathetic, curious, what...do you have an agenda here somewhere? Miss Flottie, you haven't said two words, but we have tried to treat you right."

"Yes, you have. I appreciate it. I really do. Yeah, those texts look super-hot. They really did work. They were fun. And yeah, I suppose I have some thoughts but I need to watch it all unroll. I love my husband and I'm crazy about Bayard. But, as you know, all that's a relative thing..." Her voice purposely tailed off and she was beautifully demure and sat still again, a small, tight, trembling smile creasing her face.

"It's about money, isn't it?"

"Isn't it always? Isn't that why you are here?"

Collier short-necked a tight head nod and kept moving.

In but a few minutes, Collier returned with Eddie in tow. He knocked on Broadway's door and walked in. Eddie waited outside. Flottie just watched and said nothing.

Collier explained briefly about the texts and explained counsel's reticence as to giving the cell to anyone and the two assented to their proposed handling. Collier motioned Eddie in. Eddie nodded at the two but otherwise stood mute. Judge Collier spoke.

"Gentlemen, I have read the beginnings of this particular thread and where it stands at its end at present and I have also read here and there in between. I have not read all of them as we don't have that much time but I can assure you both that I have the gist of them, shall we say, well framed in my mind. As a neutral hired by all y'all, it is incumbent upon me to take note of what I think is important to the case and I believe what y'all are getting ready to look at is very important, especially the beginnings of it.

"Eddie Terrell, please stand over here where they both can see and start and scroll from the beginning."

Eddie did as he was told and Nestor and his client leaned in close to read. They began.

As the process went forward at a slow but constant pace, Nestor's face sagged and his eyes opened wide.

Steve Shinings sucked all of his lips into his mouth and his face began to blaze red with his embarrassment.

He blurted, "Oh, damn, goddamn, that's enough!" as he shook his head violently.

Eddie stopped immediately, put the cell phone in his jacket pocket, nodded at them all and went back to his bullpen.

Bob Collier simply said to Broadway and his client, "Your move, gentlemen. I'll be on the porch."

Nestor came out in a bit and sat down next to Bob Collier.

Collier laughed and said, "Nestor, we've got to stop meeting like this."

Nestor, with an obvious grimace in his voice, responded. "Well, if I'm gonna get paid, this courtship will have to stay the course."

"Agreed. What you got? Come along now."

"Judge, we'll come to seven hundred fifty thousand. I feel bad for that young fellow in there. He's really been run hard and hung up wet and he didn't even know how bad it was until just a little while ago. Maybe he hasn't been paying attention like he should but he got bad blindsided by this.

"But we ain't throwing in the towel now, not by a long shot. Tell them in there that as far as I'm concerned, we'll keep going and they better too.

Thought about it right when you left. It's an easy suit to draft and file. It's an easy case to try. I know I'm not considered one of the masters of the courtroom around these parts, but so what? Bustings is busted but good if a suit happens so maybe that's a good sales point to drill into him right about now when he's high on all the smoke coming off those texts. Hell, say we lose. I won't have that much time and money in it. It'll make my reputation something, better, worse, who knows but it'll let loose a hell of a storm on Bustings in there. And everyone knows that so I don't think this is a good time to get too cocky."

"Nestor, those are good points you make. I will deliver them to them in just a few minutes. Now, a question. Are we having lunch brought in? I don't care one way or another. I'm just asking."

"Judge, so far this thing is moving so I'd prefer to let everyone just get a Coca-Cola or a water or a coffee out of our break room. We've got some Nabs and pretzels and such in there. I expect that'll hold everyone. Let's not hit a pause button. What do you think?"

"I agree and will go let them know. I think that will be fine. I won't be long, I don't think."

He went back to the prospective defendant and eased into a chair next to him.

"I have made an executive decision. We're moving and I don't want to break for lunch. I don't want anyone to get sleepy. Nestor has drinks and snacks in his little break room." There was no dissent.

"Good. Now, they have moved to seven fifty. Y'all are at two hundred. Mr. Bustings, I just want to talk with you a little more. Your lawyers, I expect, know pretty much what I'm going to let you know."

So, Bob Collier, never taking his eyes off the lothario, did deliver Nestor Broadway's requested message almost word for word and concluded with a tilted head nod, "And I think he's exactly right. So where do you want to go now, Mr. Yard, Mr. Bustings?"

Even with his typical bad boy approach, the reply was remarkably jocular.

"Judge, I really want to go down to South America and shoot some birds but I expect that ain't exactly what you're looking for so I think I'll go to three fifty and let's see what happens next."

Collier could not help but chuckle. The other three just looked; the guy's social skills were so crazy erratic. And, damned if he wasn't very funny at times too.

"This is all just a game to you, isn't it?"

"Yes, sir, I suppose that is so. It's the business of money. That's all it is. I hope y'all don't take no offense to my attitude. I know all you lawyer types get all caught up in the lawyering of it all and the search for justice and the truth and all that. I just want to get this over with and keep moving. It was a nice time while it lasted. It surely was."

Yard Bustings' focus suddenly evaporated. He was obviously thinking about all his raptures with Flottie.

They all watched, fascinated how this strange man could just float in and out of wherever his mind took him.

He was obviously a lot brighter than they had all initially figured, but he was still an odd duck for sure.

Eddie said, "Hey, Mr. Yard. Snap out of it. Earth to Yard. We need you in here with us now."

"I'm right here. Like I said, let's go to three fifty…boys and girls, this ain't my first money rodeo. I'm ready to buy him off and that's what they all want no matter what so let's grease the skids and get 'er done and be generous but not too generous. You know what I mean?"

Bob Collier asked, "Mr. Yard—you know I'm kind of getting used to that now—Mr. Yard, I'd like you to give some hard thought over these next few minutes as to what your top-out number is."

"Oh, Judge, I been doing that from the get-go. Don't you worry."

"You gonna let me know what it might be?"

"When the time comes, Your Honor, when the time comes."

"Fine. I'm going back across the way."

Eddie handed the judge a sheet of paper and asked that he deliver it. Collier read it quickly.

"Sweet Jesus. What else are y'all gonna whip out?"

"Nothing else, Your Honor. Just tell them we know it's more than plenty and if they want to burn down their house to burn down ours over here, then have at it. If we ain't getting at best a mediocre lunch out of this, we are about done."

"Understood. See y'all soon. Oh, Miss Patty, from here on out, you're lead counsel. These two over here have been relegated to the cheap seats." Collier smiled sweetly. Collier knew. They knew too and were pleased. It was nice to just spectate while the big wheel turned. Out he went.

Patty didn't hesitate. "Mr. Yard, let's you and me go over here and talk. Eddie and Alph, how about y'all just fool with your phones for a while, please?" She assumed the mantel of control adeptly.

Alph and Eddie loved it.

Patty took Yard into the corner and began a hard, whispered interrogation. Her client did not resist.

Collier walked through the common area. Flottie inquiringly looked at him but did not speak.

"Any questions right now?"

"No. Just watching you get after it. No, I take that back. Y'all getting close?"

"Closer."

"Good. Keep working, please."

Collier just shook his head and thought, *Wonder how much little Miss Yin and Yang wants. And to think I get paid to help out in this sort of thing. Plenty cheesy and grinding entertainment...well, yeah, lots of grinding did get us all here... Christ! I wonder if Yard has already built something like this into his formula...?*

The judge went in and sat down.

"Gentlemen. I think we really are getting closer. They are up to three fifty and haven't said 'that's it' yet. Haven't even tilted toward it so far so I believe they have more rope to run out. Now, they've given me another piece of paper to give to y'all. It is an affidavit from Miss Floretta whom, as you all know, is sitting out in the reception area. Before we go any further, I think this is another item that is not helpful to the ultimate outcome you seek here. But I'll just sit here and y'all please read it, review it and then we can talk further."

Before reading, Nestor grumbled. "Goddammit, how many of these rabbits they going to keep pulling out of their hat? This is just damn surprise city! Please excuse my language, Judge, but this is downright aggravating."

"I understand. I really do. But, you have to keep in mind, there is no lawsuit in existence and they are under no obligation to conduct themselves as though the Rules of Civil Procedure and Discovery are applicable to this process. Now, they have told me to let y'all know that they have nothing else to provide to you today. This affidavit is the end of their tangible offerings for this day."

Nestor nodded, still theatrically grumpy and laid the paper down on the table where the two could read it. It did not take long for the two of them to start shaking their heads, almost in unison. They read on down to the end of the short page, then looked up.

Steve asked Nestor, "You mind if I have a say here?"

"No, go ahead. With what we've been given today, I don't know if it'll change the weather forecast but go ahead and have at it. And damn, son, are you still sleeping with her? Didn't I tell you to get away from her and stay away from her?"

Sheepishly, Steve nodded in the affirmative. He grimaced and said, "She's hard to resist. Sorry, she just is..." His voice tailed off.

There was a pause.

Collier held up his hand.

"Nestor. Steve. Based upon what I've just been told, your case is DOA. Steve, you, by your actions, your engaging in coitus with your wife after knowing of her assignations with Bustings, have, in the eyes of, as to the rulings of the law of North Carolina...well, you have forgiven her, have physically reconciled with her. Your case would be thrown out of court. Nestor, you know that."

Nestor grumped petulantly, "Fine, I basically agree but we can still file and then the bell is rung no matter what."

Collier nodded slowly and then said, "Nestor, that's true and everything we say in here is confidential, but you had better be careful. If you file and the case proceeds to discovery, it will surely come out that Steve has reconciled, that you knew it before you filed, Bustings may be ruined, but you then subject yourself to serious sanctions by the bar and the courts because you filed what you knew to be a frivolous and unworthy action. Think about it. If everyone in this building is too aggressive, all anyone and everyone will get is a bunch of very Pyrrhic victories."

It was very still in the room for what seemed longer than it really was and then Steve spoke.

"Okay, Judge Collier, I know all this looks bad for our side of the case and I've screwed up and this whole damn thing is a damn mess. I just want this over with. What do you think we should do now?"

"Now, are you telling me that you are not inclined to have a lawsuit filed?"

"Yes, sir, I think that's what I'm thinking. If we sue him and wreck him, there may not be any money then. Isn't that right?"

"Yes, that's potentially true. I surely am going to keep your inclinations confidential. I'll not tell them anything along those lines. So, keep negotiating. Stay with it. Let's see how much farther we can go. I think they truly want to get settled here too. So let's see what can be done.

"Now, let me ask you a question. Maybe a couple of questions. You have to play straight with me now. Understand?"

"Yes, sir. Ask away."

"Do you have any understanding or agreement with Miss Floretta out there to split or share whatever money you may end up getting ?"

"No, sir. None at all. Yeah, we still sleep in the same bed, but I have not discussed any of this with her. Nothing at all."

"Alright, do you think she has an expectation that she ultimately will be able to get some of this money from you?

"Maybe. I don't know. Now that I'm thinking about it, I expect that's why she's out there. Hoping to finagle money out of the situation. I wouldn't put it past her. She pretty and pretty smart and has gotten, it looks like, pretty slick too. I guess not the girl I married, huh?"

Nestor mused. "I'd been wondering that. Now, let's say that we get this resolved. It's Steve's money. She has no legal claim to any of it, does she, Bob?"

"Not that I know of. I suppose she could charm some of it out of you." A wry smile crossed his face. "We could just tell her to leave, but I'm not sure that's wise at this juncture. I expect that would just rile her up and I rather let this play out, however it's going to play out, right here while we are all here together. Here's another question for you, Steve, and I'm not trying to be cute. Are you going to try to patch things up between the two of you or are you going to be done with her?"

"I been thinking about that too. I just really don't know. What do y'all think about that?"

"Son, we are not marriage counselors so I'm not about to go down that road with you. Now Nestor Broadway here is your lawyer and if you get some money, before you do anything else, you need to sit down with him and come up with a plan to protect your money. That is, if you are not interested in sharing some of it with her."

"What a mess. What a damn mess."

"Yes, it does look that way, but let me go back to them and keep the ball rolling and see. What number do you want me to take back to them? I have a suggestion, if I may offer it."

"Please. Go ahead. This whole damn thing is giving me a headache." Nestor rubbed hard at his temples.

"I would match their move. They came up one fifty. I think if y'all come down one fifty, that would be a good signal to them. That would put you at six hundred and it's their move at three fifty. What do you say?"

Nestor and Steve looked at each other and Nestor said, "Go ahead. At this point, I don't see how it would hurt."

It didn't and it inspired Yard Bustings to quickly dance out another move to four fifty.

His lawyers, and that surely now included Patty, just sat there. They were all just ornaments in the room, mere temporary decoration.

Judge Collier said, "Thank you for that move. It's gonna help. Let me ask you this though. Do you really have the ability to come up with that kind of money, say within thirty to forty-five days? I mean, we aren't playing with Monopoly money here, are we?"

"Don't you worry about that, Judge. Your boy Yard here got it and will have it covered. I've been in business for a good long time now and have done just fine and paid attention along the way. I promise you that."

"Alright, good. Let me go talk to them."

As Collier opened the door, Bustings called, "Oh, Judge. One more thing, if you please. That's my top-out number."

Collier closed the door. "That's it? You sure? You really might be playing with fire."

Eddie and Alph leaned forward. Patty leaned back. They were the audience for the play.

"No, sir. I don't think so. And his lawyer in there is gonna convince him to take it. Neither one of those guys got the heart to try it. Besides, when they think it through and I'm pretty sure his lawyer already has, ain't it interesting how that four fifty number divides by three?"

Bustings laughed. "They ain't gonna kill the goose that's laying them golden eggs. Now, that would be downright stupid. Please go ahead and tell them anyway you like, but I'm getting bored and hungry and would really like to just go on. I don't think this should take too much longer. Do you?"

"Well, let me go find out. I promise I'll be back as soon as soon as I can." And he went across the way with Flottie eyeing him all the way but he did not pause to update her.

Collier delivered the news. Steve asked the judge what he thought about it.

"Son, you've already told me you don't want to get any deeper in this. It is a lot of money. I think you now need to have a talk with your lawyer here. I'm going to go out and wait in the reception area. You come get me when you're ready."

Bob Collier took a seat across from Flottie. It was awkward but unavoidable. He felt if he went out to the porch again, it would feel an awful lot like he was hiding from her. He nodded at her. She quietly asked, "Still close?"

Collier gave her a one nod and looked away. He's never been in a mediation like this. He waited.

CHAPTER SEVEN

ELUSIVE ERRATIC CONTROL
Winter, a Few Months Before

IT WASN'T LONG before Nestor opened the door and nodded at Collier. Steve was standing behind him, his face a portrait of resignation and relief.

Collier was moving to bring the others out to the room so they could all be together as the resolution was memorialized and signed off on.

Flottie looked past Nestor and spoke to Steve, "How much?"

Collier had the door open and was motioning to the others to come on out. When he heard Flottie speak, he froze.

His mind whirring, he turned to try and throw a stop sign up, to keep Steve quiet.

Steve flat-voiced "four fifty" across the room.

Flottie stood up abruptly, her face suddenly tight-hardened. "Really? Well now. So you're gonna get four hundred fifty fucking thousand dollars from that fool in there because you didn't pay enough fucking attention to me! What the hell do I get out of this? This is bullshit!"

Collier started, "Uh, Ms. Shinings, Flottie, now please calm down..."

That was as helpful as throwing a barrel of napalm into the mix. The pin was already out of the grenade.

"No, sir, Judge! I am not about to calm down! I'm going in there to talk to that bastard Yard!"

"Ms. Shinings, you can't do that! I'm in charge of these proceedings," he spluttered, his face reddening.

He started to say something to the effect that he was the mediator in this case and in control, but he at the same time realized there were no formal pleadings filed, there was no real, legal case currently extant and he was certainly not in control.

"Oh, yes I can and I will! I'm in charge of my own proceedings now!"

She hot-footed it into the room where the money was. Bustings was trying to get out of his chair but she pushed him down back into it. From the other side of the table, the others just gazed on, a combination of fascination, amusement, and aghast grimacing.

A collective unspoken agreement to not physically restrain her was suddenly and unanimously in place. But she could hurt someone. Medusa was marching among them.

Judge Bob Collier, Nestor Broadway, and Steve Shinings stood in the door watching.

They were all thinking the same thing. *Is all this going to blow up the deal? My God, she just might kill Bustings right there as he sat.*

Collier also mumbled quietly under his breath, "Jesus, this harpy has hijacked my mediation!"

He tried once again, his voice a bit stronger in command, "Ms. Shinings, please, get ahold of yourself!"

She was like a sinewy gray bat, with wings fully outstretched, ready to attack Yard Bustings. Flottie rocket-shot back over her shoulder, "To hell with that. You get hold of yourself!"

Yard, face pale with concern, rocked back in the captain's chair. "Honey, sweetie, now come on. Calm down. Please. Please." He was unaccustomed to pleading but that was exactly what he was doing. He was not very good at it and he was bleaching out in the wash.

"Calm down, my ass! You had plenty of fun fucking me and now I'm gonna have fun fucking you over. He gets a pile of fucking money from you for fucking me. What a load of bullshit! What do I get outta this shit show? Looks like a big bowl of fucking nothing."

Without looking, she hurled another bolt at her husband.

"Stevie babes, you gonna share with me, your sweet mommy?" The words clipped off like rounds in a pistol.

Nestor was shaking his head at Steve. "No, no you don't, don't say anything." Nestor had already wrapped his head and his virtual wallet around his one-third fee of one fifty grand.

Steve didn't know what the answer to that blast should be and said nothing in his growing state of dismay, his shoulders hunched up as though he were protecting his neck. He was humiliated and looked as though he was shriveling. The prospect of some conjugal reunification effort was vaporizing; whatever its molecular structure might earlier have been now shattered into sharp shards on the floor of his life.

She fired back again. "No, of course not. You've always been cheap. And you've turned into a silent, sniveling pussy. Keep your hard-earned 'I got fucked' money. And by the way, fuck you, the horse you rode in on, and your dog Spot. To hell with you!"

Flottie turned back to Bustings and just stared a hole through him. Her invective was getting ready to take a different tone. The shift was almost palpable. Everyone just waited.

Eddie leaned across the table to get a better, close view of this real-time train wreck. The salacious fascination of this human earthquake was irresistible.

Alph leaned back to get wide angle on all of it and thought, *Damn, sometimes I think I have seen it all but obviously, I haven't...ever since I hooked up with Eddie, all sorts of UFOs just seem to fall out of the sky...crazy shit...God Almighty, this Flottie gal is erratic and explosive...damn nice-looking too.*

Patty wrote herself a note, "Flottie is no dummy. She has a plan and we are gonna watch it play out right now. And I bet it's gonna come out of the Yardman's ass."

Flottie pulled a chair out and turned it to face Bustings. She sat down. She settled herself and was quiet, quiet as she had been earlier in the day. The Three Faces of Eve came to mind. She leaned in close to Yard Bustings. One could see she was composing her next words.

Then steadily and deliberately, she spoke. It came out slowly and straightforward.

"Now, Yard, let's get down to nut cutting time. You've made your deal with Stevie Wonder here and you're going to honor it. Don't worry all you judge and lawyer so and so's. I'm not gonna blow the deal up. I expect if y'all pushed back on me just a little bit, you'd freeze me out anyway. Just drag me into court and get a judge to cram it down your throats and to tell me to hit the road. Now, I've blown my steam off anyway and now I am thinking, shall we say, a bit more clearly."

She slowly back and forth looked over the assembled.

"To everyone, I'm sorry I yelled and said all those bad words. I really am. Not very ladylike, I know. But..."

She shrugged. It was nice enough of her to say but it was obvious she really did not mean much of it. Just a little more window dressing. A feint here, a fake there, set up the interference and run to daylight.

"So now, here's what I'm thinking. But, first a question to you, Yard."

Bustings was again pleasantly composed and nodded, waiting.

"Yard, honest answer now. It was all exciting and lots of fun with us, wasn't it?" She smiled so her eyes did too.

"Yes, honey, it truly was."

"And, Yard, we really did enjoy each other's company, didn't we?"

"Yes, we really did." Yard nodded.

"And from time to time, I'd give you a little present here and there and you'd do the same for me, right?"

"Yes, that's true."

She was speaking softly and drawing him into her aura, ever closer. He was slightly swaying under her influence.

All the others were now leaning in to make sure they could hear her performance and it truly was performance art.

"And now, don't you agree with me that we ought to work this out so everyone can go on home quietly?"

Yard Bustings paused before he answered. He laughed a little laugh. "'Everyone' is the key word, right?"

"Yes."

"Yes, of course."

"Everyone now is you, right?"

"I think you are onto something, Yard."

All was still low-toned quiet. Bob Collier was taking it in. He was in awe. This was being thin-sliced to perfection. He quickly remembered yet another of Winston Churchill's brilliant aphorisms, 'Make sure to be able to tell someone to go to hell in such a deft way that they end up looking forward to the trip.'

"Let's just say for purposes of our discussion that something or some things might happen that would potentially be, shall we say, unpleasant if we can't get this right?"

"I think you need a bigger word and a more powerful word than 'unpleasant.'"

"I think I understand. I believe you are speaking of what some of those folks on the TV news call 'the nuclear option?'"

"Yard, is there anything else I could be speaking of?" She was eying him indulgently, her head cocked to the side.

There was silence for a minute or so.

"Honey, I can only think of the one thing that would be."

"Yard, you understand, don't you, that you have left me with but this one option?"

He cleared his throat, looked down at his shoes, looked back up. "Yes, I understand. Now, if we can work this out, we can go back to world peace, right?"

"Yes," she said.

"And you would sign off on it, just like a contract that I would get these smart lawyers to draw up. Just like for the four fifty to Steve too? And you understand it would be legally binding, that it wouldn't be something you could run off the rails."

"Okay. Yes."

"'Cause if you tried such a trick, these lawyers over here would have make you have not so much fun with that big sucking sound we always sometimes hear about. In other words, what Yard might give, if agreed to, Yard just might have to take back if you wanted to take a run down the path not agreed to."

"Right. Okay. Right. You're getting warm, aren't you?" She laughed.

He smiled benevolently. "Now my family NEVER knows about this. NEVER. You understand that and agree to it?"

"Well, I think so but I need to see what's behind the curtain or the door before I cut a deal with you. You understand that, don't you? A girl has to look out for herself, right?"

"Right, I understand."

"Soooooo...what you got in mind, Yard?" She slowly and deliberately folded her arms across her chest.

Yard called gently across the room. "Mr. Nestor Broadway. Mr. Steve. Are y'all agreed upon me paying Steve here, say within forty-five days the straight up sum of four hundred fifty thousand American and so I'm honoring our deal? And if I don't within forty-five days, there's a penalty of One G a day until there's a full payoff?"

They said that was a solid deal and they would abide by it.

"And to my fine lawyers, that's the way y'all are gonna draw it up, right?"

"Right."

Yard stood up. "Flottie. Stand up and come with me." She looked up at him and stood. He took her by the hand and out the door. He announced. "Everybody just sit tight. I'll be back in a few."

He was back in just a few minutes.

"Where's Flottie?" Nestor asked.

"She's gone on home. She's alright. Folks, our business here today is done. Don't y'all worry. Whatever trouble there was has, I do promise, passed and won't be back. C'mon, boys, let's go talk out there in the parking lot. Mr. Broadway. Mr. Steve. Thank you for the hospitality. Nice visiting with you."

And out he went with his legal beagles tailing.

The sun was warm on them as the five huddled on the asphalt. Judge Collier was exhausted and it showed. Yard slipped on his sunglasses and became less present.

Alph and Eddie eyed their client with obvious curiosity. Yard just grinned at them. Eddie said, "Patty, you are his most recent 'counsel of record.' Go ahead. Ask him whatever. I think we're all hunting in the same field."

"Okay, Mr. Bayard 'Yard' Bustings, what's the deal? How did you pour oil on those really pissed off boiling waters?

"Well, Miss Patty, boys, Your Honor, it's like this. Remember now what seems like way back when, I told y'all I had a couple of nice houses down at Lake Norman. They're both west of that big marina near the Davidson College exit, just off the interstate."

"Yes, go on."

"Y'all know that Flottie and I have a thing for each other."

"We've noticed that."

"A big thing, you know."

"Yes, go on now. Let's try to get to it efficiently. In truth, Yard, you have worn us all out."

"To sum it up, Flottie's gonna buy one of those houses from me. You know how y'all lawyers like to say, "...for ten dollars and other valuable consideration..." That sort of legal mumbo jumbo. She'll keep it confidential. No chattering. And y'all will, I'm sure, write it all up for me that way along with everything else. Right? And of course, I'll be paying y'all extra. In a way, I'm feeling like I'm putting you on retainer for the rest of the way if that's alright with y'all."

"Interesting. Well, yes, sure. Fine by us. No prohibition on your doing that. What's one of those things worth, by the way?"

"Both north of seven hundred grand, free and clear, no mortgages or liens."

Alph whistled. "Damn, you're handing out Easter baskets today, aren't you? You are a very interesting fellow and appear to be far wealthier than we had originally surmised."

"Yeah, guess so. Just needed to be done and I figured, what the hell, let's go on and get to it. I figured when she showed up, she was looking for her cut of the candy. Besides, in the long run, it's all good money to invest in putting a lid on all of it. Steve gets a nice, big chunk of change and Flottie can keep the house or sell it or whatever. I don't much care. I'm not much for fighting and or getting tattled on and helping pull down a wall of bricks on my head so this is the better way, don't y'all think?"

"You're the client and we are here to try and help you achieve your goals so fine by us." They all nodded.

Alph inquired, "That's a pretty big number on that lake house. You planning on making a gift tax filing. I expect we'd advise you to do that."

"Well, it's like this and I do appreciate that advice. But, you know, sometimes it's better to ask for forgiveness than permission. So I believe I'll wait and see which way the wind might be blowing on that one on down the line. So you see, I'm not ignoring you, just paying attention to the running on of the times."

They nodded.

"Y'all got anything else? Believe we've done a good day's work here."

Eddie paused and then asked, "Yard, it is obvious to all of us that you and Flottie, well, got the hots for each other. I have a feeling this isn't the last time you will have seen her. Do you think that's an accurate observation?"

"Might be." Bustings looked away as he tried and failed to suppress a tight smirk.

Patty popped in. "Yard. Look. You are a smart guy. But in this particular situation, seems to me, seems to all of us that you keep letting your little head lead your big head around. You are putting yourself and a lot of what you've built up at risk. Why not lay this particular hobby down and just go ride your motorcycles around and go shooting and make some more money? Wouldn't that be a good way to keep occupied?"

"Oh, Patty, yes, you are right so let's just all agree that I will keep that advice in mind. Now, if that's all we got, how about y'all get started on getting all the papers put together and also, how about y'all see about the tax deductibility of the payment to Steve? I'll be in touch."

It silently occurred to Bob Collier that Yard would have made a hell of a lawyer, albeit a notably sleazy one.

And then Yard got in his car and drove away. And the sun still shone down on them. And they had all lost control of the thing and yet, fortune, yet good enough, was still with them. They had failed and yet succeeded.

CHAPTER EIGHT

HYPNOSIS

Late March, Wednesday

EDDIE'S ATTENTION CAME back to the road in front of him just as suddenly as it had veered off into the compressed memory of Yard Busting's problems and their solutions. It happened all the time. He would be driving along and mentally just go someplace else for God knows how long and then consciously reorient to the present. He always wondered each time how long he had been "gone" and how in the world he had not ended up in a ditch or worse. It was an autopilot sort of thing it seemed. He looked it up once. It was called "highway hypnosis," the monotony of the road slowing the brain, leaving the driver less alert to the point of basically checking out. But so far, so good, no disasters yet and on he went.

He turned off the interstate at the Golden Isles Parkway and wiggled his way east to Arnold Street and there was the legendary King and Prince. Opened as a seaside dance club in 1935, she had a national reputation as a beloved southern institution and never held herself out as the equal of the more stately, nearby Cloister at Sea Island. To do so these days would be oversell though her beginnings argued that she might have been allegedly the most exclusive club in the world with the grand Brahmins of Rockefeller and Whitney and McCormick leading her roster. These days the rich might well be in attendance but if they were famous, no one much knew or cared about that.

She was very comfortable in an understated way and sprawled along the beach as numerous additions over time had stretched her along. Billed these days as a "resort" she more aptly was known as a great beach club with absolutely magnificent ocean views.

As he pulled up, again she did not disappoint.

He checked in and the desk clerk noted the call for his reservation from their friends up the way at the Ballastone in Savannah.

He was housed near the main building in an ocean front room. He grabbed his *Rumpole of the Bailey* book and slipped on some track shorts and a T-shirt that read, "I'm a lawyer. To save time, let's just assume I'm right all the time."

It was arrogant enough but also signaled something ridiculously self-deprecating. When folks saw it, they either made a face and disapprovingly turned away or then again, some were game enough to want to talk a little.

He went out to the ECHO, an outdoor, eating, drinking, sunning, lazing area that was decked up with swimming pools behind and the lovely ocean facing. The sun was out. There was only a slight breeze. It was quiet, not too many people around. Kids were at a minimum. It was one of those "just right" late mornings. Eddie found a chaise and a good sized, fluffy beach towel and proceeded to flip the little red chair flag up.

A nice looking, lanky young man, maybe seventeen or eighteen, in a white shirt and a black clip-on bow tie appeared at his side. "Good morning, sir. I'm Kevin. How may I help you? Would you like a menu?"

"Hi, Kevin. Yes, you can help me. Please bring me two ice cold Buds in the can, no glass and a double grilled cheese and some chips and a good-sized dill pickle. I'd appreciate it. Oh, I'm Eddie Terrell. I'm in 1124 just over that way." He gestured.

Kevin said, "You got it, right away, sir." Eddie figured Kevin sure did like it when the customer knew what they wanted without a lot of dithering.

Eddie settled into his towel and book. The ocean tumbled and turned, an eternal rolling of pretty, sunlit water. He had learned some time ago that this spot on the K and P's property had been named "ECHO" because of the constancy of sound the waves made as they came eternally curling in over and over again.

Kevin returned, put the food and drink down on a little round top and asked if he could bring anything else. He had been thoughtful enough to bring salt and Heinz ketchup. Southerners were known to sprinkle and sop a good grilled cheese.

Eddie replied, "Thanks, Kevin. I'm good. Oh, how about do me a favor? If you find me asleep about 2:30, how about give me a nudge, get me moving? I've got a little work to do later on this afternoon."

"Yes, sir. Sure."

Eddie gave Kevin two thumbs up and picked up the first of the Budweisers. It was, as requested, freezer cold in his hands. Eddie drank it down in just two very satisfying guzzles.

Eddie had always been a quick study and that often included quick drinking as well. It set the foundation.

Years ago, after downing more than a few glasses of whatever while visiting one late afternoon in some dark, hole-in-the-wall lawyer bar up in Winston-Salem, he had been told by one friend that he was too fast with the quaff and that he needed to practice better "liquid management." Another friend interjected. "Hell, no. First you got to fire for effect and lay in your foundation. Then, you can take it more easy and target as you like."

Eddie voted with the latter.

He dressed the sandwich, munched on it, crunched some chips and pickle, sipped on the second beer and repeated the sequence until all was gone. He leaned back as the nap in the sun he sought was beginning to come along. He was contemplative.

Man, that was good. This is good here too. Here I am, just wandering around out in the Golden Isles. They are still so beautiful even though condo worlds and big boxes and Vrbos and strip malls have started their big invasions. Sapelo, St. Simons, Brunswick, and Jekyll. Mysterious, deep swamp and dark, runaway slaves and bad guys and good guys used to hole up all over here in rickety little houses on sticks. Beautiful birds and gators, and snakes too. It's too bad the onslaught is not just coming. It's here. Just like Yogi Berra said, 'Nobody goes there anymore. It's too crowded.' Jesus, hope the folks down here don't let another Myrtle Breach happen.

And then after a few moments of mental silence, he thought some more.

Now where are we, where am I here? I do miss Mikey. But Charleston was good. It felt good to please Truck, to make him happy. I've learned to share. When I was a kid, I sure didn't like that so much. Hell, got to think that Truck might find us something good out there down Charleston way. I'd go back in a skinny minute if it had some meat on the bone. Take Mikey, Alph, Patty, the whole crew. They liked that.

Now Savannah was a bust. Not a waste 'cause you gotta go prospecting but turned out to be nothing. At least we didn't jump right in and avoided that mess... now, in a little bit, let's see if we can go and catch a better fish...

And his eyes slowly closed as the suds and the sandwich began their assigned work of settling Eddie and bringing him a little sleep. He began to quietly purr and his exhalations slowed and elongated. He was still.

CHAPTER NINE

STRONG IN THE SHADOWS
Late March, Wednesday

EDDIE'S EYES FLUTTERED open as he felt a hand lightly pressing his left shoulder. He was curled fetal, partially twisted into his beach towel. It was Kevin.

"Mr. Terrell. It's 2:30. I guess it's get up and get going time. You were sleeping so sound, I hated to do it but it's what you told me to do."

Eddie wiped some drool from his chin, scrunched his eyes open. "Thank you, Kevin. You did good. How about please sign my ticket for me and add thirty percent for you? I got to go. I'll see you later, I hope."

"Thanks, Mr. Terrell. Hope so. I'm on shift until close at midnight."

"Then chances are good. Once dark starts coming on, I'll switch over to some good bourbon. You can help with that, right?"

"Yessir!"

Eddie had quickly changed into some jeans and a collared shirt and now drove out to Highway 17, away from the old and nouveau casual opulence of the coast and swung south. The landscape was now obscured and cramped with the basic urban blight of low-end muffler shops, gas stations, night clubs, used car lots, shabby convenience and lottery stores and what city planners and zoning boards allowed to be labeled as "light business and industry."

There was blown and discarded trash sprinkled among the weeds in the median and along the side of the road. Every now and then, there would be a dead dog or deer or critter in full rigor mortis off in the weeds and litter. The signage was faded and often twisted by weather and vehicular assaults. The strip went on for many miles and was the antithesis of the high-end comfort Eddie had just left.

After a while he found the place over to the right, Clay's Granite and Stone. The office was a nondescript square, squat cinder block building and behind it was a large open-ended warehouse with many prominent holding racks. It had a large, hard-packed gravel and sand lot, big enough for delivering and departing eighteen wheelers to maneuver in. There were a number of fork lifts and small cranes of various sizes. It all was surrounded by a rusting chain link fence with large, swinging double gates. All of the fence was topped with glinting razor wire. There was a big sign that read in big, dark letters, "NO TRESSPASSING. THERE IS A BIG, MEAN ASS GERMAN SHEPHERD ON PREMISES AND WE DON'T CALL 911."

Eddie had gotten a call a week earlier from the mighty Murdaugh firm in Hampton, South Carolina. He had worked a few medical malpractice cases with them in the past. They were a good outfit that excelled in both trial skills and the enormous double throw weights of prestige and influence. Eddie did the heavy lifting and the Murdaugh crowd would vacuum the fat settlements out of the liability carries. Hampton County and all down that way was known to insurance companies as "Hell County."

Jury pools were Black, poor, resentful and very plaintiff-oriented and had been for decades. Hampton was the only county in South Carolina without a Wal-Mart. One had been planned but in-house counsel, once the on-the-ground-research had been done, waved that idea off. It was the equivalent of waving a red flag at a mean bull. Too many slip and falls, too many parking lot injuries. Too much of too much and thus, not worth the investment. But now Eddie was not in Hampton County, South Carolina, where the socio-cultural fix had long been in place but down on the coast of Georgia which had the look of a burgeoning purple state and plenty of unknown confusion.

He was told that one of their client's boys was driving a flatbed loaded with vertical, many ton slabs of marble and granite down to St. Simons. He was said to know what he was doing. He was hauling down from Elberton, the marble and granite capital of the Peach State, just northeast of Athens. He was unloading a five-ton piece that got loose and crush-killed him.

The thought at Murdaugh was that the boy did not have enough or properly trained assistance at Clay's. The matter came up in a discussion Patty had had when she was talking with them about another matter. She passed it to Eddie and he signed on. He was heading that way on other matters and the idea of cutting up and over to Sylvester did silently percolate in his head.

Eddie's task was to ascertain what had happened and if money could, more probably than not, be made out of the mess.

He went into the office. There, at a battered, gun metal gray desk, sat a good-looking but rough as a cob girl, built formidably but nonetheless alluring, smoking a Salem Menthol—always a tip off—gonna quit soon—and talking on the phone. She obviously put her makeup on with a small trowel but she obviously did it deftly. Nothing ham-handed here. There was a lot of that in the South. This was nothing at all unusual about the entire panorama. She did not see him at first.

Eddie stood in the door quietly listening. The gal was saying into the receiver, "...well, you know, she's a lying bitch, always has been a lying bitch and always will be a lying bitch. To hell with her. I don't blame him one damn bit..." She took a pull, exhaled quickly, looked up and said. "Oh, gotta visitor. Gotta go. Later." And hung up.

She stubbed the smoke out, stood up and came around the desk. Eddie looked nice enough, clean shaven and clean clothes. He presented well and was no threat, no scammer or bill collector or process server. She extended her hand for a shake.

"Hello, Mister...? I'm Brittany, the office manager here. Your name is what and what can I do for you? And that call you were listening in on? That was a friend. We were talking about my sister and her all over the place, all the time bullshit. Pardon my French."

"Hi. No problem. I was just curious. Comes with my territory. I'm Eddie Terrell from North Carolina. I'm a lawyer from there but I work all over." He handed her his card. "I'm not here to cause any trouble, I promise."

He studied her, an involuntary one two-second up-down scan. She was pretty and tightly dressed but no camel toe. Good and darn. Wink. Just tight enough.

"Lawyer, huh? Oh that...hell, I promise I'm not worried about you. You here about that kid that got marble squashed a while back, aren't you? I can't think of anything else your house call would be about. Our ass ain't in no crack about that one. We're clean and in pretty good shape so far with just about everything these days. That was just one of those things, you know."

She was straightforward in a lightly coarse, throaty way and was well worth a second look. He smiled pleasantly, continuing to check her out as he did. She looked him over too, as dogs make decisions, so were they. She was clearly confident. He liked that. But he was disappointed because if she'd been closed-mouthed, defiant, curt or reticent or downright "get the fuck out of here" rude, then he was probably on to something. Her demeanor indicated another dry hole.

But, as with all of it, all the time, once he went looking, he had to get the story and pass it on to from where the inquiry originated. It was the professional way and it signaled a thoroughness that could always engender another call, another case. The word always got around as to who was half-assed and who really took the time to look, think, and study.

Eddie for years had seen himself as the big, fat bass in a fishing tournament that aired at 2 a.m. on ESPN 3 or 4. Obscure? Sure but if it helped make the bank, then so what...a lot of folks did not understand that you had to hump and hump some more to pile up the commas. He loved the lure and would strike at it over and over again until he got caught. From the get-go, he had always been hooked.

"Well, okay, and yes, that's what I'm curious about. Would you please tell me what happened?"

She already had the winning ticket.

"Sure, come on. I'll tell you and I'll show you too." He dutifully followed her out the door into the big lot. As he did, a very big black and silver German Shepherd came around the corner of the desk and fell in next to the girl named Brittany.

They walked over to the far corner of the yard, a good fifty yards from the office door and just a short pull from the front gates. Brittany whistled sharp and commanded the dog, named Baron V, to sit and stay. It did. Eddie made a mental note to be nice and to move deliberately.

She turned and faced him and pulled her cigarettes and lighter out of her hip pocket and fired up.

"Okay, here's how it went down as best we could tell. Do you remember back in the early spring when the weather turned bad real fast on that party holiday...what was it...Saint Patrick's Day...got real cold and the wind came up hard?"

"Yeah, I do." Eddie was flat-faced and now assured of defeat. And as he recalled it all too well, he knew now that any claim here was doomed to be a stillbirth at delivery. Two death cases in a row sent down in flames by the winds from Savannah Hell. He kept his mouth shut and listened. And, the more he looked and concentrated, it was still worth the time.

"We had loose-chained the gate and all gone home on account of the shitty weather. It was about midafternoon. There are only three or four of us here at any one time."

"Why did you loose-chain?"

"We knew there were a couple of deliveries coming in. We just didn't know exactly when. It happens from time. Usually the haulers will let themselves in, rechain and park and wait for help on the unload. Sometimes if it's nighttime, they'll sleep in their cabs until morning when we can get the lifters set up to assist with the load. That's what we figured would happen here, if they got here at all, considering the shitty weather and I do mean it was shitty...wind was blowing like a son of a bitch and colder than a witch's tit."

"Uh huh. Yes. I've heard. I know. Keep going, please."

"Well, that dumb shit did get here before dark and instead of just hunkering down here or going on to a truck stop or wherever, he obviously tried to at least start to untie his load. Hell, Eddie is it, is that right...?"

"Yeah, that's right." He kept his face interested but he knew the case was already deep sixed. He felt uneasy but stayed with it.

"Hell, Eddie, when we found the slab down on the ground the next morning, at first we didn't know he was under it. But when we realized he wasn't in the sleeper and nowhere else we could see, we got two forklifts and lifted it up about a foot and a half and got down on our knees and goddamn it if he wasn't leveled out like a damn Gumby cartoon...if he was eight inches thick by then, I'll kiss your ass. It was weird. Nasty too. Lot of shit and goo and blood already squished out and it was still leaking."

"What do you think happened? I know you don't have any witness statements. But what do y'all think happened?"

"Well, look, see the stains? It's rained some since then, but it ain't completely washed away."

Eddie looked and she was confirmed. No outline but just an unnerving, spread out discoloration. Eddie had seen plenty of stiffs along the way, but this now but a shadow did indeed take on a different dimension.

"Now you just said 'we.' Who all was here? Who is 'we' if I might please ask?"

"Sure. Me, our boss, Mr. Mack Brown and one of our lift operators, Mr. Julius Peppers. Strongest, biggest man I've ever seen…he probably could pick up the slab by himself but he is so good at running that thing—like a sewing machine in his big hands"

"Right. Please go on. I suppose we are close to the not-so-happy ending?"

"Yeah. We figured he unloosed some of the ties—and I think it was cold as hell and he was in a hurry and not being careful, surely he was rushing…well, hell, he wasn't being careful no matter what and it all made it all unbalanced and more unsteady, more loosened up on one end than not and another big gust of heavy, hard wind came along, and that afternoon, there were a lot of those and one of those took that five- to six-ton slab like a big, tall sail on a boat and pushed it over on him and his ass was cooked flat in a second."

"Uh huh," Eddie murmured as he saw it happen just like that.

"Hell, Eddie, see, once he started that unclipping the ties, with that weather and wind, his chances got to be slim and none and slim had already got up and left the room. That's the way I see it, the way we all seen it and that's the way the cops saw it too, just by the way. He didn't think it through. Stupid shit like that will get you killed and it sure did here."

She smoked and looked him steady. She was now mildly curious. "Knowing what I've just told you, you got a different thought?"

"No, no, I don't think I do. No. I think you have laid it out straight. I appreciate it." The lot was dusty.

Baron V just sat without so much as a flinch or shake. He was a beautiful, big dog.

"There ain't no lawsuit here is there?" she asked without antagonism.

He shook his head. "No, ma'am, don't think so at all unless…do you think Baron V here saw it happen? Saw anything?" He was teasing but not sure if Brittany knew he was. She had been very earnest in her telling.

She never missed a beat. After a stared pause, she offered, "Of course he did. He's very alert. He just ain't talking about it." She grinned and softened.

He decided she was desirably cool. For a moment, he wondered if he might ask her out for a drink. He thought of Mikey. He shook the thought off. He wanted to get on up to Sylvester, get on up to Aiken, get on home. It was another bust, but like a fishing line, it was being played out and snagged back, pull, pull...not very well.

Another let down and he felt his mind sagging. It was all a part of this business and he had long ago learned to roll with the punches, but from time to time, especially far away from home base, there was no refuge to go into and he felt blue and flat.

They all knew that the only things along the way that were inevitable were death and taxes and lots of cases that just didn't work out. But a bad streak was aggravating and sometimes made Eddie despondent.

The last few months had beaten them all down some but it was still difficult to get used to.

It was usually a temporary condition and he had always been able to resurface and re-oxygenate so he summoned up a smile and a respectful bow as he told the interesting gal named Brittany, "Well, thank you for your time. I'm glad I could see it for myself and come to understand it. It was nice meeting you. I've got to keep moving now. Again, thank you. Take care of yourself."

"You too. Where you headed now?"

"Up the road to Sylvester in the morning. Now, back to the K and P where I'm staying the night. There's a nice young fellow named Kevin over there who is saving some good bourbon for me."

"Ah. Sounds very nice. What kind of business you got over there in Sylvester? There ain't nothing there much save a big hunting lodge. You going shooting? Don't look the type. "Oh," she tightened her lips and smiled. "... and by the way, buy me a drink? Over there at K and P? I can follow you over in about half an hour. It would be easy, you know..."

She tilted her head, blatantly batted her eyes questioningly and waited.

Eddie paused and then cleared his throat and replied. "You know, I thought about that, about asking you if I could buy you a drink, really and truly, just passed my mind in the last thirty seconds. I decided not to do that, not to suggest or ask. No good would come of it I don't think. I've got a fine girl at home up in North Carolina. Yes, great minds do think alike but don't necessarily mean what they're thinking is a good idea. I appreciate the opportunity but I believe we should pass. I hope you aren't offended."

There was what they call in the South "a studying." It didn't take long.

"No, lawyer Eddie, I'm not and you're probably exactly right so let's just make this a fun woulda coulda, maybe even shoulda memory and you keep on going. You take care of yourself now."

She summoned big Baron V and they walked slowly back to the office. He watched them go in. He wanted to remember. He always wanted to remember so much. It was a strength.

He watched a loaded-to-the-gills eighteen wheeler lumber through the gates, the big pieces of flat stone pointing jagged skyward, a rolling stegosaurus. He got in his car, drove through the tailing, stirred dust cloud and headed back to the King and Prince.

Eddie thought, *Here I am out on the edge of the Okefenokee, struck out looking again and in more ways than one.* It was bothersome and made him antsy. *Meant to be, I suppose. Sometimes I feel like that blinking red warning light that comes on in your car's dashboard with the flashing message,* Service Soon. *Ugh. Thank goodness young Kevin will have some ready medicine for me.* He needed to get the damn saturnine beginning to squat on him up and off his mind.

He punched up the Murdaugh firm on his cell, explained to a nice law clerk the facts as he had uncovered them and thusly reported that any potential case, like the driver, was a DOA. The sharp young lady thanked him. He headed for the ice cubes and some nice, synapse-calming pours.

He then called Mikey and told her about his day and asked about hers. He listened carefully to her as she did to him. They told each other they loved the other. It was a good way to end the day and slide into the night.

CHAPTER TEN

QUESTING FOR THE BEAR
Late March, Thursday

THE NEXT MORNING, once awake, Eddie put on some shorts, a T-shirt, and walking shoes and headed to the beach. He was certain a good, long walk in the ocean air before breakfast would start to lessen the pall that had fogged in over him. It was a beautiful, breezy day with a few lazy clouds well to the west.

He walked down the mostly deserted sand for thirty minutes and then turned back to find something to eat and some newspapers. The ocean's roll was hypnotic. It reminded him of those white noise sleep machines that help rhythmically the coming of sleep.

Years before it would have been a more vigorous, sweat pouring run and jog and run some more. In his salad days, Eddie could knock out seven or eight miles and he loved it. Then the endorphins had just bubbled in him.

But that was then and this was now. The passage of time and its all too well known vagaries of his body slowing down and becoming more recalcitrant to strenuous exertion had been in plain sight for some time now.

He accepted such diminutions without much grumping and did what he could. Though less, he knew it was good for him and he owed it to Mikey and his people and clients and to himself to stay as fit as he could. He could still lift some decent weights and do pushups, but it was a battle and his desk job, and courthouse life kept him more sedentary than he liked.

Eddie also had lower back issues from fights, falls, football, car wrecks, slamming into the corner of his desk or door, you name it, over the years. Eddie's physical life had been defined by all sorts of often violent physical contact—his discs had been pounded to wafer-thin status and often there would be a radiculopathy that would painfully shoot down his right leg as the nerves became sandpapered by certain movements.

He was just getting older, but the hour walk up and down the beach did help and put a little snap in his step once back to the hotel. After a nice breakfast with good eggs and coffee and a USA Today and the Brunswick News, he was sated and put his things together, checked out and headed west towards Sylvester. He called Southern Woods and made a one-night reservation. He was tempted to ask about Moon Beam. He let it go. *Soon enough*, he thought.

Eddie was a little more excited than he had earlier thought he would be. He really was looking forward to seeing her and visiting with her a little after all these years. Years before, he used to do "guy trips," though that pretty much tailed off once he met Mikey. Girls were just always more interesting to Eddie than boys.

Years before, he had gone with a gaggle of guys to hunt and shoot at a lodge with all the bells and whistles just outside Sylvester called Southern Woods. It was smack in the center of the South Georgia bird country. Eddie wasn't much of a shot and he was not at all keen on shooting animals, though he did not condemn those hunters who found it to be fair sport. His group would bring their bag for the day to the big house's kitchen and the meals that rendered forth were delicious.

Eddie had long ago theorized his trial work had brought him within so much proximity to murder and mayhem and gun and knife and pick your bludgeoning instruments of blood and violence and that was the off switch that willfully kept him away from the trail of killing an animal. It was a quiet anathema to him. And yet he loved studying wars and battles and combat and conflict, and the contradiction was not lost on him.

But he loved to shoot clays and the place had three fine setup courses, each with a higher degree of difficulty. He shot two, sometimes three times a day, blasting away, sometimes hitting the flung and rolled orange discs, sometimes not. He had a visceral love for the contest and the strength and focus and discipline it called for. He loved the crack of his over/under twelve-gauge and was always delighted when he would bust one.

It was so much more fun than golf, a difficult, exasperating and expensive sport that despite his throwing copious amounts of money at lessons and rounds for years and years, he never managed to break an egg, much less a hundred. For a long time, he was the links poster boy for golf in the context of one of the truest teachings of Alcoholics Anonymous: The definition of insanity is doing the same thing over and over again and each time, thinking you will get a different result. That was Eddie's eternal eighteen hole agony-fest.

Happily, years ago, one day his clubs were lost forever at the club. They had disappeared from or into the maw of the bag room and were never to be seen again. The attendant searched and searched and then fearfully cowed to tell Eddie that he could not find them and feared they had been taken away or stolen by someone. He waited for Eddie's rarely displayed anger to erupt, Eddie waited and waited, and then busted out laughing and exclaimed, "Don't worry, son! It's a sign from God! It's over! I am set free!"

People standing around the pro shop and caddy stand, waiting for carts and tee times heard this and as it was absorbed, people began to bust out laughing. Most all of them had known forever the shackles and the addiction of chasing that damn dimpled sphere around and they knew their foolishness about it too. And they were glad for Eddie and sort of sad for themselves too because they could not quit. And obviously, Eddie had not quit. His clubs had just jilted him and tossed him aside with no tools left to perpetrate his chronic failures. But, no matter, he was out of the links jail cell for good. And thus, that was that for golf. Finis.

Yet the big house at Southern Woods had all sorts of comfortable amenities so he had had plenty to do while his buddies hustled each other and chased birds and machismo over out in the woods. It was fun to watch them go off with the guides and beaters, some in wagons, some on horseback, some walking. And sometimes Eddie would just walk with them and marvel at their shooting skills, and the dogs at work were quite a sight too. And then Eddie could go shoot as many boxes as he liked when he liked, sit by the pool, get a massage in the spa, read a good book or two in the large library, take a nap or a stroll in the pretty gardens. So he had liked the place and had good memories of it.

They were there for about five days and each evening, before and after dinner and sometimes without dinner, they would all go to a little bar without any signage tucked away in the midst of groves of tall Georgia yellow pines, a nearby annex in the woods on the grounds of the big house that was also called Little Southern Wood by locals and visitors who were lucky enough to find it. It was run by this remarkable girl, Moon Beam, always quickly shortened to Beam once a friendship had initiated and she had been his absolute highlight of the place.

This was in no sense of the words a continuation of a hoped-for courtship or a long-ago crush. Simply put, she was engaging, delightful, smart, funny and had a total command and control presence. He had never seen any-thing like it and knew he never would again. She surely was very desirable and at the same time, utterly unobtainable. She became who she was once she was in her small, contained space behind her bar with her wipe-down towel, unique as to time and place. The phenomenon of The Beam glowed as if by a mysterious extraterrestrial until she took her leave at the end of the evening. And then she was gone until her return. She had a panache that summoned all as long as they behaved. And if they did not, one stink eye from her and the miscreant knew their time was up.

So, he was looking for her again, just to say hello and have a drink or two and see if she'd remember him and see if she was still the same. The bar always opened at five when the modest neon Pabst Blue Ribbon sign in the front window clicked on. He sure did hope she would remember him. A gal like that was not going to be forgotten.

Like a high school boy on his first real date, he did not want to be too anxious too early, so he veered his way an hour north of Sylvester to let some time burn off and grab some history at the most notorious military prison of the Civil War.

Andersonville Prison was a colossal calamity of disease and death, a lethally microscopic abattoir that had belonged to the Confederacy, and their Union internees suffered horribly and died in droves. Scurvy, diarrhea, and dysentery were the omnipresent reapers. It was open for only fourteen months, administered by one very unlucky Captain Henry Wirtz.

The captain never had enough space—the place was filled to more than four times allowable capacity—just as were the holds of the slave ships that heaved to outside Charleston—never had decent sanitation—slit trenches for offal and waste were dug through the centers of sleep and eating, not enough food, not enough fresh water, always in the sweltering breathtaking heat of South Georgia. There were none of the basic supply and support logistics afforded the other thinnest of units in the field and the whole place was at best an afterthought to his superiors who were otherwise far more deeply engaged with the end game of their certain, impending defeat.

Wirtz ultimately was the scapegoat and was the only Confederate officer participant of the entire war who was tried and convicted of war crimes and it did not take long for the drumhead to roll. He was hanged on November tenth, 1865, on a gallows next to the United States Capitol.

The grounds of Andersonville were now a national park and were carefully manicured, lawns tight mowed with mature blossoming dogwoods sprinkled about with benches and set back flowerbeds here and there and the wooden structures of the prison were preserved in orderly and neat fashion. Little signs and markers informed the wandering and curious visitors what had happened at various stops along the way. Small groupings of small headstones sprouted up like granite mushrooms and small groups were guided on tours. The day and the weather were lovely. But for Eddie, it all had a grinding, sorrowful feel to it.

Dismal horror and gut-clutching death were the order of the day at Andersonville, every day. In the well less than a year and a half of its existence, about forty-five thousand prisoners were nearby detrained and shambled in. Over thirteen thousand of them were later and continuously dumped into mass graves and the great majority of the remaining sick and desperate and dying were sent out in emaciated and broken health and future as happened later at Treblinka and Auschwitz.

He went into the gift shop, an incongruous label for this sad place. He bought a drink and some crackers and sat outside on a bench. The crackers tasted like dust. He poured most of the drink out and tossed the trash into a brightly painted National Park Service bin and walked briskly to his car and got the hell out of there. His mood was not improved.

He steered south to a more cheerful place and looked forward to finding the Beam. Sylvester the Cat. Now that was more like it!

Moon Beam's real name was Joanna, which was then shortened to the simpler "Beam." She was one good-looking tall drink of water, legs as long as the tall yellow pines that encircled the place. She was endowed with a figure that evoked the grand carvings of goddesses that graced the bows of the giant prides of the long ago British fleets.

Her blonde-brown hair was copious and full and always tied up in a ragged-over bun or a pony tail. With a high forehead and big, round alert hazel eyes, thoughtful and realistic smarts radiated off her. One of Eddie's friends had quietly exclaimed during their visit of so long ago, "My God, her lips are like the dessert buffet at The Cloister on Sunday, just better!"

In her Daisy Dukes, a tight T-shirt that almost always read something to the effect of "Fool, What The Fuck Are You Looking At?!" and her quick shuffling pink flip flops or bunny rabbit bedroom slippers, she was a classic and she knew it, and almost always in good humor. But bad manners could and would darken her mood and responses.

She was from, it was said, up around Macon. It was rumored she was from a family of history and substance, that her daddy was a prominent surgeon, her momma a regal matriarch and that she had run away from home early, that she had been around the block more than a few times with great adventures and alternately rich and trashy lovers but no one had ever confirmed a word of it. The scent of watchful wild just smoked off of her. She always danced away from inquiries, usually with a lightly dismissive, "Now, wouldn't you just like to know...?" and kept moving.

Her voice was deep and dripped with the syrup of the deep South. When she said, "Hay," it captivated in its stretching over many seconds. It was mildly hypnotic.

She laughed large, told good stories, had every come-back line that could be imagined, took no shit and took plenty of shots with the patrons and seemed to have no vulnerabilities. No one seemed to know where she lived other than behind the bar at Little Southern Woods.

Eddie arrived at the big house a few minutes before five, checked in, tossed his bag in the rustically handsome room and then drove around the back road of the place to the little bar. The "Open" sign was lit and he backed his car into a space across the gravel lot facing the front door. There were a half dozen cars and trucks already there. A couple of guys in work clothes were going in. The dropping sunlight filtered at ever-flattening angles, soft and golden through the tall trees. It was quiet. Eddie was expectantly hopeful.

He went on in through the slapping screen door. The jukebox was lowing some B.B. King. The lights were down and the conversation was mostly quiet with a random hoot and holler busting the top off. It was as he'd remembered it and that made Eddie feel good. There was an old, low brick fireplace over to the side but there was no fire in it with the season growing too warm. He could still smell the smoke and resin from the winter just past. He walked to the long bar in the back and sat on a stool at the very end against the wall.

The rows of bottles on the back wall of the bar were cheerful rainbows of color backdropped by a full-size wall mirror. Back in the kitchen, he could hear the murmured voices of the help and the rattling of pans. He waited. Oh, this was so much better than the disappointments of the last many days.

A big fellow came out of the kitchen door, great wide forearms like Popeye, bar towel in hand. He smiled at Eddie.

"Hey there, mister. How you doing? What can I get you?"

"Hey, there. Let's see...how about a double Rebel Yell and a cold Bud back...?"

"You got it." The fellow reached down into the cooler, fetched the beer, popped the top and put it down in front of Eddie.

He then turned from Eddie and pulled down the bottle of Yell and grabbed a bar glass and poured away and then with a nice pirouette, gracefully paired it with the Bud.

"There you go. Anything else?"

Eddie reached, braced his shoulders a bit and pulled half the brown down and followed with a shudder.

"Good?" asked the barkeep.

"Oh, yeah. Good. Yes, sir." Eddie nodded with satisfaction. "What's your name, if you don't mind me asking?"

"Jeremy, but most folks just call me Jere."

"Jere, here's another question? Is there a gal working here named Beam or Moon Beam?"

It was asked with hopeful expectation and with some resignation of lost possibility.

Jere paused for a few seconds, pursed his lips. "No, sir. Not anymore. She hadn't been here since maybe six, seven months ago."

"Oh." Eddie's "oh" hung in the air as might a slowly dissipating smoke ring. "Oh."

The first had some tone to it. The second rang flat. The "ohs" were followed by a soft whispered "Damn." And then Eddie just looked at Jere with a pursed, ironically perplexed, "Moon Beam is not here" face and slowly nodded the nod of comprehension.

Jere sympathetically studied his customer for a brief moment with a look of understanding.

"Well, mister, I can tell you're disappointed and I'm sorry for that. She was something and there ain't no other way to put it. Not a week passes without one or sometimes two fellas wandering in here asking about her. I've been helping out here for about three years now and when she was still here, they'd see her and light up like a Christmas tree and they have a few and yack a while and then they'd just go on, go on happy. And since she's done gone, fellas would come in hunting her, just wanting to visit with her a while and they'd find out she wasn't here no longer and well, they'd each one turn into your likeness right now.

"Sorry to take notice of it, but I tell each of them just like I'm telling you something you already know…she simply had that kind of way with men…how about let me ask you something if you don't mind?"

"Fire away. Looks like now, I got nothing but time."

Eddie grinned the tight grin of the fellow who was left standing at the altar and would, all things considered, just as soon let the trapdoor beneath him go ahead and open up. But that wasn't going to happen and it wasn't worth a blindfold and a cigarette either. That's the way it goes and that's the way it went. Some days are diamonds and some days are dust. He felt pretty foolish and embarrassed and it was as though he was mostly naked and half-ass ashamed. He thought the memory of Beam and he saw Mikey too, all in the funhouse mirrors between his ears.

"Glad to try and answer what you got if I can. I promise."

He held his right hand up in the fashion of a pledge and with his left, tossed the other half of the bourbon down his gullet. He was beginning to feel it and it was helping.

"Okay. I have asked everyone this, pretty much the same way every time. When did you meet her and how many times have you been back?"

"Fair question. And can I have another brown, please? Let's see…I met her about, hmmmm, well, I think about fifteen years ago. I came down here from North Carolina with a group of guys to go shooting and just enjoy the place. It was for about five days. It was nice and we all met her the first night and she was something else and so much fun and we just came in here every night. She made every one of us feel like we were, well, special."

Jere set another glass in front of Eddie and stood and waited.

"And, boy, this sounds pretty stupid considering what I was hoping for now. I haven't been back since. I was just down this way, over in St. Simons, on some business and got it in my head that I could come over and say hello, have a visit, see if she'd remember me, that sort of thing. Pretty much of a dumb long-shot plan, huh?"

"No, not really. You're pretty level with what so many of the others say. Seems like she just left a mark on so many. I wouldn't go beatin' yourself up over it. I don't think it's a hanging offense."

Eddie took a long pull on the Bud and again, turned his attention to the bourbon. He looked at it, studied it.

"It's like, like she was, is, whatever, is timeless. Do you know what I mean? Do y'all know where she went?"

"Oh, yeah, I know what you mean. That question is asked every time too. Naw, we really don't know where she's gone off to. Rumor for a while was she'd gone over to Albany to tend some bar at some joint called Firecrackers and a few went over that way to check it out. No soap. They'd never heard of her. You know how it is. She was, hell, she is a legend and the stories about legends fly around like crazy all the time. God only knows where she's landed this time and best I can tell, He ain't telling."

Eddie understood.

Others were coming in now, some parking themselves down at the bar near him. The pink and golden spring dusk was laying in and the cooling of the late afternoon as the sun went on down was breezing lightly through the open windows.

Jere asked Eddie, "You okay? Can I get you anything right now?"

"No, thank you, Jere. I'm good. Well, you know what I mean. I'm fine. Thank you."

"I'll be back in a few. Already figured you like a few pops. We'll find out if you are hungry in a little while."

And he went to working his way back and forth, up and down the bar.

Eddie nursed his drinks, feeling the liquids burrow deep enough into him. He was quiet and thoughtful, and the sounds of the folks coming in and settling were not at all unpleasant. A couple of pretty young ladies worked the floor, helped out by a few bar backs and bus boys shuttling along here and there among them all. He was mildly surprised at his lack of agitation over the envisioned failed reunion, but upon further consideration, he understood that he had tried to outkick his coverage and had probably gotten his just desserts.

It occurred to him that he had failed one of the key challenges of his profession and that he was the cause of the failure and did suffer that failure in the process. It was always imperative that a client's expectations be managed and kept within the rails of reason. Otherwise, the client would conjure thoughts and ideas that were unrealistic, such as "my case is worth umpteen million dollars," "that the 'other side' were always bad people," that the outcome was always going to be in their favor and so on and on. If the lawyer allowed that sort of one-sided thinking to inflate, the effect on the case could be harmful, even fatal.

And yet here he was, Eddie Terrell, the pro's pro, standing on the other side of a silly, immature and now fantasy-popped dream.

He had let it get away from him. He had not been disloyal to Mikey but he had, to recall, former president Jimmy Carter, surely, kinda, sorta sinned in his heart. It was time to move on. He was now glad that it hadn't worked out. Aiken was his last stop and it was a good safe haven. He would be home soon.

Jere came back down to his corner.

"How you doing? Hope some better. Another drink? You hungry?"

"I'm fine now. Thanks and yes to both."

Eddie pointed at the beer bottle and the short glass. "How about one more round of the same and a medium cheeseburger loaded with chips on the side?"

"I'll get that right on in for you. Glad to see you are now in recovery." Jere winked.

Eddie toasted him with an empty and waiting glass.

Later, before heading up to bed, Eddie stopped in at the big house's beautiful, paneled, high-ceilinged library. This was not a room for resort status show. This was a substantive room of long standing use and he remembered it well from long before. Absolutely full of books, this was a quiet, serious reader's room. He sat in a high-backed, old weathered leather chair and just took it all in. The books, the fireplace, the furnishings, the lamps, the concept that he was sitting with so many good and useful and pleasing and teaching words—all lent themselves to his comfort.

It consoled Eddie that though they had had a rough run lately and too, there would be others later, his mind still worked just fine as did the minds of Patty and Alph and Mikey and that, just like this room, the accumulation of their knowledge and experience would outlast and defeat any sloughs along the way. They all were a little older now but they were not weakened.

CHAPTER ELEVEN

HOMEWARD BOUND
Late March, Friday

IT WAS FRIDAY. He was alert and rested.

On his way up to "The Winter Colony," Eddie reviewed his trip. Did fine by Truck. Got out early and easy on that dog in Savannah. Ditto on St. Simons. Came up dry—just as well—in Sylvester. Now, on to Aiken to visit with old clients who had endured a large slice of hell and despite the pain of it all, had pushed on through. There was a night in store at the Willcox, Eddie's version of swaddling clothes in a manger and too a drink and dinner with a fine friend and then on home to Winston-Salem the next morning.

He called Mikey, reporting in and teasing with her and asking her what would she like to do for the weekend. After all, spring had gotten loose. She said she'd think about it. Whatever "it" turned out to be would be just fine by Eddie. They exchanged "love you's" and rather than asking to be passed on to Patty, he rang off after deciding to call back anew and see if he couldn't have a little fun with his "Command Central."

He punched in the office and waited. It rang a couple of times and then came the clipped answer.

It was Patty and he could hear and see the smoldering cigarette lodged in the corner of her lips as she intoned the flat, disinterested greeting offered from every office on earth which signaled that the recipient of the call was looking at and thinking about something else. First, she exhaled expansively with a great blow of breath.

Then, "Law Offices of Eddie Terrell. This is Patty speaking. How may I direct your call?"

Eddie started singing, "Your boyfriend's back and you're gonna be in trouble...Hey La Dee Da...your boyfriend's back..."

She hacked out a laugh. "Christ! The Angels sang it with style, then the Chiffons and now you've wrecked it...Where is Phil Spector when we really need him...? Oh well, what the hell...okay, you foolish boy, where are you and how was your foray into the woods of South Georgia?"

"Thank you for your constructive criticism of my warbling. I believe that only because I caught your caustic ass off guard have you denigrated my efforts."

"Blah blah blah. Where are you?"

"I recall there were two questions. I am on my way to Aiken to visit with the Douglas family and spend the night and then come on home tomorrow. As the workweek ends this afternoon, how about y'all get us organized to make some hay while the sun does shine starting on Monday? Please lay Cameron out on one of the work tables. We need to really start putting that one together."

"Copy that. Understand and will do. And please give all the Douglas crowd my best. And Georgia? Hmmmm...?"

"It was fine. Nothing more than a trip down an old memory lane."

"Any old flame on that old lane?"

"Nope, none at all. In truth, there was an old friend there—just a friend, nothing more— I had hoped to see but she had long since left the place and I just enjoyed where I had stayed many years ago with a crowd of guys. It's a hunting lodge and grounds, lots of grounds and it's a good place to just take it easy and settle the mind."

"Well, God knows yours could use the work. And last time I looked, you didn't hunt birds and such, but of course, way back when, you sure as hell did hunt...oh, never mind...so, when will you be back?"

Eddie laughed. It felt pretty good.

"Coming home Saturday by lunch and will see y'all Monday morning."

"We'll be waiting for you."

"I know, oh, I know."

After his loop of travel culminating in his beloved Aiken and all its myriad and jeremiad of experiences, bad, good and strange and mysterious and discomfiting and hideously frightening, Eddie drove home to Winston-Salem. He was feeling better. His fears and worries seemed to be dissipating. They were there but they were not a distraction to the point of rendering him frozen and useless as he had been earlier that morning. His mind was pushing forward.

Thinking about everything from over the past three, four months, he theorized it was all just a cumulative blow-out and that with the passage of more time and lots of effort with their work and cases ahead, the afterblast would subside and settle.

As he passed into the city limits, he called the Willcox and left a message of his safe arrival home with the front desk for delivery to Tina as she had requested he do. He also asked that they tell Tina that he said thank you so very much for her calm help and that he was doing fine and would be back to visit soon, especially if she would find him a new case to chew on down that way.

He told the nice girl that it was all code and that Miss Tina would understand.

Eddie always loved to have cases in places that he loved. He got to go travel to those places and stay in those towns and got to work the conflict many times in pleasant and trusted surroundings.

He pulled into the driveway at the little house on the lake on Lynn Dee Drive and quick- stepped to the front door. Before he could make the salutary knock of the returning warrior, the door swung open and there stood Mikey with open arms. She always took his breath away and made him jerk back, just a little. It was never feigned. It was an involuntary reflex. This time was no exception.

They had been together now for some twelve years and time and genes had been kind to her. Eddie had become with age, a more handsome, stately fellow, but she was in the category of different. She was still and probably always would be a spectacular, natural beauty. A little gray at her temples, a small wrinkle or crease scattered about, some minor aches and creaks from time to time mattered not. She was, simply put, a bomb and a head turner and he was still so crazy about her.

Lucky for him, the feeling was mutual.

They had never married. They had never had children. It was a mutual decision and she was faithful to her and their health. Once it became apparent that she was a happy settler, Eddie had lined her up with his old friend Dr. Harry Pollard, head of a fine OB-GYN service out on Lyndhurst. She delighted at Eddie's attentiveness on this and on so many other scores and was punctilious about her appointments and birth control pills and such. They both shared the viewpoint that only everyone else's children were just fine. They had plenty on their plates and were selfish about each other and that suited them just fine.

And Mikey took Eddie's health seriously too. Learning that Eddie was at best lax about his rarely scheduled annual physicals and also vaccinations and exercise and diet, she became his proprietary health guardian. She made them walk and ride bikes whenever they could and she shaped up his necessary medical appointments. When he ordered a heart-busting bomb of a meal, she would simply shake her head and murmur, "No, sir," and Eddie would without resistance retreat, usually to a salad or a piece of fish. It appeared, on the other hand, that Mikey could scrape the enormous buffet at the K&W slap clean and add nary a pound.

They were both in good shape and she was determined to keep it that way. He liked so much that she cared and he bought right on in. They were invested in one another.

And they had discussed all that and more early on and decided that whatever they had worked just fine and there was no reason they could see to complicate it by the constraints of marriage. It was a fine example of the old saying about hold the dove in your hands totally but not so firmly that you hurt it. They loved each other fully.

Now, every now and then but not often, they would have squabbles and grumps and disagreements and even a good old-fashioned argument, replete with raised voices and arm waving and dramatic expositions and declamations and stony silences—after all, these were people who sometimes ran hot and too, very hot—but like blossoming summer thunderstorms, the clouds rose up, cracked and rumbled, sometimes heavy rain fell, and then the sun came back out and rainbows often appeared.

She made all over him and he made all over her, their never leaving the front hall, their hands and lips never leaving the other. It was an excellent grin and grope, a homecoming of warmth and heat. It was another very pretty day and of course it was a happy day too.

"Well, hello! Glad to meet you. So glad to see you...well, have you thought about it...What you wanna do?"

"I dunno. What you wanna do?"

It was damn close to a "who really cares" moment, the sort of which was initiated and imitated over and over again all over the earth for time in memoriam as what true lovers do.

They were sweet to each other, sweet on each other.

Their melded, swaying quiet was interrupted only by Eddie's quickly assented to observation that they better get moving on or they would end up vertical and ultimately spent, thus wasting the better part of a very pretty day. Maybe that was not such a bad idea for the moment, but they were older now and knew the other's rhythms and as is so often said, timing is everything.

Mikey took his hand. "Okay, mister. Let's get going. Hungry?"

"Come to think of it, yes, I am."

"Okay, first stops, Village Tavern and a walk in the gardens. Walk first or later?"

"Uhm...walk first. Much to tell you."

"Oh, I bet. Yes, I do." She grinned at him and stole his heart blind again, as always, when she did.

CHAPTER TWELVE

TRANSITIONS
Late March

THEY WALKED, BARELY a slow stroll, languidly in the trees and flora in Reynolda Gardens, part of the old, sprawling R. J. Reynolds estate, slotted between the center of the city and the nice neighborhoods of Buena Vista. Dappled sunlight shone through the canopy that sheltered the path. The leaves were new and freshly green. The weather was soft and lovely. They held hands as they passed the now almost dried up, but still lovely, with muddy reeds Lake Louise and headed up toward the university. The jonquils and dogwoods were fulsome and their scent was tart sugary.

He thought of his dolorous time in law school. Simply approaching the plain architecture of the law school up and over the hill, knowing it was "just over there" triggered a cascade of thoughts.

It had been much closer to misery and melancholy than anything marvelous. It was a hard slog and his thirty-plus months there were almost always akin to being held against his will, dangled over a whirring, arbitrary academic blender whose blades were deep-sharp engraved with The Rule Against Perpetuities, Agency and Partnership and Bailments, The Rule in Shelley's Case, Dred Scott versus Sandford, Internal Revenue Service Administrative Ruling—Section 7206(4), Hadley versus Baxendale and

Palsgraf versus Long Island Railroad to cull but a few from a gigantic herd of "things that one must know."

He grew to hate the television show *The Paper Chase*. He wanted to hit that arrogant bastard Kingfield in the face with a pie and/or a bat. When Perry Mason would pop up on the screen, he would irrationally shout, "Bullshit!" and he had no idea why he did that. *To Kill A Mockingbird* poisoned his heart and he did not understand that reflexive response either. *Twelve Angry Men* made him more angry. He grew to detest "all things law" and as there was no antidote, he insulated and encapsulated.

The books were too damn big and heavy; they had to be lugged from a parking lot that was over in Stokes County, it seemed. There was too much paper, uncontrollable reams of it that flapped and got loose, and there were always a pound of nickels in his pockets which tipped him more sideways (often to counterbalance the dragging gravity of the massive tomes of law …) to gorge into the Xerox machines just outside the law library's entrance because somebody's else's canned briefs were always better than his.

His stomach hurt each day—until right at the end of his 3L year—when he emerged from the seemingly inescapable drowning and gasped in thankful, wondrous exhaustion that he had finished another set of classes. He could not wait to get off the campus as the day wound down.

There was a force field, an invisible, giant barrier that stood between him and the acceptance of the place and its potential purpose in his life.

But upon reflection down a long, long hall of time, Wake Forest University had been good to him though he had not understood that at the time of his attendance at the law school. Then, now so long ago, he again and again pictured himself sloth-like trudging from mediocrity to the edge of the precipice of failure, doing his duty to his father, doing a penance as well. Big Doug had recognized right away that graduation from Chapel Hill had meant basically that he was still very good at reading and drinking beer.

Eddie quietly recognized that his taking possession of his undergraduate diploma at Hanes Hall, after of course paying off his more than a few outstanding parking tickets, simply meant that he was just a more well-educated incomplete though he did dig much deeper academically into his junior and senior years and it showed. To what good end, he did not know. And oh by the way, the receipt of that sheepskin symbol of success was accompanied by a Bible and an American flag—artifacts of a time long since passed. He thought, *Can you imagine? My God! Get the torches and pitchforks!*

His father flatly and plainly and pleasantly told him that he needed to go to graduate school, to mature and season, to grow up enough to go out into the world and accomplish "things." Eddie knew his daddy was right, though he had no idea what those "things" were—no sense in asking as he would just show his need for all the things his daddy already knew about—and besides, Big Doug had never steered him or his siblings wrong. He was amazingly accurate and farsighted as to this business of parenting, advising, and guiding. He was their patient and steady shepherd and oracle. His tank commander in war credentials served him well. They respected him so enormously.

Big Doug was a smart coach and innately understood what his son's intellectual pay grade was. He was kind but blunt when he told Eddie, "Son, look, you are terrible with the sciences so medical school is out. Too many will get sick and die at your hands. Same with math. No architecture school for you. The buildings will fall down too often and too early. I'm not worried about your shortcomings with foreign language. I'm not sensing there's ever going to be work in your world that calls for a lot of French. I'm thinking law school for you. Lots of reading. Lots of analyzing and thinking. You're still an avid reader, right? You have always done well with English and history. Let's shoot for law school."

So Eddie took up the mantle of his daddy's offer of self-penance.

It helped that Eddie was naturally competitive and found that when challenged with a hard task and especially prospective failure, he doubled down with his mind and his effort. He understood all that in the sense of athletics and physical contests, but undergraduate school had been a pony ride in the gentle woods compared to trying to hang onto a bucking, angry overbred, inbred thoroughbred named Law School where there was an unforgiving premium on accuracy, and precise thinking and writing and the freeform wanderings of the liberal arts were disdained.

More by luck than pluck was he admitted to Wake Forest and also the toss in of favors called and entreaties made as part of the launch that landed him in what was called "The Bastard Class," for those entering in the middle of the first One Law academic year. Everyone else was already one semester ahead and the invisible linkages of one course feeding into another were disorienting, dismaying and off-putting.

The sink or swim approach was tailor-made to wash him out but he fought the riptide just enough and he made it, just by the skin of his teeth but he did make it. And too, having gotten married at the foolish age of twenty-three to a gorgeous gal used to the high-toned life did not assist him in his need to focus. In truth, Eddie carried so much distraction and scarring from yet another self-inflicted wound. Suffice it to say, the immature union did not last long.

But he graduated with decent grades (truly only at the very end, acquired in his last semester) and then remarkably with the intercession of God and ghosts, he passed the North Carolina State Bar.

Little did he know it but he was on his way with the great help, push and shove from his great friend, classmate and original issue, sturdy and smart-as-hell law partner, Tommy Rumpler.

T.R. was a paper-pushing, real-estate-binging, commercial-deal-making powerhouse, a superb lawyer and counselor and a wonderful guy to boot. He was integral to their success and that with a capital "I."

They carried the ball together for enough years to set their hooks, both individually and collectively before it was decided that each needed to solo. It was not that they were getting in each other's way or that they had gotten cranky with one another. It was simply the nature of how their practices differed and that each of them needed to now set up the correct boundaries to ensure that cross-pollination did not dilute or pollute their work.

They always did laugh, only amongst themselves, of course, that as the practice grew, how their waiting rooms began to be crowded with constant odd couple assemblages: T.R.'s clients in crisp white shirts and poplin suits and cashmere jackets and silk ties and buckled loafers or gleaming wingtips, carrying reams of architectural renderings and plat rolls; Eddie's in wife beater T-shirts, knockoff designer jeans, many with the sagging drag-ass drawers of cool, unlaced Nikes or Jordans, on backwards ball caps and bright bling and the ever-present, always being counted and recounted rolls of cash and too, many on crutches or casted or bandaged.

The former with no bulges ever to be seen rising from their breast pockets were always sent itemized bills; the latter, almost always adorned with a large, battered wallet lash-chained to their belts loops, either paid long green up front or in installments or, if a wreck or injury case, signed on for a piece of the action contingent fee spree.

Often as the days began, the suits were brought to the back for coffee and preamble chat. And the more unwashed stayed in place in the front because court appearances were on the rosters just down the street; folks had to be on time and it was a counting house in the spirit of Jim and Tammy Faye Bakker's PTL Club.

And after a while, it just got to be time to split the herd. So they did.

T.R. joined up with, as a highly sought, instantly invited partner, a wonderful mid-sized office in a tall, weirdly phallic downtown high rise, illuminated by rows of fluorescent light and desks to which were attached lots and lots of support staff, a silk stocking, carriage trade firm which needed a burst of energy and contacts and networking, and T.R. became their rainmaker par excellence over the ensuing decades, attracting white collar work, clean and too often confusing deals of ownership and control, Gordian knots that he would massage and maneuver into clear strands of success with the language of the law. Under all lay of the land and onto that land, T.R. did lay his hands and brains. He became their indefatigable trace horse. And he loved it.

Eddie found an old gabled, gingerbread-styled house with just enough history to intrigue, called the 1885 Rogers House and it stood pretty much on the cusp of where Winston formally met Salem in the very early twentieth century. Facing due east, it was on a nicely elevated rise a couple of short blocks up from the county and federal courthouses and the police and sheriff's departments and the county jail. On ramps to the interstate were just adjacent.

It had adequate parking and a gigantic, towering, shading oak in its front yard. It needed paint in and out and the nice touches of cleaning up, fixing up, and dressing up. It was owned by the somnolent trust department of the most important bank in town Wachovia (which depending on one's mood and circumstances was pronounced "watch over ya" or "walk over ya") and the bank was in no hurry to move the property. The "For Sale" signage was at best small and desultory, hung crooked on a fence on the far southern end of the lot and had a green, slimy moss and mold build-up on it that signaled seller neglect and disinterest.

Eddie liked the property and wanted to get it. So Eddie got the bank's attention and created the impetus for a deal.

After walking the long-vacant property and peeking in the windows a couple of times and standing still in the front yard and getting a sense of its feng shui, Eddie asked T.R. to run a title search on the property, which Eddie indeed did pay T.R. for with a check and a handle of good vodka. The search came back with enough information to guide Eddie to its heirs.

There were two, an older gentleman down in Charlotte named Hines and younger sister, a Mrs. Caldwell who lived in Richmond.

Eddie got in touch with them and told them of his interest and intentions. He contacted the sister first and told her of his interest in the house. She was very nice and a little surprised.

"Oh, Mr. Terrell, you've caught me off guard. I haven't thought Momma and Daddy's property in so long. It's, well, it's as though it no longer exists. But of course it does. Momma and Daddy loved that place and we did too. Sometimes I think we don't mind hanging on to it a little while longer. Sort of a way to make the memories live on. But I know something has to happen with it. Please do me a favor, would you?"

"Yes, ma'am, I will if I can."

"Would you please get in touch with my brother Charles down in Charlotte. He'll be the one to speak to about it. Here's his number." And she recited it out slowly and carefully.

Eddie took it and called the fellow and introduced himself to Mr. Hines and explained what he was thinking.

Mr. Hines admitted that while he thought about the property from time to time, it went off his radar more often than not.

"I'm pretty busy with my own business and operations down here and hell, you know how big banks are...they move as though they're running in mud."

Eddie told him that it appeared the bank wasn't making much effort to move the property though it was in a fine piece of real estate in a fine location, allowed that he respectfully felt it needed the ever ubiquitous "work," noted his rationale for those presumptions, explained his distrust of big bank trust departments as they loved to charge their management fees as their time clocks ran. Eddie discussed with the gentleman in Charlotte the fact that it had been in the bank's inventory for over three years and opined that just did not make good business sense and opined that the bank's apparent lassitude bordered on willful abuse of a trustee's fiduciary duties.

Eddie wanted to rile the man up a bit. He suggested that a call be made from Charlotte to the third floor of the Wachovia Building in Winston-Salem to express whatever feelings might be coming to the fore because of these conversations.

The man agreed with Eddie and volunteered that he would make that call in just a few minutes. Eddie counseled that Trust Departments get very nervous when assigned beneficiaries make reference to potential failures of asset management.

Eddie also told him he wanted to buy the property, get it fixed up properly and make it his law office. He felt the asking price of three hundred thousand should be reduced by about twenty-five thousand as repairs and painting and such needed to get done. And here was the kicker. Eddie told him he was willing to pay cash for a clean title and a deed. If the bank could be persuaded to get off its ass, it was a quick and fair exchange.

Mr. Hines agreed with Eddie.

After that it all went quick enough. The call was made, Eddie showed up at Wachovia's Trust Department offices later that afternoon, met with the VP in charge of the oversight of 1885 Rogers House who immediately knew the snare had been set, having earlier spoken with one of the heirs down in Charlotte, a testy Mr. Hines who was more than pointed in his sentiments that the bank had been "screwing around." In a flat monotone, Mr. McShack lamely initially clung to the "these things take time" company line and he used puffing on the cigarette, a Vantage, he was smoking along with a few racking coughs to help slow the pace of the "conversation" down. McShack was perfectly suited to the trust office genre of work. He was affable, smart and as to nature, tortoise slow. "And, there are so many intrinsic factors that warrant further…"

Eddie quick-stopped signed him with his hand and began the fast forward.

"Here are the current factors, Mr. McShack. Your weather forecast is pretty sunny right now but unless y'all get off your duffs, a storm is coming."

He made his proposal for three hundred twenty-five thousand, explained it and within ninety seconds, slid a cashier's check (a Wachovia-drawn negotiable instrument) for a hundred grand (issued by Wachovia's Senior VP of City Affairs, the genial Ruffin McDalton just downstairs on the first floor) in good faith onto McShack's desk who peered at it and made a "hmmmm" sound. (Banks always said there was "Chinese Great Wall" between their trust operations and the rest of the commercial bank. That was bullshit.)

Everyone knew everything all the time and Eddie easily and calculatingly spilled the beans to his old, long-time family friend Ruff to start the, "Hey, did you hear...?" cascade that would soon seep up to the third floor. McShack knew how this worked—the "Wall" was nothing more than a sieve.

Eddie continued. "This offer is good for seventy-two hours. As of this hour, 3 p.m. So y'all either accept it by then, no strings attached, as I have proposed it or I'll be visiting soon thereafter with your beneficiaries and discussing how big the stick of dynamite needs to be to stuck up y'alls' hatpin-tight assholes. No personal offense intended but collectively y'all are as constipated a bunch as I've ever run across and we need to get the MiraLAX bus rolling here."

McShack nodded slowly. He, recalcitrant and quiet by nature, knew there was no need to elucidate his thinking.

"And keep in mind, I'm an impatient guy and if I have to do what I'm surely thinking is Plan B, I'll do it quick, loud, and expensive. The numbers will go up, not to mention y'all having to add in all those white shoe defense lawyer billable hours—and y'all know they'll drag it around to bill it heavy—and the costs and expenses and my attorney's fees and bad publicity and embarrassment and in the house finger pointing and blame assigning. By my early calculations, the cost to y'all will go from net winner to a double number loser. I think you understand all that?" Eddie cocked his head at McShack. Eddie had indeed spoken very pleasantly.

McShack slowly nodded and stubbed out his cigarette. "I do." He grimaced. "Well, as you well know, I'll need to go to my superiors and they will have to go to our internal oversight board about all of this for vetting and approval."

"Sure. Better move quick I'd suggest. Oh, and one more thing. If we do this deal as Plan A, y'all are gonna cut your compiled, excessive trustee and management fees in half as calculated from the get-go. No quibbling. Now I got to go. You see any reason why you can't get this done or do you see problems?

"The way I see it, I'm gonna get the property one way or another and these folks in Richmond and Charlotte are gonna get their money right soon one way or another like the guy in the Fram Oil Filter ad who says, 'You can pay me now or you can pay me later.'"

McShack's large head was still. He grinned the lip-pursed grin of the cat and moved his head, almost imperceptibly to the left and then to the right.

"Thank you for your time. I'm looking to hear from you—soon."

Eddie stood, nodded, walked to the elevator banks and went down.

He knew it was all over but the shouting.

Patty went with Eddie.

Patty loved T.R. Hell, they all did, but Tommy's work involved more paper than not—and as his work grew, there would be more and more other unknowns—often boring ciphers— assisting as well and the intimacy would be evaporating. It would be more "corporate"— and it would be more quiet than not-raucous behavior and spontaneous bad language would be verboten, the verbal expression straitjacket being immediately applied—and the place allowed employee smoking only out on a landing near the parking deck underneath the bunkered lobby floor which invited too hot, too cold, too windy, too blank and Patty instinctively knew all that.

And Patty did love the rough and tumble of Eddie's practice, the God knows what's next, the "what the hells," the carrying of the bloody pelts after victory, the sadness of the "didn't work outs" and most importantly, Patty was Queen Bee and ran the show from her perspective and got to smoke when she wanted and got to help Eddie and then later, Mikey and Alph.

T.R. went Big Law, while Eddie stayed rogue.

And thus it was born and thus it did grow and go.

Eddie really did not understand the enormity and depth and breadth of the door Wake had opened for him. It was all simply unimaginable and then, all of a sudden, the doors were flung wide open and he just walked in and went to work. Going to the courthouse just suited him. If Linus had a blanket, then Eddie had the trek to court.

As things went along, Eddie ended up with handsome, just-right, grass cloth wall coverings and brass sconces and all the other accouterments of power-lawyer offices, but his eternal favorites were any courthouse where he was working and all of their adjuncts, be they jails or opposing counsel offices or judges' chambers or mediator's conference rooms. Working a case became an every time wonder to him. And he did know there was still time on the clock and the clock's moving was interminable until there it was and then it was no longer. The horizon was indistinct, but like ozone in the air before the storm, O3 was in his mental nostrils.

So much hard work and attention to detail over the years, so much perception and understanding, so much success, so much money, so much prestige and respect, so much self-affirmation. It all kept surging and growing. That cornucopia of gratitude had come to him late, so self-absorbed had he been for such a long time, had finally ripened and was now solidly centered in his mind. He wondered more than idly...fear of losing it all, fear of having it taken away, snatched from him...was that the genesis of that awful, invisible specter that haunted him so horribly just a few hours ago?

They walked up the hill and Mikey finally said, "So, Eddie. Exhale now and tell me about your travels."

"Sure. I'm ready to do that. By the way, did you remember that I went to law school up this hill here?"

She was patient, indulgent. She could tell he was distracted.

"Yes, my dear. I do of course remember. Let's send them a nice check tomo. Okay? Now please tell me things. Let's sit on this log now and I want to hear all about it."

The sunlight fluttered and filtered through the leaves. Some birds tweeted. Her curiosity was there. He wanted to tell it right. Not too much but still, right.

CHAPTER THIRTEEN

HORIZONS

Late March

H E SAT AND fidgeted and settled. She eased in close to him.
"Okay, my Eddie, tell me about your trip. I'm hungry and surely, this ain't gonna take that long. Is there something bothering you?" She turned and looked at him with serious inquiry.

"Mikey, well, yes...yes, there is...something happened while I was gone...I need to tell you about it."

She was quiet for a moment and then asked, "Another woman?" She froze and held her breath.

"No, no, nothing like that. Lord, no! I love you, baby. Ain't nobody else out there." He short laughed. She relaxed.

"Here it is but I gotta go through the travel just pretty quick to get to it. Helps me order it in my mind. Okay?"

"Okay, but how about get to it...?"

And he did, he told her about the nice time in Charleston and giving Truck his well-earned and unexpected bounty, his dead end explorations of potential cases in Savannah and St. Simons, his uncomfortable, dismaying history moments at Andersonville, his back-to-past visit at Southern Woods which he put in years gone by context (he did omit the Moon Beam part—no reason for its proffering), the nice visit in Aiken with his old clients and his old friend Tina at the Willcox and the innocuous drive of coming on home today. And that, pretty much was that.

"Except, 'pretty much' doesn't mean 'all,' does it? You're sneaking up on something, Eddie. You're circling. Time to land."

She crossed her arms and waited. She was intense. And was going to yank it out of him if he didn't get forthcoming and right now. Her antennae were up.

He swallowed and he could feel his gut tighten.

"Mikey, early this morning I had two really odd, strange dreams... well, one was a dream and the other was, well, it was a black hole of what... fear, fright, terror, I don't know...all three and more...scared the hell outta me, really scared the shit out of me...I just don't know, but the second one whatever it was, was awful. I'm still scared, well, scared enough. Certainly shaken up."

He looked at her and then looked down at the ground. She could see his worry.

This was when Mikey played some of her strongest cards. She was no sniveling weakling in a storm. And she could see this was a storm. She was foxhole-tough and perceptive. She could see that her man was troubled. She had seen this over the years when cases or witnesses or people or situations went bad south and it often weighed hard on Eddie. He was usually good at fighting the disappointment or the upset back and he always popped back up, but this creature sitting now before them was a different kind of beast. Before, when he had just gotten home, he seemed pretty good. Now as he was telling her all this, he seemed sagged down, bent.

This was no time to tell him to snap out of it, grow a pair, shake it off, all that call to the macho in him, all of which was surely still there but had been submerged by this unusual vision or no vision or whatever it was. He was wounded by something and held captive, hopefully just for now. She had never seen this in him or on him and she knew it was a time to be careful and to tread slowly. But she knew she had the touch and she was now going to apply it like a salve.

"Eddie, honey, how about this...? How about you tell me about this dream and this fright in more detail and let's see what we can cipher out of them? Take your time now. Tell me first about the dream..." There was no command of imperative, only a soft request for understanding.

She knew he had had drinks and dinner with his old friend Tina the night before. That was of no concern to her. Eddie had known Tina for a long time. That a guy like Eddie would have good, close female friends longstanding for many, many years was not a thing to be worried about. To Mikey it was a strong sign of his good emotional health, even maturity. As an off thought, she wanted to go down to Aiken and see the place, meet the gal. They'd never done that. It would be time to do that soon enough.

He told her about the dream in more detail, his walking down Boundary Road, how pretty it all was, the horses in the pastures and paddocks, the coming storm, the red barn, the stall with fresh hay in it where he had fallen asleep as the storm approached. He told her about passing a pretty girl on his walk near the red barn but omitted the details of his further encounters with the girl named Blaze; its proffer would serve no good purpose and would only obscure the trail, wherever that trail might be going.

Even in his dismay, he was strategically evasive. It was a plus. It was a minus. He was protecting her. He was protecting him. He knew.

He told her about the storm exploding over him, how he lurched awake, disoriented and dizzy, mentally flailing in the dark. And then he told her about being immediately and suddenly gripped by an unseen, inexplicable anaconda of fear and bleakness, a foreboding that signaled an invisible disaster that he could do nothing to escape or avoid. He was not sensate. He was frozen as he went over the falls into oblivion. It was horrible. His words failed him. He, a very articulate and convincing trial lawyer, a story-teller without compare, a stem winder when needed, a preacher, a fine and thoughtful speaker sat mute. He pleadingly looked at Mikey.

She held his hand and stroked his neck and sat and watched him for a long minute.

"Eddie, honey..." she began, her rhythmic reclamation program beginning in her sing-song of comfort. "Do you think this all has something to do with the pretty crummy last many months we've gone through as a firm? Do you think it's got something to do with our failures, at least by our standards? Not you and me. You and me are just fine. You know that. I'm talking about the firm, your practice, our practice."

"Maybe..." Eddie was halting in his reply. Eddie had no "Eddie" at his disposal at the moment. Eddie was in the process of surrendering in hope to Mikey.

"Eddie, are you fearful, maybe, that it's all going to just blow apart and disappear?"

"Maybe..."

"Are you worried that as you're getting older and that the time for more lawyer success is running out?"

And she was gently circling him now.

"Yes, well, well...maybe..."

"And that if that happens, everything is a failure and you're washed up and your star goes dim and then dark?"

Eddie, leaning forward, had put his elbows on his knees and balled his hands under his chin. Tears began to drip from his eyes and roll down his cheeks. Mikey carefully wiped them away. Eddie squeezed his eyes tight shut and a few more splashed out.

"Mikey, maybe that's it." Eddie spoke in a soft monotone. "It was as though everything was ending and very soon too. But, Mikey, it had a feel to it that it was us, you, me, everything, everything was going into some black hole. It was total emptiness."

Mikey nodded.

"Eddie, look at me, please. Am I here right now with you? Are you here with me right now?"

Chastened, Eddie nodded and said, "Yes, yes, we are here."

"And you do know Alph and Patty are down at the office and there are plenty of cases and work to be tended to? And it is a beautiful spring day and we are hungry, aren't we?" She giggled.

"Yes and yes. Yes, all that's so." He involuntarily smiled.

"Eddie, here's what I think. You have been tired, worn out, worn down. You put so much pressure on yourself. You always have. I can still count on my fingers pretty good and by my count, you're pushing forty years into these never-ending fistfights. Last time I looked, stress in this business, lots of stress, comes with the territory. You try to ignore it. I've seen you ignore it, push it away. That's natural for a hard charger like you. But, every now and then, it builds and builds and you're not checking your gauges and the bolted pressurized door blows out and you just don't let off steam, it explodes. I think that's what happened here.

"The last many months have been not so good by the way that you and we look at things. And too, we have got a ton of good stuff to do and to get done, both down at the office and for us. Our lives are pretty full and we don't, you don't want to let it go, except, a big except, on your terms and mine, whatever we share and that's a damn gracious plenty and whenever that is going to be is a long way down the road. I'm pretty sure. You're still plenty young to me, don't you worry." She wiggled her lips ever so slightly and edged up on the limb of romp.

She winked at him and he realized that she had surfaced him and that it was no longer a drowning doom but a reasonable explanation she was working on and that heartened him.

"I think and I'm pretty sure I'm right, you just had the big boiler blow up dream and because you are a really big force guy, you just had a really, really big one and like all bombs going on, it leaves a mess and a mark. And I'll bet you are oh so tired…aren't you?" She patted his knee and then gave it a good squeeze, the maternal melding into the eternal.

Eddie nodded and knew she had an answer and that she was right. It was an answer, maybe not the answer but it would have to do and that was fine. It was working.

"Oh, Mikey. I really am tired, tired into my bones."

She took his face in her hands and kissed his forehead and his lips and nuzzled her face into his neck. Some walkers passing by snickered, "Get a room."

Mikey shot back. "Oh don't worry, we got one, actually more than one and in just a little bit, we're going home to bounce around in all of them!"

The couple, eyes widened, laughed, kept moving and Eddie was again in awe of her.

"You think…?" Eddie considered near time without fear.

"In due time, my Carolina lawyer man…"

She took his hand and pulled him up off the log.

"Come on, Superman. Time to start cleaning up this mess and scrubbing off that mark." He nodded. He would have followed her anywhere.

CHAPTER FOURTEEN

CALMING EXPECTATIONS
Late March

THEY WALKED BACK to Reynolda Village, taking the long way back up and around past barren Lake Louise and then back down the hill, passing the snazzy housewares and better than gimcrack specialty shops and the florist and fine ladies clothing and high-end artistic photography and haberdashery stores and went in and sat at the long bar at the long-well-established and deservedly so, Village Tavern.

This whole layout, tucked just down the hill from the quietly magnificent Reynolda House and her lovely grounds. (It was a "Keen" house, the locals liked to chuckle—and indeed it was as it had been designed by the renown Philadelphia architect Charles Barton Keen.)

The collection of stores and shops and food courts was one of the university's very successful retail outlets. No Dollar Store or starving student theme here. This was for extra disposable, by choice, not necessity money. And the VT as it was affectionately known by its regulars was a small, tight and classically Georgian bar cum pub cum comfort food station. It had been around just right after Eddie had fluttered out of law school. He knew it from the beginning and the proprietor, Rich Scott, knew it too in his very thorough, quiet way. Some food and beverage people have the touch. Rich had it.

As they walked in, Eddie saw a couple of familiar faces. He smiled, waved, nodded, touched a shoulder, shook a hand here and there as he took Mikey by the hand and led her through the crowded path of the seated, the waiting, the standing, and drinking.

There was a NCAA tournament basketball game on the big screen behind the bar. The entire country was already knee deep and beyond into the annual saturnalia known as March Madness. The bar was crowded and its patrons groaned and cheered as the whistles and calls and high-wire flyings and rimmers in and out went their way or not. You could tell there was some money being wagered here and there as one or another anonymous soul would review his odds card or exclaim, "Come on over!" or "Damn, I need three-and-a-half! Just a damn measly three-and-a-half." Mikey and Eddie could see that Valpo was playing Indiana but that was not near enough to capture their attention. The TV set screen squiggled and wiggled and they found some seats down at the end, around the corner where the game really could not be seen unless some serious neck craning were uncomfortably attempted.

Eddie was glad they'd not come when Chapel Hill or Wake or Duke or State was playing; otherwise, it would have been Chick-fil-A up the street at best.

They ate double crispy chicken wings slathered with the classic Buffalo/Lake Erie drench of one-half melted salted butter and one-half taste snapping, piquant Texas Pete hot sauce, the city's definitive answer to McElheney Island Tabasco. They crunched on fresh celery and comforting made inhouse ranch dressing. They smeared their mouths up copiously. They napkin-wiped their burning lips and flaming cheeks vigorously. Eddie's pate popped with perspiration. They pointed at their faces and laughed at and with each other. They teased each other. And they drank glasses of good, cold Chablis. And then, drank a couple more. They got slightly dizzy and satisfyingly full.

They ate their feelings, feelings akin to "Did you get the number of that train?" and "I think it's gonna be okay." And "If I eat and drink enough of this, I will become purposely dulled down and able to rest."

They were both being pulled into the cozy sleeping bag of release and relaxation. Neither were resisting.

But before their creeping somnolence came completely up and over their ridges of consciousness and enveloped them, Mikey had thoughts that she offered. "Damn, Eddie, that was good! Sure helped me. Did it help you?"

"You bet. Damn good!"

"Now, are you sleepy? I am. Don't you think we ought to get on home and take it easy for a while? This has been, well, quite an interesting day…"

"You'll get no argument from me on that, Miss Mikey."

"Good. And after we rest and refresh and so forth and so forth…" She eyed him with a combination of coy and "oh boy!" "I would like you to take us downtown for a wander and drink and a light bite. Let's go to Aperture and see a movie. We haven't done that in a while and I do believe some change of pace is good for us on this day. Please and thank you. What do you say?"

"I say that sounds like a fine idea."

"And, Eddie, I'm thinking about the office and how to get our ball rolling again the way we like it to roll. We all know things haven't gone the way we like these last months. We've got some big stuff out there up ahead and its coming at us sooner rather than later and I've got a few ideas as to how to get our mojo pumped up as we get ready for the big shows. But can we hold that until Monday? I think we need to smooth our minds down for the rest of this weekend."

"Honey, I'm all for all of that and will stand by. I do understand that you and Patty want to visit with me and Alph on Monday."

"Good. That is so…I'll drive."

They went home, drew the curtains and shades and fell tight close to one another into bed. And they slept.

CHAPTER FIFTEEN

BEAUTY IS ONLY SKIN DEEP

Three Months Before...

THERE WAS NO way to dress it up. The last three months had been a punchbowl full of turds, large and small, and it weighed Eddie and all of them down. Even cheerful Alph noted and sorrowed over it. Patty was guarded and watchful; she knew this was but one more stage in the arc of their work but that did not make it any less discomfiting. They were low, introspective and quietly sullen. Things just had not gone well. It was uncharacteristic. Uncomfortable. It seemed they were collectively wearing an itchy set of clothes that just did not fit right. They tugged and turned against it and it was still intransigent.

In that time, Eddie had tried two cases, set damn near back to back—he had been forced to try them before they were properly ripened. It was a version of the litigation Torquemada, being lashed to the rack as the tumbrils rolled through the courthouse was courtesy of a senior superior court judge named Solomon Martin from the way on over eastern part of the state who came to town to show these slickers who was boss, whose fecal cavity dimensions had never really been determined; they just seemed endless and random. He was a judge with a stink eye, a controller who asserted his lofty preeminence, who enjoyed seeing the suits before him scramble and squirm. He had long ago forgotten what it was to be a lawyer.

He wanted to be known as King Solomon but that was not ever going to happen. He was arbitrary, petulant, and he was basically a son of a bitch, privately known as "The Mart," short for "Martinet." And the longer he sat on the bench, the more he became known as "Mart The Fart."

The judge was cold, gimlet-eyed and did not give a damn about a trial lawyer's need to breathe between hard focus assignments. He was one of those old grouches who sadistically savored the lawyers begging him for more time, knowing all the while that he would not be helping them out, at least not until hell froze over. And he was hell-bent for leather on beating that tectonic shift to the finish line of retirement, his cranky sinecure secure.

All of this ate up about a month and a half in prep time and trial and work time and thus squeezed a lot of the oxygen out of the room needed for "all the other things."

A "boxcar job" like that stretched a fellow and his helpers thin, real thin, but no whining or groveling for Eddie. It signaled weakness and vulnerability and Eddie was not about to be labeled as losing his drive, much less his sharps.

While at calendar call for the month's term, the clerk barked out Hazard versus Perkins, M.D.

Terrell for the plaintiff, Crocker for the defense. The lawyers stood.

"Ready to go, Your Honor. Three days to a week, give or take."

"Aright, Mr. Terrell, what's the judicial interpretation of 'give or take' and by the way, aren't you going to ask for a continuance or delay or some such like so many of your brave boy colleagues in here have already done?" This little cuffing of course being accompanied by a dismissive eye roll.

"Your Honor, I have every expectation to get it done within three days to a week but as Your Honor well knows, not all trains run on schedule. I can assure you we will all be efficient."

He nodded to his opposing counsel across the way who nodded in assent to the judge and then also to Eddie.

"As far as asking for extra time, Your Honor, no, I am not."

"Alright then, you are first up a week from this coming Monday; we'll go that Monday afternoon after the morning's motions are heard. You'll be before Judge Patterson. Any settlement discussions?"

"No, Your Honor. Nothing."

The opposing counsel looked down, embarrassed, a prisoner of his whip-cracking insurance carrier. They never offered. Not this particular outfit.

"I'll so report to Judge Patterson."

Judge Lawrence "The Hacker" Patterson was a good guy, a lawyer's judge who ran a tight ship and gave a fair trial. He could get riled at you, but if you had the law or the equity or good reason on your side and were willing to stand your ground past his initial call-down, you'd be fine. On the other hand, if you were lacking in substance or were weak-kneed, well...you get the picture. He respected the stand-up guy, not so much as to the dissembler and whiner. He was competitive even from the bench as a neutral.

The nickname "The Hacker" came from his crazy-ass basketball playing days at Clemson when his windmill defense and raw competitiveness earned him the moniker. He had played against the likes of Billy Packer and Lennie Chappel at Wake and Art Heyman at Duke and other luminaries across the firmament of Tobacco Road and had been an All ACC selection. He was tough as a pine knot, a true banty rooster. Truth be told, he was beloved.

Had Judge Patterson been calling the calendar, he would not have been jamming blivets into all these lawyers' ears but sometimes, acceptance and resignation were the cards that got dealt.

Eddie sat down and waited. It wouldn't be long before he'd be standing again.

He watched as the case roll was called and the lawyers would pop up and down like a big game of Whac-A-Mole, just that the moles were all in suits and ties. Plenty of excuses, asking for this and that, some resplendent, some rumpled, some steady, some obviously frightened, agitated, some cases near settlement, some settled. And this kind of mean-spirited judicial diktat accomplished plenty of resolutions. Plenty of lawyers figured, "What the hell. Let's get her done at a wherever number and just get the hell out of here." And that pleased The Mart as he could brag about how well he was clearing his assigned calendar to the administrative office of the courts.

Just because you were a lawyer with a case that needed trying did not mean you knew what you were doing and as Eddie looked the room over, there was plenty of that in view.

Eddie and Alph did try the case as scheduled and instructed by the Court. There were no settlement discussions. Defense counsel was an angry, young whip of a fellow but he sublimated his sarcasm and scorn pretty well as Judge Patterson eyed him in warning.

It was a medical malpractice that, in retrospect, they should not have taken on. A young infant, just a few weeks after his entry into this world, had a routine surgical procedure done at a local, private hospital, one owned by a group of surgeons. A profitable venture, it was to be sure, but its policies and procedures as to pre-op and post-operative care were lax and poorly supervised, something well known in the small sub-community of lawyers who plowed in these fields, and many of its surg nurses were, shall we say, overworked, underpaid, detached, and disinterested.

After the procedure had gone well enough, an intravenous line that had not been properly inserted and monitored in a vein in the little fellow's arm infiltrated and there was much pain and swelling and a significant compartment syndrome occurred with the blood supply being blocked off, causing tissue deterioration. If not addressed promptly and effectively, this sort of complication can lead to amputation.

Subsequent emergency remedial surgery was required and a mandatory fasciotomy was performed which relieved the pressure and there was some plastic surgery follow up as well. The child made a fine recovery with but a little scarring and no loss of use. There was no question that had the situation been attended to from the get-go, none of the ensuing problems would have occurred. The medical bills were sizeable and the pain and suffering component was certainly there, but the spokesmen as to that were the parents.

The child's parents were understandably upset and agitated and angry, even with the passage of a year and a half, though constantly being cautioned to be calm in their recitations as to how this affected their child, they were overly-dramatic, verging on the hysterical and took the tone of this was all about them in their testimony and this was off-putting to the jury.

And it did not help that the surgeon, who did the initial procedure, caught the nurse's mistake, and who undertook the successful remedial repair, was empathetic and forthright and took responsibility for the hospital's negligence in his testimony, all of which came as the offending nurse sat behind the defense counsel table quietly weeping in guilt and regret from her actions.

The plaintiff's expert was adequate in his explanation of the violations of the standards of care but also voluntarily conceded, without much qualifying, that while the child had been through an ordeal, it had been of short duration and noted that the child had made a fine recovery.

The defense expert mirrored the plaintiff's expert. The case had become Hemingway's *The Old Man and the Sea*; what had looked like a good catch at first had been eaten away to the basic stripped-down carcass.

And of course, the young boy, now almost two, was adorable, cute as a button, burbling and charming and looked fit as a fiddle as he sat happily wiggling in his parents' laps and wondered what in the world was all this about. Eddie and Alph had requested of the parents that the child be in the courtroom only for a few minutes to display his scars and then he was to be taken away and out to a babysitter, but the parents felt and said it was imperative that he was not to leave their sides. They were hell-bent for the jury to see how badly their beloved golden child had been hurt; the problem was that their mountain looked more like a molehill to the eyes of strangers. His continual presence before the jury softened all hearts and gutted any dramatic damages enhancing the impact the case might have had.

On the afternoon of day four, the jury deliberated for a few hours and came back with an award for the plaintiffs. The number was the exact dollar amount of the total medical bills and nothing more. And of course, the fine folks at Blue Cross Blue Shield had their presented liens as well.

The parents, fairly educated and sophisticated people, knew the pie they had expected to receive had shrunk and that after fees and costs and expenses were taken out, it was going to get smaller. They were cranky and ungrateful to the edge of being put out and there was little Eddie and Alph could do to assuage them. And they really were not inclined to try all that hard to that. Their relationship had stratified. They just wanted for them to go on, for it all to go away. Everyone needed time to cool down. And it was getting ready to do just that. Everything would be revisited soon enough when time for disbursement came. *Exhale*, thought Eddie.

It was a victory but it was not. Eddie regretted that he had not had more time to prep his people, to get their focus on being straightforward and settled and not on themselves. It wasn't about parental hurt and worry. It was about the kid's responses to being injured.

Eddie wished he had been more firm, even adamant with them about minimizing the child's exposure in the courtroom. He wanted to blame old Judge Mart The Fart for this jumbled up mess but in truth, the shortcomings were theirs, mostly his. This case was his, his responsibility. He was supposed to lead and to guide, not just go along with what suited the clients, especially when it came to cosmetics.

He recalled with a brief grimace but dared not repeat to the clients the old, so true line from Shakespeare's *Julius Caesar.* "The fault, dear Brutus, is not in our stars, but in ourselves, that we are underlings."

Eddie had failed to have a serious "come to Jesus" chat with the parents, had failed again to manage expectations, this time client conduct and expectations.

He made a note to remember his failings here and, also, to make sure the clients, when the disbursement sheet was prepared, received more money than did the firm. He learned early on that if the lawyer netted more than the client, it was a bad public relations fumble with the potential for ugly ripples.

The clients stiffly, curtly said their "thank you's and goodbye's" and trundled huffily out of the courtroom with their bundle of joy in tow.

The defendant hospital folk departed quickly, like wraiths. Defense counsel packed up his brief bags and nodded cursorily at Eddie and Alph as he left. He was smart enough not to gloat. He could and would go back to his office and do that soon enough.

It would later be explained to him by the elders in his shop that he'd done a nice job, limited the damage but it wasn't exactly a pelt to nail to the wall; so go on and get back to work and remember, you may have bloodied Eddie Terrell a bit but you sure as hell haven't killed him. In an insurance defense firm, especially for the young Turks, the billable hour was that which reigned supreme, and accolades and hosannas were few and far between.

Judge Patterson sat patiently on his bench as was his habit to always watch his courtroom empty for the day.

Eddie asked, "Your Honor, may we approach?"

"Of course."

Alph and Eddie extended their hands in true gratitude for The Hacker's smooth, air traffic control of the proceedings.

"Thank you, Judge Patterson, for a fair shot. We appreciate it."

This was not just a perfunctory courtesy. This was heartfelt.

As they shook, Judge Patterson deftly noted, "Well, a sort of mixed bag, I think. I can tell your people were grumpy. And, yeah, y'all too. But, they're going to get some money and so are y'all. Get up with defense counsel and get me the paperwork and we'll get the judgment entered. Now, the weekend's coming. Y'all go get some rest. Y'all look tired to me."

"Yes, sir. Thank you, Your Honor."

They turned to go.

"Oh, boys, one more thing..." There was that knowing pause.

"Yes, Your Honor?"

"By the way, that sure was a cute kid!"

They all could not help but laugh.

CHAPTER SIXTEEN

EVERY NOW AND THEN

Three Months Before...

TEN MINUTES LATER, Eddie rolled through the calendar call drill again.

Stand up. Sit down. Fight fight fight.

The clerk monotoned, "Monk versus Beautray, M.D."

"Terrell for Plaintiff, Olds for Defendant."

"Again, Your Honor, we're ready to go, but would only ask for a setting in the fourth week of the term. That would give us all the necessary gap time to retune and reframe our focus."

Defense counsel Johnny Olds, a good guy trying to be helpful, said, "I agree, Your Honor, and respectfully and further submit that a setting in the fourth week of term might give us a real chance to resolve the matter, thus relieving the Court of the time needed to try the matter."

"Are you telling me there have been settlement discussions? In a medical malpractice case? In this state?"

Judge Mart pushed his bifocals down his pernicious, mottled nose, and stared wide-eyed questioning at the two statues before him.

"Your Honor, yes, there have been some. Yes, Your Honor is correct. This is an unusual case and hopefully a compromise can be achieved."

"Well, boys, you better get along and quick because as you can tell, time waits for no man and certainly not you two. Third week of the term it is. Period. End of story. Trial judge yet to assigned so stand by, boys. That's it. Next!"

The clerk called out from his list.

Johnny Olds shrugged his shoulders weakly. "Yes, Your Honor." He stood and grappled his brief case down the row to the aisle, playing bumper car knees with those still captive.

Eddie just curtly nodded, ramrod straight as he did and then, with only a bit more grace, hustled out of the courtroom and caught Olds as he went down the hall to the elevators.

"Johnny, I appreciate your trying to help us out in there. I really do. You got a minute? Let's talk a little bit?"

"Sure, Eddie. Sure. Where you want to talk?" Olds had a look of relief on his face. He knew and Eddie knew that he knew that discussion of some kind of settlement discussion was in the offing.

"How about let's go downstairs and get a cup of coffee and then go to the counsel set aside rooms in the probate courts next to the canteen. Those usually aren't too busy most of the time."

Olds nodded and they fortified themselves, found a drab, empty room behind probate and pulled a couple of creaking old chairs up to the chipped Formica table.

"Well...here we are again. So what shall we talk about? And by the way, damn it's good to get out of there, get away from that old bastard, don't you think?" Olds intoned affably.

"I agree. Let's work this damn thing out. Whadaya say?"

"I concur. What do you have in mind?"

And another dance, another minuet began.

It was another medical negligence case and the insurance carrier was loath to ever discuss resolution. It had been the company's longstanding policy forever. Doctors were gods. The Carolinas were poor, cowed, and needy. Everything was always going to have to be balls to the wall. Everything was going to have to be tried. Most legitimate plaintiff's claims and their lawyers got run off, intimidated and neutered.

In the Carolinas, they were an insurance shell game sponsored by the states. It had all been shoved through the legislature many years ago when both bodies of solons had turned hard right just as the doc lobby screamed "crisis" for the umpteenth time. Chicken Little would have blushed.

They were called JUA/PCF and had rigged their books for years of "kick the can down the road" and treated the courts as their Visa card, pushing whatever liabilities that sporadically appeared on their accounting sheets forever into the slow maw of the future by the stall ball of the appellate courts. They were the classic quasi-Ponzi scheme, robbing Peter to pay Paul. They had 80 to 90 percent of the docs in the state insured, charged lowball premiums, and even touted premium rebates they would toss back to their insureds every three or four years.

But things had begun to change and there were cracks in the walls of this and other big malpractice insurance monoliths. The public was more and better informed about medicine and about medical screw ups and failures. The wire services were running more and more articles about medicine and medical problems and medical malpractice too.

National reach newspapers such as *USA Today*, the *Wall Street Journal* and *The New York Times* lent themselves to the cascade of information. *The New York Times Sunday Magazine* had even run a mega-article which asked to the effect: "What would the government do if a jumbo jet carrying three hundred people plunged to the death of all every week for four-plus years? Well, that's what medical malpractice fatalities look like in this country right now..." and so on. The general public was starting to pay attention.

The major television networks piled in. It was becoming obvious that the barrage of advertising for all sorts of prescription medicines was creating heightened consumer interest to all things medical. With the population of the country spending almost twenty percent of its gross domestic product on healthcare, on everything from Dr. Scholl's foot inserts to MRIs and cardioversion platforms and pills and capsules by the score, healthcare had become a huge public consumer issue and as such, the customers' attitudes to doctors and hospitals were undergoing a huge, tectonic shift.

And then the publication of the meta "Harvard One and Two Studies" by the revered, respected and high authoritative New England Journal of Medicine specifically showed that the national rates of medical negligence causing serious injury or death were in the hard specific range of two to five percent per each hundred patient encounters.

Of course, some were minor injuries and some were catastrophic and ultimately deadly. It was not hard to multiply that figure with the millions of patient encounters that took place across the country each day.

The Harvard School of Public Health had inspected tens of thousands of patient records from twenty-plus hospitals, big, small and in between from the upstate New York area. People were shocked. Most doctors had known for years and had just shrugged it off as part and parcel of their white coat abattoir. And now, that Band-Aid of falsity had been ripped off and by an institution supposedly on their side.

Eddie had subscribed to the *NEJM* along with Great Britain's *The Lancet* for years and when he laid hard into the two Harvard studies, he knew there was now a new way to set a hard bar of negligence from the get-go. The physicians had to recognize the authority of the journal—or look like functional idiots for the rest of their lives—and thus functioned the expansive credibility of the immense and far-ranging article.

And so, it began to go like this:

"Doctor, I hand you a complete copy of the recent article from the *New England Journal of Medicine* entitled 'Harvard One and Two Studies.' Are you familiar with this article? And I have the original issue here at hand if you find the copies to be suspect."

"Yes" or "no"—it didn't matter. If they did, move on; if they didn't, give them time to carefully read it.

"Doctor, based upon your background, training, education, and experience and your knowledge of the professional world in which you work and your own personal knowledge and the contents and substance of this highly recognized, respected learned treatise and authority, are you willing to acknowledge that medical malpractice injuries, deviation from proper and accepted standard of care injuries do occur regularly across this country and in this hospital as well?"

No matter the answer, the foundation was laid and the medical profession was booted off the pedestal. If they accepted the credibility of the article, one just plowed on; if they wanted to try and spit the bit, just consider all the possibilities. It was all just so ineluctable.

And so the plates shifted, for once in favor of the Good Guys.

The mantra was now "the customer is always right" and that meant the customer wanted whatever the health transaction might be to come out with a safe and healthy result. No longer were doctors placed on a high pedestal. The high cost of procedures and prescriptions engendered consumer resentment as did the new physician business models which made office and hospital visits both "hurry up and waits" and cattle calls as well.

So the pendulum had swung in favor of the patients and against the medical community and it was a great time to be a plaintiff's lawyer. The deck was no longer stacked.

The insurance carriers were finally getting the picture. Losses were starting to happen. It was decided from on high that there needed to be efforts made to resolve some of these problems before turning them loose on a now suspicious and resentful public which might amplify their growing social cultural distaste for the medical phalanx. Juries were on the prowl and that was potential bad news for medical malpractice insurers. There was uncertainty in the wind and if there was any one thing that insurance companies dislike, it was and is and forever will be uncertainty.

And so, in this evolving world of denial and accommodation, sat Eddie and his opposing counsel Johnny Olds.

The case had evolved into what was called a "gotcha."

A nice lady named Jordan Monk in her late sixties had gone to a same day surgery center for a regular, "let's just take a look" colonoscopy after having been referred by her internist. This was simply routine. No red flags had been raised; no alarms sounded.

She had taken overnight, as instructed, the nasty but necessary gallon of bowel prep fluid and had gotten some but only minimal results from her ingestions. When she arrived that morning at the appointed time, she worriedly explained her lack of pre-procedure productivity to the gastroenterologist and his nurse. The doctor, a fellow named Beautray decided to proceed. After some strenuous contorting of the scope, replete with audible grunting and groaning on the part of both parties to the transaction, the proctologist relented and gave up, declared that she was hopelessly impacted, that he could not make much progress and so he rescheduled her with further instructions about diet and the use of more powerful bowel cleansing solutions.

She went home, felt increasingly unwell and by the late afternoon was extremely ill with significant lower abdominal pain and sever cramping and when a bowel movement was attempted, the results were de minimis save for obvious, frightening blood in her pitiably meager stool.

She called her sister who took her immediately to the large teaching hospital in town.

She was admitted through the emergency room and declared "stat" for immediate exploratory surgery. She was rapidly transported to the operating suites. Upon opening her up, the surgeons found that she was indeed almost totally impacted and also found three significant rents at the juncture of the sigmoid and descending colon. Fecal matter had spilled into her peritoneum and she was rapidly growing dangerously infected.

They cleaned her out, irrigated her copiously and repaired the tears. A portion of her colon was removed. She was given a temporary colostomy bag, mega-dosed with antibiotics, and taken to the ICU where she was closely monitored for four days until she was moved to the stepdown floor. She spent another week there and upon discharge, was very weak and frail. Her medical bills were north of three hundred thousand.

The attending surgeon was appalled and adamant as to what had happened. He opined that scoping her should never have taken place and that the attempted performance of same was manifestly reckless.

"How in the hell could he have seen anything to begin with? She was worse than calcified chocolate pudding. We almost needed a hammer and chisel to get her cleared so we could go find the tears. And the tears were not physiologic from straining. They were pointed, sharp point tip of the scope injuries."

He told Eddie he would so testify under oath in open court. This was an enormous plus for the case and for Eddie. Rarely did local physicians testify against one of their own.

But of course, there were problems too.

The lady had a history of longtime alcohol abuse and though now recovering and doing well in that regard, her years of drinking, it would be argued, had made her intestinal system friable, brittle and fragile, with heightened susceptibility to injury. She had not disclosed this to the proctologist and had neglected to put any of this history down on the standard intake sheets that are to be filled out before the procedure. And her diet was, simply put, just awful, unhealthy, loaded with fats and sugars. She was not morbidly obese but she was close.

And she was a timid thing and had not much backbone for the fight. Her sister had brought her to Eddie and was her spine and encouragement throughout.

All of this had come out and become clear during discovery. The in-procedure films labeled with Ms. Monk's name and date of birth and date of procedure were blurry and while showing some impaction, they were not alarming or definitive. They did not show any injury occurring. The paper records in her chart were benign. Nothing worrisome or ominous there.

The defense expert, an arrogant but effective explainer, an oleaginous, hired gun whore from the Eddie Haskell School of Charm was from a medical school in the eastern part of Virginia, close enough for good old boy status.

And so this is where things stood until about two weeks before the roster call. The defense ploy was to nibble at it from the edges. The doc had clearly injured her but was acting in good faith and she was responsible in significant part for her injuries too as she presented as susceptible and told no one. It was the old contributory negligence play. She contributed to her state of affairs, to the disaster which befell her.

Eddie had made a demand of a million and a half. Johnny Olds got authority from his carrier to counter at one hundred grand. This was not a bad sign. It signaled that something here was troublesome to them. A mediation yielded no progress. The mediator, selected by the defense with Eddie's assent as a gesture of good faith and good will, was a limp bust, a waste of time.

The mediator was vague, weak and detached. He was an inheritor, a rich boy with a law degree from Cornell and a stock portfolio and inheritance of big trucking that bred ennui, disinterested ignorance and as much noblesse oblige as might be found running in a muddy gutter on a torrential night in New Orleans. But it wasn't all bad. Eddie made a mental note to never use that useless guy again.

And then one afternoon, Patty came back to Eddie's office and stuck her head in the door.

"There's a nurse out here who wants to see you."

"How do you know she's a nurse?"

"How do you know she's a she? And, yes, she is. She's got her scrubs and Velcro strap white tennies on and a name sewn into her smock followed by the letters R. N. Let's just say you can't fool me every day!" Patty snorted derisively.

"Okay. What's it about? What's her name?"

"Her name is Phoebe Shannon. Says she will only speak with you but that it's very important and that she thinks you will want to hear what she has to say. Oh, just by the way, she's pretty cute…" Patty winked, again derisively.

"Hmmmm…doesn't ring a bell, but so what? Let's see what she wants. Okay, you sold me. Bring her back here, please."

Soon enough Patty ushered Ms. Shannon into a captain's chair in front of Eddie's desk, made the introductions and backed out of the office and quietly closed the door. As she did, she stuck her tongue out at Eddie and flipped him the bird for good measure.

Eddie smiled kindly and just shook his head at the departing digit and turned his attention to the pretty girl sitting before him. They shook hands.

"Hello, Ms. Shannon. Nice to meet you, I think. I'm told you have something you want to tell me about. What might that be?"

Eddie waited. Ms. Shannon did too, just for a moment and then spoke.

"I'm, well I was, Dr. Beautray's nurse."

Eddie leaned forward. "Tell me more, please."

Her correction in mid-sentence from present to past tense signaled the potential uncovering vein of something, something of value.

"I know you are Ms. Monk's lawyer. I was there when Dr. Beautray got served with the papers."

"Yes, that's true. How did Dr. Beautray take it?"

"Not too good. He was angry, cussed a lot, stomped around, went in his office and slammed the door. He's been mean and bitter ever since."

Eddie paused, the pregnant wait to see if the fruit, whatever it might be, would fall to the ground on its own accord.

Shannon bit her lower lip. Eddie studied her gently.

She reached into her carry bag and pulled a set of films out and handed them to Eddie. Their top margins had Jordan Monk's name and date of birth on each of them.

He looked at them intently and saw immediately that they showed extensive impaction and at least two and maybe three sites of injury. Free air was present. It had begun to gush out of her.

"He switched the films out. He doctored them, mislabeled them. I knew what he had done and I switched them out again the next day and took the originals. And here are my notes and my drawing of what happened. I have been really careful with this. My note is time stamped by me and dated. I made it that same afternoon all this happened. This has been eating at me for too long now. I asked him many times to stop the scope. I even at the end pleaded with him, shouted at him to stop. Obviously, he never did until he knew he had royally screwed it up."

Her notes and drawing were damning.

"Well, my goodness…" Eddie was kindly and soft spoken with his words. "Two questions, please?"

"Yes?"

"First, will you testify as to all this?"

"Yes, I will. I know it won't be fun but I will. I promise you I will."

"Thank you. That's very courageous of you. Thank you. And, may I please put these films and your notes and sketch in my safe until it's time to use them? Of course we will have copies of all made carefully now as there, of course, is the need to provide them to the court and opposing counsel."

"Yes, of course. I understand. I'm glad you have them now. The whole thing just keeps giving me the creeps. Dr. Beautray has pretty much turned into a raving asshole—pardon my French—and kept talking about how the trial of his case was getting closer and closer and he was all over the place and I had to get away from him so I quit a few weeks ago. Couldn't stand it, couldn't stand him any longer. I've been stewing over this for a year and a half now. It's been eating me up."

"No offense taken, I promise you. Words far more potent than that get used around here all the time and I understand. "

"How is Ms. Monk?"

"She's coming along. It's been a tough road but she's coming along."

"Well, that's good to hear. He almost killed her. I remember she was a nice lady."

"She is that."

They watched one another for a few moments.

"You sure about all this, Ms. Shannon? Everything is on the straight up?"

"Yes, sir, it is and I am."

"Good. Thank you." He buzzed for Patty.

As Patty came back in, he told Shannon, "Patty will get all your correct contact information and so forth. I expect you realize we will be issuing a subpoena for you real soon to assure your appearance in court. We do it with everybody. I hope you understand. You've become very important now and we sure don't want to lose you."

"I understand."

Patty raised her eyes in silent questioning of Eddie, knew something good had happened and took Ms. Shannon out to her desk.

Eddie studied the gifts he had been given and buzzed Mikey and asked her to get Johnny Olds on the phone for him.

CHAPTER SEVENTEEN

THE NECESSITY OF TALKING

A Few Months Before...

S O, AS OLDS and Eddie sat, Olds was now up to speed. He had copies of all of Ms. Shannon's materials in hand. They had also been provided to the carrier.

"Johnny, let's get this thing moving. You know I've got you by the short hairs now. Your doctor is a caught liar, a deceiver, and as I understand it, a loose cannon with a short fuse. He's probably going to blow up in your face. And God knows this case can and probably will blow up in your carrier's face. I know it and you know it. Why don't you do yourself a favor and help them cut their losses. They'll thank you when it's over, I bet.

"I'm sure you remember way back when y'all were first served with written discovery which included a Motion to Produce Mrs. Monk's original file and all records, notes, and films for our inspection and copying."

"Well, yes, I recall that." Olds deadpanned but the grimace was in his eyes.

"What you provided me way back when did not include the film copies I recently sent over to you. Now did it—or is my memory faulty on that?"

"Well, no, you're right on that."

"Johnny, I know you can't make the true items just materialize out of thin air. But your client is supposed to help you round all this stuff up. Hell, you damn well know and I'm sure you explained to him it's his duty, an obligation to the court and a requirement of the rules. And it looks to me like he tried to play 'hide the ball' and now has gotten caught and gotten his fingers burned and there seems to me to be only one way to make the fire go out.

What does he say about all this, if indeed you can explain it to me?"

"Eddie, there's that lawyer-client confidentiality problem here so I don't think I'll be able to answer that one. I think you understand that."

"Well then, what do you say to that? Ain't no lawyer to lawyer confidentiality between us." Eddie laughed. "I did think that maybe, just maybe, since you and I are trying to not keep secrets from one another that you might give me a hint as to your current mindset on this little problem..."

"Wish I could but that's a negative, makes me uncomfortable..."

Eddie thought, *Oh, I bet. Better be careful, Johnny. You don't want to get swept up in the appearance of helping your defendant tamper with very material evidence...*

But Eddie just nodded and held his tongue. Time was short for the reckoning. There was no reason to speak further of the interrogation to come. Furthermore, he understood that Olds needed to stay far, far away from this rotting pile of shit lest it all fall in on him when the avalanche started. Olds did not want to get ensnared in a shared spoiling of evidence fiasco. The doctor could well suck Johnny under...

So Eddie instead floated just a little hopeful, diversionary bait to make Olds wonder about the trail Eddie might take.

"Well, I guess we may never know. It'll all speak for itself anyway. No need for much explaining. I'll get all the new material in through his former nurse and after that, through the surgeon Carter who repaired her. Curious. How come you didn't want to take Nurse Shannon's deposition ASAP once all the new stuff come to light?"

"That one I can answer. Like you said, it all speaks for itself. No reason to let her really cut loose before now. I expect she'll do that anyway...hell, I don't know. Maybe she won't show." Olds tailed off. Eddie saw no need to flay him.

Eddie and Johnny went way back and had jousted many times. They respected one another and liked one another and could talk straight with one another.

Olds continued. "Yes, Eddie, I know all that and I agree with you, privately of course—not for public consumption—but you also know that my hands are tied to a great extent. Dr. Beautray, while not exactly the epitome of a reasonable gentleman, does want this thing settled and put behind him but he has no authority over the mighty and haughty payer of my billable hours. He, like so many, signed off on their complete control of the policy's purse strings when he took their coverage.

"You know I've been at this business a long time. He has let them know that he wants the case settled but at present, he's but a small voice being ignored by a big wind.

"Hell, we all know that any of us who do this kind of insurance defense work live in a very uncomfortable twilight zone of conflict of interest.

"My client is the doctor. I have an absolute duty to him. I have a fiduciary duty to his interests. But my real client is this damn insurance company, the big dogs with the money and I have to dance a tight rope when they call the tune. It's all a legal fiction and yet, there is no other way. The courts allow it now. The issue has been long since settled with plenty of Sparkle Pony and lofty language. And once we defense lawyers become their peons, we are forever lashed to them. Usually can't get out. Hostages to their steady money."

Olds shook his head in clear dismay and too, shrugged his shoulders with a clear sense of resignation.

"Johnny, you ever give any thought to getting out, to coming over to the happy side, to working without a net but without the continuous ethical conundrums?"

"Yes, of course I have. Most of us have. There are very few 'true believers' left and in truth, they're just blinded by the light. But I'm too old, set in my 'paint by the numbers' sinecure and while I'm pretty good at what I do, I have no prestige, no flash factor to offer anyone like Alph brought when he joined up with you. Hell, I just have a bar number. Alph Baron was the president of the state bar. Big difference there. And even if I tried to take the leap, open my own shop, hook up with a promising rookie or an older successful, fat chance on that shit—my wife would kill me. Too much uncertainty, the loss of steady money, too much disruption at this stage of the game."

"I know and I understand. You have my empathy. I appreciate your candor. It'll stay only with me. So, what can we do here? I'm frustrated and I know you are too."

"Yup. And not the first time either and it sure won't be the last…"

Eddie nodded.

Johnny Olds sighed. "Well, here's a little something. You know how we are required to regularly update the carrier with comprehensive 'status of the case' letters and always with copies of same to the defendant doctor or healthcare provider?"

"Uh huh," Eddie nodded.

"I don't think it would surprise you to learn that my assessments have not been very sanguine about this mess and I have been pouring it on each time out. And their review of your recently provided copies of films and notes and so forth have, it seems, stimulated their attentions. So, it seems that my efforts in that regard have borne some fruit. As well as your pulling that golden horseshoe out of your ass. You know you are sort of making my job easier, don't you?" Olds smiled pleasantly.

"Oh, Johnny, I sure hope so. Now how about put some meat on that bone."

"I have been instructed to offer you three hundred thousand dollars, but you have got to come down a good lick. And if you won't, then I am instructed to withdraw the offer."

"I see. I'll consider it. Of course I will but I must speak to Ms. Monk about it."

"Will you recommend it to her?"

"I will recommend a reduction in demand but I will certainly not recommend that she settle at that number."

"I understand. I figured that was what you were going to say. Eddie, here's a little more that may help."

"So we aren't at take it or leave it, drop dead, go to hell yet?" Eddie grinned.

"No, we are not but we're getting closer. Here's what else I have to tell you and this is totally confidential for now. No bullshit. You may not tell your client about this until I say so— so now here I am trying to compromise you, messing with your ethics. Can I have your sworn assurance?"

Eddie laughed. "What the hell...in for a penny, in for a pound. I promise my mouth is closed until you green light me. What are you talking about now?"

"Well, first, as I have earlier said, you gotta come off your $1.5 million, you need to make a generous move. Once that happens and once we complete jury selection, I will offer you half a million payable within thirty days. I really do not expect any more authority than that and if y'all balk, the number can and probably will be yanked. And, Eddie, we have easily picked up early on that she's real shy and skittish about all this—no reason to put her through the wringer. This could be real hard on her."

"Johnny, I don't disagree with you, but keep in mind her sister has been a great strength to her and y'all know that too from taking that lady's deposition."

Eddie thought, *This is interesting enough and he's wishy-washy on yanking the offer. Happy to play but gotta prep it hard now for trial. This is such a pain in the ass but maybe we can make a chicken sandwich out of this chicken shit of fast scheduling to please this asshole of a big zeal judge...*

Olds thought, *The company treats all alike. How stupid. Eddie Terrell is not an amateur. They've walked me into having to try a big chunk of this one. Just to get to a half and then I'm gonna get stretched. I just need to go home and have three big drinks. Shit.*

Eddie followed on.

"Johnny, I appreciate all this. I will talk with Ms. Monk in just a little bit and I will call you as soon as I have conferred with her and you have my word I will not disclose Part B until you say so."

"Thanks, Eddie. And, oh just by the way, Jesus, how in the hell did we get into this line of work in the first place?" Olds was thoughtfully serious.

"Oh come on, Johnny. Cut yourself some slack. A long time ago we were all starry eyed, weren't we? I know I was."

"Yeah, I guess, well, I know...you're right. But it sure seems though that all that time has taken the bloom off that rose."

"Well, sometimes that is so, but seems to me, we just gotta keep plugging along. It, after all, is the nature of our beast, ain't it?"

Olds considered it. They were all prisoners of their work and the embrace was always tight and sultry too.

"True, you got that right. So it goes. Glad we could talk."

They shook hands and went their separate ways.

Eddie called Ms. Monk, let her know about the three hundred on the table and got her permission to drop their demand to $1.25 million.

He called Olds and relayed that information. Olds grumbled a bit and wanted the demand brought further down, but Eddie knew it was all part of the show and simply and politely and quietly demurred. There was no push back from Olds.

He went back to the office and they went to work on the final trial prep. Eddie was put out with all this hoop jumping and it had soured his mood even though the money meter was moving north.

Eddie let everyone know what was going on and where they were after his visit with Olds save for his intentional omission of the climb to five hundred that was coming up next. They were pleased and it felt good to hold the forthcoming lagniappe on his hip. He asked Alph to be with him at trial and just observe and share his thoughts with him. And he asked Patty to line up a temp for the week of the trial to sit at Patty's desk and greet visitors and answer phones. He wanted all of his people with him. They were to him as Linus's security blanket. They all, each in their own way, comforted him, calmed and soothed him.

Alph Baron said, as always, it would be his pleasure to try to be of help. And that helped lift Eddie's spirits. It was a professional routine. And Patty called and lined up a nice gal from the agency they used for such from time to time who had helped them before, a gal named Polly who was bright and attractive and engendered confidence that balls would not be dropped or fumbled while she was there playing center field for them while they were in the courthouse.

They were soon thereafter all informed by the clerk's office that Judge James Little of Orange County was assigned to be their trial judge. This was good news. Little was smart and steady and thoughtful and understood human nature. He could be seriously stern at times but he never ran roughshod over lawyers or clients; he was well-known to reason with all, the over-enthusiastic and the recalcitrant too. He had a great poker face and his judicial mien was perfect for the part.

Eddie had been jerked around by Mart The Fart as to the calendar clock but Eddie had his Irish up and was going to show them, but there was a resentment in him for the moment that clouded his usual joy of going into combat. He hyper focused for the next weeks and crafted a clean and simple presentation. As he did, he would walk and talk it by Alph and the others and they'd nod or shake their heads or offer brief commentary. It was called "collaboration" and it felt good.

CHAPTER EIGHTEEN

AN INTERREGNUM/ ASSIMILATION

Eddie and Alph

EDDIE AND ALPH had grown very close over the years. They treated one another as beloved brothers. Alph had picked up the world of the plaintiff's lawyer very quickly and adeptly and had become damn good at it. He understood that all he needed to do was flip the board and then he got to read out of the back of the book. He did not know many of the adjusters or the younger Turk defense lawyers but he knew their bosses and senior supervising partners and he was adept and quick at making the short calls that mined long green. He made lots of money for himself and all and had flexible freedoms and opportunities that he had never had in his straitjacketed former world of insurance defense and corporate work.

Alph was a graceful lawyer athlete and made effortless plays that were anything but. He was a natural but would not have been so for his many fancy years on the other side of the fence. He had natural balance and in his dusking years, he had become beyond legend. And it made him giggle in an innocence that he and all, save for the "other side," came to love. He was a lethal legal trial man child now, a power switch hitter and now, an even bigger lock for the hall of fame he had long ago earned.

Plus, now he had Eddie the Engine. Eddie was a stone cold sweet-faced killer. Alph loved him. And Eddie loved Alph. They drank from the same cup as the two faces of Janus, with beginnings, endings and all in between. Alph added class to their sleek rough and tumble. Eddie the Shark and Alph the Gentleman. Hell, Alph would never deign to drink his coffee from Styrofoam—only good china cup and saucer for him. There was an "old worldliness" to him.

And, oh, the prestige and status he brought to the firm and to Eddie's side were truly palpable. When the two walked in to whatever room they countenanced, the odds to be paid on the bet for them began to shrink and did so quickly. What a ten strike Eddie and the firm had hit when they implored and convinced Alph to join them.

Alph was reinvigorated by the new and wildly fun sandbox he had jumped into with both feet and it was as though he had shed years from his chronology. He loved being the hunter instead of the hunted. He loved being able to help pick the cases they would take from a variety of offerings instead of being told by the insurance company masters they had to take them all or the masters would take them all away.

He loved the range of freedom that came with the initiating strategy and tactics from the inception of the fight. He loved the happy informality of their office. The teasing, the give and take, the honest commentary and assessment, the comings and goings of so many characters and especially, he loved the laughter. Even in its most serious moments, that laughter, that humor always stood just behind the door or around the corner.

This was a far, far distance from the forced sterility of bill-by-hours law, always marking the sixty minutes in six-minute increments, always adjusting those ticks upward, nudging the totals in order to pile up the time and validate one's worth to the greater machine. In that green shade world, there was little humor save for the shallow, de rigeur exchanges of banality and resignation.

It would be fair to say that Alph was also renewed and refreshed by the re-emergence of one Lee Ann Jepson. Years before Lee Ann had been Eddie's live-in squeeze, but that was more than a decade ago and they had parted company, if not cheerfully, then at least efficiently and there had never been any hard feelings that lingered.

Alph had met Lee Ann in a local, "nice enough" dive bar (most likely as in Li'l Abner's Sadie Hawkins Day, she had chased him until she snared him) and they had taken a serious shine to one another. This now was a good while ago.

It wasn't a great leap of logic to understand that Lee Ann liked older, attractive, well-to-do men of substance and obviously, trial lawyers held a great appeal for her; ass hard and tough and steely-eyed as they could be between the lines. When off-duty they were doting and not demanding if handled correctly, and Alph had the sweet disposition that enabled those outcomes. One look at Lee Ann's smiling, batting eyes and Alph Baron was malleable and compliant.

And Lee Ann was still arm candy to the max, still quite the classic looker. Not quite buxom, her carriage was still bountiful enough and her shock absorbers still worked magnificently.

She had an apartment in an older, very nice set of buildings draped with old oaks and maples over near the big hospital campus. Though Alph was extremely generous, Lee Ann was not kept and she kept it that way.

After her departure from Eddie, Lee Ann quickly reclaimed and thus re-warmed her receptionist's perch with her wolf whistle fanny down at the Department of Forensic Pathology at the medical school's teaching hospital; its chief, the courtly Pole, Dr. Georgio Podgorny—whose descriptions of death and its causes and its variables were virtually symphonic, always with the lilt of Chopin hovering over his musings and presentations—had moved on. His successor was a mild-mannered, unassuming, unhurried, absent-minded sort of big brain, a very tall guy with a shock of pale yellow sprawling hay on top of his domed pate who gently lurched about and quietly mumbled to himself more often than not.

And she had learned, over the bumps and grinds of earlier years and travails that she was smart enough to know she was only so smart so she always underplayed her hand. She, at heart, was a reasonably simple girl because she had willed herself to be so and she had learned to simplify whatever she could. She had grown to detest drama and Alph was anything but drama. And that was true of her work as well. There was no drama there because most everyone there was already rigor frozen stiff at degrees well below room temperature and slabbed out on sliding trays in hollow stainless steel drawers with locker latches that snapped finality.

That frigid holding climate well suited the dead and the few, blue scrubbed upright heartbeats that busied about on the above death shredding linoleum in the running of the place were all quiet, introverted types who did not need a lot of chit-chat. Much training shoe squeak and more cigarette breaks. And there was no odor save for the chemicals used so if one pretended to be in a dry cleaners, it all worked out just fine. The pay was fine enough too. It was one of those few places where the customer was not always right and there was no suggestion box.

So Lee Ann and Alph took up with one another, always at a respectful distance in public, always in a happy embrace in private and it worked. Every now and then, there would be brief moments of PDA—sometimes when Lee Ann would pop into the office for a lunchtime visit, sometimes when the third glass at the bar propelled them into their hugging more than a little bit zone but mostly, it all quite proper.

When such excitations would break forth, Patty or Mikey would admonish them with exclamations of "cold shower now!" and "more saltpeter now!" and Lee Ann and Alph would giggle and blush and break the clinch.

It also "worked" in great part because Alph's wife of longstanding years, known uniformly to all of them as Mrs. Alph, being known for years as a hard ass, imperious bitch which of course had from the beginning propelled randy Alph into the quick shadows of philandery.

After the long ago, grinding times of coming to grips with her spouse's wanderings (and she recognized this as she continued to think it all through as time passed—they, neither of them, could quite remember why it was that they married in the first place; legitimating security they supposed…), she quite pleasantly accepted her role as the top of the totem.

That was not a resignation but rather simply a small scar that had healed and keloid strengthened long ago. Of course, Mrs. Alph knew "about" Lee Ann but did not interrogate nor snoop. After a while, she never did think about it much. She felt herself to be, after narrow introspection, to be quite French and nonchalant about it all and that pleased her.

She had her charity events to which Alph would happily and dutifully accompany her, her ladies' luncheons, her benefits and dinners, her travels and tours, her bridge games, her hit and giggle tennis matches, their lovely house in the mountains near Roaring Gap, occasional strolls with him, her Mercedes SUV, her furs and jewels and her manifest accoutrements of higher living and above all else, her status.

Long ago, the two of them had set up camps in bedrooms far apart from one another but they were pleasant and kind to one another and took more than a few meals together. They shared much of their thinking and advice.

Of course, there had been whispers and cut eyes and rumors across the many years but after a while that all subsided and there was a legitimate peace in the valley. There was always someone else to scuttle. And the train of tattle and gossip always did move on.

Alph and his missus had become over the years as the soldiers of the South and North had been in early 1865. Truce was called and the boys in butternut and blue would leave their lines and go visit with one another. There was plenty of visiting and news sharing, card playing and drinking and usually some nostalgic singing and then after a while, the soldiers shuffled back to their trenches and redoubts and dug-ins and resumed the wait for the next spasm of conflict; something they all hoped wouldn't be too bad and something they could all get through.

Eddie actually had come to think well of Lee Ann as did Patty and Mikey. They just didn't care about the appearance or morality of it all. It was an interesting curiosity at best. After all, they were all grown-ups and Alph worked his ass off and he was fun to play with too. Mrs. Alph never came around and the only time any of them saw Lee Ann and Alph together was when they'd have brief visits at the office or when they'd "bump into one another" when they were all out having a few after a day at work. No one worried about it. There wasn't anything to worry about. Everyone just let it lay.

CHAPTER NINETEEN

GAME DAY

Back to a Few Months Earlier

S O EDDIE AND Alph went off to try the case against Olds.

Earlier, Patty and Mikey made sure the brief bags and trial boxes were put together and that there were abundant office supplies at hand.

Nurse Shannon had earlier been served with a subpoena to appear with an accompanying note to arrive at Courtroom 6A by 3 p.m. that first afternoon.

The repairing surgeon, a nice fellow named Heath Carter, had also been subpoenaed and instructed to arrive at 1:30 p.m. Eddie had met with him a couple of weeks before and his candor and forthrightness were sincerely appreciated.

Eddie was going to call the defendant Beautray as his first witness and as he was the defendant, Eddie would be able to remove the kid gloves and get after him with a good snapping cross-examination. Beautray was an adverse witness and did not qualify for the usual, more banal routine of direct examination.

A lot of lawyers stayed away from this move, fearful that it could back-fire on them if the witness made a good impression and also, it gave the defendant two shots at testifying, the second when called back to the stand by his defense counsel to dance the dance of the "3 C's"—the charade of "clarify, correct, contain" which might help clean up whatever messes had been made on the first pass, created at the behest of the upstart plaintiff's lawyer who dared to do something impertinently different.

Eddie felt strongly that he could cut Beautray and mortally wound him early and often. He so wanted him to lie and obfuscate.

Eddie knew that he had backup help in the personages of other witnesses, thus making the maneuver less stark. So the plan was firmly planted in his head. *De l'audace, encore de l'audace, et toujours de l'audace.* And strike to kill, always strike to kill. The ancient rule of regicide endured.

Eddie also wanted to make sure that Dr. Carter was there to watch Beautray squirm and evade and lie and thus instill in Carter some more animated and invigorated righteousness.

Mrs. Jordan Monk and her sister Mrs. Delores Rhyne had come to the office and Eddie and Alph sat with them for thirty minutes explaining again the basic procedures of the days ahead. He asked again for their resolve and their patience. Mrs. Monk was naturally apprehensive but promised Eddie that she would stay the course.

"I've come this far. I might as well keep going. I know you'll tell me what to do and lead me fair. It's all in the Lord's hands now."

Her sister nodded firmly in assent and they were both told that they were going to do just fine.

They were told that they would be the last two witnesses presented so they could watch the case unfold and hopefully over the next few days that would increase their comfort level in the courtroom. Trial lawyers often forgot that their comfort zone was for most lay people a mental chamber of constriction and apprehension.

Not Eddie. Not Alph. They truly had compassionate pulses and loved working with their clients.

And too Eddie reminded Mrs. Monk that they were working with something of a money net already beneath them and he was hopeful that more fruitful discussion between counsel could bring more cushion.

Polly the temp had already arrived and was alertly on station at Patty's desk.

It was a nice, chilly but sunny end of winter day. They all put on their coats and walked down the hill to the courthouse, went through security and took the elevators up to the sixth floor. They went into the big courtroom. The Clerk of Court and the court reporter and a few other administrative folks were organizing their papers and materials for trial. Two bailiffs stood by. The plaintiffs took the counsel table closest to the jury box and settled in and waited.

It was 9 a.m. and Judge Long would start the proceedings at nine-thirty.

Johnny Olds and his assistant and an irritated-looking Dr. Beautray came along a few minutes later, rolling their few trial boxes in on a small-wheeled trolley.

Eddie and Alph and Johnny all shook hands. Olds said a pleasant "hello" to Mrs. Monk who nodded shyly and looked away. Her sister stared straight ahead. Eddie knew that given half a chance, sister Delores would just as soon strangle Beautray.

Eddie offered an overtly cheery, intentional, little too loud chirpy "Good morning, Dr. Beautray," who side-mouthed muttered in return, "What's so good about it?" with not-so subtle contempt glowering in his face. Eddie had gone to get a rise out of the guy and it had worked.

Let's just keep popping his blood pressure up little by little, Eddie thought.

Olds frowned and narrowed his eyes at Eddie in disapproval but did not speak to his displeasure.

Alph shrugged his shoulders in the apathetic fashion of Alfred E. Neuman and was amused and Olds and Beautray knew it.

The game was on.

Eddie knew, as he had always suspected, that as deceitful and evasive as the good doctor had been in his brief deposition some months before, that he would be more of the same and even more when he sat naked and alone in the witness box.

Eddie had always longed for the English rule that applied to their witnesses in their box. Across the pond, unless they were under a physical infirmity, witnesses in the UK were required to stand. That gave the jury the full view, the full display of nervous twitches and hands clutching and shoulders drooping and feet shuffling—a more thorough and comprehensive method to see the witness and all their telling body language in full.

Here in the States, the seated witness was only in half view. That was unfortunate.

Judge Long and his clerk came in to the high bench.

"Before I bring the jury pool in, would counsel please approach the bench."

They all did so and stood beneath Long's gaze.

His Honor nodded at each and added, "Well, Alph, been a while. How are you liking the rough and tumble of the trashy and tawdry side of the aisle?" Long grinned and winked at Alph.

No disrespect was intended as it was an old lawyer joke.

Insurance defense lawyers were allegedly respected. Plaintiffs' lawyers were allegedly scurrilous scoundrels and these days, all the lawyer advertising on television added much shabby grasping to the latter.

Eddie and Alph did not advertise on television or anywhere else for that matter. They just did not need to. They were the top of the mountain. They were not smarmy, nowhere close to it; they were classy, smart, effective and damn lucky too. Good fortune sought them out. They were the poster children for Officers of the Court.

Alph was happy, enervated, and enthusiastic. "Hey there, Judge Long. Hope you and yours are well. Recall I last saw you at the bar meeting at Wrightsville summer before last. And I'm good, really enjoying working on this side of the valley. I keep asking myself what took me so long."

His eyes shone.

Long replied, "Alph, I've heard you are indeed getting along with all this real well and I'm glad to hear it."

Olds was apprehensive. The bonhomie between the old warrior and the respected judge signaled a tiny but perceptible tilt in the plaintiff's favor. Olds sighed in his heart.

"Now, gentlemen, I've read over your pretrial briefs and submissions and proposed areas of questioning for the venire. I see nothing but straight forward there. I also see there are no pretrial motions outstanding. Have I got all that correct so far?"

The lawyers chorused, "Yes, Your Honor."

"Now, have there been any settlement discussions?"

Eddie slightly raised his hand.

"Yes, Your Honor, there have been some. Not enough, but some so far."

"Interesting and somewhat unusual considering it's a malpractice case in these parts. Where are y'all? You going to tell me?"

Long was like that, never inclined to just yank it out of them; it would all come along in due time.

Eddie nodded to Olds to pass the baton of response to the judge.

"Your Honor, the defense has offered three hundred thousand in response to the plaintiff's initial demand of $1.5 million. Plaintiff has reduced its demand to $1.25 million and that's where we stand at the present."

"The basic facts as I have read them and think I understand them are quite serious. Don't y'all think it would behoove each of you to keep moving the meter here?"

The lawyers then all knew that Judge Long was going to be intent on helping them move that needle, something he did not always do.

Olds nodded. "I think that's what we've got in mind, Your Honor, but I think we need to get started here so we can see how it all looks to be playing out."

"Fine. I understand. Let's bring the jurors in. Oh, and Eddie, Johnny, and Alph too. I know that Judge Solomon has rushed y'all along here and I appreciate everyone getting ready to go on shorter than usual notice. I just wanted y'all to know I'm mindful of that pressure."

"Thank you, Your Honor. I think we are good to go. At least, I think so." Eddie smiled.

Eddie had not filed an updated supplement to his pretrial brief so the Court was unaware—for the immediate present—of the high explosives that Nurse Shannon had recently delivered. This was an intentional oversight but not a hanging offense. He knew he might be later chided for the omission but he was willing to get his hands slapped in order to have the Court experience the surprise along with the jury. Eddie was betting that the latter would outweigh the former.

Olds had not either, just because to do so would seal his client's fate early and he then could be accused of not effectively representing his client and too, it depressed him to think about it. Might as well just let that sleeping dog lie until it soon enough got up and took a lunging, bloody hunk out of you.

They all turned back to their counsel tables and got to work.

As Olds sat down and adjusted his half moons and reached for his trial notebook, he automatically reflected on the small vignette that had just played out with Judge Long as its lead player. As to their all being hustled to trial by that son of a bitch Solomon and their being the recipients of that collective recognition of that unfortunate forced timing by the Court, Olds replayed the tape and saw that Judge Long had only faced Eddie Terrell when he spoke and he knew it was with Eddie that the Court's sympathies fell.

Olds was having a queasy feeling. *Jesus*, he thought, *where else would I rather be right now...? Hell, just throw a damn dart at the map...* He sighed quietly again. It seemed such was becoming an involuntary habit. This case was comparable to having dog shit on your shoe that you could not quite scrape off.

Johnny Olds felt rumpled and shabby. And his clerk looked at him to see if he was all right and his client picked at his cuticle and silently seethed and felt sorry for himself.

CHAPTER TWENTY

THE MINUET OF NEGOTIATION, DECEIT AND DARE

A Few Months Before

A GAGGLE OF FORTY prospective jurors was escorted into the big room by the bailiffs, shuffling into the narrow passageways of the pew-like rows, and the benches creaked as they rustled and settled. Eddie and Alph watched them carefully to see how they were dressed, how they carried themselves, what newspapers and books they carried and for any other signs that revealed something about how they might think, further developing their impressions of these individuals.

Earlier, all the lawyers the week before had gotten access to the juror information cards for that term. Patty and Mikey went down to the clerk's office and picked up a complete copy and brought them back up the hill for a complete analysis and scoring at one of the round conference tables in the office.

The information received was basic and helpful.

Each juror provided the following: name, address, race, sex, current employment, spouse's current employment, previous jury service if any and if so, what kind of matter—civil or criminal—did they participate in.

Every lawyer had a manner, a technique of noodling all this information.

In Eddie's office, four notebooks were prepared and then they all sat together and reviewed each sheet. Commentary and vigorous discussion were mandatory.

They used an A-B-C-D scoring system for each name. A's were the most preferred and D's were the least. This was as good a starting point. They all knew plenty of it was, at best, a crap shoot.

Insurance and professional employment were basically anathema to a plaintiff's side of the case as were the wealthy and the inconvenienced and distracted. Minorities and the less affluent were preferred. And gender always counted depending on the tilt of the one who is gored or the gorer.

Once the venire was brought in, the questioning by counsel was, as always, exploratory as to prejudices and also, temptingly alluring as the lawyers fed small pieces of bait to the panel, telling the story here and there. But in this case, Eddie chose not to let the big cat out of the bag. There was huge sex appeal in keeping it on a leash.

One of Eddie's favorite lines of questioning was asking what kind of bumper stickers and decals did these folks have on their and their family vehicles. He had learned that approach long ago in a seminar where the presenter was a superior court judge from Seattle. It was fair game in that all such rolling expressions and declarations were intentionally displayed for the general public to see and process. The logic of such open and will-ful declarations had always been immediately obvious to Eddie, but in the beginning, many hidebound old grumps would just say, "Not here, not now, not ever."

But Eddie stayed with it and finally got some traction on it and then some more, using the piggybacking of those assenting and allowing to convince the doubters that these days it was standard operative procedure.

So, from the political (Jesse Helms for U.S. Senate) to the collegiate (Let's Go State!) to the preferential (I "Heart" my such and such and so and so) to the provocative (Go ahead. Hit me. I need the money.) and let not be forgotten the random and goofy (Honk if you want to nuke a whale for Jesus), this sort of passive-aggressive signaling was always a treasure trove.

And often, expanding on the theme, Eddie wanted to know what kind of car the jurors drove. The same sort of judicial pushback was there (along the lines of "No, because I say so...") but as the wise man said, you can't make an omelet without breaking some eggs. And Eddie was nobody's fool. During trial time, he always drove his Chevy Impala to and from the office so he could honestly preface his inquiries with "My car is a Chevy Impala" as opposed to a Mercedes SUV or a BMW.

And last, but certainly not least, in the algorithms that swirled about in the selection and dismissal process was the lawyer's instinct about the people under scrutiny. Eddie and Alph knew this was Holy Writ even if a juror checked all the favorable boxes and the lawyer had a sense of unease or distrust or even something as basic as "I just don't think this one likes me or likes my client. And/or there's something here that ain't right. I just don't like her all that much," that juror had to be let go.

This was what Eddie called "dog smarts." He had learned it at a seminar years before when a very sharp lawyer named Craig Spangenberg from Cleveland explained that he had a savvy bulldog named Buddy that would go downtown with him to the city center of "The Mistake on the Lake" (Among many moments that helped create that pejorative moniker was the seemingly endless fires that would spontaneously combust in the polluted, chemical cesspool of the nasty Cuyahoga River) when he was a kid to prowl around, buy candy and basically check out the big city.

He and Buddy would approach a corner. Before turning, sometimes the bulldog would growl; sometimes it wouldn't. Sometimes there was another dog on the other edge of the corner; sometimes there wasn't. If there was another dog coming around the bend that did not evoke a snarl, then that dog was okay by Buddy. But if Buddy, even before turning the corner, began to agitate before any other dog came into view, that was the instinct of dislike. Buddy knew and Spangenberg explained, "If you have any sense that you don't like a prospective juror or that prospective juror doesn't like you, then you've got to follow your gut and get the juror off the panel."

Thus, over a few hours, the panel was scrubbed and winnowed and a jury was picked, sworn in, seated and instructed as to their conduct and responsibilities by the Court. It was approaching the noon hour and Judge Long told all to go have an early lunch and to be in their seats ready to go at 1:30 sharp. He sternly admonished them to do no research or study, electronic or otherwise, about anything or anyone having anything to do with this case that they were now an integral and critical part of. And then the judge sent them on their way.

"All rise," squawked a bailiff and the courtroom began to empty. The jurors were led out first to the back hallways and the elevators before anyone else was allowed to depart, each of them wearing a large, bright, red and blue badge which clearly identified them as current possessions of the

Court as the finders of fact and which also signaled they were not to be communicated with, questioned or inconvenienced in any way.

Judge Long, arms folded, standing in his long-sleeved black robe and watching from the bench, was satisfied the break had begun in orderly fashion, turned, and went out toward the long hall and his chambers. As he went, he eyed the two lawyers but said nothing. The bailiffs and Court staff had also departed. The courtroom was growing still.

As the Monk group began their shuffle to the exits, Olds called across the way quietly and asked Eddie if he could spare a minute or two. Eddie nodded his assent and asked Alph to escort the others to go on a few blocks down Main Street past the Wachovia Building and across 4th Street where he would meet them at the Katherine, an upscale eatery which also had a fine bar, something that was certainly not in this day's mix of thought, word and deed. Eddie asked that they only order him a grilled cheese and a Diet Coke. He had little appetite during trial.

Eddie wandered over to the bench behind the defense counsel table and sat down. Olds asked his assistant to take Dr. Beautray to find some lunch at the little deli spot down 4th Street in the O'Hanlon Building and said he would be along shortly, adding that he'd like the Greek salad, light on the garlic dressing please.

Eddie made a note that he was glad to not be Dr. Beautray sitting next to Olds after lunch.

Olds then sat down next to Eddie. Everyone had gone on by now and the courtroom was quiet.

Olds smiled lightly. "Eddie, I have to note that you just sent your troops down to a pretty snappy, fancy place to eat while I have instructed a far more modest repast for my little crowd...already counting and spending my money, are you?"

Eddie slowly shook his head in mild amusement but the crack surprisingly popped him. He flared.

"Now, Johnny, you know better than that. You're on your carrier's dime, chained to their expense account stipend. Just yet another benefit for you of playing dialing for dollars on that big clock that rules your life. And I will, just for the record, be buying my crowd's lunch with my money as I haven't gotten a dime of yours so far and if we don't get this thing worked out, I may never see a nickel of your bank roll. I doubt it but as you know, life is uncertain so eat dessert first. Remember, eat, drink and be merry for tomorrow we may die. Now, are we still playing by your rules and your move? Our jury is seated."

Eddie was teasing but it was hard teasing, though only just a little bit, and some contemptuous snarky had seeped into his words. Regretting this and wanting to show good faith and reel the calm back in, he followed on quickly with, "Sorry, Johnny, that was meant to be a little joke and it just came out wrong. I apologize. My bad."

"No problem. I understand. It's okay. You know, Eddie, dammit all, you are right." Olds' dissatisfaction with the constraints of his suit and tie share-cropper world frothed out. Johnny Olds paused, reordered his thoughts to the issue at hand. Eddie waited, trite penance his companion.

"So now on behalf of Dr. Beautray and his practice, we offer Mrs. Monk half a million dollars (Half a million always sounded bigger than $500K), which surely is no inconsequential sum, for a full and final release as to all matters at controversy here along with a dismissal of her action with prej-udice and whatever other paperwork is necessary to conclude the matter. There, of course, will be no admission of liability on the part of Dr. Beautray as this as always is a compromise of a disputed claim. You know the drill."

"Well, yes, you did do what you said you would do and I appreciate it."

"Eddie, this is as much as we are going offer. There's no more going back to the well for more. I really hope you will encourage Mrs. Monk to accept it. I know she's a nice lady and has been through a lot, but that's a pile of tax free money to her, even after your fees and costs are paid. And let's get this over with. What do you say?"

Olds was earnest, too anxiously earnest. Eddie knew Johnny was tired, worn out and a bit blinded by the big hopeful hope of laying this one down and going on home and wrapping his heart and hands around an Old Fashioned glass of whisky. Olds was situationally broken but he would never admit it and would stay on the rack until his pension kicked in. Eddie felt sorry for him but not for so long as he measured the veins in his neck. This was not a bean bag.

"Johnny, you know I need some time to go over this with her and I can't keep the sister in the dark and we can't keep the Court in the dark either. We are required to keep the Court well informed. You understand that, don't you? And talking to her at lunch in a crowded restaurant during this short break doesn't give me much time or the atmospherics I feel I need. She's, as you are well aware, a bit skittish right now and needs to be handled with care. Seems to me you got one of those too, right?"

"Well, I get it. And yeah, we both got Mexican jumping beans but the difference is you got to keep her informed. I just gotta keep the company informed."

He sighed again. Jesus, was Olds going to need supplemental oxygen? He was almost imploring in his tone of voice.

"Let me ask you this. Are you going to recommend it to her?"

"I'll put it this way. This is different from the initial three hundred. It is a bigger number but I'm not going to cram it down her throat or be forceful or push her. I think that would be counterproductive, and remember and as you also know as well, her sister is pretty strong-willed about all of this, has marched her all the way to where we are right now and will be a big part of any decision-making. If she sees or perceives me as being willful, she'll liable to freeze it up.

"But I promise you, Alph and I are going to talk with her and Delores, confer with her very seriously and I'll have an answer for you either late this afternoon after Court is concluded for the day or first thing in the morning before Court reconvenes. That's the best I can do right now. Now, if you feel the need to rescind or pull this offer, I got it and she knows nothing of this right now so I'll have to figure how I'm going to handle that... and we'll just go on from there. My peril. Your peril and so forth.

"Hell, no matter what happens, you're gonna get paid for all your hours so carefully columned and hell, I've got enough to get by for a while.

"And also what is and damn more important for these present moments, no matter what too, I'm going to need some quiet time with the two of them and we have to let the Court know what's going on. So now, Johnny, what kind of time can you allow me or are we done here?"

Eddie waited.

Olds sighed. "You know, Eddie, I wish you'd just go ahead and give the offer a strong recommendation but I know you can't do that considering the time box you're in right now. But God knows I hope you do soon. My client is a surly asshole and yours is a wimp with a lead-by- the-nose drill sergeant. Okay, I'll give you until 9:30 in the morning. If it's not a go by then, tell your lady the five hundred thousand is gone. The best she's going to do is the three hundred. I will hold the line on what we've agreed to there and what we have represented to the Court."

"Thank you. Fair enough. And just so you can tell your carrier you're boxing me in and wearing me down as we move toward a potential finish line, I'll reduce our demand to a million one and we can report that to the Court as well."

Olds nodded.

"Now, let's run off and grab a sandwich and get back in here and at least do a little lawyering before the day is gone. We can't ask the Court to give us the afternoon off. Judge wouldn't allow it anyway. I promise I will make only a brief opening statement and you can hammer away with your damages defenses. It's all going to be pretty pro forma. Your guy will do fine. He's attractive and I'm sure you'll have him prettied up and it's already 12:50 and we need to hustle. We got a deal as to how we are going to proceed, right?"

"Deal, and Eddie, one last question...what are you going to do about the altered X-rays? That's a big concern on this side. You know that. Kinda that nuclear thing, you know..."

Johnny's face was a little pallid, a bit more twitchy and active once the key nub of the trial matter had been broached. He knew the pin was out and Eddie was just holding the grenade polite and tight.

"Fair question. I plan on getting those in through Nurse Shannon and I seriously doubt we will get to her today. And of course, I will cross your doc and your expert on them when the time comes. But maybe, hopefully, I just don't know, we'll be done before then...and if we're not, then we will all just keep on keeping on..." Eddie's voice tailed off as he finished.

The world was a hateful place, full of landmines and traps and snares.

Olds stood up and Eddie followed suit.

"Okay, Eddie. Thanks for the time. See you in a little bit and we can talk with Judge Long briefly before we get going with openings."

And so, off they went.

Olds was guardedly, gauzily hopeful, with the ludicrous, foolish optimism of the lonely fellow buried deep in the cave that somehow, someone would break through the thick-crusted seal of the landslide and save him. As he gasped unto unconsciousness, would provide oxygen to him and give escape and succor and comfort to him, but deep down below on his many subcutaneous mental, emotional layers, he knew better.

He sensed he was fucked. He was a senior partner but a minor one too, on his own in this courtroom, left only with a very nice, hard-trying and ineffectual assistant. He was not even provided with a hot shot associate, a ladder climber that he could share shit shoes with.

Johnny did feel legitimately that the hook was well-baited with enough spendable spinach. He also knew he could make one more call for one more hundred grand, something he knew Eddie knew too and something he figured Judge Long would push for as well. He would talk with Dr. Beautray, key him in to what was going on and would warn him to be totally honest and humbled straightforward about the doctored films when his time came, if it did come at all.

He prayed vaguely that time would not come, of course.

It would be suggested by Johnny Olds later that evening to a bored and dismissive and annoyed Beautray, only suggested of course, though Olds wanted to grab Beautray by his three hundred dollar shirt collar and shake him and tell him in a loud and fierce voice to "pay fucking attention," that it might help if he professed an innocent helplessness and overwhelming panic in the face of her impenetrable wall of stratified shit and that he always felt he could find the crease and opening to get the scope through and let's not forget you're looking for killer cancer here, I repeat "killer cancer!" and that it was so vital that you push the edge of the envelope as we're trying to save people here, and also he needed to throw himself on his sword of apology and good intent while all at the same time indicting Mrs. Monk for her deceitful providing of misinformation and her previously deleterious lifestyle of booze and benders, a neat trick of two-faced embrace—love you while I wreck you...and so forth, maybe...

Eddie quick-stepped it to lunch. He looked at his cold, congealed cheese sandwich, took a lame, half-moon bite and a long draught of the now lukewarm nasty soft drink, did not even remotely note their dietary deficiencies and quickly called his bunch to huddle, gesturing their heads in tight toward the center, looking like a badly designed prayer wheel and closed them into a tribal quorum, shushed them into a silence while the rest of the room around them laughed and loved the pretty day and led themselves in what they thought were normal lives.

Offhandedly, Eddie knew there was no such thing.

Even though she sat across from him, he missed Mikey so much. No time for that now.

He told them quietly of the increased offer with set time limitations and told them that they would discuss it all after Court was concluded for the day and that there was no necessity for it to be discussed and accepted or rejected until later; certainly not now. He was firm in that they should all should be patient and pay attention as things unfolded over the afternoon.

He was cracking precise, sharp-toned and it was clear that he wasn't trying to jumpstart any conversation just yet.

Alph and Patty and Mikey understood. They all knew Eddie was working, trying to get to the corner and run to daylight, trying to get the tumblers to fall in and click in the correct sequence. They could tell his engine was on a hard idle.

It was abundantly clear to them that Eddie was a bush hog in the scrub. He was clearing things away in his mind, getting lean for the start of the trial.

Mrs. Monk looked at her sister and asked, "Oh my, Delores, what do you think? This all just makes me so nervous." She had a look of decision-making anguish on her face.

Delores faced her sister. "Honey, here's what I think. I think we need to do as Mr. Terrell here says. We can always pull away from the insurance company later if we feel we want to play shoot for the moon. We ain't chasing for money right now. Well, we kinda are but they seem to be coming our way right good with it so let 'em come on. They've fucked you plenty good but you are on the comeback trail. We've got time to decide whatever whenever we need to. Try to relax and eat your chicken salad. You want some more sweet tea? In the meantime, you just gotta sit tight and watch how it unfolds. Okay?"

Mrs. Monk nodded warily. She was a little scared.

Delores turned to Eddie. "You still got some unfolding to do, right?"

Eddie grew fonder of Delores each time out.

"Yes, ma'am. That's right. We are going to try and cut them off at the pass."

He, around the table, winked at them all.

Delores raised her hand, summoned the waiter and asked for a double Early Times on two cubes in a short glass. She told the fellow to hurry. It was 1:15.

The four of the office smiled. Mrs. Monk didn't look surprised; she just pursed her lips. Everyone knew what was going on. The short glass of brown water arrived in but a minute and she held it and shook it colder for thirty seconds and it was then swallowed down in two neat gulps.

Delores shivered, smiled her benediction for the moment, waited a few seconds and then slowly extended her hands out over the table in the manner of a séance or a Ouija board. No one moved. The hubbub all about them noticed nothing.

"See, y'all. Steady as a rock. Now, I'm ready for some surgery."

Eddie called for the check. It was time to see if their hiding in the trees and gullies in a quick ambush that ought to be in plain sight just might work.

CHAPTER TWENTY-ONE

THE STARTER'S PISTOL IS NOT FIRING BLANKS

A Few Months Earlier

WHEN THEY WALKED into the courtroom, they were right on time. Johnny Olds and his assistant were there but Dr. Beautray was not.

Eddie asked, "Uhm, where's your boy?"

"In the can. I think he's got a touch of the nervous stomach." Olds rolled his eyes.

"Okay, how about let's go back and see the judge."

Eddie thought, *He has the guts of a coward. He'd shit out of his ears now if he could. Good. I'll tear him a new one soon enough.* Eddie throttled himself back. Be not so strong, not yet.

Alph and Eddie and Johnny Olds went out the side door, down the hall and knocked on Judge Long's chambers' door.

"Yes? Come in."

They did so and his Honor looked them over and smiled beneficently. "Have you come to tell me the case is resolved?"

Eddie deferred to Olds with the tilt of his head.

"Your Honor, no, we can't tell you that right now but we can tell you that we have raised our offer to five hundred thousand, Eddie here has come down to $1.1 million."

"That's good. You're making progress. Keep making it."

Olds hesitated a moment, then spoke further. "Judge, I've been instructed by my carrier that the five hundred is it—that there will be nothing further. I've given Eddie here until 9:30 in the morning to tell me yea or nay. He'll have plenty of time to confer with his client. This is serious money now, Judge."

Eddie stood mute. Judge Long asked, "Johnny, how much coverage you got? Two million? I believe I recall that correctly from your pretrial submissions."

"Yessir, that's right."

"Johnny, we're going back in here now and get this ball rolling. I'm not going to keep our train in the station wasting time. But when we have a break, I strongly suggest that you go make a call to your people. You can do better than five hundred and you ought to and you know it. I'm not requiring you to make that call but I think you know what I'm telling you. Don't you?"

"Yes, sir, I do."

"Good. Everybody ready to go with their opening statements?"

"Yes, Your Honor. I will not be very long. Johnny here can speak for himself."

"That's pretty much the same for me. I plan on being brief."

"Good, let's go." He led them back into the courtroom. Taking the bench, he gave the seated jury an overview of what was to come and then called for the plaintiff to give the opening statement on behalf of Mrs. Monk.

Eddie said, "Hello, everyone. We are all glad you are here. We know and understand and appreciate there is inconvenience to you because you are taking time to be here with us for these next few days. And I expect you will quickly come to understand this is an important matter that warrants you close attention. And we all thank you for that close attention."

He then stood and placed himself behind Mrs. Monk and gently put his hands on her shoulders and introduced his client and everyone else as well. That included the defense table. It was a good way to show a jury that this was his show, his production and that he was the master of ceremonies. He had long ago been taught that the courtroom must belong to him and that he was in control of it, of course, always being respectful of the judge.

Once his introductory comments were in place, he stepped over and stood in front of the jury and continued. "Mrs. Monk here is a sixty-year-old lady who has lived here in Winston-Salem almost her entire life. She was married but her husband passed away many years ago. They had no children but luckily, she has her younger sister here with her, Mrs. Delores Rhyne. Mrs. Rhyne, would you please stand so these folks can know who you are. Delores did, nodding with a slight, pained smile on her face.

"Mrs. Monk worked for over thirty-five years at Hanes Knitting and was a senior loom operator and also watched over and supervised a number of other operators when what we are here to talk about happened. She made good money and wanted to work until she was sixty-five. Instead, she's had to take an early medical retirement. All things considered, her health was good, especially for the last long time. It is true that during and after her husband's difficult illness and death, she did wrestle with alcohol for a while but she never missed a day's work over it and she has long since put that bad habit behind her. Along the way, she will tell y'all about that and many other things as well. I think y'all will find her to be a lady of solid goodwill and strong and truthful as well. I can assure you she wished she was not here now. But she has to be. It is, sadly, required of her.

"She was referred to Dr. Aviv Beautray by her family doctor for a routine colonoscopy which is the running of a scope up through the rectum and then on up into the large intestine where the lining of the large intestine, the colon is inspected for abnormalities. Cancer is one of those abnormalities they look for, but please remember, Mrs. Monk was not sick or ill, did not have cancer then and does not now.

"The night before the procedure, Mrs. Monk drank as prescribed a lot of laxative solution, very unpleasant stuff it is too, which was supposed to clean her large intestines out so the doctor could get a good look with his scope. Most of the time the laxative gets the job done; sometimes it doesn't. It was readily apparent or certainly should have been readily apparent to Dr. Beautray from the beginning, from the get-go of the procedure that Mrs. Monk was not properly cleaned out. How is it they say it? What you see is what you get? There is the old truth: 'there are none so blind as those who will not see.'"

Eddie knew these last lines were objectionable but he didn't care. The bell had been rung and nothing was going to unring it, and Olds did nothing except watch Eddie while Dr. Beautray stared straight ahead.

"The procedure should never have proceeded, should have been stopped, halted right there but recklessly Dr. Beautray pushed on and on and that is why we are all here today. You will soon learn the details of all this and I believe, no, I know you will figure this situation and the ensuing damages she has suffered out in good short order. Please allow me to note but one of Mrs. Monk's permanent, I emphasize permanent problems from this, as you will soon see, a classic case of medical malfeasance. She has to have a colostomy bag because of all this and it cannot be reversed and so she will have to live with that bag and all that it entails for the rest of her life.

"You will hear of course from Mrs. Monk and her sister Delores and also hear from a lady named Miss Phoebe Shannon who was Dr. Beautray's attending nurse in the examining room with them when all this happened. You will hear from Dr. Heath Carter, a surgeon at our Wake Forest Medical Center who repaired Mrs. Monk's injuries and who she follows as his patient to this day.

"And when the time comes, I suppose you will hear from Dr. Beautray and he can, as he wishes, give his version of these events. I will examine him in due course. So here it is in a nutshell with much more to be revealed. My opposing counsel, Mr. Johnny Olds, will now give you his opening statement on behalf of his client, Dr. Beautray. I thank you very much for your attention."

Eddie walked back to counsel table and sat down.

Johnny Olds approached the jury. As he did, he loudly, mightily cleared his throat in a resonating harrumph, torquing his head above his neck to the side. Then he shrugged his shoulders and reset himself. It was such an obvious sign of discomfiture. And of course, it pleased Eddie's team.

He perfunctorily went through his traces, told the jury what a great and fine doctor Beautray was, told them he would never be reckless with a patient. He said of course she was a very nice lady. He told them Mrs. Monk never told Beautray that she wasn't well cleaned out, that she had not been able to adequately evacuate her bowels and he also told them she had, by her unfortunate and excessive drinking over time, thinned the lining of her bowel out, thus making her more susceptible to injury during an otherwise routine procedure and that this heavy drinking on her part had not been explained or told to Beautray before the procedure commenced. He told them that her injury was well-repaired and that she was able to lead a very close to normal life, that she could have gone back to work if she had chosen to but she had decided otherwise. He asked them to remember there are always two sides to a story. And then, abruptly, he sat down.

Eddie looked at Alph who returned the glance with but the slightest of nods. Eddie thought, *Jesus, what a load of bullshit. He just mailed that one in. But then again, he doesn't have much to mail in the first place...*

Judge Long thanked the lawyers and instructed the plaintiff to call his first witness.

Eddie stood and called Dr. Aviv Beautray to come to the witness stand and be sworn.

There was a sudden intense stillness in the courtroom. It was as if everything had frozen in time. Seconds that felt like minutes passed. Everyone was watching. Judge Long had his hands and fingers steepled in wait. And then the silence was broken by feverish, rapid whispering from the defense table. It was plainly audible for all, certainly including the jury, to clearly hear.

"What? What is this?...What in the hell?! I'm not going up there now, not right away! You never told me something like this was going to happen...can he even do this? This is insane...I thought you were gonna get this whole damn mess taken care of..."

"Yes, he can do this...yes, I did tell you Terrell might call you to the stand...you obviously don't remember. You haven't paid much attention along the way, have you...? I'm trying my best on this...but..."

"Why, dammit all, I ought to..." Beautray's face was locked in an outraged anger. Olds face had drained, lost all its color and was, at best, a faded shade of graying beige. Beautray had his hand tight gripped on Olds' arm as they were leaned hard into one another. Their chairs had merged into one another, a love seat of recrimination and resignation.

They were hissing at each other like vipers about to strike. They were agitated and their volume was rising. It was obvious to all that they were adversaries now.

Judge Long simply in his voice of calm authority said, "Dr. Beautray, please come forward and be sworn."

Beautray stood and sagged at the same time. Olds slumped in place. Both had gone quickly silent now, as a radio switch snapping to off, both understanding that their rips at one another had not been discreet or private. Both looked like they wanted a cigarette and a blindfold. Beautray slowly, in what appeared to be thoughtful deliberation, walked up to the clerk who had a Bible with her. She spoke to him.

"Will you be sworn or do you prefer to affirm?"

"Sworn, please."

"Place your left hand on this Bible and raise your right hand."

He did as instructed and at the same time, he looked over her shoulder at Olds with the most obvious, unvarnished, seething hatred.

"Do you swear to tell the truth, the whole truth and nothing but the truth, so help you God?"

"Yes, I do."

"Please be seated and state your full name for the record."

"My full name is Dr. Aviv Placide Beautray." The doctor took his seat. He seemed to be elsewhere.

Judge Long said, "Mr. Terrell, I presume you want the defendant witness declared to be an adverse witness?"

"Yes, please, Your Honor."

"I do so find him to be an adverse witness. Please note it for the record. You may proceed, Mr. Terrell."

Dr. Carter and Nurse Shannon were riveted, leaning forward. Delores had a beneficent, sweet smile of oncoming satisfaction glowing on her face. Mikey held Patty's hand. Alph was dialed-in, watching Beautray carefully. The jury waited.

In North Carolina, the rule when addressing witnesses in trial is that counsel must remain seated unless granted permission by the Court to stand or approach. Before beginning his first strafing run at the doctor, Eddie was seated and carefully ordering two X-ray sets, holding them up to the overhead lights just a little longer than was necessary, then layering and clipping them deliberately with a snap into their respective groups. The jury watched him. Eddie wanted them to watch him. He wanted their curiosities stimulated.

Thus, there was a pause. It was a good thing to let anticipation build. Eddie looked at Judge Long. He did not speak but gestured his head in the direction of the doctor. Judge Long said, "You may approach." Eddie first showed the exhibits to a sulking Olds who cursorily glanced at them and nodded sourly. Eddie then went for Beautray. He handed the doctor the films in the two clipped sets. Beautray's hands shook slightly as he took receipt of them. And Eddie stood away to the side of Beautray to make sure the jurors could see the tremors.

"Doctor, please look at the time stamps and the dates on those films. Mrs. Jordan Monk was your patient and you, assisted by your nurse Miss Phoebe Shannon, performed a routine colonoscopy on Mrs. Monk on that noted date. Are the dates and times accurate? They, to me, appear to be the same."

Beautray studied the sets briefly. He seemed to have come back into focus. "Well, yes, I did, we did perform a colonoscopy on Mrs. Monk on that date. But this set I recognize and the other I don't. This first set shows everything looks fine." He held one set up. His affect was desultory, almost apathetic.

"Doctor, the jury can't for now see which set is which, so how about explain to them what each set shows? They both have Mrs. Monk's name on them and they both have the date and time of the procedure on them, don't they?"

"Yes, that's right." Beautray reddened, was more alert. He sat up straight in his witness chair. "Uhm, well, this set shows a good, clean colon. The other does not."

"Did you take these two sets that showed two different situations?"

"Uhm, well, no. Just took the acceptable one. This other one I have never seen. I don't know where it came from." His eyes flinched.

Two jurors stifled short bursts and quietly laughed out loud and more than a few were shaking their heads in skeptical disbelief. It appeared it had not taken long for the lance of the picador to be barb deep.

"Doctor, do you see your former nurse Miss Phoebe Shannon sitting just over there just behind the bar?"

"Yes." He swallowed.

"Doctor, do you see Dr. Heath Carter from the Medical Center at Wake Forest out in the courtroom sitting next to Nurse Shannon?" Eddie gestured to help Beautray locate him.

"Yes. Uh, I don't know him but I'll take your word for it." He nodded and swallowed again.

"Doctor, have you read Dr. Carter's emergency surgical and operative notes of exploration and repair?"

"Well, I have but it's been a while..."

"Do you recall what they said, what they described?"

"Yes, I think I do, generally of course..."

Olds felt physically ill and had shrunk down into his chair to constrict and ward off the spasm of cramping that had seized his gut and his mind. He hated his work right now. Jurors were peering at him and then going quickly back to Beautray.

"Do you know why your former Nurse Shannon is here?"

"Yes, I suppose I do…" His responses were flatlined and desultory and almost trance-like.

Eddie handed a copy of Nurse Shannon's notes to Olds, to the clerk and to Judge Long. He held a copy of them in his hands. They bore at the top Dr. Beautray's name, office and email address and telephone number.

"I'd ask that that this be marked as the next exhibit in order."

"Any objection, Mr. Olds?"

Olds shook his head to the negative, almost an imperceptible shudder passed his unhappy face. "No, Your Honor."

"Fine. Thank you. Counsel, you may proceed."

"Doctor, do you recognize the paper these notes, these writings appear on?"

"Yes."

"They are from the notepads you regularly and daily use in your offices, correct?"

A glum "yes" uttered forth.

"And, do you see your handwriting anywhere on these pieces of paper from your office?"

"No, I do not."

"Can you tell us whose handwriting appears on these papers?"

"Yes."

"Whose handwriting is it? Please tell us."

Beautray sat silent, scanning the words and then looked venomously at his former nurse.

"Doctor, tell us now, please." There was a dart in Terrell's tone.

"This is the handwriting of my former chief nurse, Nurse Shannon sitting just over there." He nodded.

"And the diagram on the paper…?"

"Yes, that's her drawing. Yes, she made drawings regularly during procedures. Yes, that's hers too."

It was as though a valve was being loosened in Beautray's mind and the stench of the deed was leaking out more freely.

"Now, we're going to discuss your nurse's notes and drawing in just a bit, but for now, I'll ask you some basic, general questions, alright?"

"Alright."

"Now, did Mrs. Monk get injured during the colonoscopy you performed on her?"

"Well, I think so but I didn't learn about it until later. I felt everything had gone fine."

"What do you think Dr. Carter and Nurse Shannon are going to tell us about that?"

Beautray again sat up straight and looked around, seeming to reorient himself to the time and place of the present. Everything went still again. Everyone waited. He then held his hands up as though apprehended and said, "Wait."

Eddie waited. The courtroom waited. Beautray then waved his hands about his head as though he was warding off bees. "May I start over, please? I want to, I need to get this right now."

Eddie could see it coming, cocked his head theatrically and quietly said, "Why, yes. Please do. What is it that you want to get right?"

Judge Long interjected. "Yes, let's get it right. We're waiting."

And then, the flash flood cascaded out of Beautray. As if reading from a list of prepared remarks, he ticked his culpabilities off in clear cadence.

"Everybody, Judge, I just want to get this over with. I hurt Mrs. Monk. I didn't mean to but I do. I'm so sorry I hurt her badly. Mrs. Monk, I don't know if you can ever forgive me or even if you should but I truly am sorry.

"I was stupid, foolish, reckless and wrong. I was negligent. I broke the rules of my profession.

"I was in a hurry. I had my mind on a big business deal, my wife, children, my God knows what else...I wandered. I was not paying attention. I was in a hurry."

Visions of glory sure gone now.

"Phoebe, bless her heart, had gotten Mrs. Monk ready and we had given her some light sedation, but Phoebe had warned me that she didn't think the overnight prep had been very effective and on my first attempted pass,

Mrs. Monk was unusually uncomfortable despite the sedative and she was clearly unacceptably impacted.

"Oh, and that stuff my lawyer told you about Mrs. Monk not telling me she wasn't good and cleaned out so this ought to lie on her and not me—that's bunk. She told my nurse who is part of my office and besides, it's my job to figure that out. I'm the guy with the scope.

"So I kept trying to pass the scope on up and I couldn't see at all and I just started probing—really stupid—and in essence what I was doing was stabbing blindly into the muck and I guess I just got frustrated and kept doing it thinking I could find an opening. Mrs. Monk was miserable and Phoebe was yelling at me to stop, even screamed, hollered at me a couple of times. It was as if once I got it in my head to keep going, I couldn't stop. I've wondered about that since—do I have some sort of Superman thing going on? I'm a doctor so I can do anything? That's nuts.

"Also, that thing about Mrs. Monk's alcohol consumption making her more susceptible to injury. That's nonsense. Sorry, Mr. Olds, but nice try and all that, but again it's our job to deal with that—we see and process all sorts of patients and are required to deal with anything like that—and my after action procedure notes make it pretty clear that I didn't note any friable tissue or anything like that.

"So I hurt her, hurt her badly and didn't even recognize that I'd done it…that's bad too. The sooner you get to these things, the better the chances are to address them effectively. I recall just a little later on Dr. Carter called, didn't get me and he left a message explaining who he was and what was going on and what he had needed to do and asked that I call him back. I never did. Just too chicken, too ashamed, I suppose."

Beautray just shook his head. He had taken on a bearing of peaceful calm. Johnny Olds had folded his bowed head into his chest. His assistant was astonished but also silently admitted to himself that this was better than television or a movie. Beautray continued.

"And then I wasn't quite done with my stupidity. Once poor Mrs. Monk—still sedated—had been taken from the office by her sister I think, the Delores lady over here, Phoebe was real upset so I sent her home and proceeded to switch some normal, regular looking films for Mrs. Monk's and relabel them.

Now, I want to make this real clear. My lawyer Johnny Olds over there didn't know anything about the doctoring—isn't that an ironic word for all this—of the films. He only found out about it a few days ago after Phoebe had, after snooping around in the file cabinets as she probably should have done and she found them—I deserved to get caught—did it on her own and she took my magic tricks to Mr. Terrell here who then got everything copied and secured, and alerted Mr. Olds about it all and Olds after that confronted me. So, Mr. Olds had and has nothing to do with any cover up; that's all on me."

Olds looked up at his client and spoke quietly, "Thank you for that." Olds' eyes were smoldering and his face was now battleship gray.

Beautray was wrapping his soliloquy of deceit and responsibility up. "Oh, one last thing. I also dictated my procedure notes as though there had been no problems. Not only had I messed up, now I was covering up. I guess I just thought I could wallpaper the whole mess over and get away with it... how stupid. So that's the real story." He exhaled long. He said again, "I just want to get this over with."

"And well, now here we are but I'm pretty sure I'm no longer gonna be here for long. I'm pretty sure my ticket to practice medicine is going to get pulled. I have royally screwed up. Please ask me any more questions you might have for me."

And then he closed his mouth and sat still and waited as did they all.

CHAPTER TWENTY-TWO

SQUEEZE AND RELEASE
A Few Months Before

JUDGE LONG HAD the lawyers in his chambers. He had already sent the jury home for the day with the usual admonishments and instructed them to be in their jury room at 9 a.m. the next morning. He made no mention or reference to the strange and unusual events of the afternoon. There was no need to. Everyone knew something big was afoot; just nobody quite knew what that was or was going to be.

He had the bailiffs put the sisters Delores and Mrs. Monk in a small, closed-off lawyer conference room on one side of the courtroom and did the same with Dr. Beautray on the other. Olds' assistant sat with him but neither spoke. The judge told anyone left in the courtroom they were free to go or free to wait. He cautioned he did not then know what was going to happen next or when it might happen so any estimates of time and decision or ruling was indeterminate.

It made no difference to Patty and Mikey. They just kept sitting. A bomb had gone off and it was not in their blast zone but they did have front row seats to watch it when it had suddenly detonated.

Judge Long looked at Johnny Olds and Eddie Terrell over his midway-down-his-nose glasses. He was renowned for his neutrality, his natural ability to play all cards close to his vest. He betrayed little in his face, but if you were able to look carefully, some small muscles at the corners of his eyes would give away displeasure. Alph, farthest from him, but not too far, felt those subcutaneous feathers fluttering.

"Fellas, I don't remember seeing any information about the newly discovered set of procedure films in either of your Pretrial Briefs. Is my memory correct on that?"

They both responded, "Yes, sir."

"Eddie, I'm guessing you were so close up to the rump of this trial, you just really wanted to include me in the 'shock and awe' of it all and you are just, shall we say, slow in getting your supplement into the file?"

"Yes, sir, I suppose that's about it," Eddie mumbled his response. He looked down at his shoes and wondered how bad this was going to be.

"And, Johnny Olds…I suppose you just 'forgot' that was something you needed to do…?"

"Well, Judge, I suppose it would be fair if I said it sure was all something I'd just as soon forget…" He smiled ruefully. "Apologies, Your Honor. Bad joke. I've never had anything like this ever happen to me in my entire career and I think it has just floored me…sort of froze me up…"

Long nodded. "You know, Johnny, I understand. That doesn't mean I'm crazy about it but I do understand. Seems, considering your situation and what your client has just done out there, well, it just seems more reasonable than unreasonable. Alph, what do you say about all this?"

"If I may, Your Honor, that's the damn craziest thing I think I've ever seen. Long time ago, there was a young lawyer who stormed into our old offices up on Summit Street…Madder than hell at Bill Maready because Bill was stiff-arming him on some discovery in a malpractice case. They got into an absolute cuss out blow out and they were gonna fight and the younger guy was starting to turn Maready's desk over on him when Norwood Robinson came in a broke it up…thought, until today, that was the topper…but now…?"

Alph was in the reverie of fine, exciting old memories.

Judge Long broke the recall. "Alph, now that's all pretty interesting, but let's get back to this business at hand—what do you say about all this? About what has happened today and what didn't get done before today? I'd appreciate your input. You are more of an old pro than me…" There was more than enough crisp snap to the judicial inquiry.

"Ah, yessir...well, how about some continued negotiations, a slight pause of the trial until in the morning and sanctions for all, until they, uh, we all get our procedural acts together?"

Olds thought, *Oh, great, now comes the Hari Kari express complete with career ruination and lovely parting gifts for our contestants...damn these old farts.*

Long thought quietly as they all stood there watching.

Long said, "You know, Alph. Not bad. Thanks for jumpstarting my very startled brain. But here's what's going to happen. No, this is what needs to happen I'm pretty sure. Johnny Olds, you need to go call your carrier. Your case is in crash and burn mode and worse. I presume that is not lost on you?"

"I understand, Judge."

"Eddie Terrell, what's your finish it off number?"

"Uhm, Your Honor, I don't know...a million?" It was racing past him. Even though he had seen it all coming, it was all still going very fast.

The Court was in the air traffic control tower mode. Judge Long stated, "You know what they say, boys, a pig gets fat and a hog gets slaughtered. Nine fifty is your solid number for now. No budge. Now Johnny you need to make your call. Go outside and get it done. If you need my help, I'll speak with them as well."

"Judge, I'm not sure they'll go that high. I appreciate your offer of help. I really and obviously do but..."

"No buts. No! We are way beyond that stage. Explain, please explain to your company that I am in command and control mode. I will brook no peevishness from them and if they want to try and kick over my traces, feel free to explain to them that hell hath no fury than a slighted woman save for a very riled up judge. Here's what going to happen if you don't get that number and we get this thing settled. Listen carefully. I'm going to reconvene Court in the morning and anyone can examine, cross-examine, call any witness they like. And when all is said and done, I'm going to charge the jury on both compensatory and punitive damages in my very pointed and firm judge's voice—if you get my drift—and I'm also going to give a very heavy, pointed charge as to evidence tampering. Johnny, you're lucky I have not yet, not so far yet, struck all of your pleadings, decimated your answers and just hung you out to dry. You and I know that the chances are good that that jury can blow you to kingdom come well past the two million number and then here comes the ineffective assistance of counsel and bad faith claim..."

Olds knew.

Eddie and Alph suppressed little smiles. What had been expected to be a long, messy slog had now launched them into the catbird seat. They had never seen anything like this as well.

Judge Long level snapped at them, dosed them with more reality. "Stop with the playground giggling. Y'all aren't off the hook, not by a long shot. Remember, I can and just might declare a mistrial. That means, as you well know, back to square one with a new judge, maybe even someone as 'understanding' as Judge Solomon Martin...and plenty more drudgery and work. You get my drift, I think."

They all gulped quietly, considered that new foreboding landscape and nodded.

"And if we don't get this resolved here right soon, I am going to sanction all of you, in equal and not insignificant portions, including that damn fool doctor out there and Alph, that means you too. And let me mention that this misconduct by all of you ought to be reported to the state bar and the state medical society. I'm not saying I'll be the one to do it but feel free to take that into consideration as well. Do you all understand? As you can tell, this has agitated me...and I am not happy about any of it. And by the way, both of your supplements to the initial Pretrial Briefs need to clocked in with the clerk's office first thing in the morning and they better be complete and in full. Now, let's move this ball and see if we can end this strange day."

They were unsure as to whether or not they had been dismissed. They hesitated and just stood there.

Judge Long grumbled at them in irritation and as he waved them away he told Olds to go make his call, reiterated that he was available to help shove the carrier along and told the others to go on but stay close.

It did not take long. The threat of the hanging by a horsehair sword of Damocles was not hypothetical. One did not have to be on law review and the Order of the Coif to understand that they all were standing at the nearest edge of a very unwelcoming precipice and could be split open like ripe melons if the final pieces of this uncomfortable puzzle could not be firmly fitted for the finish.

Olds told Beautray what was going on.

Beautray's response was simply, "Finally. It's about goddamn time some-body listened to me. All I had to do to get something done was wreck my career...and at this point, I'd just as soon drag all you sharp suits down with me..." Olds privately noted that his client's gentle contrition of but minutes before had now instantly morphed into angry bitterness and more self-destructive invective. Olds grimly nodded, said nothing in response and hurried to make the call.

Eddie and Alph quickly visited their clients and the others. They were completely candid about what had taken place so the message delivered was anything but soothing.

Mrs. Monk was unsure, frightened a bit. It wasn't the amount of the money that hung on the near horizon that troubled her; rather it was the speed of it all happening so fast. She had finally come to be ready to screw her courage to the sticking place, to climb into the witness stand and say her piece. Now, it appeared she would be denied that chance. Also, she was worried about her lawyers; they had put themselves in harm's way for her and that bothered her too. And she thought of the other lawyer, the Olds fellow. He had looked miserable and now he was in trouble too. And that darn Dr. Beautray. Well, he was a foolish one but she felt sorry for him. It was just her nature. But she was reticent and shy by nature and would not speak to any of it now. They all had enough to worry about.

Delores saw the frustration in her sister's eyes and face. She understood. Delores had been the captain of their ship for a good, long time now so she took the rudder again and tried to pour some oil on the roiled waters of her sister's churning mind.

"Honey, be steady now. It's out of our hands, but we will know soon enough and I think it's gonna be okay. Think about it. That Judge Long has got all these fellows by the short hairs. They aren't so stupid as to want to jump off a cliff just to spite him and themselves. Let's just sit back and wait. It ain't gonna be too long now."

Alph said, "Mrs. Monk, for what it's worth, I think your sister is right. And yes, this is a bit of a scary time for us all but I think we'll get through." He reached over and patted her hand. She quietly thanked him.

Eddie asked, "Delores, a question, if you will. Do you carry a real Magic 8-Ball with you?"

They all laughed a little.

"I say this in all honesty. Your ability to sort it all out is pretty impressive. We are all glad you are here with us."

There were nods all around. Delores just smiled. "Well, boys and girls, we will just have to see, won't we?" And they all sat silently because there was nothing else to do.

And soon enough, it was indeed over. Olds knocked on the door, stuck his head in, said, "It's done at nine fifty. Let's go see the judge."

Judge Long was obviously pleased and relieved. He told them that if their supplemental answers were properly filed by 9:30 in the morning, he would find a good case of amnesia to enjoy about whatever else he might have said earlier. To make sure the resolution was firmly finalized, he wanted all the lawyers and their clients back in Court tomorrow about noon so just before lunch, they could memorialize the settlement in open court. He told them that it made him uncomfortable when he had to lean on lawyers, especially good lawyers. He apologized for what he felt were his harsh, curt words. He instructed Olds to get the dismissal and the settlement paperwork together. And he asked if he could go have a brief private word with Dr. Beautray. He also told the clerk to inform the next panel of jurors to be present and ready to go in the morning.

Olds returned and said Beautray would speak with Judge Long. Long waited for all the shaking of hands and the hurried departings and said he would see them in the morning to wrap matters up. Olds asked Judge Long if he should stay and the judge responded to everyone.

"Please go on all home now. It's been a long, interesting and trying day." He called for his clerk and instructed that the currently seated jurors be called at the numbers indicated on their information cards and told that their service would no longer be needed, that the case of Monk versus Beautray is concluded by compromised and confidential settlement.

"Do I need to stick around, Your Honor?" Olds asked.

"No, not necessary. I promise you, nothing outside the lines. On your way out, just ask the doctor to wait for me in the courtroom. I won't take much time."

Patty and Mikey and Alph and Eddie walked back up the hill.

Mrs. Monk and Delores hugged each other and Delores said, "Come on. Let's go to my place and you can watch me take a very big drink. You know, Jordan, you just might want a small one..."

Mrs. Monk, still tentative but now releasing, nodded slowly. "Yes, maybe, just to, you know, settle my nerves the way Momma used to do…"

Johnny Olds saw Beautray as he departed. Their parting was blank and barely cursory. Even though the doctor had gotten it all concluded, it still felt like betrayal and impertinence to Olds. He went back to his office, reported the barest of facts to the few who were still around, cynically reporting "I only got half my ass ripped off" and then retreated to his car, went home in search of a glass and ice cubes.

And Judge Long, still robed, went out into the now empty courtroom and asked Dr. Beautray to come and sit with him for a few minutes on the benches.

Beautray rose very slowly and moved even more slowly the few feet needed for the visit. He sat down heavily, clumsily, all the starch washed out of him. He bore the exhaustion of a total adrenaline burn-off. He was spent. It always happened to almost everyone involved in trials such as this and the revelations of intentional misbehavior were no different than dumping a bucket of gasoline into the fire.

"Your Honor…I'm so sorry. I'm so sorry. I…" Beautray tailed off. He was now the miserable confessor to his calm priest in his black judicial robes, the cassock of the Court.

"Doctor, I know you are. I appreciate that…very much. I don't want to take a lot of your time but I do want to tell you a couple of things. I know you've been mad, angry, upset, lots of things through the course of all this. It's natural. Understandable. I know you've been put out and off by your relationship with your lawyer. That's understandable too. Try not to be too hard on him. You surely know he got dealt a very hard and harsh hand here."

"Yes, sir. I do know that. Everything is on me. I am responsible."

"I'm glad to hear that. Now, I'm not going to sanction you, not going to sanction or penalize or fine anyone and we are going to wrap this matter up tomorrow, as neat and clean as can be. Do you understand that? Can you hold your moods in a tight line for that?"

"Yes, Your Honor. I do. I will. I promise."

"Good. Alright. And one more, no, two more things. First, I am not going to report you to the State Board of Medical Examiners. I don't think that's my role here no matter what but…I do think you need to drive down to Raleigh in the next couple of days and self-report this quickly and thoroughly. You well may need a lawyer to help you later on down the road with this as the specifics of the matter become clearer so keep that in mind too. And now, well, I did not tell you what I am about to tell you—do you understand that..." He paused.

"Yes, sir, I understand—whatever it is..."

"Good. I think Mr. Alph Baron whom you have met along the way in this matter would be someone who could be helpful to you as these matters unfold. He is a fine man and a fine lawyer and is very well-respected in the halls of power in this state, if you get my drift...and, now that the matter is soon concluded, there will be no conflict of interest problem..."

Beautray nodded slowly. "Oh, Your Honor. Thank you for that. I will keep it in mind, keep it between us."

A bit of life began to seep back into Beautray. Maybe there was some light at the end of this dismal tunnel.

"Now, one last thing. No matter what happened along the way—and that's all done no matter what—at the most critical point in these proceedings, you told the truth without flinching and you told it straight and without excuse-making. That counts a great deal for me and Lord knows I've seen a lot of dissembling and evasion over all these years. Yes, you did lie and cover up to get you to the crucible but when it really mattered, you came through and took the bullet. So if asked by you or whomever when and if the time comes, I'll send a letter to that effect to the powers that be. You took the bullet when it had to be taken."

Beautray's eyes began to water. He grasped for Judge Long's hand and whispered, "Thank you. Thank you so much."

Long simply rose and quietly spoke. "Most everyone deserves a second chance. I think that includes you. Now, go on home and tell your wife and family about this as you see fit. But keep your honesty always in sight. I'll see you tomorrow. I believe I've told all the lawyers we should assemble here at noon."

"Yes, sir. Thank you, sir." Beautray could barely hold back his tears.

"Now, go on, son. It'll take a while but I think you'll be fine."

Long headed back to his chambers, his exhaustion beginning to blanket him as well.

Beautray wiped his eyes with his sleeve and left the courtroom. As he walked into the large, now dimly lit lobby, two people came toward him. One embraced him. The other stood next to them in support. Phoebe Shannon and Heath Carter.

The night was coming on but it was not full dark just yet.

Alph shook Eddie's hand and told him, "Great job, great job. Now, I'll see everyone later but I've got to scoot." There was an irrepressible twinkle in his eye. "I have an appointment, if you know what I mean." They all laughed and Alph briskly headed down the stairs.

The remaining three gathered up their files and papers and bags and took the elevator down to the ground floor and went out the back of the courthouse, nodding and murmuring their thanks, as they departed, at the deputies who ran security. It was getting chilly and they pulled their coats in close. They walked up the short hill to the office in silence. Alph's car was already gone. Polly the temp was waiting for them. She had turned the front porch light on. She opened the door.

"Well, how did it go? Y'all got your poker faces on…"

Patty grinned. "It went fine, Polly. Had a little excitement along the way but got a nice, fat finish."

"That's good, that's real good. Congratulations, y'all. Hey, Eddie, you're looking a little flat-line. You okay? You're pleased, right?"

"I am good, Polly. I'm fine. Thank you. I'm just tired. Comes with the territory. Hell, you know the drill."

"True. I indeed do. Well, I need to go. Glad I could help out today. Call for me whenever you need an extra hand. And again, congratulations!" And she waved as she went out the door and down the steps and was gone.

Eddie dropped his brief bags down with a thud and sat down slowly on the waiting room couch. He rubbed his temples and squeezed his head in fatigue, motioning for the ladies to sit down across from him and they did. They watched him. They knew he was going to talk.

"Ladies, thanks for your help. I really appreciate it. I hope y'all know that. I am tired and today was good and we got a good enough result, but honestly, it was not satisfying for me. It was like eating cotton candy. Everything dissolved so fast, too fast. Like getting my pocket picked. Beautray, in doing the right thing, and he did, took the sledge hammer out of my hand. They say, 'Confession is good for the soul.' Well, maybe for him but not so much for mine. I wanted to see if the jury would just light his ass up. I think they would have. Dammit. I'm frustrated, frustrated all the damn time these last many days. Everything is going too fast. Good damn thing I got my ride around the countryside coming up in the next few months. I love all this, I love what we do but I've gotten stale, jaded, spoiled, what...?"

He paused. "No, please don't answer that. I'm going to figure it out. I promise. I'm sorry. I should be grateful but I'm doing a damn poor job of it. Why in the hell is everything so sort of empty now. I'm just in a shit mood..."

Mikey asked, "Do you want us to respond to that? I'm not sure I can do much with it right now."

Patty said, "I'm with Mikey on that. Oh, and don't worry. I'll come in early in the morning and get the supplementals on Shannon's materials done for filing and delivery to the judge first thing."

"Thank you. Always on top of it. Thank you, Patty. And no, no, no. I understand. I'm just running my mouth. I've just got a burr under my saddle and I gotta find it and get rid of it. And I will. Let's just go home and finish this thing up tomorrow."

Patty nodded and simply said, "Court is now adjourned."

CHAPTER TWENTY-THREE

REFLECTIONS
Present Day, Late March

AND SO, THE recent months were distinctly troubling—the last months had slid, tumbled rapidly and without warning off a short ledge and it was on their minds. Things had gotten slow and irregular and stunted. So it was time to get started on rectifying that.

This was as good a place as any to get that new ball rolling; in truth it was where they were and so it was the only place to begin the renewal of their excellence.

In this unpleasant interregnum had come so many distractions and happenings.

They had gotten short sheeted on some settlements; they had too much going on and just were too damn busy, and if the adjusters got close to a number that worked, they needed to go with it. Their success over the years had built-up momentum that had turned into a multiple bumper car rear-ender. They were getting in their own way, stepping on each other's toes. They were so popular that good cases came flying at them and they took them all, and after a while it was too many and the abundance of it all began to weigh them down. They needed to hire and train some good help to alleviate the pressure but they had gotten so used to being so small, so insular, it was just something they all knew was "out there" but no one spoke of it. They were working long hours and would not relinquish their excellence.

It had ruefully and amusingly reminded Eddie of his first day of kindergarten when he had come home and dutifully stood next to his daddy who was not well and in bed. "Well, son, how was school today? What did you learn in school today?"

"I learned to share and I don't like it."

There was constant worry about a statute of limitation getting missed. Such could truly get your ass in a tight bag and was an unpardonable sin and one that could get very expensive on both the money and reputational ledgers of the firm. The trust account was getting balanced to zero only every three or four months now, not monthly as was optimal. Everything looked good but an unannounced audit by the State Bar would cause much hyperventilation and hypertension. A recent growing ever more notorious case down in South Carolina where the high profile, high influence, powerful Bid Daddy senior partner had been revealed to have over many, many years skimmed and stolen tens of millions from his partners and firm and their clients had sent chills down many lawyer spines.

They had neglected their regular black book tickler meetings, holding them now and for a long time barely sporadically and when they gathered, their case reviews were all too often rushed and cursory. They were zooming about too much; this had been incremental. Now, it bordered on a growing malignancy. They were not doing as many site visits as they used to do.

Eyes on the prize was often vital and now it too had been significantly shunted to the side of the road. They had let their once formidable, legendary habits of going to clients' and witnesses' homes lapse greatly. The same was regrettably true of treating physicians.

All their technology needed upgrading; the idea of fewer wires and cords strangling across the floors and snaking from behind desks and potted plants had not yet seriously crossed their minds just yet. And there was the lurking sensation that somewhere along the way, they had individually and collectively lost some of the fire in their bellies and that was privately shaming and something that was studiously ignored. They had been drinking from a fire hose for a good while now and those gushing, throbbing waters had hypnotized them and had begun to quench their better and best fires around the edges. They were still a formidable manse but there was fraying at the mostly hidden edges. They were behind a lot of curves and they had gotten upright flabby; they sucked their stomachs in literally and figuratively. The clothes fit but it was a tightening waist band and collar. It could all be remedied but they needed to get to work on a broad front, and dawdling was not going to help.

And, God knows, it wasn't for lack of money that a lot of this fell into neglect. They were rolling in the stuff. The unthought, ignored irony was vulgar.

A recent story, apropos of nothing and also everything told a tale that was instructive and potentially apocryphal. A Mrs. Sullivan and her reticent, gawky daughter of thirteen years had come to see Eddie. The young lady still on crutches, nobly named Alexandra, had recently had knee surgery and so far, her recovery was uncomfortable and uneven and the mother was adamantly convinced that the surgeon had screwed it up.

The mother was angry, full of spitting venom. She would instruct the child to tell Eddie what had happened and then repeatedly, before the kid could open her mouth, proceed to lead the way. The child was nonreactive and less than desultory in her body language. Eddie had seen this drill before, more than a few times. He always just let the Momma Bear burn out and then would explain the whatevers as were needed.

When it became apparent that the parent was in full filibuster mode, Eddie raised his hands in submission and spoke.

"Mrs. Sullivan, I understand and appreciate all that you are saying. I'm sorry Alexandria is having a tough time with this right now and I know this is of great concern to you. I hope and trust that her recovery will progress and that she will be back in tip-top shape sooner rather than later. But, right now..."

"But what?!" sputtered Mrs. Sullivan. "But what?!"

Eddie leaned sincerely forward. "It's too early to see if there's a case here. We have to see what the end result of Alexandria's recovery looks like. These cases cost a lot of money to put together and pursue and we have to be careful and watchful before..."

Before it was out of his mouth, Eddie painfully realized he had opened with an enormous red flag waving at the bull and the bull was on go. He had put their money before her problem and he knew he had, well, fucked up and so, here it came. He resignedly and quickly braced and almost closed his eyes and waited for the hot blast.

"Before what?! You are such a money whore! You are no better than those television lawyers. Hell. You're not even gonna get us what we deserve. Well, mister, here's what you deserve…A big bucket of shit and a small rag… Come on, Alexandria! Mr. Terrell, you are fired!!" And Mrs. Sullivan jerked the girl up and yanked her out the door, slinking her at jet speed around the corner of the door like a cartoon character. They vanished like apparitions. The sound of two doors slamming in quick succession and the curdled yell of "You all go to hell!" echoed in the hall and the waiting room. And then it was still.

Eddie just sat there and thought, *Well, there goes another satisfied customer…*

Mikey came back and said, "Uhm…I would be remiss in the exercise of my curiosity if I did not ask, what in the hell was that all about?"

Patty and Alph peered in behind Mikey.

"Well, I tried to tell Mrs. Sullivan that her inquiry about her daughter's bum knee case was premature but it appears that held no truck with her so she called me names and departed…"

"Shit happens."

"You know, she fired me before she hired me. That's a first."

They laughed and shrugged their shoulders.

The phone rang. Eddie said, "Since we are all here together, let me get it."

He picked up the receiver and said, "Hello, this is Eddie Terrell." Before he could put the phone to his ear, a torrent of invective roared out of it, all of which involved money lenders in the temple, filthy lucre, prostitution and Eddie's deep complicity in all of those aforesaid topics.

"And I'm going to tell all my friends and family what a cold-hearted bastard you are! All of them! Good fucking bye, you cheap ass son of a bitch!" Click.

"I guess that's really not much of a ringing endorsement, now is it…?"

Giggling, they all wandered off, leaving Eddie to wonder if he was short on his game. Their recent roads had been getting bumpier it seemed.

CHAPTER TWENTY-FOUR

A LITTLE RECHARGE
Late March

WHEN THEY STIRRED awake blanketed in groggy, the Saturday afternoon sun was morphing into a purple and pink sinking sky over the lake. They held hands and studied one another. They were still sleepy.

"Mikey, what are you and Patty going to talk to us about on Monday?"

"Curiosity killed the cat. Satisfaction brought him back. Monday morning will bring satisfaction. In the meantime, pleasure will just have to hold the door."

"That's interesting. Any chance I could tickle or tease it out of you?"

"No. What do you think your chances are about getting tickled and teased if you try to press that line of inquiry?"

"I'm guessing slim and none and slim just got up and left the room."

"Congratulations! You've just won Final Jeopardy! Now, let it lay. Please."

"Okay. What would you like to do now? We could just stay in bed..."

"Nope. We will spend more than enough time in here in the morning. It'll be Sunday—some days are high church, some days are low church. You'll get to pick which fork in that road you want to take." She smiled sweetly, beatifically.

"Right now, we have a plan. Let's execute it. I want to get out of here, go downtown, get a drink, something to eat and go to a movie." And she hopped out of the bed and went to the bathroom and finished her ablutions in brisk order before sliding into some very skinny jeans and a T-shirt and a light jacket. "Come on, lazy bones! Let's go have a little fun!"

He marveled at her, admired her. He was devoted to her. "You know, chances are good I would follow you into hell. You know that, don't you?"

"I sure think I do, but how about get your lawyer ass on the move and follow me pronto Tonto to the car...?"

"At your beck and call. At your command. On the way. Yes, ma'am!" And he roused himself up into the charms of a nice Saturday night with his best gal.

"Where you wanna go?"

"I've got some ideas..."

"Well then, lead the way." It was a graciously pretty dusk.

They drove down Reynolda Road back into town, hooked a left on Fourth Street and went about halfway down the far hill, parking near the once deserted and dilapidated Bailey Power Plant that had once juiced all the engines and machinery that mighty R.J. Reynolds Tobacco Company had jammed into its big, sprawling side of the slope footprint.

Bailey Power was now being reborn as Bailey Park and that entire area of town, once empty tobacco warehouses and factory sheds, was beginning to fill with the new age industries of high-tech and gene splicing and organ regeneration and people were moving into converted lofts and apartments. There were bars and restaurants and music and something that would have been unimaginable a decade before—there were thousands of people living and working down across the railroad tracks that used to feed the tobacco factories.

They went into a darkened yet inviting dive bar called Fair Witness and studied the drink menu chalked up on the board next to the bar. For a place like Winston-Salem, this was beyond exotic. It was fun and was but a small part of what had been taking the Twin City off the Podunk Map for a surging last few years. Eddie and Mikey loved the place. Patrons were indoors and also scattered on the sidewalk, others were standing in a line at a little gelato shop next door. Jazz and indie music played, just loud enough to be enjoyed, not so loud as to be bothersome.

Mikey got a couple of pops that featured iced tequila and herbs. Eddie opted for a couple of concoctions of rye whiskey and a house-made orange syrup, delivered with plenty of ice.

They hopped up onto a wide window sill bench with a big window for people watching and enjoyed their rips and the chill vibe. After forty-five minutes or so of quiet, pleasant, not much need for much conversation, Eddie wondered, "Should we have another drink?"

"No, honey, I don't think so. You've had long days and we need to get you fed."

"I'm not gonna fight you on that. I think you're right."

They returned their glasses to the bar, paid their ticket and stepped out into the night. There was the nice, human hum to the place.

"Come on. There's a terrific Mexican just up the way. Very up-end with a great look and great food. I read about it in the paper called Alma...you up for a little legit south of the border?"

"Sure. Lead on. How do you know about this one? In the paper...?"

"Yup, it was in the paper. Good reviews. It's nearby. Let's give it a shot."

And they did and enjoyed real chips and salsa and guacamole and chicken enchiladas, washed down with some nicely potent mescal margaritas. The décor was slick and bright and pleasant and again, there was both indoor and outdoor seating.

"That was nice. Thank you. Now, a movie down at Aperture?" Mikey gently inquired.

"That sounds pretty good, but may I please beg off on the movie and offer a more expansive raincheck when the sandman is not sitting in my eyes?"

"Not such a heavyweight any more, eh? We've obviously got to toughen you up, Mr. Terrell. Don't want you to lose that fighting trim. You know you're going to have to go more than a few rounds in the morning, don't you?" Mikey's happy teasing was enticingly lovely. "You get a pass this time but you better steel yourself for tomorrow is another day."

"I'll tell you this, Miss Riewy, all I need is a little recharge and I'm gonna be all over you like a duck on a June bug when the morning comes. And you better believe it. And you better prepare to be boarded."

"You got a deal. Let's go find the car and blow this pop stand."

"K. How about you drive?"

"Deal on that too."

Eddie was sound asleep before they passed the library on Fifth Street. His head tilted left on his shoulder, quiet, slow exhalations blooming through his lips. If he had not had on a seat belt, he would have been in Mikey's lap.

Sunday came along and was a gray, rainy day. They didn't care. They had each other and they proved it.

CHAPTER TWENTY-FIVE

THE HORIZON APPEARS
Late March

MONDAY MORNING SHONE brightly. There was some cool in the air and one could sense a coming change in the season. Mikey and Eddie had some toast and coffee and picked through the *Winston-Salem Journal*. Eddie always went for the sports section. Mikey for the comics, Dear Abby, the horoscopes, and the rest of it all, they just rustled away with it.

Eddie asked, "Okay, what's my horoscope today?"

Mikey found that particular page, pulled down the half moons snugged up in her coif, peered down over her nose and leaned into the print, peering.

"Let's see. Here we go. Well, isn't this interesting…it says, 'If you stay focused, you will have a good money day and will be very productive. Marshal your assets and pay attention to future needs. Be a good listener and be willing to be flexible. Don't be afraid of the uncertain.'"

"Is this interesting because of what we're going to be talking about in just a little while?"

"You'll just have to wait and see."

"What does yours say?"

"If you and your partner Patty can get Eddie and Alph to keep their eyes on the prize, it will be a good day. Romance is not featured but grasping the realities is."

"Well, I know that's made-up bullshit." He grinned. "But you did it very well and I am beginning to think that this morning with you all will form up as some serious self-analysis and strategic planning session. A firm retreat that turns into an advance? Am I close?"

"Not bad and it won't be long now. You ready to go on down?"

"Yeah, you got my interest up. Let's go."

As they pulled into the office, Alph was just ahead of them.

Eddie called to him, "Alph, wait up. I think I know what awaits us."

Alph did and they whispered and tittered to one another like little boys. Mikey went right on in and found Patty laying out legal pads and pens in the large conference rooms. There was a tray with ice water and coffee and soft drinks off to the side along with a bowl of peppermints and jaw breakers. Eddie loved Heath bars and Butterfingers so if they were within reach, he gorged; thus they were banned.

Soon, Alph and Eddie wandered in. "This looks serious...like some kind of negotiations, some kind of peace talks..." Both men were very curious now.

"It is serious, but it's not conflict resolution if that's what you got on your mind. Alph, would you please go lock the front door and tape this sign on it?" Patty had finished her set up and handed Alph a stiff piece of block-lettered top stock.

"We are closed today for a private firm meeting. Please call our office phone—336-971-1999—and leave us a message. We will get back to you no later than this afternoon. We apologize for any inconvenience. UPS/FED EX please leave all deliveries on top step. Thank you."

Alph did as he was asked and quickly returned. They were all standing, waiting, grabbing a cup or a piece of sweet.

Patty spoke solemnly and sonorously. "Shall we park our asses and get to it? Please." Patty laughed at her failed formality.

"So we shall. But, first, in order that even as we further evolve from the lowly caterpillar to the beautiful butterfly, I want to make sure our minds are still right and that we retain our understanding of the real world. Therefore, I have a new joke to tell you." Eddie smiled and looked them all around as they sat and rustled on in. They were attentive.

Eddie cleared his throat in the "ahem" manner of a Baptist minister preparing to sermonize. He began.

After a particularly wild company Christmas party, the vice president woke up with a terrible hangover. He turned over and groaned to his wife, "What in the hell happened last night?"

"As usual, you made a fool of yourself in front of the chairman of the board."

"Piss on him," the man answered.

"You did," she said. "And he fired you."

"Fuck him," the man replied.

"I did. You go back to work on Monday."

There was the briefest of pauses in the sunlit room and then came their delighted explosion of laughter and tearing eyes and applause. It was vintage.

Alph caught his breath and wheezed out, "Eddie, do you think our next few prospective hires will enjoy something like that as much as we just have!?" He swiped at his eyes, sparkling with the humor.

"Well, they better or they're not gonna make it..." He was satisfied and after a brief smirking pause—always let the good stuff sink in—he continued.

"Now, Patty, as our senior wrangler, why don't you start the drive?"

"Okay, but only for a moment of some introductory comments. Then I'm lateraling the ball to you, Mikey." The ladies nodded to one another in assent. Patty looked down at her notes on her pad, cleared her throat and began.

"First, I know we are a small outfit so I suppose we could just do this sitting in Eddie's office or out in the front, but we think this is pretty important so we wanted it to be more formal-like. And that's why we are in here with our big, fine table and all our important and fine books and big, brass chandelier. Helps, we think, to get our minds lined up."

"Second, we think this is for all of us, not just you fellas. We haven't done anything like this in as long as I can remember and we think it's time we oiled and greased all our brains up. We want us all in the game on this. More to the point, we think we must be.

"Third, we are as good an outfit as there is, anywhere around. No one wants to bet against us. But we have gotten soft and short here and there, and we think it's time to regain what we have let slip and let slide and at the same time, get even better. And we think that's gonna take some work on all our parts. We have over all these years become a family and this family needs to be pulling in the best and same directions. We can and will be better.

"Lastly, we're gonna keep it simple. We're got some central topics and then we are going to study on them and address their needs. I think we will all see that this ain't rocket science and that there are good answers for us to come to and use.

"And we want you to know that this is a serious, very serious effort to help us become more profitable, more efficient without burying ourselves or killing ourselves along the way. We ask that this be treated like a comprehensive top-down analysis and we really do need to put our shoulders to the wheel and accomplish what needs to be accomplished.

"One last comment. This little gathering was Mikey's idea and I think she deserves big credit. In these—what?—ten or so years, she has more than earned her spurs and has become such an important part of what we are and what we are going to become and I'm proud as the devil to work with her and call her my friend."

There was a murmured assent from all as they turned to Mikey who, with head down, was obviously blushing.

"Thank you, Patty. Thank you very much. That means a lot and I really do appreciate it." Her face rose to all of them. She paused. "So let's get to it."

And it began. There was an efficient review of their accumulated shortcomings and omissions which had become increasingly apparent over the last many months. They all participated. They all contributed. There was no arguing, no rancor. In about an hour, a good, working list was made. Mikey kept the discussions between the rails and had done so with a smooth, light touch.

Alph giggled in his kind way. "This kinda feels like what I left a decade ago over in that tight shirt collar jail I used to wear. Very organized, very corporate. But it is still a damn sight more fun and interesting. Over there, we used to do this kind of meeting regularly, quarterly. Plenty of substance in all the hot air, I guess, but damn little of it ever meant anything much in the way of change. Office managers and all sorts of mostly anonymous folks took care of most everything. Basically, plain and simple, the almighty billable hour and the patronizing and schmoozing of the all-important insurance companies were always first, front, and center. So, that surely is not us and I'm so glad it's not. Good meeting."

"Deal. Yes. First, let's stretch our legs and then, keep moving." So they did.

After a few minutes of wandering about and bathroom breaks and cup refills, they sat down again.

Alph, as was his constant preference, would never drink from Styrofoam. Years before he had brought a set of five (for the five regular working days of the week) fine Limoges china cups and saucers to the office and he babied and treated them gently. He was his own servant to them and washed and dried them and always laid them back up on the shelf carefully. He always said with a little twinkle in his eye that they brought "even more class to the classiest outfit in town."

Eddie would from time and to time tease him and ask him if they should create some grandiose firm monogram or symbol and slap it on everything. Alph would just laugh and shake his head and respond, "Now, Eddie, enough is enough and too much is too much and that would not only be tacky but also too much!" Over the years, it came to be playful shorthand as they passed from time to time wherever in the office.

"Monogram time yet?"

"Certainly not. Tacky and way too much."

They settled back into their seats and began to work through the core and most important distillations of what they had come to put together.

At the top of the list was one item that once discussed and kicked around, basically just glared at them. It was so obvious. They were always and at an ever-increasing rate, taking on too much work, too many cases, too many small-fry cases and it was becoming self-defeating. They were being stretched too thin, trying to do everything for everybody. It had become an ingrained article of faith that they could do it all and so they went out and tried to do it all. It was taking a toll. The monetary results were still good, but the time and organizational inputs necessary to move the files—and there were hundreds of them—were stretching them uncomfortably administratively and professionally. The business was tough enough and then the piling on of matter after matter, tort after tort, crime after crime invited further exhaustion and aggravation. This was making them downcast and grumpy and did nothing to help morale. It had always been a Godsend that they all had good and sharp senses of humor and could dig away at each other and the files and papers which lay always at high flood before them.

Eddie wryly and ruefully noted that it was like trying to herd cats or like Lincoln once said, it was like shoveling flies across a barnyard. And

Patty said, "Come to think of it, we're sorta like the frog they put in a pan of lukewarm water and then they slowly turn the heat up and the frog just gets sleepy and then gets cooked."

Mikey grimaced and made a face. "Let's just not go there. Okay, what are we gonna do about it?"

Alph started in on the problem and the others joined in. They were, beginning the next day, going to start culling the herd they already had in house. They estimated that the culling process would take at least a week. Smaller cases, those with a realistic appraised value of less than $15,000 were going to be pushed for settlement.

Some of those were going to be farmed out to other, usually younger law firms, with a small reasonable referral fee of ten percent attached. Nothing wrong with ginning up some goodwill among others as they streamlined.

And some of the smaller ones were to be set aside for their new (hopefully) lawyer hire. That greenhorn was going to need some real case and courtroom work to cut teeth on. They would be the first set of training wheels. When Eddie and Alph needed to try a simple—well, nothing was ever simple in this business—car wreck or slip and fall or contract case to regain the feel for what that was like, the newbie could watch them and learn as well. They were going to cross-train each other and it would be beneficial for all.

They were no longer going to take on all comers. No more plunging. Anything that looked dubious or too much work for too little return or something that was just too damn little to be messed with was to be politely declined or sent elsewhere.

Eddie laughed and noted that this was fun, that he could already feel the load being lifted. He recalled that for years he had often compared himself to the bass in the fishing tournaments that aired on ESPN 3 in the middle of the night. The bass was always striking at the lure, always getting hooked. Eddie had been the bass. He did not want to be the bass any longer. He did not want any of them to be the bass anymore.

An important exception was offered and accepted. Family and close friends always were to get close attention and a discount on fees charged, no matter what.

It was decided that a case screening committee of Patty and Mikey should be established for both current and proposed incoming matters. After all, they were the two that had to put the files together and manage them. If they could not agree as to whether something was a "go" or a "no," the tie-breaking vote was to be cast by Alph after brief consultation. There would be no appeals for any edict handed down by Alph. One of the great benefits of being a small firm was that it was light on its feet and solid decisions could be made on the fly.

This plan on case maintenance and intake led immediately to another area of weakness and need they had all known about for a long time. Again, they had kicked the can down the road without even acknowledging the existence of the can. They needed help. They needed support staff help. They needed lawyer help. They needed fresh blood and fresh eyes. And all understood that money was not an issue here.

Patty cut to the chase there. "Hell, y'all, we're rolling in dough and have been for years! Now it's time to spend some of it!"

It was decided that two people would be promptly found and that the unanimous preference of all was that they both be female.

Patty quickly suggested to nodding acclaim that Polly Webster, the sharp and smart temp that had recently helped cover their phones during the Beautray trial be approached and offered a salary and benefits equally commensurate with those that Patty and Mikey were receiving and toss in a nice signing bonus as well. These were not inconsequential sums.

Patty said she would invite Polly for lunch in their offices tomorrow, adding that it was always nice for others to see the worker bees buzzing happily away in their hive.

"Patty, please tell her that Eddie will 'make you an offer you cannot refuse' and that we would like her to start as soon as possible, like yesterday."

"Yes, sir and thank you! We really need her and we already know she's good."

"Let's not bank that good money just yet but let us hope, let us hope..."

Attention was then turned to finding the next young lawyer. It was decided, after considerable discussion, that the prospect should be someone coming fresh out of law school, not someone who had already been out in the fields. The consensus was they wanted to mold her from the get-go to their ways of practice, to their approaches, to their attitudes and aptitudes. And they did not want reticence or a tentative shrinking violet; they needed self-confidence and a willingness to realistically chase the golden ring. They needed a stand-up gal who was worthy of the "foxhole."

The "foxhole" was their "inside baseball" code, for an imagined bastion where smarts, creativity, toughness, tenacity and loyalty were front and center, not to mention a thick skin, a comfort zone that welcomed bad and worse language and jokes, a good sense of humor and the ability to laugh at themselves. They needed more of those who emulated all of those qualities constantly and persistently and this was going to be that start.

Alph suggested that he and Eddie soon make a trip out to the law school at Wake Forest and check in with Dean Bowman and see if he had any thoughts as to who might fit their bill. If they found a live one, they would first have a visit with her and then they would make arrangements to get the candidate to the office for a thorough vetting by Patty and Mikey and hopefully Polly as well.

"This is getting exciting! We are shedding our old skins. What's next?" Eddie and Alph were pleased and impressed with their Girls Friday.

Mikey dragged her finger down her list. "Technology. As comfortable as we are with what we use, we might as well be using rotary dial in the iPhone age. We need upgrades, probably across the board. Patty and I suggest that our good friend and brilliant IT guy John Adams down in Atlanta, whom we haven't used in years, be promptly scheduled to come give us a thorough look-see once-over and make suggestions and proceed from there."

"Yup, we surely need to streamline our tickler black book system and our trust account maintenance and I suppose there is so much more. Line it up please, ASAP. I expect this is going to end up exasperating me and Alph pretty good, but we need to go ahead and jump up on a new learning curve and we might as well go on and get to it."

Alph rolled his eyes in mock horror. "Sure, why not? In for a penny, in for a pound. Gotta keep learning or we get stale. One of these days the feds are going to go with computerized filing and the state will too…" He winced and shrugged his shoulders in anticipated obeisance.

"Consider it done. As soon as we finish up here, I'll make the call."

"And please tell him that plane tickets, car rental, hotel, etc. are on us, of course. Next?"

Mikey responded, "Yes, next. Next is social media. We have no presence, incredibly, not even a website or a Facebook page. This is not a suggestion that we upgrade in this area. This is a suggestion that we just begin to do something in this area. We are behind the times here and in a big and bad way."

"Yes, I know. It could be asked why do we need it. We are already and always busy as hell with more coming in all the time. That's true but and to us, this is a big 'but,' we need to begin to show everyone out there that we are active and current in these times and that we know what we are doing. We need to put a face on us."

Patty got up, wandered into a far corner of the big room, lit a cigarette and pointedly gesturing with it, added with more than a little emphasis, "Yes, we sure do. Hell, my kids know more about all this social media stuff than all of us put together. This is so important and think about this too. We're going out to hopefully bring in Polly and also, a young, savvy bright young thing. We are not going to want to try to sell her on our lack of this kind of thing. And if she's who we hope she turns out to be, she's the next generation. None of us are getting any younger. We're at the point where we need to start building the next generation and we have to do that by being up to speed with the times. Plus, she, and Polly too can help us put together what we need. Besides, Eddie and Alph, isn't it about time that we flashed your ugly but charming mugs to the world across the world wide web? Mikey and I are pretty revved up on this."

Eddie nodded. "I understand. Needs to be done. So let's do it and do it right. But we haven't the expertise to pull something off like this by ourselves. Sort of like me thinking I can dunk a basketball; wishing and hoping just don't make it so!" He laughed at himself. The mental picture of that effort was embarrassing.

"I'm gonna call my old friends Mark Clore and Sam Allen. Mark knows more about maternal fetal medicine than most OBs out there and we call Sam 'MacGyver' because he can hook two desk chairs up with a coat hanger and a five volt battery and drive it around a room. They are great guys, have no hesitancy about sharing and they are technology freaks and geeks of the highest order and they'll put us in touch with who can help us build and put together what we need. They are very social media savvy."

"Okay, what else?"

Mikey exhaled. "There is not a whole lot left here so I'll try to bundle it up. We need to go back to being baby lawyers, of course never being tentative or unsure, but being thoughtful and thorough and consciously checking the boxes as we move through our cases and our work.

"We need to renew old friendships and make new ones as well. We need to not only drink after work with each other, we need to invite others outside our circle for a drink or a meal. We need to make this something we do regularly, not every day or even every week but regularly and we need to remind each other to do it, individually or in pairs. We need to resocialize ourselves and this firm. And we will need our entire group to pitch in on this as it goes. We say to you, Eddie and Alph, with all due respect that the trial lawyer world is being pollinated with damn good lady lawyers and we want to be out front on this for sure."

"We agree and affirm. I promise we do."

Mikey continued. "And as my daddy used to say, 'It's a damn poor dog that won't wag his own tail.' We need some good and constant PR being pushed out to the public. We need to get in touch with the county and state bar associations and the trial lawyer groups and offer ourselves for speaking engagements. Hell, I think we ought to, once we get these new foundations in, set up an annual one day seminar with cocktails and good food afterwards and invite, say four of the best lawyers we know, plaintiff and defense, and we'll present along with them."

"I like that. Good stuff. Eddie, I think we need a press agent."

"Agree, Alph, but I think these days they are called publicists. I'll get a line on one or two from a fine independent editor I know over in Raleigh and we can go from there."

"Okay." Mikey continued.

"We have club memberships and access to tickets to games and events and concerts. Those are unused assets that need to be used, and to our benefit. We need to go back to hitting the bricks. And we need to sharpen up, get back in shape physically and mentally. By the way—a suggested new practice here. Bring your walking shoes tomorrow. Go buy another pair to keep at home. The ones you bring are gonna stay here in plain view so they get used. We all need to get outside and get a little cardio and fresh air.

"We really, really understand that what we've laid out here and agreed to is going to be a lot of new effort and we gotta be ready to deal with it effectively. This is going to be some serious transitioning and it's going to put more than a little strain on us. But, if we do it right, we will be better than ever. Okay. That's it. I'm zipping it up now."

And Mikey theatrically snapped her mouth shut with a nod of finalization.

Patty and Mikey looked at each other and were pleased. Eddie and Alph looked at each other and were pleased as well and then they looked at the ladies. Eddie simply said, "On behalf of the two of us, you two are beyond great and we appreciate you both more than you know and before we get started on these various projects, I want to reward all of you with a, shall we say, negotiable instrument that must be considered only fun money for y'all's chosen amusement. I'll attend to that in just a minute.

"Now, before we become renewed social butterflies, how about let's check the phone messages, keep the sign on the door a little while longer and just the four of us go over to the Katherine for a drink and a good lunch? We've now got a whole lot of new plenty on our plates to think about and work on so let's call it a day to let everything sink in. I've made what I think are good notes along the way and of course, we got Miss M and Miss P to keep us up to speed. So let's go choke and chew and talk sports and the weather and some such.

"Oh, and Patty, please go write out three checks for five grand each for you all. Nothing for me, please. Thank you."

They grinned their smiling appreciation and Eddie was glad to be doing it. They were all giving him more presents and he wanted to reciprocate.

"Oh, last thing. Since we are going back to baby lawyering, and that is a damn good idea I think, we need to be doing some good, instructive reading about that to help us on our new, improved way, along with our usual doses of advance sheets and case reports and all the rest of it. So as it hopefully appears we are going to be growing, Mikey would you please order six brand new copies, whatever the latest edition is, of James McElhaney's *Trial Notebook*. It's as good a trial work Bible as there is out there and I want us all reading it and reading it some more."

Alph laughed. "You know, you're right. I haven't thought of that in years. It's a damn fine book. Very well and simply written. Very useful. Great idea, Eddie!"

And they were all smiles and when those few initial things were done, they headed down the street. Eddie had a strong sensation that the clouds were lifting. They were moving forward and it felt good.

CHAPTER TWENTY-SIX

A NEW EVOLUTION BEGINS

A Few Months Later...

AND SO THE rebirth began.

Then in due time, they received and began to flip through the pages of *Trial Notebook*. At first, they were a little hesitant and scattered and would look here and there and pan a nugget out of "cross-examination" and then wander over to "pretrial motions." Once they realized that they had no organized master plan and course to their readings, they intuitively let it proceed anyway and would ask one another what topic they had recently studied on. Discussion, basically disguised as "Q&A" on the fly, usually ensued.

This was regular in its unannounced, rapid fire "game show" format. But it worked. It did not happen every day but it did begin to happen then happen consistently.

Patty asked, "Okay, Alph, what's the best rule for cross-examination?"

"Never ask a question on cross that you don't already know what the answer will be," Alph responded with emphasis and alacrity.

"Not necessarily. How about when you don't know what the answer will be but no matter what, the answer will come out to your benefit? Like in *Witness for the Prosecution* when Charles Laughton asked Marlene Dietrich after catching her in an enormous, compromising inconsistency. 'Well,

Frau Vole, were you lying then or are you lying now or are you simply a pathological liar!?"

"Damn, Patty, you just yanked my chain but good! I need to get back to the good lawyer movies!"

"Well, Alph, I'd suggest you start with *My Cousin Vinnie* with Joe Pesci and *The Verdict* with Paul Newman. Those two will start your new engine but good!"

Mikey asked, "Eddie, what is a good way at trial to get an adverse witness who is on the 'I don't recall' default button to refresh his recollection of a critically significant event, such as where he was at the time of his patient's death?"

"Well, you gotta stay after him, gotta come at him from more than one angle of approach."

"C'mon, Eddie. I know you are intuitive as all get out and can pull plenty of rabbits out of the hat but that's a pretty mushy answer. How about this: ask him, in precise order, if he remembers where he was when Kennedy was shot, when the *Challenger* exploded, when Reagan was shot, when 9/11 happened...get him to acknowledge these were "very significant, very memorable" events in the course of his life, right? If he stays with the 'I don't remember, I don't recall' shtick, the jury is going to find him full of shit no matter what, so you've already won the battle if not the war. And if and once he admits that he remembers exactly where he was when 9/11 happened—and we all do, we all do, don't we—then ask him wasn't the death of his patient, his very own patient something very important, very significant in the course of his professional career—I mean after all, Doctor, you don't lose one very often, do you? Again, another high and tight fast ball zinger for the jury—so, Doctor, where were you when Mrs. Smith died? Et cetera... he'll give it up."

"You know, Mikey, you are hotter than a two-dollar pistol and I mean in more ways than one." Eddie beamed at her.

And then all sorts of other salubrious things began to happen.

A few days after their "reinvent the firm" meeting, Eddie and Alph were chewing the fat in Alph's office when there was a knock and there framed in the doorway, Patty had Polly Webster, their temp, in tow.

Polly was a lady of substantial carriage and not at all blocky, instead rather smooth and supple. She had clip-cut frosted brown hair and sleepy eyes. She was the definition of attractive and winsome. Pressing nicely into a comfortable middle age, she was taller than average and there was a pleasant quiet strength to her bearing. Polly was the eldest daughter of the late, legendary JAW, James A. Webster, Chaired Professor of all—things—real estate law at the law school. (JAW had taken Eddie over his traces years ago and had basically busted Eddie's ass. But Eddie made it by a hair and grew to adore the old curmudgeon.)

And when Eddie's class had finally finished the "Raleigh on the rack" of the three days of bar exam essays and multiple choice questions in the towering and Arctic unto freezing livestock pavilion at the North Carolina State Fairgrounds, they then repaired to The Mosque, a wonderful restaurant owned by law school classmate Nick Dombalis's family to drink beer and then, in exhaustion and relief, drink more beer, it was JAW who appeared at the big glass door, backlit by the eye-squinting, setting sun with a case of beer on each shoulder who brought tribute and succor to his beloved wounded.

Polly's voice had none of her daddy's gravelly crack-the-whip to it; rather it was straightforwardly calm. She wore an Eve Arden—like "Our Miss Brooks"—long, bejeweled eyeglass chain around her neck. You could easily tell she was alert and composed and stayed clean as a whistle all the time. With very little adornment, she wore only her wedding bands on her right hand. She had been widowed some years before and lived alone, her two children long since grown up and on their own—she was close to becoming a grandmother soon. She sported a stunning ruby brooch on her dress just below her left shoulder. It was eye-catching just like herself.

Eddie and Alph stood and courtly nodded. Eddie said, "Polly, we have sent Patty to fetch you. We want to hire you full time. We know you already do plenty of P.I. temp work. We'd like you to join us full time. By the way, full time here means you set your own hours and you take time off for vacations and whatever as you wish. You are a grown up. You know how to work and to be responsible about it. No clock punching here. And Patty will fill you in on the money and benefits and how we basically go about doing and approaching things. I promise we will be happily generous."

"Eddie, I am complimented and very interested in all this. Patty has filled me in enough to set the hook. I don't want to go too fast but let's just see how the next couple of hours go. I know you don't beat around the bush and neither do I."

"I appreciate that, Polly."

"Eddie, one more thing before I go off with Patty now and visit with her and Mikey, is it?"

"Yes, that's right. And, what is the one more thing?"

"Well, Eddie, how about tell me a good joke?"

Eddie, as usual, squared his shoulders and intoned the ribaldry.

"The bashful bride and groom were delighted to be finally alone in their honeymoon suite after a courtship highlighted by intense celibacy. Blushing, the bride asked her new husband, 'Johnny, now that we're married, could you tell me what a penis is?'

"Pleased to discover that his new wife was naïve unto the point of probable virginity, he proudly pulled his penis from his britches and showed it to her."

"Oh," Polly interrupted. "It's just like a dick, only smaller," she deadpanned.

Polly waited, watching their curious eyes, then spoke with a sly, eye-twisting, head tilting, sweet little girl smile. She purred with the calm of a benign predator. "Hmmmm…not too bad. Not bad at all. Maybe one of these days I can share one or two of Daddy's old chestnuts. Now, you know he wasn't too bashful, especially after he'd had a few…and oh, yes, if we can find a good place, it would be fun to have a drink with y'all."

Eddie knew she was not hustling, not at all; she was a delightful surprise. She was simply looking for the strike price while she marked her territory. She had played him well with Patty's wanting information and her own fine instincts and it made Eddie happy. There was no resentment, just appreciation. What man could resist being nicely played by a smart, skilled lady.

With the blandness that comes with knowing, she dryly said, "Come on, Patty, show me the inside works of around here." They went out the door and Polly turned as they did and leered an exaggerated wink at the two warhorses. Still silence sat upon them as would a newly dug grave of a happily departed…a visitation of pleasure was within reach.

"Eddie, I believe she'll work out just fine." Alph giggled.

"Alph, I believe you are correct. Good God, seems we are tracking… yes, seems we are…"

Eddie pleasantly mumbled into a promising nowhere and Alph was pleased. Here in this home, he was challenged, charged, and always pleased.

CHAPTER TWENTY-SEVEN

PUTTING MEAT ON THE BONE

Late Spring

POLLY DID SIGN on and she pleased them all, was an immediate natural and good fit and the reinforced trifecta of smarts immediately went to work on the evaluation of every case in the office. Polly acclimated quickly. Case evaluations encompassed the whole of it all, the soup to nuts look-see of every facet of a case and thus, the scope of the office's work came to light fully. It was rapid fire education for Polly and damn revelatory for Patty and Mikey.

Some cases were sacrosanct, untouchables and of course, some were so obviously "what in the hell were we thinking?" and thus quickly moved to the toss or refer-out column.

They referred nothing to cheap, all hat, and no cattle firms in the nature of the proverbial "Dewey Cheatem and Howe;" nothing was proffered to screeching advertisers and hokum chest beaters.

Rather, they sent plenty to the promising young up and comers who had plenty of recall as to who was good to them before they found their salad days. The upright "Glenn Lynch and Graham" bunch and also to the amusingly named but damn fine outfits of "Ewell Screws Hobbs" and "Grace and Tisdale" got the cultivating calls with but modest referral fees—usually no more than ten to fifteen percent—and alliances were cemented. It was understood that when a "whale" came around, Eddie and company would be called to man the decks and sharing of work and money would be the flag of the day.

It took almost a week to plow those fields but it was done efficiently with little blather but with plenty of precise, thoughtful analysis. Polly lent her comments and observations but was not yet a voter. If there was disagreement as to keep or toss, and there were of course some of those, Alph ruled thoughtfully and that was that.

John Adams came over from Atlanta and mystically and mysteriously did his computer and IT magic as though he rode on a silent electronic fog. He would seep into the offices and stations and as if by sleight of hand, huge screens and keyboards would appear along with delicious apps and software upgrades. Bundles of wire and cables shrunk tenfold. He was the calmest, smartest, most patient fellow they'd ever seen and he truly was a savant, a wizard. He was "now you see him, now you don't" and just quietly chuckled his way through their mess.

Eddie called his old buddies, the brilliant trial lawyers, as good as they could be, Mark and Sam and they right away pointed him to a High Impact, a very high quality website producer out of Denver. Eddie also got a lead from Alice Osborn, savvy book editor friend of his over in Raleigh, who put him in touch with Hannah Turner, a snappy and smart publicist who worked out of Chapel Hill and Charleston. She was interviewed and immediately retained and turned loose to burnish and tout them.

She was but a slip of a pretty young girl and could if she tried pass for barely twenty but her brain and contact and idea lists were mammoth. Her mind churned. She worked and coordinated with the website guys and also started lining up speaking gigs and press placements. No more hiding their light under the proverbial bushel basket. They were now on the way to being a glittering public offering, and the push included their fine squad of polished and fascinating legal assistants.

They all consciously started the taking of others to lunch or out for a drink. It was a time of social lubrication and they were all good at it. And it was fun.

And after a short while, Eddie and Alph drove out to the Wake Forest Law School late one morning and met with Dean Bowman to begin their search for their ideal young lady lawyer. The dean promptly guided them to Dr. George P. "Mad Dog" Walker, the head instructor for moot court and trial practice studies. They conferred for about fifteen minutes, reviewing the hoped-for criteria of their search.

"Professor, what do you think?"

Without further comment or preview, the "Mad Dog," known for his laser-like intensity and exuberant, barking voice picked up his office phone, called the law library and asked if Miss Strulip was nearby and if so, would she please come down to his office to meet two gentlemen whom might be of some interest to her. He listened and then nodded. "She's on her way." Eddie and Alph met each other's glances.

"Be patient, gentlemen. Do you wish to interview her with me present or would you prefer that I absent myself? I am happy to do whatever suits you."

"Professor, please stay with us for our visit and also, I must note that we seem to have a candidate," Eddie observed. Alph nodded.

"What can you tell us about her...before she gets here?"

"Only this. I think she has the potential to be a superstar, but you two will have to determine if I am prescient."

There was a light tap on the door and as Mad Dog barked, "Please come," in walked a tall, slender, sleek glass of water with prim, short cropped red hair and heart-shaped lips. She had what might be green eyes but their identification was clouded by thick round lenses encased in horn rimmed frames which seemed to circumnavigate her face. It was as though she was in disguise. She wore a fuzzed up, bulky, nondescript cowl-necked sweater of desultory gray, a black and white tartan over-the-knee skirt, black tights and a pair of clunky black wedgies. She appeared less than even pedestrian but there was something else there.

All three men stood and looked at her and she stood there and looked at them. It was that moment of first impression. There was just enough of a pause to admit to appraisal. Was she diffident or was she serene or was she just something else, another alleged sheet of mica and less? Were the two visitors interesting or just a couple of older suits, old boring suits, paint by numbers suits?

Mad Dog cleared his throat and with obvious, loud and aimed gallantry, made the introductions.

"Please make the acquaintance of Miss Cheryl Ann Strulip, an only recently graduated Juris Doctor Summa Cum Laude from this august institution. She's been doing part time helping in the law library upstairs and has also been doing the same with the local legal aid office. The rest and substance of her will be up to you to divine.

"Cheryl Ann, these two fellows are Mr. Alph Baron, a former president of the North Carolina State Bar and Mr. Eddie Terrell who, it would be fair to say, has cut a wide and very successful swath for many years through the courts of North Carolina. They are both trial lawyers in the surest sense of that description. I have taken the liberty of suggesting that they meet you and if you so choose, submit to their interview of you. I will be present for whatever takes place for no other purpose than as you well know, I am quite interested in your future path and they have asked me to be present for your conversations. If you are all right with all this, I will be only silent and watchful. Oh, and she has passed the North Carolina State Bar examinations and was sworn in to the bar last month by His Honor, Judge William Freeman. She is actively licensed."

Cheryl Ann paused, pursed her thinking lips, furrowed her highbrow and quickly unwrinkled it all and steadily said, "Why, yes, of course and well, this is very interesting and I am very complimented, Professor Walker, that you have arranged this visit. Hello, Mr. Baron. Hello, Mr. Terrell. I'll be more than happy to answer whatever you wish to ask."

There was unexpected frisson over the desk. The room held an electric charge.

The shaking of hands was anticipatory with proper confidence and firmness. And then they sat. Cheryl Ann took off her glasses and cleaned them with a yellow cleaning cloth she removed from her handbag and like lightning strikes on a clear summer day, her eyes were indeed captivatingly emerald green and luminescent. And in that instant when her head raised to prepare to look at them as they asked questions, she went from ugly duckling to beautiful swan.

Her innate pulchritude now readily and delightfully established, she was composed and alert but not guarded. She certainly would not offend or repulse those who might come along to treat or contest with her; quite the opposite. At worst, she would distract and at best, she would melt and mold. Eddie and Alph were now hopeful but knew then would come the hard part. They presumed she was smart. Mad Dog Walker had straightforwardly indicated that. The word "superstar" was rarely tossed out in describing a greenhorn, newly minted lawyer. But how was she smart? She surely was book smart; that came big, very big within her territory. But was she street smart, intuitively smart, tough and creatively smart? Did she have that elusive and ephemeral "it?" They were getting ready to find that out and hopefully, a whole lot more.

Eddie asked Alph to begin.

"Well, here we go. May we please call you Cheryl Ann?"

"Of course."

"Please let me cut to the chase, if you will, and then we will scratch around with your history and so forth. You are attractive, obviously very smart, so impressive that you are the person that Dr. Walker has called to visit with us and you do not display any of the nervousness or edginess that is so often apparent in situations like this. This surely is as close to impromptu and off the cuff as it gets and seems to me with little time to anticipate or prepare, well, I'm not so old as to have forgotten my time of interview..."

She nodded slowly and gave away nothing. Alph Baron smiled his charming, avuncular smile. Eddie never took his eyes off her. He watched her eyes and her hands.

"So, how does it come to pass that you have not already been landed by a prestigious, well paying, nice-sized firm and put into training and work already? Instead we find you in the library and at legal aid? Is there a problem, a something going on?"

Mad Dog smiled as did Cheryl Ann. Her smile was one of the sincere and politely tolerant sort.

"No, Mr. Baron—or may I please call y'all Alph and Eddie? There isn't a problem other than a lot of folks think I ought to have my head examined for not having already gone down the path you have just described. I have had a number of such opportunities and have, I hope with good manners, declined them. Now, may I ask you both a question or two? And once y'all answer my questions, of course I'm glad to explain and answer further." She held herself with a comfortable aplomb.

"Of course you may."

"Will you please tell me about your firm? I have the impression it is not large. You obviously go to court a lot. You obviously are good at what you do. And, Alph, how did a past president of the North Carolina State Bar end up in what looks to me like a pretty—no offense intended—small outfit?"

Eddie's heart rate quickened a tad. Her speech patterns did not signal a bookish effete. She spoke clearly, efficiently, and to the point. And the unhesitating use of the words "small outfit" were from the mind of an observant realist.

Eddie offered to take her first inquiry:

"When I came out law school some thirty-plus years ago, I started and stayed small. I found the courthouse early on and found that I loved it and still do very, very much. I've had the same legal assistant for what seems like time immemorial, an incredibly smart and sharp lady named Patty Cherry. Lots of times, I feel like I'm her Man Friday. Yes, we are very small. Have our offices up on the hill over near the courthouses. It's an old house we put together, dates back to 1885. We're comfortable. We also have another legal assistant by the name of Mikey Riewy whom I found out in Montana many years ago—that's a story for a different time—who Patty has trained and who has trained herself and I suppose I have helped some too along the way with my mistakes and omissions.

Mikey and I live together. We've been together for over a decade now and no, we have no problems living together and working together. And we just in the last few weeks have added another very skilled lady named Polly Webster who used to do part-time, freelance trial work but we got lucky and have convinced her to come on board full time. We have a lot of work, lots of cases, lots of personal injury, medical malpractice, business litigation, et cetera and we need help.

"We are mostly plaintiff, work off contingent fees and too, don't mind doing civil defense work and do some here and there, bill by the hour there. Criminal? If it's interesting and the clients are good, we'll take a go. Drug work, not so much but every now and then...

"We are in the process of streamlining and upgrading every aspect of our practice. We are also cleaning out a good number of our case files as they no longer fit our newly revised practice template. But we want to keep some smaller fry in the pool for us to always work on and help anyone new with. Nothing like cutting teeth on the real thing.

"As the old master sergeant at Fort Bragg says when he's got his babies down in the mud and the real bullets are sparking over, 'Low crawl your ass to Bulldog Hall. This is live fire, boys and girls!'

"And oh by the way—and this is a fun fact—Polly Webster is the daughter of the late great JAW, the legendary Wake Law School professor James A.

Webster. I'd presume you have run across his name in this building from time to time."

She quick-nodded in appreciation, interested that it was all so incestuous. These people were as much of a tribe as her Lumbees back home.

"And, we have no employee handbook or book of office rules. We do get to and will holler at each other and blow off steam. Maybe that's a rule? We had a cuss jar once...a dollar for a cuss word. We filled it up on its first morning...so much for that...got rid of it then and there. It was a useless exercise in self-imposed self-restraint. The only real rules we have are do your work and work hard and have some fun along the way. Whew, that sure was a mouthful. Now, Alph, please tell her how you came to join our little menagerie and whatever else comes to mind."

There was a look in Cheryl Ann's eyes and on her face that was radiant. Eddie and Alph knew they had found what they were looking for; now, could they reel her in?

Alph leaned forward and with great, good humor began his truthful self-deprecation.

"Miss Cheryl Ann, I got here to practice with Eddie because, well, Eddie just flat out—and please excuse my French—Eddie just beat my ass into the ground in a legal malpractice case involving an air crash death and a badly missed statute of limitations that I was trying to defend. I was flailing and then Eddie here flailed me but good."

"No offense taken. I'm a country girl." She nodded for him to go on.

"Well, one thing led to another and Eddie and I got along very nicely and we spent a little time together and then a little more and after a pretty interesting and intense mediation down in Charleston way back when, Eddie asked me to join him as 'Of Counsel' and then Patty and Mikey tag-teamed me but good and I happily folded and here I am, still am after all this time and still enjoy it all so much. Now, please tell us more."

"Fair enough. I have no interest in working in a billable hours pit, grinding always for the clock. Sure, you get a nice salary and bonuses from time to time and you get a secretary and sometimes a legal assistant and you get nice benefits, but they own you and you are chained to them and you have to take every case they hand you. You instantly become their indentured servant. You have no choice. Once you're in, they pretty much own you. You become a nicely dressed sharecropper. I want none of that."

Alph exhaled an audible, "Mmmm…"and looked at Eddie and asked if he could go ahead and walk out on a limb.

"Hell, yes, go ahead and walk out long. By the way, Cheryl Ann, you've already told us that some bad language doesn't bother you. What about off-color, sometimes raucously bad dirty jokes?"

She tittered. The sound of doves slipped from her lips. "Fine by me. Like I've said, I'm a country girl. Rough language in its place gives me no start and if it's good stuff, then all the better."

They nodded in pleased unison. Mad Dog was proud, almost aglow.

Alph resumed. "Well, Cheryl Ann, here we go with the sixty-four thousand dollar question. Hope I don't blow it, overreach it…what would you like to do? What kind of law practice would you like to have?"

"Sitting here with y'all, I am reminded that if y'all think you are interested in me, then I need to be selling myself to you with good reason. First off, I've been a real good student here at Wake and I don't know what all Dr. Walker has told you but I've been on Law Review for two years and am in the top three placements in moot court the last two years. It took me my first year to get tuned up and settled. I love moot court. I can't wait to try cases, cases that I believe in. I've always wanted to be a lawyer. You know, those Perry Mason reruns on WRAL in the afternoons…everybody has always known that about me." She looked down with honest modesty.

The Mad Dog noted he had told them nothing more but that he thought she had "good potential."

"Admirable. Please go on if you like."

Eddie thought he just might faint.

"Yes, of course. You see, I grew up small. I'm from a little, real little place right on the North Carolina side of the South Carolina line called Rowland, population barely a thousand and shrinking every year. As someone once said, there is no there there. It's just a few miles from that weird crazy place, South of The Border that's right off I-95. Funny, I guess they need to change the place's motto, 'The Home of a Thousand Friends,' cause it sure has not gained many along the years. In truth, it's pretty much a dead end and getting deader. Something out of a Southern gothic picture book. My daddy is a tobacco and cotton farmer and my mom is a school teacher and helps out at our church. I'm used to small but I knew I needed more stimulation. I'm used to hard work, worked on the farm all the time. I expect we've got some

Indian in us but my folks have always teased me about how, well, white I am and my hair and eyes. I was never much good at biology and glad it doesn't show up here on any course lists…I'll accept maybe I'm just a little different.

After high school, went to Campbell over nearby in Buies Creek. Liked it fine and did well. My folks wanted me to go to N.C. State, but once I took a look at that place, it gave me the willies—just too big for a pretty naïve kid like me. Being a Campbell Fighting Camel—now there's a picture just by the way—suited me just fine."

She was loosening, telling her story. The men wanted to listen. She was articulate and comfortable in her skin.

"My last year at Campbell, a professor at the law school there had gotten wind of me, how I don't know but I surely am glad he did. He asked to visit with me and I did and he told me that while he wanted to recruit me to stay in Buies Creek, he thought it was time for me to spread my wings and keep moving on. He suggested that I apply to Wake Forest, said he thought it was a good fit for me. I was growing up some and I was game and he helped me with my application and my recommendations and I made it and now here I am in Winston-Salem. Oh, and this—I think it's important for y'all to know. I like guys just fine but this just isn't the time or place in my life to be cultivating a steady boyfriend or getting married or having kids. I just need to start getting after what I've started, what I've always wanted… "

Her voice softly tailed off. She looked off into the distance, wherever that was. They just watched her. She came back to them.

"So, what do I want?" She looked at them squarely and silently, resolutely gulped. "Well, here's my sixty-four thousand dollar answer. I think I'd really like to be with y'all."

Alph looked at Eddie and nodded. Eddie looked at Alph and nodded. They both looked at Mad Dog who nodded and then all three looked at Cheryl Ann. Eddie broke the silence.

"Miss Cheryl Ann, we think that's a fine answer and I believe we will all gather at the river. But, there is one more thing. Do you have a little bit more extra time to spend with us today?"

"Oh, yes, of course!" The color was rising up in her face and she beamed.

"As you can tell, ours is a pretty tight crowd and again, this is pretty off the cuff and impromptu. I think we'd like to take you down to the office so our bunch down there can meet you and you can meet them. Fair to say, we think this is all going to turn out fine but also think this is a necessary thing to get done."

"I understand. I'm ready when you are."

"Then, let us proceed. Professor Walker, thank you so much for your, shall we say, hospitality!"

"Lady, if I might and gentlemen, the pleasure was all mine. Knock 'em out, Cheryl Ann!"

They all shook hands again with vigor and headed to the final exam.

A while later—once she entered the double doors of the office—Cheryl Ann felt as though she had just been transported into a warm bath of fur and bubbles—all four ladies went into the small conference room and shut the door. After much muffled laughter and pleasant exclamations and whispered observations, Patty with a grinning two thumbs up led them out and it was game on. Eddie then took Cheryl Ann into his office and offered her $75,000 a year to start plus all benefits and also the opportunity to receive regular bonuses and also access to the exercise of "eat what you kill," that being whatever good cases Cheryl Ann brought into the office that concluded successfully, she would receive a proper percentage of the fee generated. Cheryl Ann happily accepted.

Eddie's last benediction before they went out to join the others was, "Cheryl Ann, I hope you realize that you are not just a hire, just an addition. You are our reach into the future, a future that we think and fervently believe you will lead. In time, if all this works out and God knows we believe it to be so, you will lead this firm, make it grow or go slow as you find it to be, add or subtract as you think best and hopefully with the help of others that you identify and seek. Alph and I will be around a good while longer and we want to help but we are now going to work on you to be the lead sled dog. Remember, if you ain't in the lead, the view never changes. Do you understand, this isn't just a big deal for us, it's a really big deal for you...?"

She silently nodded as the moment required and was jelly inside.

"Okay, let's do this." Eddie opened the door and swept his arm out in presentation and there she was and hugs and happiness flowed forth from a cornucopia of relief and excitement.

She asked Eddie if she could start the following Monday. Of course. She wanted to go home and tell her parents. And she did. And she was button-busting proud. And scared to death.

CHAPTER TWENTY-EIGHT

SOME WILD-ASS SHIT

Present Day

MONDAY MORNING MADE its introduction in a grim gray suit that was spitting rain. Cheryl Ann's hair had always been a ravaged victim of humidity and her rain slicker was stick stuck to her dress. She felt misshapen, lumpy, and odd. She pulled into the parking lot apprehensive and more than a little bit fearful.

"Oh what have I done? Can I really do this?" She parked, killed the engine and sat very still, her hands still gripping the wheel that no longer needed gripping. It seemed minutes were passing.

Then Patty glided in alongside her, waving and grinning as her smoke plume enveloped her. Her door opened, the nimbus preceded her and she called, "Come on, Miss Cheryl Ann. Time to get to it and make some hay!"

"Well, no time like the present," Cheryl Ann mumbled to herself and out onto the lot she stepped. Patty took her arm and steered her up the curling brick walk and onto the porch landing.

"You nervous?"

"A little, I guess, I think..."

"No problem on that. Understandable. We're gonna shake those butterflies right off your tree and right soon too."

Patty guided her on in through the tall doors, turning on lights as she went, reset the thermostat and opened many shutters and curtains to let the gray light of the day in. She started a big pot of coffee, explaining, gesturing and pointing out for Cheryl Ann's benefit as she rumbled about the office.

"Cheryl Ann, honey, we know you are a quick study, but always feel free to ask about anything. It doesn't cost anything and getting helpful information usually pays off real good."

Cheryl Ann nodded. Her jitters were starting to subside. Patty, hands on hips, eyes sharp alert, swiveled about and surveyed the morning's beginnings.

"Now, I have a thought. What do you think about this? We run a tight but loosey-goosey shop here and we really do have a lot of fun as we go. I'm not trying to offend you or your momma and daddy but I'm of the mind to change, well actually shorten your name to 'Cas' like Momma Cas though you sure are a damn sight prettier. Makes it easier for us all and I believe nicknames or whatever are a good sign of familiarity, of belonging and, honey, we surely do want you to belong." Patty grinned and continued.

"Listen to this. Eddie was Edward. How stuffy is that? Alph was Ralph. Plain, plain that...I was Patricia. Hoity toity I'm not. Polly used to be Dorothy and not from the Wizard of Oz and Mikey, God knows where that came from...it sure ain't from that TV ad, 'Let Mikey eat it' but it sure is out there."

She paused. "So, what you think? Would you let us hijack your given name for the sake of office unity and fun?"

Cheryl Ann nodded. "You know, I think that's a pretty neat idea. I like it. Cheryl Ann has always made me feel, well, like a magnolia tree and that sure isn't me. I've always wanted a nickname so now, I'm Cas. Pleased to meet you."

They shook hands and Patty started the roil. Polly and Mikey and Eddie wandered in. Alph wasn't far behind. Patty quickly explained that their new hire had been renamed. That was fine by all. Eddie surveyed.

"Okay, kids. Here's how I'd suggest we get this ball rolling. Time to baby lawyer as we decided earlier. Of course we need to acclimate...so now, Cas, is it? There's nothing more bracing than a long run off a short dock into cold water to brace the mind. So, into the tank you go Patty, Polly, Mikey. Would y'all go into the big conference room and just pick up where you left off and get Cas tuned in on how we evaluate our cases, one at a time, sort of a shorthand look-see for her? Alph, would you please sit with them and comment whenever you see fit?"

Alph responded, "My pleasure."

"Let's spend the morning on that project, get her a good overview, then get lunch brought in. This afternoon, Alph, how about you make some calls on some cases that are ripening up nicely for settlement? Get opposing counsel or adjuster on speaker phone so Cas can listen in and get the back and forth of it. Tell whoever some basic bullshit that you need to be hands free cause there are a bunch of documents in another case that you need to be going through. Shouldn't be a problem because these days we all multitask. Obviously, do not let the other side know Cas is with you. Cas, remember, in this part of things, silence is golden. Soon enough, you'll be doing this sort of thing solo. And, oh yeah, as y'all go through cases, how about we set aside three or four that Cas can go try in due time? And later on this afternoon, let's sit together and see what we've gotten done and Q&A each other and go from there.

"So, all good?" They all nodded. Patty asked, "Eddie, you're pretty much telling us to freestyle it, right?"

"You got it. Now, I'm going to lock myself in my office, read a bunch of medicine, think a lot about Cameron, call Kermit and start our serious, hard game planning. Its day certain setting is just about nine, ten weeks away and those days are going to melt away quickly. Alph, I'd appreciate if you pretty much took over most of what we've got going on for now. As you know how it goes, I've got to get my head wrapped around this thing just right. I'd really appreciate it and of course I'm always around for whatever but please be our trail boss for these next few weeks."

"Your wish is my command. We will get things done, I promise."

Polly raised her hand and asked the questions that both she and Cas had in mind.

"What's Cameron? And who is Kermit? Gosh, I'm getting old. I remember when my kids watched Kermit the Frog all the time..."

"Patty, why don't you do the initial honors and then I'll come along and give a good overview."

"K." She went to the corner, opened a window, and fired one up. She was wreathed in smoke that then tunneled out and away.

"Here you go. Cameron is a wrongful death medical malpractice case and I think it's fair to say it's the biggest whale in the office right now. It certainly has Eddie by the serious brain short hairs and he and Kermit are really fired up to get after it. Defense counsel for the doctors and insurance carriers have treated Eddie and Kermit like dog shit on a shoe and it appears they ain't gonna offer a dime, so it's looking like it's balls to the wall on this one, all or nothing.

"It's going to be tried over in Greensboro, next door in Guilford County. And yes, Kermit King is our co-counsel. He's from Columbia, South Carolina, and is a legend. Eddie swears it seems that Kermit knows where all the bodies are buried all over the Southeast, if you know what I mean, and says he's smartest, sharpest lawyer he has ever come across. And for Eddie to say that is really saying something. Has a photographic memo and can call up all sorts of case and statutory law in the blink of an eye...North Carolina, South Carolina, doesn't matter; he's a walking encyclopedia. We haven't met him yet but looking forward to getting that done soon. His chief assistant is a cool, smart gal named Traci. Haven't met her yet either but we've been on the phone a lot and of course, there will be plenty more of that too."

"Okay and Columbia, South Carolina? How does it come to pass that we have gotten into what sounds like a big-time case and there's a lawyer from South Carolina helping us?" Cas asked.

"Eddie's licensed in South Carolina and has been for a long time. He'll explain. Eddie, please take the controls here."

Eddie leaned forward, took a few moments to order his thoughts and then began his exposition.

"Okay, y'all. Here you go. And by the way, give a good listen here. This is, as Patty says, a real important case to us and it's truly a heavy lifter and it's got a little bit of everything so it's a good learning, how-to-think-and-evaluate-and-get-things-done case so there is much value added here as well. So, feel free to take notes. And by the way, long, long, long time ago, I was chasing a gal around down in South Carolina and ended up with a case....

Cas was in a spinning thrall but on the point. She had been dropped into the eye of a hurricane and she could see in every direction.

"Cameron is a med mal case involving the death of a young infant, an identical twin. Soon after his and his brother's birth, he repeatedly presented with a condition that was totally curable, but the docs and the hospital staff and nurses missed it over and over again and that failure caused this little fellow to become suddenly and manifestly brain damaged and after months of being in what they formally call a 'vegetative state,' he died about a year later.

"This case came to me in an unusual way. I got a call out of the blue about all this from the parents who are from Greensboro. They are some of the nicest, finest people you will ever meet. And they're smart and good to work with. They had been told to call me by the wife's brother who is an OB-GYN in California at University of California San Diego. I had gone out there about a year and a half before, before little Cameron and little Charlie were born, to attend a week long seminar on maternal-fetal medicine. Funny how chancy life can be. I had gotten a random brochure about the seminar in the mail—I guess my name was on some trial lawyer organization or publications mailing list.

"I learned so much out there. Really enjoyed the experience. This was no slap-dash deal. We—there were maybe twenty-five of us—were in class six to seven hours a day for five days. It was intense. The wife's brother was one of our instructors and he and I talked a lot along the way once we figured out our shared Southern roots. Of course, I had no idea about his sister and brother-in-law.

"When this disaster began to unfold, he told them to call me. They told me that he told them that I knew my stuff. That scared the hell out of me. I realized right away that if it was going to be a case and proper, neutral experts were going to make that call, then it was going to be a put-your-big-boy-pants on case. Sure, I knew some stuff and had learned some more stuff, but I also didn't know enough stuff and I was going to have to start studying like crazy. I knew I was going to need help. The case was going to be just over in the next door county and while I know plenty of folks and lawyers over there, I have, it's fair to say, an affinity for Kermit.

"I met with the parents, we got along fine and they retained me. We got the records. There were a pile of them. We got them put together and I got a wonderful pediatric surgeon over here at Wake Forest by the name of Wayne Taylor to review them. He, after he completed his review, told me that the medical folks in Greensboro had seriously breached the standard of care and that there was significant negligence in the child's care and he said, thank God and remarkably, that he would come over to Greensboro and testify as to same.

"It's usually a cold day in hell when a local physician, so close to the action if you will, will step up and publicly call negligence on whatever happened. Usually, once you get a positive opinion from someone local, it's a private opinion and then you go out of state, hopefully staying in the South, to find the guy or gal who will testify.

"I pointedly asked Taylor about that, asked if he was concerned about making enemies, being intimidated, harming his reputation and his patient flow and so forth. He told me he wasn't worried about that, that he was an old pro with a big reputation well-earned and that since he's senior faculty in a private institution of highest standing regionally and nationally, that helps plenty as well. He was also emphatic that the negligence he saw in the case was very, very bad.

"So the game is on and I immediately know I'm going to need a good, solid co-counsel to help me. This is pretty much the dog has chased the bus and now caught it. Uh-oh. What's the damn fool dog need to do to get to a good ending?

"So I settle and quiet myself and think about who I would like to get to work with me on this and it was pretty simple. I had found Kermit years ago, even before I had found Mikey, and I got him to help me on some med mals and some other cases that had come my way out of South Carolina. And, yeah, I've been actively licensed down there for a long time. As I recall, we won one, lost one and got a bunch of the others nicely settled and along the way, we got to be damn fine friends. He's about twenty years older than me. I consider him my greatest lawyer mentor. He's as quick a study as I have ever seen. Patrician as they come. Fabulous public speaker. Takes notes in, get this, Spencerian shorthand. He's always perfectly and precisely dressed and can walk through Hurricane Hugo without a hair out of place while I on the other hand can walk to the front door and my shirttail flies out. He's yin and I'm yang or put another way, he's Fred Astaire and I'm Pig Pen. But we do get along and complement one another. Obviously, I adore him."

Patty laughed. "Obviously..."

"Anyway, I go down to Columbia, have an always fun and interesting lunch and visit with him and Traci and tell them about the case and ask them to come play. We are very comfortable with each other, have been from the long ago get-go. They sign on and off we go and here we are. And by the way, Cas and all, lawyer lesson here—never be hesitant about getting other smart, effective folks to help you. Half a good fee is better than a one hundred percent empty wallet.

"Point well taken. What's the case about?"

"Right. Of course. This little fellow named Cameron was born with a well-known, recognizable birth defect called a tracheoesophageal fistula that is not, I emphasize, not a death sentence. You fix it. Move on. It's a small but discernible opening between the child's trachea and esophagus. So when he was breast or bottle fed, liquid would drip during swallows or suckings from the throat into his trachea, the passageway to the lungs. Once that fluid gets into the lungs, it can and often does cause acute onset pneumonias, usually relatively mild but not always. So as with so many things that have to do with these little people, Rule One is pay attention.

"There are many early warning signs—frothy, white bubbles in the mouth, repeated coughing or choking while feeding, repeated vomiting while or soon after feeding, trouble breathing while feeding or struggling to breathe after feeding, a bluish tint to the baby's skin while feeding—that lack of adequate oxygenation, a very rounded full stomach. The Good Lord does provide clues.

"Properly trained and experienced pediatric surgeons, pediatricians and neonatologists should spot this thing early. Barium studies with contrast can rule it in or out. That's what little Cameron had, they found it, and they fixed it with a surgical repair. The little opening was closed. Story over? Nope.

"Now, in about one to two percent of such repairs, and this is well-known, this is no mysterious secret, the repaired opening will reopen, will reoccur. When that happens, the surgical repair is a bit more extensive, somewhat more complex but a recurrence is a known complication and is almost always completed successfully and the child goes forward, feeds well and thrives.

"Soon after his initial repair, Cameron began to display the same signs and symptoms but they were discounted by his doctors and the neonatal nurses and the hospital's pediatric radiologists. Among the many culprits, and there were many, was the off and on use of a feeding tube. The feeding tube, when used, blocked the hole and so Cameron would do well. Fluid couldn't get to the hole and the lungs. They'd then pull it and the same problems would start all over again so back in goes the feeding tube. They couldn't and wouldn't see the forest for the trees. Radiographic studies with contrast showed inconsistent views; sometimes there appeared to be leakage into the trachea, sometimes there seemed to be none. Those inconsistencies were never explored; rather and incredibly, in depositions we were told that since the majority of the frames seemed fine, there was no reason for alarm.

"It literally rained symptoms for forty days and forty nights—as biblical a theme as I've ever been handed—and sadly, on the forty-first day of all this, the reopened opening enlarged significantly and spontaneously, blew out if you will, his lungs were acutely soaked, drowned if you will, flooded with secretions and formula. In a matter of just a few minutes, he developed a huge, oxygen depriving, irretrievable chemical pneumonia which ultimately rendered him manifestly and globally brain damaged. And he died about a year later.

"He stayed in the hospital for another couple of months, but his parents, after the initial, horrible shock had grown increasingly and understandably embittered and had Cameron taken to a straight shooter of a pediatric surgeon at Duke, a very nice man, an absolute old-school Southern gentleman named Bieman Otherson for second opinions. Those gently and specifically delivered were of no solace so they took their boy home until he expired about six months later.

"And remember that Cameron was an identical twin and his brother Charlie needed looking after too. Just think too about the stress on these parents. Our experts tell us this whole damn train wreck was completely preventable."

Eddie came to a temporary stop and was gripping the back of his chair and looking down. He was shaking his head ever so slightly and his face was reddening. It was obvious to all that this one had gotten to him bigtime.

Polly exhaled, "Jesus! That's just awful! So sad!"

Patty and Mikey and Alph nodded grimly. Cas's eyes were red around the edges.

Eddie jerked his head up and plowed on. "Yes, so many cases like this are really sad. I've handled, as has Alph, all sorts of wrongful death cases over the years but when it's a child or an infant, it just tears at your guts. There is a surreal quality that accompanies them. Things are out of cosmic order. Older folks, adults are supposed to go before children. That seems like it should be nature's progression but sometimes it's not that way. Parents are supposed to go before their kids and when something like this happens, it's a horrible reversal of what should be the proper path of life's chronologies. It's as though everything gets stood on its head in the cruelest of ways. It just doesn't seem fair.

"And, dammit, these people need to be careful all the time, not just some of the time or most of the time. It's hard work to be vigilant. According a recent meta-study in the *New England Journal of Medicine* and a great big article in *The New York Times Sunday Magazine*, mistakes in hospitals are estimated to cause at least two hundred fifty thousand unnecessary patient deaths annually here in the United States and that makes it the fifth leading cause of medically caused and induced fatalities after cancer, heart disease, and flu and opioids, and dammit, most of it is avoidable and preventable. Beyond frustrating."

Alph nodded, lips tightly pursed.

"Now, I need to tell you about the parents and the family and the doctors and the players and will here in just a minute; I want to paint a complete picture for y'all to work off of in your heads. Yeah, Kermit and I are going to carry the ball with Patty and Traci's good help but any and all ideas and suggestions are always appreciated.

"The parents here are really fine, nice people. Their names are John and Susan Andrews. They're very attractive, well-mannered, well-educated people. John went to Chapel Hill. Susan went to Hollins. These are educated people. They are unusual in that they are upper income folks who don't very often fall into the snare of sloppy, negligent malpractice. Well-to-do folks always get better and more attentive medical care. It's just the truth but obviously and always there are exceptions to the rule.

"In spite of this crushing disaster, they have picked up and gone on about their lives to good effect. John is a textile executive with Burlington Industries. Susan is a stay-at-home mother, does some charity and school sorts of things, primarily tends to Charlie who by the way is cute as a button. He's about four now and a bit of a character. His parents both have nice senses of humor. They live over near the Greensboro Country Club off Cornwallis. It appears they care very much for one another and that it is a consistent care and love which is very helpful here because lots of times when something like this happens, it tears families apart. That does not seem to be the case here.

"They love Charlie a ton and a half, but they have admitted in private, they sometimes look at Charlie and see Cameron and realize how much they miss Cameron. That hurt and pain and longing is permanent, the always stark reminder on the never-ending horizon. Their medical bills from this are enormous and because John had to be away from work off and on for the better part of a year, there is some economic loss and also losses at opportunities for advancement.

"Now, there are our plaintiffs. The defendants are as follows…

"The pediatric surgeon who did both repairs is an arrogant, haughty, smartest guy-in-the- room type, named Seamus Narcy. Been around a long time. Fair to say, time has not been kind to him. He has the look of a mountain coastal landslide down south in Italy, just everything crumbling and falling away into a sea of flab and fat. Bloat would be a kind word here. Look at him from the side and you get a forty-five degree angle running north to south. He does not like me which suits me just fine. He wouldn't like me worth a damn from the get-go, but his lawyer has tossed a lot of coal in his boiler and really jacked up his enmity about me. He is a snarky guy, long divorced—heard that was an ugly one—sloppy with plenty of money being wrestled over, has that hard look of basic mean, malevolence about him like an aura. He was competent long ago, so I have heard, but his gaffes here are so many and so blatant, it looks to me like he's lost a foot at least on his fastball. I don't like him either but my disdain is objective, evaluative, and from afar. I am of the belief that when all is said and done, he will have become an unwilling asset for us. And since he knows I don't like him worth a damn, his sneers and knife-thrown looks grow greater and more pronounced and it amplifies his distractions.

"He's got a creepy assistant, Robert Pirright, a Man Friday type who is not a named defendant who goes by R.P., but we call the "The Abacus." Apparently handles the good doctor's affairs, money and so forth, and Dr. Narcy demanded of his lawyer that R. P. to attend all discovery, depositions, motions, and hearings. We don't think assigned defense counsel was all that crazy about that condition but we didn't oppose—which we easily could have—because it's a weird relationship, sort of a mini-me deal and they just look at each other all the time, nod and affirm one another with shared sneers and signals and glances. We think it's a plus for us when trial time comes. He is represented by a perpetually angry guy, a big guy who also hates my guts, named Don Richardson. Interesting component there.

"Why do these folks dislike you so much? I can understand the unpleasantness of getting sued but this sounds more personal." Cas was curious.

"Fair question. And accurate too I think. Don Richardson, whom Kermit and I have named The Prince of Darkness is an unhappy, black and bleak heart guy to begin with, is used to getting his way, is a bully and is used to pushing people around to good effect. Has been doing it for years. He's senior partner in his firm so wears his power and influence like a Roman toga. The quintessential attack dog. Kermit is cool and is not the kind of guy Don's going to go after. Don knows Kermit would flick him away like a flea and that would be embarrassing, if not downright humiliating, for old Don. Remember, he's a bully and bullies always worry about getting put down. So here I am, the younger guy who he doesn't know much about and he figures he can steamroll me. Wrong. Too bad, fatso. I'm taking Narcy's deposition and Don doesn't like the way I'm asking questions—I'm boring in on Narcy good and hard with it—and Don starts hollering and raising sand and saying he's going to stop the deposition and this is all highly improper—which by the way, it's all just as proper as can be—and he figures I'll back off and take the sharp off my spear, but not a chance.

"Kermit's sitting over there cool, calm and collected with a little amused smile on his face as I tell Don, 'No, now you be quiet and only object as you are allowed to by our rules. And nothing more. It's you who are intentionally misbehaving. See. Look over there. See that telephone? Feel free to call the judge and we'll get our court reporter here and we can all go over there and he can hear the read backs and rule on my conduct and yours too. And then you can stroke me a nice, fat check after the Court tells you that you are way out of line. And you'll get a not very subtle dressing down so bring your client and your serf too. I expect they'll enjoy the show. And you know right now that you are the one out of line and just because I ask hard questions of your client does not mean I am out of bounds and you know it. So. We're waiting. Go on and write a check your mouth can't cash. Go ahead and make your call.'

"And we sat and waited and Don wiggled about in his chair to point where the poor chair creaked and strained under his less than svelte physique and Don was sweating and mumbling to himself and then said with a staged disdain, 'Just go ahead but watch yourself. You just better watch yourself.'

"'Thank you, Don. I believe I will.'" And I went right back to drilling holes in the good doctor. Don had been caught, jumped and called out in front of his client and it shamed him and chastened him, all in front of his client and hod carrier. You know how you can sense when someone doesn't like you. Well, he never liked me from the beginning of the case. And once all that happened in those few minutes, he grew to black heart hate me and his defendant surgeon just followed Don's lead. So there you go."

Cas said, "Gee, I wish I'd been there. That's exciting stuff."

Patty chuckled and looked at Polly and Mikey. "Us too. We could have sold popcorn."

"Okay, back to it. There is also a neonatologist, a lady named Marina Ostroff. Dr. Ostroff along with Dr. Narcy followed Cameron throughout his course. She's a little bitty lady, nice but talks all the time. Constantly nervous like a sparrow with a cat coming up the tree. She's represented by a nice fellow named Donnie Cleveland, laughs a lot, lots of time inappropriately, pleasant enough, nothing like Don Richardson but is also Richardson's parrot or his Senor Wences hand puppet in the box. When Richardson speaks, Cleveland almost follows on every time with the 'Salright' chorus.

"And there is Holy Cross Hospital's in-house pediatric radiologist and head of neonatal nursing, Dr. Andy Petser and R.N. Frances Williams. Both seem nice enough. Petser is pretty much the stereotype for a pediatric radiologist; no need to develop people skills—he deals with pictures, not people—and so he has none. He's pretty much a flat plate. And Nurse Williams has a nice way about her but seems to be in this situation a bit of a nervous Nellie. It's obvious that what happened here bothers her greatly. It was on her watch and it troubles her.

"Petser and Williams are represented by one of those IKE kind of guys— you know, 'I Know Everything.' Guy loves to make pronouncements that just hang in the air with no meat on the bone. Has lots and lots of hair just slathered in product which is sculpted and styled and swept back into a good-sized dove tail shag. Tells me a lot. He just might have more hair than ego and he's got a ton of ego...if you get my drift. Guy's name is Fabian Fahtly. I've named him The Fart. He's the closest thing to Foghorn Leghorn I've seen in a long time."

They all had a good laugh. It helped.

"I think that the three defense lawyers along with Narcy and The Abacus have created a five-headed hydra and they all feed off of one another and have failed to recognize that ever-enlarging, malign problem. Now let's also remember we like what we've got so far but this is no time to get cocky or take it personal. We need to play the golf course and not the golfers. We need to avoid the distractions of their toxins. This is no slam dunk. They have three pretty stout experts, with nice, big-time credentials who say this is just one of these unfortunate things, that no one did anything wrong, that this poor little fellow was damaged goods from the beginning, et cetera, et cetera, and the public is generally, more often than not, doctor friendly. And there is so much plaintiff lawyer advertising on television and billboards out there and so much of it is just cheesy and tasteless and bombastic so that doesn't help out at all with public attitudes either."

Polly quizzed, "Well, it's obvious that you have some pretty strong feelings and observations about the defense lawyers. How do you think they feel about you? Not about the 'dislike'—about your ability to effectively try the case?"

"Well, they know Kermit is courtroom and polymath brilliant, but I think they also know that Kermit has not tried a malpractice case here in North Carolina before so to them, that's a big edge to their side of it. That doesn't trouble me at all. Kermit, more than any lawyer I have ever encountered, has the gift of simplification and identifying with the core issues. He is one of the most elegantly and effectively articulate trial lawyers I have ever had the pleasure of knowing and seeing in action. If words are tools, then he is Michelangelo with his hammers and chisels. He doesn't get hung up on jargon or chasing rabbits down trails. He just gets to the nub of it and then doesn't let go. And he has studied and studied on this and knows it cold.

"And me? They just think I'm a cocky asshole. I smile too much, crack too many jokes, laugh too much, goof around too much, and do not take their bullshit. I push back and call them out. It clearly annoys them. They know I've been around but they discount me because they think I'm at best a guy that has always just picked the low-hanging fruit and this is, of course, the big leagues. Doesn't bother me a bit. I think we've already gotten under their skin and will burrow under lots further before the day is done. It helps I didn't much pay attention in law school. I just wing it the way normal folks would in a good, bare knuckle argument. Hell, I'm not getting younger and have plowed many fields along the way. They can't see my forest for their trees. Suits me. Fuck 'em!"

Eddie laughed. He was revving up.

"Now, let's wrap this up so y'all can get to work with Cas and files and such. But let me tell you about our trial judge now. His name is Bill Traxler and he's one of the best around. Davidson guy. Smart, perceptive, even-handed, firm with a fine sense of proportion and a terrific, subtle sense of humor. Never too heavy-handed. He does not dither around when making decisions. He knows the law. This is a day certain setting with a fairly estimated trial time of about two weeks, give or take, before jury deliberations and we got lucky and he got assigned to us. If you show up prepared and ready to go, he's golden. He does not suffer, if you will, foolishness lightly. We are real happy to have him as our ringmaster.

"Lastly, the defense and the insurance carriers have made it crystal clear that they are not going to pay any money here. They will not even offer a token sum and in one way that's bad because our clients are worried and intimidated and more than a little scared about going to trial and would really just like to receive some small tribute and then they would be acknowledged and in their minds validated but it's way too late for that.

"Kermit and I have already advanced costs and expenses for expert witness fees and travel and court reporters and depositions and medical illustrations, and the like, close to six figures and by the time we try this, it would not surprise me to see that number double. Our clients are aware of that, respect that and understand the full game is going to have to be played. Honestly, it helps us for we have no choices to make. We're obviously not going to drop or dismiss the case now. We are going to try this thing and give it our best and we will just see what happens. The other side does not respect us now. But by the time this is over, I swear they damn sure will. So, kids, for now, that's all I got." Eddie leaned back in his chair, a bit wearied by the lengthy presentation but he enjoyed it too as it helped bring a big picture of the case into a tighter lane.

There was a sense of necessary grimness that lay about the table. It was inevitable. A very sad story. A lot at risk. A lot of loss. A very uncertain outcome. The building blocks of worry lay all about them.

Patty pulled a cigarette out of her pack, put it behind her ear and put her lighter on the table in front of her. She shook and rustled her notes to change the mood from concern to determination.

"Now listen here. We have got an awful lot to do still but the good news is we have the time and we will get this thing put together. As far as getting our witnesses to trial, I will coordinate with Eddie and Kermit. Gotta get 'em to the church on time. We will house whoever needs to be housed at Graylyn over across from Reynolda, and Eddie's Old Town Club is just across the way for feeding times. All will be comfortable.

"Most all the depositions have been taken but they needed to be broken down and summarized and then shared for review and comment. Their people, our people, their experts, our experts. Pretrial motions. motions in limine, exhibits lined up and marked and shared with the other side. A good, solid pretrial brief and an accompanying supplemental medical brief. Thinking out loud here. Medical illustrations, radiographic films, view boxes.

"Cas, how about I give you a couple of older, only slightly used pretrial briefs, law and medicine and y'all read 'em over and start putting something together? And Eddie, I know you've got some strong ideas about how we are going to show the Court and jury how the symptoms, the red flags piled up for so long."

"True." Eddie nodded.

"So, let's get to it. Battle stations, everyone."

Eddie headed to his office for his sequester. The rest stayed where they were and began to arrange stacks of files for review and evaluation.

Cas kept shaking her head and mumbled to no one in particular, "Law school and moot court were interesting and even fun and all but praise baby Jesus, this is heavy lifting and the Super Bowl, all playing out in suits and dresses! This is some wild..." She paused, halted with the phrase on her lips frozen.

Patty laughed and lit one up. "Go ahead, Cas. Say it. It's good for your head, I promise."

"...some wild ass shit."

"Attagirl! You're in."

And so with the recent pieces all now in place, it had started anew. Eddie was pleased. They all were.

CHAPTER TWENTY-NINE

WAR STORIES AND BASIC TRAINING

Present Day

EDDIE CALLED KERMIT. As with each call, their dialogue began with the usual.

"Mr. Terrell, what state are you in today?"

"Why, Mr. King, as you well know, I am always in the state of constant confusion."

"Is it remediable?"

"Hopelessly not."

"Then let us nonetheless proceed."

And they did as always discuss and parse and think about their case.

Kermit was a creature from another time. In his mid-eighties, sometimes it seemed he may well have been from another solar system. He was unique. Born and raised in tiny Cameron, South Carolina, he as a young boy began going to the courthouse in Orangeburg County with his uncle, who was a general practice lawyer, riding over in a mule-drawn buckboard. He liked to sit in the front row of the balcony, often the only Caucasian in the crowd up there. He explained that by looking down at it all, he could get a more total feel for the cases and the players. He was obviously both precocious and a sponge and he observed diligently and with analytical thinking.

After college at the University of South Carolina, where he was a debate champion—oh, and he learned shorthand to make note-taking more efficient plus those precise notes were often sold to other students, thus helping pay his academic way, he went into the army, became chief assistant to the base commander at Fort Jackson and developed profoundly effective clerical and organizational skills to a degree that his superior would not allow him to be shipped off to Korea. After that came law school where he excelled and then out into the real world. It is still to this day said as was spoken by the great Alabama football coach Bear Bryant, "He could take his'un and beat your'un and he could also take you're and beat his'un."

Later, as the scope and substance of his practice expanded and expanded some more, it was also regularly acknowledged that he "...knew where all the bodies are buried."

One late night many years later, Eddie and Kermit were sitting on a worn out and ragged Naugahyde bench, their backs to a cinder block wall in front of a still empty gate in the barren, dinky Columbia airport. This place was not Destination A by any means. They were working one of their first cases together and still didn't know one another well. They were waiting for an expert witness coming in from Atlanta whose flight had been held by a lengthy weather delay. Eddie and Kermit had grown to really like and enjoy one another but Eddie was often more than a little intimidated by him. Kermit was just so damn smart and Eddie did not want to be clumsy and fumble the brain ball when with him.

They sat in silence. Then, Eddie made small talk. "Kermit, when did you decide to become a lawyer?"

A low, flat tenor murmur eased out of Kermit's throat which he then cleared and he spoke to the question. "Eddie, long ago when I was but a very young child, I learned two things. One was that I was going to be a lawyer and the other was that I was always going to be very thin."

He told Eddie the riding to the courthouse story and *too* there was no doubt as well that Kermit, trim as a yardstick with never a hair out of place, was always going to be thin; Eddie had always watched in amused amazement when, at a working lunch or dinner, and even in the midst of a nerve-wracking, gut wrenching trial Kermit would elegantly and at an always restful pace ingest prodigious quantities of food. No course would elude him. Dessert was always de rigueur. Starches and butter and creams and biscuits were his friends. He was no trencherman; he was a gourmand.

And while certainly not in case prep or court time, only the best champagne and vodka would do.

Eddie grew to absolutely love him. And Kermit grew to love Eddie too. Their differences played into their mutual strengths. They played off each other and then with each other. They were the equivalent of lawyer jazz. They riffed and held the bass line, could improvise while sticking to the script and could rise and fall in rhythm and in off beat too.

One day they were in a very intense second round of mediation involving the horrible murder of their client's son at the hands of some gangbangers in a poorly supervised and secured night club. There were four sets of lawyers arrayed against them. Three of those lawyers were good guys, understood risk and reward, were smart and savvy and had good senses of humor; the fourth was a pinched nose, pernicious, self-satisfied, self-important fellow—in other words, an above-it-all asshole.

The mediation was approaching its conclusion. They were getting close. The mediator, the magnificent Bob Irwin, had nudged and cajoled and wiggled and knitted the adversaries into the bell lap. Irwin came to Kermit and Eddie, filled them in as to where things stood, made them acknowledge they were very close and then asked, more in command than in question, "Don't you think one more hundred will do it?"

Eddie and Kermit huddled with the parents and responded in the affirmative and Bob Irwin was out the door to seal the deal.

A little longer than was initially anticipated, Irwin returned, laughing and shaking his head.

"Well, we've got a deal but I gotta tell you…listen to this mess. I tell them all we need to wrap this up for another twenty-five Gs from each carrier. The three good guys—you know who they are—quickly jump in. The jerk—you know who he is too—what a pain in the ass!—sticks his nose up in the air and says, 'No way. Nothing more from me. I've exhausted, against my better judgment by the way, my authority and we're not putting another penny in. That's it. I'm done. If y'all want to make up the last twenty-five between yourselves, have at it.' And then he sat down, looked away from all of them and pretended to be no longer present.

"There was an aggravated silence and then the great Bob Brown started yelling at Smarty Pants. Now, please forgive my French but this is close to verbatim. Went like this.

"'Listen, asshole. You are going to pay in your last twenty-five. Don't you understand? Kermit King is the smartest lawyer in the building and Eddie Terrell is the craziest. There is no telling how badly Kermit is going to cut our nuts off in court and there is no telling what Eddie will do with our balls once Kermit castrates us. We don't need that shit. We need to finish this up now and get the fuck on out of here. "'Now cough your twenty-five up, and I mean now, or two things are going to happen and quick too. One, the word is going to go out from all of us across the state as to what a completely unreliable turd you are—and you know, your rep ain't exactly stellar to begin with—and two, I'm going to count to three and if I get to three, I'm going to come over there and jerk your cheap ass in a knot. So, one, two...'"

He folded. Everyone shared in the pain of the give.

Kermit beamed at the description given him. Eddie wondered if he could get it on his tombstone. In their sadness, the parents were pleased and relieved.

So Eddie and Kermit kept moving forward, getting the Cameron case ready to go. And the rest of their world of tort and tension kept moving forward too.

In the back of the office, Alph and Cas settled in as Alph dialed up an adjuster on a minor car wreck case and then next would go hunting another friendly lawyer on the other side of a nice sized whale.

"Hey, Mr. McKinney. Alph Baron here, calling about the Newell car wreck case. Got you on speaker so I can shuffle away while we talk a little."

"Hey, Mr. Baron. Let me pull that file."

The adjuster, after a few minutes of desultory conversation, asked, "Jesus, Mr. Baron, let's not go round and round here on this ten cents worth of nothing. I got a stack of these on my desk as long as my arm and I'd like to close a lot of them out and I bet you wouldn't mind picking up some nice go-to-the-beach this weekend money. Are you with me?"

Alph laughed appreciatively. "You know, Mr. McKinney, I just might be so inclined but please...none of that ten cents stuff; I know you don't mean to demean the honor of my client's claim."

"That, sir, was never meant to be so. Please pardon my indescretion. That was just meant to be shop talk between the two of us."

"Oh, hell, McKinney, I was just gigging you. You and I both know this is just drying mortar between many bigger bricks of disaster. Now, let's see.

My demand was for seventeen five hundred. Your open, made many, many weeks ago, was six thousand. Now where shall we go?"

McKinney spoke in sotto voce, as though he had his hand secretly over the phone. "Look, I really want to go to lunch now and I need badly to take a leak sooner rather later, if you get my drift so how about this...?"

Cas grimaced and grinned in amused unison.

"How about you reduce your demand to fourteen thousand and I'll come up to nine thousand? That's it for this day. Gotta show them I'm working the file, always working the file. Always fending you prick P.I. lawyers off, defending Nationwide's money. But, if you call me next week, no make that in about two weeks, I think we can get it done for eleven thousand dollars, after I have worn your greedy ass down some more." McKinney chuckled.

"Indeed I do and I appreciate the rough and tumble of it. I really do. Now, I think the courtesy of the impending big finish here calls for only another five hundred to go on top of that 11 and then I'll gladly relent."

A pause. "Oh what the hell. Done. Deal?"

"Deal done. Box checked. Thank you, Mr. McKinney. I'll call in a couple of weeks."

"Look forward to it."

And as they were unhooking, Alph and Cas heard McKinney grumble, "What a damn money dance of predictable shit..." and the line went silent. Alph held his "Shhh" finger to his lips just to be on the safe side. Cas paid attention.

"Alph, so that's how you do it, huh?"

"Well, close enough. Small talk. Polite courtesies, patience. Build relationships with good manners, good humor. You have to let the dough rise slowly. You rarely get anywhere trying to rush the process. And always remember, a pig gets fat but a hog gets slaughtered. Don't overreach and always have some give room. Before you make your initial demand, make sure you have fairly and reasonably evaluated your case.

"Very soon, you will be handed files like this and you will be making calls like this. Do not use that special times three or four multiplier. One size does not fit all. Come up with a figure and kick it around before sending the demand letter. Discuss it with us. That's why we are here. We teach each other. We are here to help.

"And remember to keep yourself out there, cultivating the garden, bringing the cases in. We need to have plenty of decent, smaller ones. Not piddling but decent. We ain't gonna win no war with nothing but big battleships. You'll get the hang of it soon enough, I promise. So what do you think?"

"Real life is more interesting than a classroom, that's for sure!" Her enthusiasm was obvious. She smiled thoughtfully.

"Okay, let's make another call. This is a larger value case. It has already been filed and the liability carrier has assigned it to one of their regular retainers, a fine fellow and fine lawyer, Bobby Elston. You'll get the gist of it as we talk along the way."

"Hey, Bobby. It's Alph Barron. Hope you and yours have been well."

"Hey, Alph. Nice to hear from you. So far so good with one and all. So, what shall we talk about today? If my memory serves me correctly, you have the moderately banged up lady with the Country Squire station wagon with the fake wood siding that got tangled up with the city bus on your mind...?"

"What a memory, Bobby! Impressive! Yes, Mrs. Flately. That's right. I'm hoping we can move along on this one and get it finished up sooner rather than later."

"Hang on. Let me pull my cover sheet. Hmmmm."

Papers rustled. Alph waited.

"Alph, the answer to your thoughtful entreaty is yes and no. Yes, we eventually can but no, not right now. Your demand is reasonable and is a number we can work with as we go along. Your client checks out clean as a whistle. Nice lady by the way and there is, just between you and me, no question as to our liability. But..."

"Bobby, I appreciate all that but what's the 'but' here?"

"Alph, as you well know, timing is everything and by my count, there are, between treating physicians and a couple of other related fact witnesses, about five or six more depositions I need to thoroughly work the file up in order to make my value recommendation to the carrier. By my rough estimate, and I know you know this drill very, very well, that's twelve to oh, maybe sixteen billable hours to my credit. You remember those days, don't you? Sure you do."

"Oh, man, of course, yes, I do."

"Please remember I am chained to these insurance companies and chained to my time slip binder and desk. With over twenty-plus paper pushers over here, I still have to hustle. And you know, I've got to produce at least fifteen hundred billable hours a year and if I don't, I am as expendable as crummy leftovers in the back of the fridge. Thus I must, on this one, press on a bit longer. I hope you understand."

Bobby was apologetically soothing.

"I understand and I appreciate where you're coming from. I'm being prodded by our legal assistants to roll some more balls and Mrs. Flately's file is among a number that have been handed to me to do something with. So I promise to be patient and not nag and will sit through these upcoming depositions and think of this one as a nice annuity accruing on down the line. And come to think of it, we have a fine new lawyer who has just joined us and she'll be able to sit in and learn a bit."

Alph winked at Cas.

"Good analogy. I like it. I know you've enjoyed being over there with Eddie. Please tell him I send my best. I'll tell you what...get your folks to get up with my Debbie over here and let's get these depos scheduled over the next ninety days and I'll have authority to work with you soon thereafter. We, you and I, will then get it resolved. I promise I will not push us into a delaying expensive mediation when we know what needs to be done here. Your demand is a fair chunk above two hundred grand. That's not horrible. I promise we will get this one done the old fashioned way, lawyer to lawyer."

"Bobby, that sounds fine to me. Thank you. And I needed that pleasant tutorial from you. Got a little ahead of myself."

"No problem. So, now, just between us girls, moving on to more sala-cious matters and speaking of whales, some scuttlebutt on the street is that you're getting ready to give battle next door over in Guilford in a slam-bam-thank-you-ma'am heavy duty med mal with Dapper Don Richardson and Chirpy Donnie Cleveland on the other side. That close?"

Trial lawyers loved to bullshit and fish one another all the time. It was there webbing, their netting. One never knew when one might pick up a useful or piece of hot information, plus it was fun and always expanded one's worldview.

Alph chuckled. "Yeah, that might just be so...what else does the scut-tlebutt say?"

"Well, that Don and Ronnie think y'all are riding a stone cold loser and that y'all are in too deep. And that you've made a pretty tactical error by bringing in an outside lawyer from South Carolina, fellow named King, who has little experience with this type of complex litigation...death of a little kid, right?"

"Yeah, an infant actually, an identical twin...and isn't that all pretty interesting?" Alph mused, then paused. "Bobby, let me make you a little deal. How about this? If you'll tell me where that scuttlebutt came from, I'll give you the story from our point of view and will ask you to quietly seed a few clouds for me. First, let me ask you this...Don't you think Don Richardson is pretty much the biggest, bullying, pompous ass in these parts?"

"No doubt. No doubt at all. Now, where we going here?"

"Hang on. Do you know Dr. Seamus Narcy? He's a pediatric surgeon over in Greensboro."

"Yeah. A little bit."

"Thoughts on him?"

"He's a pretty frosty guy. We repped him years ago. Thinks his shit does not stink. I don't remember the details but we helped him walk. I didn't do the work. One of our partners over here did. Steve Galetti. Interesting, at least to me, Steve gets along fine with both Richardson and Narcy. The scuttlebutt came from Steve. Now tell me your story."

Alph laid it all out. Trial lawyers like all the details. And then Alph added a finish-it-off piece.

"Bobby, how about do this for me? When you can, go tell Steve Galetti that Eddie thinks Richardson and Narcy are complete and total assholes and I know they don't like Eddie worth a damn and he doesn't like them either. Tell him that Eddie and Kermit King are hot to whip their snotty, cheap bastard asses. How about lay it on thick as cement...? We want them to see dead red whenever they see them or hear either of them speak. You get my drift? We'd really appreciate it."

"Oh, yeah. I'll do it. You want me to help mind fuck them, right? Get them distracted, keep them chasing the case and your guys too. And that's two different roads to run down too. I like it. Sure I'll do it. We already agree that fat Don is a turd and Narcy is a jerk of an egomaniac. Happy to play Mata Hari in this approaching drama but when it's all over and done, you're buying."

"Deal. Thanks, Bobby. I'll get lined up with you on this other matter and help make the wheels turn and the hours burn. I promise."

And off they went.

Alph was serene and sat quietly for a few minutes. He then said to Cas, "Now listen, please. You are not to tell anybody in this office working on that case about that bit of conversation I just had with Bobby. There is no need for our side of the good guys to be aware of the venom we've just planted. Understand?"

"Yes. I understand. I promise. Do you think it will work?"

"Well, my dear girl, probably it will. Bullies and better-thans usually take the bait and that's what I'm counting on. Plus, the good Judge Traxler didn't fall off the turnip truck yesterday and he'll take notice and I expect the jury will as well. And we'll be over there watching. It will be a fine tutorial for you and for all of us as well. In this business, if you're going to be worth a damn, you have to keep watching and listening and learning. You can and must never stop."

Cas nodded her understanding and thought to herself, *Good God! What a wild ride this is going to be.*

And thus did Alph take their young star under his avuncular wing.

CHAPTER THIRTY

D-DAY MINUS ONE

A Few More Weeks Later...

A S THE LAST few weeks went by, they all worked hard and smart on Cameron and the case began to coalesce tightly. It was as though an inevitable infection had swept over them. Patty and Alph and Eddie knew it to be so. Polly observed it was like making good boiled custard; you just had to keep stirring and paying attention.

As the time for trial grew closer, more and more of the collective office's focus and energy was devoted to it. It was as inevitable as a rock rolling down a hill. All the other rocks simply had to get out of the way. The physics of momentum had taken the wheel.

Cas's tutorials with Alph on basic torts, auto, and slip and fall and the like, were speed shifted to reading and marking and commenting on various Cameron depositions, a review of all pertinent Rules of Evidence, an assembly of on-point cases and the juggling of please do this and please do that. She was being branded with the sear of heat and fire of heavy litigation. There was much discussion about every facet of the case—much of if this, then what—if that, then what.

Both a regular, as required by the Rules of Civil Procedure, pretrial brief and an extensive and well-illustrated supplemental medical brief were prepared. They wanted to get them to the Court with enough time to allow them to be read and studied and appreciated. In truth, they hoped they would be admired and silently applauded. This sort of striving scored positive points with the referee, well beyond the perfunctory hand-ups which Eddie and company knew would be the rote, just another day at the office, defense pitch.

It was the same process as distilling. Get your crushed corn and malted barley, water and bread yeast together (your law and facts and rules and exhibits and jury instructions and God knows whatever everything else might be needed) and heat them all up and chill it all down and pour it back and forth and breathe the air of more and more thought into it, and then the bubbles and useless particulate will work themselves out. Everything goes down into a big funnel into a master container, and goes round and round and round, and then it all settles down and then it sits and rests for a couple of days—and this was intentional; the case is "off limits" to talking—only more quiet thinking applied to it and then, after all that, there was step-by-step review and the application of algorithms and then there was their good case to try.

Eddie decided in a good "what the hell" moment that they would all go to Greensboro to be together and help one another and to give the Andrews family some moral support. And too, it would help counterbalance whomever the defense would be bringing in, other doctors and nurses, folks who might "know" jurors or who just might have a "influence."

So Eddie called his old friends Rise and Kenny and Curt and asked them to tend to the office and mail and calls for the days of the trial, which they figured would go well into a second week. They could watch television and order out for food and drink, have reliable friends over to play some cards or chess and checkers, do whatever and spell and rotate with one another as need be. They were all eminently reliable and neat as could be. They were pleased to be asked and thus that cover was in place. Eddie told them each a little about the case and asked them to meet with him at the office at eight o'clock Monday morning so he could hand off a few sets of keys.

Rise giggled and said it felt like old times. Curt, recalling the excitement of those "old times," asked more rhetorically than not, surely there's some bigger action in here somewhere. Eddie told each of them that they were hunting serious big game, had just one bullet in their gun and that this was a kill or be killed deal. Second chances had taken the 605 to Cleveland.

There was murmured approval all around. Eddie was getting older but he still carried his slash like a street man.

All supplies were rounded up and put into good-sized toolboxes. This included aspirin, cough medicine, tissues and screwdrivers, extra pens, pencils, Sharpies, clips of all sizes, duct tape, staplers, Scotch tape, Wite-Out, scissors, rulers and legal pads by the score. And too were the large sized 3M adhesive backed strip pads carefully stacked for transport. Patty had helped Eddie create these. They would be important pieces of ammunition when the shooting started.

And just days before trial was to start, it was all ready to go. The briefs and exhibit lists and proposed jury instructions were delivered to the Court and to opposing counsel. The up-to-date lists of prospective jurors were checked over and scored for "accept," "reject," and "maybe" with the accompanying notations soothsayers, fortune tellers, and Ouija board hopefuls. Many of the other in-office cases were checked to make sure they could hang fire for a few weeks and here and there, calls were made to explain to clients and opposing counsel what was going on.

Kermit arrived on Saturday afternoon and they all spent Sunday at the office going over everything. As the sun rolled off to the west, Kermit, as was his practice and habit, steepled his long fingers thoughtfully beneath his chin, smiled and pronounced he was pleased and felt all should be too. They had also met with their clients earlier to buck them up and make sure they knew to be where and when and to offer the assurances of all-out effort. The clients went home and the rest went to a quiet dinner at Old Town Club that Sunday evening. Afterwards, Kermit was comfortably ensconced at Graylyn. Everyone else went their separate ways to rest and prepare for the long slog beginning the coming morning.

As Eddie and Mikey prepared to turn out their lights, she looked at him quizzically with a tilt to her head.

"You, okay? A little quiet you are. I know this is a big one. You all have prepared beautifully and thoroughly. Are you worried? Maybe, just a little?" She walked around the bed and embraced him and kissed his forehead. "I love you. You know that for sure, don't you?"

Eddie returned her sweet embrace and kiss and sighed, "Yes, I know that. Thank you so much. I love you back. I surely do. And yeah, I'm a little worried just like always but maybe a little more. It's a big case. Jesus, I've been at this a long, long time now. Just hope we've got enough gas in our tank...hell, just hope I've got enough gas in my tank."

"You do, honey. I'm sure you do."

Eddie let her go, sat down on his side of the bed and looked thoughtfully at the floor. "Well, I believe you are right and so let's go prove it tomorrow. Come on, honey. How about you go turn off that light and come over here and find me in the dark? It's almost showtime."

Mikey cooed, "What do you mean 'almost?'" And her satins and her scent slid effortlessly across their sheets.

And in a click, the room was black and they folded into mutual alliance and tightly sealed their borders.

CHAPTER THIRTY-ONE

BATTLE JOINED
Present Day

MONDAY MORNING WAS the beginning of a bright, sunny day. The weather outlook for the next couple of weeks bode well for more of the same. It was ironic. All this nice, lovely weather, the coming on of spring and yet, like moles, Team Terrell was headed into a windowless underground labyrinth of courtrooms and back hallways and meeting rooms and judge's chambers and the bleak, plastic snack room run by the cheerful Association For The Blind.

The modern day wagon train caravan was packed up and assembled in the office parking lot. They all took their own cars so folks could come and go as needed. Cas rode with Alph. The tutorings were ongoing and Cas was learning on the fly. Rise and Curt and Kenny were given keys and a thousand in cash for food and incidentals. Eddie told them no matter how things turned out over in Gate City, he'd take care of each of them in full once it was all over.

They drove the twenty-plus miles to the Guilford County courthouse. These were mostly thoughtful rides save for silences being punctuated by Johnny One Note Case questions and answers and musings. The case was now, as it had been for a good while, paramount and all invested and consuming.

They wheeled into the parking deck, slotting side by side near the freight elevator. A G.C. sheriff's deputy working lot security helped them round up pushcarts and they loaded their trial boxes and bags and easels and exhibits up and went up to the 5th floor to Courtroom 5A.

They settled in. Everyone necessary and pertinent to the proceedings was already there or coming flurried in save for Judge Traxler. There was much unloading and organizing and settling down and settling in. Defense counsel and their doctor and hospital defendants did not so much as offer a mere nod of acknowledgement, much less a cursory greeting.

It was obvious, as it had been for a long time, that enmity and hostility had infected the defense team. Eddie and Kermit were delighted. They hoped to build on it, exacerbate it, accelerate it and turn it into a slow scorch and burn wild fire. In the meantime, Eddie's crowd were going to conduct themselves as the poster children for Miss Manners and Emily Post. The contrast would prove helpful.

Things quieted down. All the lawyers had their trial notebooks at the ready and their pads and pens lined up neatly. The staffs and random spectators waited. The lawyers just stared straight ahead. (There were always curious railbirds in courtrooms; they had a solid sixth sense as to the potential for a big one and would confirm their suspicions by asking a bailiff, a) what kind of trial was it going to be and b) how long was it estimated to take. Of course, here the tantalizing answer was a) medical malpractice/wrongful death and b) ten days +/−. Reality TV has always been with us it seems.)

At 10 a.m. sharp, the bailiff called, "All rise!" Judge Traxler, affable by nature, took his seat in his big bench chair, said, "Good morning, all," and instructed counsel to approach and gather.

Eddie cheerfully and briefly introduced his team including Mr. Kermit King from Columbia, South Carolina who had been signed off earlier pro hac vice by Judge Bill Freeman.

Richardson and Cleveland did the same. They were unable to avoid the flat in their voices.

"Nice to see all of you. Nice to meet you, Mr. King. Thank you for joining us. Now, everyone ready to go?"

A unanimous "Yes, Your Honor" was spoken in chorus.

"Have there been any further settlement discussions?"

Don Richardson spoke tersely. "Your Honor, there haven't been any such discussions and there will be none going forward."

Traxler cocked an eyebrow. "Well, that's interesting. You sure about that, Don? You know, conditions and situations do change in trials of this scope and nature."

"Your Honor, we have been given our instructions. No settlement offers." His parrot companion nodded, a little too vigorously. Traxler noticed. These guys were on a tight, short leash. Their insurance company masters had clearly growled at them hard.

"Alright then. Fine. A fight to the finish it will be. I have some doubts about that prevailing wisdom here, but we are off the record and I am not allowed to inject myself into these proceedings and I promise I will not. So, let us proceed."

Fahtly cleared his throat. "Uh, Your Honor, may I note that my client is under no such, shall I say, constraints as indicated by these other defense counsel."

"So noted. Thank you for that information." Richardson and Cleveland frowned.

Eddie nodded and held his tongue. Kermit briefly, tightly smiled. Divide and conquer? And so they went to work.

A jury was selected, sworn, seated, and instructed.

Eddie Terrell was no fool. He was a very effective advocate, had been for years and was at his best when he bored in on a recalcitrant, evasive, deceitful or reluctant witness. He was, especially when his wheels were greased and limber, a smooth fighter, could punch and counter punch. He could play chess on six levels with witnesses, always swooping ahead of them or leaping from behind or besieging their flanks. He would find the weakness and he was feared. He was a fine shaper of points and arguments on the run and a superb cross examiner. And from time to time, Eddie would switch things up and shoot with a scatter gun, not a rifle, which often flushed the covey for more than just one good shot. Variety's spice of life kept things more fulsome.

So now was not Eddie's time. It was time for the calm, measured, precise laying out of the facts of the case against Narcy and Ostroff and Petser and Williams and the man for that job was the orator, the brilliant and masterfully complete and organized Kermit King. As best Eddie could tell, the only time Kermit winged it was when he flew to New York or Paris or Rome. And thus a few days before, Eddie, laughing appreciatively at his good sense, told Kermit that he needed to initiate the proceedings for the Andrews. Kermit, clearly amused and pleased, did not disagree. They had, long before, become a damn good team and here was one more piece of that mysterious puzzle of yin and yang.

Kermit gave the opening statement for the plaintiffs, beginning graciously with the introducing of everyone who was with them including Alph and Cas and all staff. He added a gloss, a little history for each one. He humanized. It was a classy and well-mannered beginning and the jury liked the opening soft touch. Kermit King was not just good; he was deeply engaging in the most Southern of ways. The team looked good, not wooden and mannequin-like. The defense crowd could not help their stern, stiff, stick-up-their-ass glower.

Those introductions also tossed that particular ball into the court of the defense who later might omit such introductions, leaving the jury to wonder "who those other folks were" or if so matched, would illustrate to the panel how there was going to be an effort by the defense to influence and muscle which almost always is found to be offensive.

Kermit introduced Mr. and Mrs. Andrews, simply and cleanly, and showed the jury one photograph of the newborn twins and one photograph of Cameron.

Then described a step-by-step forecast of how the trial would proceed and who the witnesses would probably be. He pointed out the thick, black notebooks of tabbed and indexed medical records, telling the jury of their substance and importance. He reviewed all of the pertinent anatomy, using an enlargement of a drawing that Eddie had made Dr. Narcy create during his deposition. (Kermit omitted the discomfitures and protestations of the defense when this elicitation occurred.) He described little Cameron's brief life in some good chronological detail but purposefully omitted much, saving those particulars and specifics for trial itself. This technique is called putting up the Christmas tree before it is decorated. He defined the legal definitions of negligence and medical malpractice and outlined what the plaintiff's allegations and accusations were as against the doctors and hospital. He then held up a large chart that read as follows in large cap lettering. He reviewed it with the jury.

ACKNOWLEDGED SIGNS AND SYMPTOMS OF RECURRENT TRACHEOESOPAGEAL FISTULA (TEF)

1) Choking/coughing during feeding;
2) Bradycardia (a slowing heart rate) when feeding;
3) Pulmonary infections and pneumonias (inflammatory conditions of the lungs) during and subsequent to feedings;
4) Respiratory distress—such as wheezing, gasping, rhonchi (secretions/obstructions in larger airways), rales (small clicking, bubbling or rattling sounds in the lungs);
5) Apnea (breathing stops and starts) and cyanosis (bluish discoloration of skin resulting from inadequate oxygenation);
6) Drooling while feeding;
7) Gagging and vomiting while or after feeding;
8) Wheezing;
9) Difficulty in swallowing during feeding;
10) Aspiration (the sucking of food particles or fluids into the lungs);
11) Abdominal distension (a very rounded, full stomach);

At the bottom of the chart, there were four categories of medical records pertinent to this case. They were listed as follows:

M.D.'s Progress Notes
Radiologic Findings/Barium Studies
Respiratory Therapist Notes
Nursing Progress Notes

Kermit assured the jury that all the information would be carefully reviewed with them.

He described the pertinent anatomy. He told them of the simple, initial discovery of Cameron's fistula. He told them that the baby had, after the initial repair, trouble feeding and he was not thriving as he should have been and he then told them straightforwardly and simply that little Cameron, for literally forty days and nights, suffered from these listed signs and symptoms of a recurrent TEF—that they were overlooked and/or ignored and/or misinterpreted by his attending physicians, these defendants, until the fistula, the opening widened from the pressure of yet another forced feeding, and collapsed during that feeding and he became immediately and manifestly and irretrievably brain damaged as his lungs were flooded with fluids and secretions and thus totally compromised. He told them Cameron could not recover from this massive insult and that he did not and he died eight months later. This never should have happened yet it did and the responsibility for this sad tragedy lies at the feet of this group of intelligent, educated, sophisticated doctors and medical people sitting at the defense table.

Kermit concluded, "Ladies and gentlemen of the jury—this is why we are here. And at the conclusion of the case, we will ask you to deliver monetary verdicts—for that is all the law allows in civil litigation matters such as these—in favor of John and Susan Andrews and on behalf of their brain damaged and now, sadly deceased little son Cameron. We greatly appreciate your participation and your attention. Thank you."

With a graceful, funeral solemnity, he walked slowly back to counsel table, shook hands with John Andrews, gently hugged Susan Andrews and sat down.

As Kermit settled quietly, Don Richardson immediately marched rapidly to the jury box, set his feet wide, tugged at his shirt collar, adjusted the knot in his tie and tried to settle himself. He was indeed a big man, a human monolith. He flipped through his yellow legal pad, glancing and glancing some more. It was a rushed and clumsy effort. He was in a hurry; hungry to refute and could not slow himself down. His words began to machine gun spray forth.

He began with a wave of his hand, "These lawyers..." fired out in a tone of too loud and angry. He caught himself and backpedaled. He paused, inhaled and started anew with the proper trial lawyer words of preface. "If it please the Court..." but his enmity towards Eddie and Kermit was already revealed. Judge Traxler watched and realized it.

His statement consisted of here is a coin, it has two sides as does this story and the harsh accusation here is that the doctors and this hospital killed this child. Richardson was grim.

Then he suddenly thundered there is no sympathy allowed in a courtroom and certainly not this one. He told them that basically Cameron was damaged goods from the beginning, that he had multiple birth defects. He told them that a fistula is nothing more than a little hole and that it was hard to find. He told them the doctors tried to look for it. He told them that once Cameron suddenly headed south, they worked desperately and heroically to help him revive and recover. He sourly reminded the jury that this case was about nothing but money and that's what these people and these lawyers are after. He told them to pay close attention, he thanked them for their service, he pounded back to counsel table, sat and glared straight ahead.

Narcy and Pirright looked well satisfied and their body language and expressions twinned one another. The others looked blankly concerned.

Donnie Cleveland rose to take his shot. He had always been the kinder of the defense pair and he tried to unsting Richardson's venom. He spoke with heartfelt sympathy as to what good doctors and good people their clients were. But again, he played Richardson's second fiddle and parrot. He could not help it. Richardson held tight sway over his head; Cleveland was intimidated by Richardson—and he soon wandered into an albeit softer recitation of what had just been presented. Cameron was damaged goods, we tried to save him, this was just about dollars. Remarkably, Cleveland even said that "loving attempts" were made to help this child. He repeated that the accusation that the defendants killed this child was grossly unfair and that they wanted a verdict that vindicated their people. He sat down.

Eddie and Kermit glanced quickly at each other and short-nodded and resumed their attention, taking exacting notes. They would later remind the jurors of these words that had just been spoken.

The hospital's lawyer, the overly plumed and coiffed and with an ego on steroids, Mr. Fabian Fahtly stood and addressed the jury from behind counsel table. His clothing was expensive. His watch was heavy gold and prominent. His shoes were lustrous. He adored the sound of his own voice.

He intoned with a dramatic nod, "May it please the Court. Again, I am Fabian Fahtly and I represent the hospital here and the interests of its employees, radiologist Petser and Nurse Williams. I will be brief."

Fahtly proceeded to blame pediatric surgeon and neonatologist Drs. Narcy and Ostroff for this disaster. They were the captains of this ship and primarily in charge of this patient. His people only carried out their orders and instructions.

And he emphasized that in any and all circumstances, the jury should not get carried away as they must keep in mind this was only an infant with no economic value whatsoever. And too, there was the surviving, identical twin and that surely now was of even greater value to his parents. And he unctuously thanked the jury with a slight bow and seated himself, unconsciously smoothing his suit front and too, was clueless as to his ill-mannered and tasteless remarks.

The judge then told all they would now be in a fifteen- to twenty-minute recess to give everyone time to prepare to present their evidence and direct and cross-examinations.

Eddie leaned close to Kermit. "Can you believe all that dogshit?"

"Yes, I can. I'm delighted and I expect you are too. Nice to see they do not have a unified defense. Let's put your tools together."

CHAPTER THIRTY-TWO

PLEASE, CLIMB IN MY BARRELL

In the Courtroom

NOW, IT WAS going to get interesting and quickly too.

Eddie, with the help of Patty and Mikey and Polly had created four large charts tightly lined and easy to see and read.

As the time period leading to Cameron's acute injury was an exact forty days, each poster was laid out in ten-day increments, from September sixth to October fifteenth. Beneath each date there were four blocks and along the left side margin were the four types of medical providers as listed in the chart that Kermit had shown the jury in his opening statement.

The five tall easels set up lined the long wall beside the jury box and could be seen by everyone in the courtroom. No obstructions. They looked like formidable, lean silver cranes awaiting their cargoes.

The jury returned and Judge Traxler called all to order. "Mr. Terrell. Mr. King. Please call your first witness."

Eddie Terrell stood. "Your Honor, we call the defendant Seamus Narcy to the stand."

"Alright. Doctor, come forward and be sworn."

Narcy looked hesitant but Richardson, with an obvious impatience, waved and nodded him forward. The walk down the short green mile had begun. Narcy had a surging sense of foreboding. The lawyers had worked with him and worked with him for hours and hours, drilling and testing him and challenging him and that had helped him feel confident only moments before. Now, that confidence was receding and evaporating with each step. The Abacus, sensing his master's discomfiture, looked on, stricken and frozen. The sword of Damocles hovered. Narcy went before the clerk, hesitantly put his right hand on the proffered Bible and slowly raised his left hand.

"Do you solemnly swear to tell the truth, the whole truth and nothing but the truth, so help you God?"

A nearly inaudible, "I do," slipped from Narcy's lips.

"Please be seated in the witness stand. State your full name for the record." Softly, it came.

Eddie briefly wondered if they had prepared Narcy for what was coming. He didn't care. He was just internally curious.

"Your Honor, I asked that the Court declare this witness, as allowed by our Rules of Civil Procedure and our Rules of Evidence, to be an adverse witness and as such, subject to my potentially leading questions and full examinations including cross-examination."

"It is so ruled. You may proceed."

"Good morning, Doctor. Your Honor, may I please approach the witness? We want him to have these fully tabbed and indexed and complete notebooks of medical records to refer to as we proceed. There are two notebooks which totally encompass the days of care and treatment in significant question. Long ago, Plaintiff and Defense counsel agreed to their thorough uniformity. We also have sets for the Court, and opposing counsel and individual defendants all have been provided the same. They have been earlier been marked and agreed upon as Exhibits 1 and 2. We ask that all follow along carefully as they wish. We want also to alert the Court and all others that this will be a long but steady and substantive process. And, please, may my assistant Miss Cherry stand by the easels to work with them as we go forward?"

"Yes, it appears so. Go ahead. Yes, she can. Proceed." Traxler knew the lengthy perp walk would start now. And so did Narcy and anyone else who was paying attention.

And proceed they did. Narcy was now in the barrel. The snare had been tripped.

CHAPTER THIRTY-THREE

A LITTLE FOOLISHNESS OFTEN NEVER HURTS

In the Courtroom

"DOCTOR NARCY, YOU are very familiar with Cameron's records that now are placed before you, correct?"

"Yes," stated Narcy.

"Over the course of time, how many reviews of them have you undertaken, both individually and with your lawyers?"

"Objection. Violative of our lawyer-client privilege," said Richardson.

"Overruled. Mr. Richardson, you well know that Mr. Terrell has not asked about your communications, only how many times the reviews took place. Proceed, Counsel."

"Well, many."

"How many? Your best estimate please."

"Oh, at least fifteen, maybe more."

"You have seen the large chart Mr. King presented in his opening remarks. Do you find it to be demonstrably accurate and complete?"

"Yes."

"Patty, please put the chart on the third easel, the one in the middle. Thank you. Doctor, do you now know and understand what you and I are about to begin doing?"

"Yes. I think so." Narcy was internally angry at all of these assholes and especially Terrell. He had been led to believe there would be some questions, maybe a lot, but this now looked like a very long slap and snap line.

"Good. If along the way, you feel you do not understand something, please let me know. We will start at the beginning, start in the records on September sixth. Are you there?"

Resignedly, Narcy nodded.

"A spoken answer, please; always a spoken answer, please."

"Yes, I'm there."

"Thank you. Now for September sixth, please review the physicians' notes, the radiologic findings, the respiratory therapy notes and the nurses' progress notes. In any of those four categories, are there recorded signs and symptoms of a potential recurrent TEF?"

"Yes, but not in the radiologic findings."

"So no film studies were done that day, correct? But there are known and acknowledged signs and symptoms of a potential recurrent TEF in the other three categories for that day, correct?"

"Yes."

"Patty, would you please take your red marker and color those three boxes in? Thank you."

And she did and for the next two full days, the records for each day were steadily examined and discussed and the number of boxes colored in grew to virtually fill the wall. The defense hated it. They could not object. Narcy was sullen and hated it too. But he knew he had to endure. Lawyers who have been around long enough understand that ass whippings do occur from time to time, but such occurrences were basically foreign to a fancy pants surgeon such as Narcy; it was beyond the realm of inconceivable and yet, here it was. It was beyond distasteful. Where in the hell had his immunity from such insults gone? For God's sake, he was used to being handed things.

There was nothing to object about. They were restless and frustrated, and they rustled about in their seats, a visual and constant virtual silent groaning before the jury. The Abacus, the strange Mr. Pirright at first looked straight ahead but then, he began to have facial tics and twitches and would look at Narcy imploringly and then turn away and then stare at the jury.

Narcy never really resisted or tried to spit the bit. He disliked Terrell with a fuming passion and that was clearly obvious but he moderated his voice and kept his responses in check. His face was too taught and strained. He was being pressed, squeezed, and it clearly did not agree with him.

Eddie treated Narcy as a ripe and tasty orange. And the juice flowed and could not be stopped. If Narcy had been bleeding, he would have been declared room temperature long ago.

The jury was attentive. They were not bored. They were engaged and interested.

Kermit and the rest of Team Terrell sat still and paid attention. Narcy was knotting his own rope and it was a big, long, thick one, a navy rope. And then came the first of many providential events. During a break in the middle of the second day of the record review, the Court took a brief recess. After a few minutes, Judge Traxler returned and with some abruptness, told all the lawyers that he wanted to see them in his chambers. He wanted the court reporter to come with her machine and he wanted the clerk to join them as well. There was some hard intensity in his voice.

When all were assembled and all were curious as to what this was all about, Judge Traxler told the court reporter to transcribe the meeting in its entirety and then asked the defense lawyers, "Who is this fellow sitting just behind you all? The odd-looking man, well to me anyway, with the facial tics? Is he one of your legal assistants?"

Don Richardson, with a reddening face, replied, "Your Honor, he's not a legal assistant. He's Dr. Narcy's assistant; his Man Friday if you will. He attends to Dr. Narcy's personal matters and affairs."

Traxler stared incredulously at Richardson for a moment and then held up a small slip of paper.

"Gentlemen, the foreman has sent me a note. It reads as follows. 'The man sitting behind the defense table is beginning to make ugly faces and they are directed at us. He does it when you are dealing with the trial. Can something please be done about this? It is making us all very uncomfortable. Thank you.' It is signed by the foreman on behalf of the entire jury." Mr. Richardson, what say you about this?"

Don Richardson looked at his shoes. "Your Honor. I had no idea. Obviously, my back is to him. I have not seen this. I will make him stop that immediately."

"No. No. That's not good enough. That's not satisfactory. He is not even in your employ. I thought he was one of your assistants. I'm amazed that you would think such a thing would be even remotely appropriate. He is not even affiliated with any officer of the Court and he should not be beyond the bar in the first place and now this. So, here's what's going to happen. Before I bring the jury back in and we continue, you are going to escort that man out of the courtroom and tell him he is not to return. Tell him he is to leave the building immediately. No, you walk him out. If that does not happen quickly and efficiently, I am going to hold him in contempt and punish him and of course banish him and, Don, I'm going to hold you in contempt too. Do I make myself clear?"

"Yes, Your Honor. I extend my apologies for this. I'm very sorry." Forced contrition had jacked a torpedo hard in below Richardson's water line. He was not used to being knocked about but he knew he had brought it on himself because of his complacency. He asked the judge in a small voice, "Before I follow your instructions to the letter, may I tell my client what's going on?"

"Yes, you can but be quick about it. Now, go on and do what I have instructed you to do. Now!" Traxler growled. "The rest of us will be at ease until Mr. Richardson returns without that man. Madame court reporter, madame clerk, did you all get all of that down?"

"Yes, Your Honor."

When Court resumed, the weird Abacus had disappeared for good and, of course, the jury and everyone in the courtroom knew something serious had happened, and the foreman and jury nodded and smiled gratefully at the judge while Dr. Narcy looked despondent as if his chair had been yanked out from under him. And Don Richardson began to have increasingly bad feelings about the proceedings.

Eddie looked at Kermit who simply and quietly said, "Well, that was just marvelous," and there was delight in his voice.

Court then resumed and the record review continued. The hits just kept coming. The signs and symptoms kept mounting up. About four o' clock, Eddie finished up with the terrible day of October fifteenth when all hell had broken loose and the child had been cast into eternal oblivion, and he paused and Dr. Narcy looked spent.

It had been a virtuoso beginning and all knew it. Eddie Terrell then handed Dr. Narcy a pad and a pencil.

"Doctor, would you agree with me that we have reviewed these records thoroughly and completely?"

Wearily, he nodded. "Yes, yes we have…" His voice tailed off.

"Would you agree with me that we have gone over forty days with four categories each for a total of one hundred sixty potential entries, potential opportunities, if you will, to see and study that which was there to be seen."

"Objection! Objection!" Richardson and Cleveland were on their feet. Fahtly did nothing.

"On what grounds, gentlemen?" Traxler asked.

Richardson complained, "We submit that the use of the word 'opportunities' is prejudicial and improper."

"Denied. Mr. Terrell, you may proceed." Traxler was obviously peeved. Don Richardson's credibility had ebbed.

"One hundred sixty opportunities were present, correct?"

"Well, yes."

"Now, by my count, by our count, one hundred nineteen of one hundred sixty of the boxes along the wall have been colored and marked in. Is that correct? Feel free to take the time to count them all if you like. We are almost finished here."

"No, I'll take your word for it."

"Thank you. So please do a little math for us. What percentage of the boxes have been colored in and marked?"

Narcy scribbled his computation and looked up. He looked angry and whipped.

"So, Doctor Narcy, in this crucial forty-day period that we all acknowledge is so important in this case, what is your computed percentage of opportunity?"

"A bit over seventy-four percent."

"Just under three-quarters, correct?"

"Yes."

The trap door on the gallows was opening.

Terrell began to walk backwards toward the wall of red. He was wearing what were routinely called "lawyer shoes" or "clodhoppers." He was always uncomfortable in them but they were considered part of the "uniform of the day" in this type of setting. Eddie always felt them to be ungainly. They then picked a moment to justify his sentiments. He suddenly clumsily stumbled and then lurched into the line of easels and they collapsed in sequence like dominoes. He took a thumping pratfall to the floor, landing on his backside as the five charts and easels fell all about him. He was instantly mortified and mightily embarrassed and turned a searing crimson.

Oh, God, he thought. *I have ruined everything! Damn! Damn! Damn!*

The courtroom was silent. All eyes were back and forth from Terrell to Judge Traxler and back to Terrell. And then Judge Traxler started to chuckle and then laugh and laugh hard, not in a derisive way but in the way of happy enjoyment. And the jury understood that it was really funny and it was okay to laugh and they began to laugh as well and Eddie and Kermit and Alph and Cas laughed and everyone in the courtroom busted out laughing—save for the defendant and their lawyers.

They sat stone faced. The courtroom slowly quieted down from its reverie and as the silence came back over them all, Don Richardson who had been loudly crunching ice while slumped back in his chair spoke loudly and sharply for all to hear.

"You are so stupid!" he sneered.

Cleveland seconded as always, "Yes, you are so stupid!"

The jurors heard this invective. Their faces showed clear disapproval.

Terrell hopped to his feet. "I apologize to the Court and to everyone. Yes, I can be clumsy. Oh, I am really sorry and embarrassed too!"

Judge Traxler, his shoulders still shaking and wiping tears of good humor from his eyes, said, "Eddie Terrell. It's okay. Things sometimes do go bump in the night. No apologies necessary. None at all and by the way, are you alright?" And as he asked, he then took a cold, warning look at the defense table.

"Yes, Your Honor. I am. Thank you." He could have hugged Traxler for his kindness.

"First, let's put everything back in its place." Patty and Mikey quickly reassembled the displays.

"Good. Now, have you completed your examination of this witness? It's getting late in the day and I'm thinking this would be a good place to stop if you are done and defense counsel can begin their examination as they wish in the morning."

Eddie Terrell took the proffered guidance as gold. Kermit and Alph both nodded their assent.

"Yes, Your Honor. I pass the witness."

"Thank you. Alright, everyone. We are adjourned for the day. Please do not discuss this matter with anyone. Go home and rest and let's all be back here in our places at 9:30. Hope all have a good evening."

The bailiffs took the jurors out. Traxler asked the lawyers, "Anything, gentlemen? No, well then, see you all tomorrow." And he was gone off to his chambers.

Richardson, lugging his brief bag, side mouthed sotto voice to Eddie as he passed, "Yeah, you really are stupid."

Eddie laughed. "Come here, Don. I have a sweet nothing to whisper in your ear."

Richardson, never one to leave well enough alone, turned back and stepped toward Eddie. Kermit knew that Eddie was going to fuck with Black Hearted Don's head. He tried not to smile.

Don took a few steps of return and leaned in, leading with his cranky jaw. "Yeah? What is it?"

"Don, I may be stupid. I can go with that…but this jury and judge love Kermit and they love me, and they also think your little playmates are your butt-kissing parrots and peacocks, and you, they think you are a turd so go fuck yourself and get the fuck away from me."

Eddie grinned, leered at Don. It was a dare that Don could not rise to. Don's face tightened and he stalked away. The Andrews looked shocked.

Kermit explained, "Our friend here, Eddie Terrell, is getting into Richardson's head. He is becoming Don's great distraction. It is an exercise in mind control. We think it helps us. Please don't be alarmed. No reason to be. There will not be any fisticuffs, at least not in this courtroom for this trial. Don just detests Eddie so we want him to grow that feeling, expand on that. That's why Eddie taunted him. Looks to me like it's working. Do you understand?"

They nodded tentatively. Alph said, "Oh yes. Kermit King is right. We've all been seeding this field for a while now."

"Good. Good. Now, go home and get some rest. As you well know, there's much more to come."

As the Andrews walked out of the courtroom, Kermit laughed. "Eddie, that was bold and effective too. I like it but suggest it now gets throttled back. You have pulled the pin on his grenade. Let's just let the seconds tick. You know, Don's an unhappy guy. He is angry and selfish by nature. He reminds me of the bull who carries his china shop with him. Good. Let's stay after the case now and get a drink and unwind and plan our tomorrow.

CHAPTER THIRTY-FOUR

FLANKING

In the Present

THE NEXT MORNING, Judge Traxler told the defense the witness was now theirs. Don Richardson rose and said they had no questions at this time, signaling that they would put Narcy up when it was time for them to present their case in chief. This pleased the plaintiffs as they knew they could take other bites out of that apple in due time.

"Plaintiffs. Call your next witness."

"We call Dr. Marina Ostroff to the stand. Again, Your Honor, we request that the witness be declared adverse."

"So ruled. Proceed."

Kermit took the nervous, bird-like neonatologist through a brief but pointed affirmation of the previous exercise with Nagy. She was uncomfortable and tried to talk around and about most everything. She talked in circles. It was obvious that she had been coached to motor mouth and evade and obfuscate. King stayed with her and slowly pulled the necessary admissions out of her. But she persisted and finally, after yet another question was being randomly fluttered, exasperated, King rifle crack-slapped the table and snapped, "Doctor, I ask you what time it is and you tell us how to make a clock!"

"Objection! Objection!"

"Overruled. Yes, Doctor. Now, my first very firm, do you understand, instruction to you is listen to the question, understand the question and directly and without all this dithering, answer the question. We do not need that sort of non-responsiveness from you or any witness on either side of this case. Have I made myself clear? Please answer Mr. King's questions. Now."

Chastened and now greatly quieted, she retreated, relinquished her strategy and was quickly and finally efficiently eviscerated by Kermit. She left the witness stand and Cleveland asked that she be excused so she could go check on her duties at the hospital. In truth, she just wanted to run away. Judge Traxler opined that it was an unusual request and asked the plaintiff what their response might be.

Eddie and Kermit put their heads together and then quickly Eddie stood. "We have no objection, as long as she comes back to participate one of these days coming in the future."

Traxler smiled and said, "Well then, off you go..." The jury laughed and the defense grimaced.

Cas observed quietly to the others, "That was a good move. Pieces keep getting taken off the board. Looks like their boat is emptying. Rats deserting or being forced to desert their sinking ship..." They admiringly affirmed her.

It was now obvious to the defense that the hospital's radiologist Andy Petser and Nurse Frances Williams were to be next in line. Fabian Fahtly looked perturbed. Petser, as always was blank but he appeared pensive. Nurse Williams looked worried.

During Kermit's cross of Petser, the X-ray reader admitted under tight questioning that two barium studies had been performed in the last ten days before Cameron had blown out and that some of their films showed a leak and some did not. Petser opined that they were thus inconclusive. Kermit looked at him as an owl might peruse a mouse.

"You were concerned? You were looking for something? Looking for a fistula. A recurrent TEF?"

"Yes. That was what the doctor's orders said."

"And you found substantive evidence that showed there was a TEF in a number of your films, didn't you?"

"Yes, but some of the other films did not show anything."

A fluorescent view box was put on a table next to the witness stand. It was turned on. All the films were attached to its illustrating light. Petser then had to show which films revealed a possible leak. There were a number that did. Petser also had to admit that the films were taken from different angles and that would surely affect that which was to be seen and studied and that some views might be obscured.

Kermit then pulled out his wallet and took two photographs from it. He approached Petser and laid the photographs on the rail. "Let us say it is your job to know who these people are, your job to identify these people."

"Okay."

"Who are these people?"

"I have no idea." Petser showed some sign of life. He was both annoyed and dismissive. He clearly thought this was a stupid exercise.

"How are you going to find out who these people are?"

"Well, I suppose I'd have to do some looking into it, some investigating."

"How would you do that?"

Petser's light bulb was beginning to come on. "It would be up to the doctors, Narcy and Ostroff to do that. The boy was their patient."

"Did you ever take it upon yourself to call the doctors and discuss these films with them?"

"Not that I recall."

"Did you ever meet with these doctors to discuss what these films showed?"

"No. I just dictated my findings and I guess that was just put in the chart."

"You 'guess?' Do you know?"

"No, I guess I don't but that's standard operating procedure."

"Did Dr. Narcy or Dr. Ostroff ever request to meet with you and look at these films to see what they showed?"

"No, I don't recall that. I don't think so."

"Don't you think they should have?"

"I don't know. That's up to them."

"Do you know if either or both of these doctors looked at these films, investigated these films?"

"I don't know."

"I see. Now, how are you going to identify who those people are in those two pictures?"

"I guess I need to ask around." He looked befuddled.

"Don't you need to show those pictures to people? Don't you need to ask around, as you just said? Doesn't that make sense?"

"Well, yes..."

"You know they are my photographs. The people in the photographs are different. They are not identical twins. Aren't you going to ask me who those people are?"

"Well, yes, okay. Who are those people?"

"They are my two daughters. You see, you investigated, didn't you?"

"I suppose so."

"You did what you were supposed to do, right?"

His silence was better than a "yes."

"I pass the witness...oh, one last question. How often did you see Dr. Narcy and Ostroff when you were working at and in the hospital?"

"Well, I saw them all the time."

"Thank you," Judge Traxler interceded. "Please answer any questions the Defense may have of you. Counsel, please proceed."

Cleveland asked, "You say these films were inconclusive, right? So nobody could tell from them what was going on, right?"

"That's right."

"Inconclusive, right?"

"Yes."

"They were not helpful, thus they were useless, not useful, not determinative."

"Yes."

Kermit was jotting on a long legal pad. Eddie Terrell decided he had had enough of this circular loop de loop and also he wanted to stir their pot some more. He stood.

"Objection, Your Honor. Asked and answered. Overly repetitive."

And thus ensued a good, confused squabble with Richardson, Cleveland, and even Fahtly talking loudly, talking over one another, objecting, objecting to objections, complaining and basically venting their mounting frustrations which had been building for a good while now. Eddie just put his arms out in the classic Alfred E. Neuman gesture of "What, Me Worry?" Judge Traxler put his hands momentarily over his face, then sternly instructed all to be silent.

"Objection sustained."

Nancy Aherns, the court reporter said, "Judge, they were talking all over one another. I couldn't get it down. I need my record to be complete. I need to do that. My tape recorder will be all jumbled up too."

"Yes, I understand. How do you propose to sort that out?"

"Ask the lawyers?" She looked perplexed.

Kermit King stood. "Your Honor, I think I can be of some help."

"How so?"

"I take verbatim notes in short hand. I learned to do so a long time ago in high school. I believe I can give us all a thorough read back. It's all here on my pad."

"Mr. King, may I please see your notes?"

"Of course."

"Please come forward."

The legal pad was handed up. The jury was watching with great interest. Judge Traxler studied it, flipped a few pages over and peered, obviously intrigued with them.

"Mr. King, is this shorthand in Spencerian script? I haven't seen this sort of thing in years. And in ink, not pencil too! My grandmother wrote in a beautiful Spencerian hand. Impressive, it is. Hard to do too. Out of date now. Would defense counsel object to Mr. King giving us a read back?" The judge held the pad for all to see. They were again neutered and could not resist. The read back was done. Everyone was impressed. More good points fortuitously scored for the plaintiffs.

There were no more questions of Dr. Petser. He came down. Judge Traxler called for a recess. Hospital counsel wandered over and asked to speak privately to Terrell and King. Eddie motioned for Alph and Cas to join them and they all went out to one of the private conference rooms just off the entrance to the courtroom.

Don Richardson looked at Donnie Cleveland and Dr. Seamus Narcy and said, "Shit!"

Narcy's dislike for Eddie Terrell was blooming into a virulent, vengeful hatred.

CHAPTER THIRTY-FIVE

CULLING THE HERD
Present Day

FAHTLY WAS A man in a hurry. King and Terrell knew that when the ask to meet was made. He made no effort to conceal his ardor for a release and departure. He might as well have been spread eagle naked lying before them.

"Boys, I'd like to wrap up our participation here. My clients and my carrier have given me authorization. Would two hundred fifty thousand get it done? It's a healthy sum."

Terrell and King looked at one another. King's head barely moved sideways but his signal was obvious.

Terrell agreed. "Fabian, you know you have plenty more rope and we do too. You don't even need to make a call. No disingenuous prattle now. You get it?"

"I'm not so sure about that."

"Let's now get on to nut cutting time. In order to cut your bunch loose, we will need 600 K. Of course, our clients need to assent and that's the rule. And we all know that's highly probable. They don't want to be here but y'all forced them. So now, we want your pin money."

"Uh, I can't go that high. I really can't."

"Yeah, right. Now, we don't like Richardson out there worth a damn and he despises us, especially me, and Cleveland is just his butt boy. You, you're okay, a strange okay, but still okay. So, here's the deal. It's a two-parter. Listen carefully now."

Fabian Fahtly looked as would a dog hopeful of being released from an eminent beating. An anxious "Yes?" was his response.

In a flat voice, Eddie drilled. "You are going to pay half a million to get the fuck out of here now. And you are going to agree to that in thirty seconds or we're leaving and all bets are off. We are sick of dealing with all of you. So, what say you? You've got the authority and we've got the whip hand. And you know it…"

There was no hesitation. He caved like a cardboard suitcase in a summer thunderstorm. To his credit, he did not whimper.

"Okay, you got it." Curiously, he asked, "What's the other part?"

Kermit was watchful, curious too.

"We are all going back to the courtroom and all, including those other assholes, go back into chambers and let Judge Traxler know what we have agreed to and he will get it on the record, out of the presence of the jury. And then you and your people, before the jury returns, will go on and get out of the courthouse and go away."

"Well, sure, that's just standard operating procedure. That's the second part? That's it?"

"No, here's the second part. You are required, as you depart, to pull them aside and quietly tell Richardson and Cleveland that we want them to know they're alone on an island now and that we are coming for them. You are to tell them that, exactly that. You gonna do that? If not, we have no deal. Understand?"

"Yes. Of course I'll do it."

Kermit was pleased.

And over the next few minutes, it was done. The three packed up and departed, leaving their spaces emptied. Traxler again asked defense counsel if they didn't want to discuss terms. They just shook their heads, saying they had no authority. Traxler told them, "You two are playing a shaky game, aren't you?" They just shook their heads and looked away.

Now, all that was left were the two defense lawyers and Dr. Narcy. Cleveland told his assistant to summon Dr. Ostroff immediately back to the courtroom. Their outlook was grim resignation. Their optics were terrible and sinking. They looked to be but a defiant, fragile few, huddling together as the storm surged toward them.

The jury came back in. They knew instantly.

CHAPTER THIRTY-SIX

PLOWING A STRAIGHT FURROW

Present Day

THE PACE QUICKENED. Ostroff skittered in a bit later.

Dr. Bieman Otherson, the head of pediatric surgery at Duke, who had done the post-disaster evaluation and examination of Cameron, and also reviewed his records, politely and neutrally discussed his medical findings and his opinions as to Cameron's situation. He was the ultimate gentleman and no one would be foolish enough to assail anything he said. Eddie Terrell intentionally made no effort to evoke standard of care opinions from him.

Richardson let Cleveland take the lead on the cross. Cleveland, after some mundane preliminaries, and always too anxious to prove his worth, asked Dr. Otherson if the care Cameron received was medically adequate.

Otherson with a slow, measured, mournful voice and demeanor replied that he would prefer to not respond to that question. Cleveland was then mute for a few seconds. Richardson hissed, "Leave it alone. Sit down!" Narcy looked at Terrell with deep bitterness.

The plaintiffs then called their pediatric surgery expert, Dr. Wayne Taylor, from the well-respected and nearby Wake Forest University Medical Center. He was efficiently qualified to speak to his specialty and also to neonatology since he had worked closely with those professionals for many years. Thus, both Narcy and Ostroff became fair game.

Taylor, without a doubt a good-looking fellow which surely did not hurt, steady and unwavering, laid out the case of many deviations of standard of care against the two doctors and the hospital as well. He listed them all specifically and in clear and cogent detail. Basically it was a shared debacle precipitated by many, but defendant Narcy was primary and in charge. Taylor calmly described the collective conduct as "gross negligence" and said if they had acted within the well-known and proper standards of care, the recurrent TEF would have been found, repaired, and the child would then have been able to thrive and grow. Click. Over and out.

Terrell passed Taylor to Richardson.

Richardson attempted to nibble around the edges of Taylor's testimony, probing to find a place of weakness that he could chew on, but Taylor gave no ground, conceded nothing and was charmingly and totally Teflon. Richardson was almost at the end of his rope. Cleveland had the look of the guy who had checked out. Narcy and Ostroff just looked down.

In frustration, Richardson asked in a whining and plaintive tone, "Doctor, I'm curious. Do you even know these two fine physicians?"

"Only a bit. Mostly by reputation. But I am only one county over and we do all share information and opinions and knowledge with one another. There seem to be more than a few of us around. We are lucky to have so many good hospitals and medical schools here in North Carolina."

"Then they do have fine and good reputations."

"Yes, of course they seem to be well-thought of but they failed and failed badly here."

"How can you, like this, turn on your people as you have in this case? They are, for all intents and purposes, your colleagues and neighbors!" Richardson was angry.

"I can explain that." Dr. Taylor calmly leaned forward toward the jury. "In addition to doing what I do as a doctor, I also farm. The farm belonged to my late daddy and then was passed on to me when he died. I have a few acres up near Saurtown Mountain and grow corn and peanuts and such, even some pretty flowers.

"It's therapeutic for me. Pulling stumps and rocks. Preparing fields. That sort of thing. Mr. Richardson, when you took my deposition, you never asked about my hobbies or interests outside medicine. I take no pleasure in criticizing these people, but what they did was wrong and harmful. I'm not going to cover for them or minimize this. This child should be alive today.

"My daddy taught me long ago when I was to begin to plow a furrow, I was to do it completely so I have laid my hand on this particular plow and I cannot quit until my task is done."

Richardson blanched and sat down, saying nothing more. Traxler asked, "Anything further?" The two lawyers just shook their heads. "Well then, the witness is excused. Doctor, you may leave. Call your next witness."

Mr. Andrews described how all of this had fallen on them like a ton of bricks. He described his and his wife's loss and devastation and their love for the surviving child which also and always reminded them of Cameron. He also told of a meeting he'd had with Narcy at Narcy's office about two weeks before everything went off the tracks. He recalled the office in specific detail, down to the layout, the furniture, even the magazines. He said that considering all the trouble Cameron was having, he specifically asked Narcy if Cameron did indeed have a recurrent TEF. He told how Narcy said he didn't think so and confidently reassured him and told him he thought they were on the right path. Andrews asked for more testing and was curtly told there should be no doubt that there would be more. He said he departed—it felt more like being dismissed—doubtful but what else could he say?

Richardson crossed him tightly on the meeting and more, but Andrews, while doleful and far away, was definite and resolute.

Mrs. Andrews, when her time came to speak, mostly wept and struggled to speak and tried to dry her tears with little success. She was so sad and pitiable. Terrell passed her quickly to the defense who declined to question her.

She came off the stand and rushed sobbing into the arms of her husband.

Traxler quickly declared Court to be in recess until the following morning and instructed the bailiffs to take the jury out.

The plaintiffs rested their case.

CHAPTER THIRTY-SEVEN

LIAR LIAR PANTS ON FIRE
Present Day

TO OPEN THE defense, Narcy was presented again on direct. The hope, of course, was he could stanch the bleeding. He testified on behalf of himself and Ostroff, thus making it clear that Ostroff would not be heard from again. The litany of "we looked and looked," "it was hard to find that little hole," "the child was compromised," "we are good and conscientious doctors," the aghast "we have been accused of killing this infant" and the intimation of the baby's unknown prospects for life and success in the distant future resonated dully again. From time to time, many jurors simply looked away in resigned boredom. There was nothing new here.

On cross, Eddie Terrell told Narcy he promised to be brief. Narcy looked hopeful and relieved.

"Dr. Narcy, do you remember the meeting you had at your offices with Mr. Andrews about little Cameron?"

"Well, yes."

"What did you talk about then?"

"I really don't recall."

"You really don't recall?"

"No, I really don't." Narcy was haughty, spitting the words out.

"Really?"

"Yes, that's right."

Terrell, raised his eyebrows to the jury and nodded the "well, there you have it" nod. "The witness may come down."

Narcy went back to the counsel table. No one would look at him. On that side of it, no one liked anyone.

Richardson then called a defense expert, a pediatric surgeon from Columbia Presbyterian in New York City. His name was Dr. Malcolm Painter. He was tall, stately, and handsome with a mellifluous voice. He was straight out of central casting. His expertise was to be showered on the two defendant doctors.

The obligatory presentation of his credentials and prestige and acumen and stately appearance were impressive and substantive. Obviously, it was hoped that he would be the firewall, the break to halt the run of hard luck that had dogged the defense from the beginning.

He, with professorial chapter and verse explanations, walked the case through its particulars and declared emphatically that Cameron's providers had more than met the standard of care. The defense passed their star witness. Could his testimony save their chestnuts? Could he make the diving, acrobatic game-saving catch in center field?

Kermit and Eddie huddled briefly.

King asked, "Well, what do you think?"

Many years ago, his type would have struck some cold fear into Eddie. This type of fellow could often be "way back when" an overwhelming missile.

Eddie smiled, patted Kermit's arm. "Watch this. I think I got this guy." Eddie stood up.

"Dr. Painter, to tightly sum up what you have said just now—you say that these doctors are blameless, that they are not responsible, that they provided state-of-the-art care, that they clearly met the appropriate standard of care here. And also, you strongly indicated, that little Cameron was badly compromised before all of this happened, that unfortunately and as indelicately as it might be put, little Cameron was 'damaged goods' from the time of his birth. Is that a fair and total recitation of your opinion given here just now?"

"Yes, it is." Dr. Painter smiled benignly at Terrell.

"That they did it by the book, so you say...well, just as you have written in your book, your widely regarded medical text book entitled, *The Surgical Evaluation and Treatment Of Pediatric Birth Anomalies.*"

Painter's kindly smile tightened a bit. He looked around, looked specifically at the plaintiffs' counsel table.

"Yes, that's right."

"Now, do you have your briefcase with you?"

"No, I don't have it here with me." Painter's face was no longer sweet.

"But it's here in this courthouse, isn't it?"

There was a long pause. "Well, yes."

"It's outside this courtroom, isn't it? Pushed up underneath the sitting bench to the right of our doors here. It's where you put it, right?"

Painter's face went instantly to blushing red, then to graying pallor. He knew he had been caught. He sat silent and waited for the next blows.

"Dr. Painter, just to help you out here, I was sitting across from you out in the hallway. You paid no attention to me. I watched you. I watched you reading. You don't know me. We never took your deposition. You had no idea who I am. Is that correct?"

The sullen "yes" was uttered.

"Dr. Painter, in your briefcase, there is a large, thick medical textbook with a blue and black binding. Isn't that right? Isn't that what you were reading from?"

Painter nodded his agreement and murmured, "Yes."

"It's your very famous and well-respected, earlier referenced textbook, the one that you authored and edited, right?"

A pause and then louder, firmer "Yes" now. He was now going to take it like a man. There was no use in ducking. The thought passed his mind, with great regret, that he was getting ready to now forever forfeit at the very least an easy hundred grand in extra, annual expert witness fees and too, his long, well-earned good reputation was in tatters and he would never be used as an expert again. The stark irony loomed up before him, came slamming into him hard that he was now the "damaged goods," he was the whore sitting lonely in a courtroom in North Carolina that felt very cold.

"Your Honor, may we please have the Court's permission to send Dr. Painter out in the hall to get his briefcase and textbook?"

"Yes. Doctor, please go retrieve them and return to the stand."

Terrell quietly asked as Painter started to move out of the witness box, "Doctor, I expect it has now occurred to you, hasn't it, that I have read and studied the book you are about to bring to us?"

"Yes, I believe you."

Defense counsel and their forlorn doctors watched glumly as their last hope, their once shining star was walking past them, flaming out as he went. He would soon return but a cinder. He would then read certain passages as instructed by Terrell that utterly contradicted his initial testimony and then at least, it would be over and he could go home. He departed marked as a liar and a fraud.

And so, it did all finish that way. The defense rested.

Narcy was beginning to think it was all a conspiracy, some grand and effectively nefarious plot to ruin him. He was internally unhinging.

Kermit asked Eddie, "I'm curious. Was that a case of good luck, something providential or was you're being in the right place at the right time part of your plan?"

Eddie grinned. "Part of my plan. I was taught a long time ago, always get to the courthouse early. See who is coming in. See what the jurors look like. See what everyone is carrying and reading. You never know. This time, we hit the jackpot."

Judge Traxler called them back to chambers. He was standing with them, among them. His arms were crossed.

"Now, Defense Counsel, I ask again and ask with great interest, if you get my drift, will you now make the call that will get serious settlement discussions underway?" There was an intense edge to his voice, his impatience flaring up.

"Your Honor, we have already been instructed by the carrier."

Traxler shook his head, pursing his lips in disapproval. "Doesn't your recommendation carry any weight with those people?"

Cleveland, embarrassed, shook his head. "No, sir, not really."

Traxler looked them over for a moment, then spoke with disdain. "Well then, you have allowed yourselves to be castrated. You are professional, intellectual eunuchs. I feel very sorry for you both. Now, so be it and maybe it'll all work out for you no matter what. We will see. But what I see is a complete disregard for the risk out there...that's not lawyering. That's not being good counselors. Is it?"

There came no reply.

"Alright. So now you argue, then I will charge and send them to deliberate. It's early afternoon. I'll let them go until 5:30 and if need be, will bring them back at 9 in the morning. Who is arguing for the Andrews?"

"Mr. King is."

"Fine. You will have thirty minutes total."

"Understood and thank you, Your Honor."

"I have already reviewed your requests to charge. I find them to be acceptable. There is some redundancy to them which I will clear up in the next little bit. Each defense counsel will have twenty minutes to argue. I will call time breaks at five minutes, three and at end of time. When I get to time is up, I promise your time will be closed up, even if you are in mid-sentence. You all now have thirty minutes to prepare, assemble, put together, whatever your closings. Any questions?"

There were none.

CHAPTER THIRTY-EIGHT

LATE ASSESSMENT
Present Day

"SO, ALPH, WHAT do you think? Where do things stand?" the younger inquired of the elder.

Alph and Cas and Patty and Polly and Mikey had moved to back of the courtroom while the conferencing was going on in chambers.

"Okay, here's what I think. I've been where those defense lawyers have been, more than a few times. God knows this is just my opinion but I think they're in trouble. They should have cut their losses long ago, should have been allowed to settle this thing and get the hell out of Dodge. If this had been a prize fight, it would have been called on a TKO and stopped way before. I don't think that jury much likes those four over there.

"But here's what they do have going for them. Society generally likes and respects doctors. And as we all know, lawyers as a group are not beloved or respected. And here, where we live, society is conservative. The damnable 'tort reform' movement has been politically and culturally effective and it moves the needle to the right.

"And they have said repeatedly that they tried and they tried to find out what was going on, that they were in a tough spot. That may resonate with some of these folks. Remember, it just takes one holdout to hang a jury. I've seen it happen.

"And this too. If they lose and the number awarded is unsatisfactory to them, they can always appeal and keep running a long clock, usually at least a couple of years. Now, applied post-judgment interest is hefty here, set into place to encourage resolutions and discourage appeals, but this crowd has always used our appellate courts as a Master Card or Visa. This is their unyielding mindset. It's going to take more than a few plaintiffs' victories to break that manner of approach.

"And I'm sure there are other reasons of theirs up in the air as well but this one stays with me. I have to think the insurance carrier strongly believes that the very youth of this infant holds any award number way down. This little fellow has no economic history of success, no history of supporting a family, no lost wages. The argument is, 'Hey, let's not get carried away.' This is "the other side of the coin" feature that Richardson spoke to in his opening.

"So, I think we win but I can see how we lose, either flat out lose or lose on a small number awarded."

Alph sighed.

Cas was mildly exasperated. "Alph, you had me all positive when you started and now, you've got me bummed."

"It's the nature of the beast, honey. Wonder when I can go grab a smoke…" Patty was pragmatic. "I've seen rabbits pulled out of a hat. I've seen chicken salad turned into chicken shit. That's just the way it is…" She tailed off.

Mikey was hopefully rubbing her hands together, imaginary worry beads being folded over and over again. "Eddie always worries more than he lets on. Y'all know that. I'm glad Kermit King is here to help on this, to help us all on this. He is one helluva lawyer—I'll surely say that!"

The nodded assent was emphatically unanimous.

Polly ruminated. "Y'all know I've done a ton of piece work legal assisting over many years but this is first time I've been in Court watching it all go down in full and at full tilt. I trust my instincts pretty good. I say we win but I am concerned about the 'just a baby' Alph has described."

Eddie and Kermit came back in to the courtroom and asked their crowd to come with them to one of the conference rooms. It was time to help put a big finish together. They had, in what seemed like a very long time ago, hit the silks when the green light blinked "GO" over the LZ. Their boots were getting ready to hit the ground. They needed to make a clean landing and move the jury to vote with them. They went off to the task.

CHAPTER THIRTY-NINE

KERMIT BRINGS A BAT
Present Day

KERMIT OPENED AND closed.

Richardson and Cleveland were center of the sandwich but their meat was old and dried. They laid out all that had been said before and hit hard over and over again on the child's lack of monetary value, economic and otherwise, all the way giving the jury their apologies, that it was hard for them to speak of such matters but that it had to be done, but it sounded oleaginous, had that under feel of slimy.

Kermit, always well-paced and quietly eloquent, opened with the analogy of caretakers of a most valuable property. They inspected regularly, most always multiple times a day. On numerous occasions, smoke seemed to be coming from the property, easing from underneath its doors or from underneath the eaves, wisping from its chimney. The caretakers knew there was no one inside the property who could address what might be going on. And though the caretakers speculated continuously about the phenomenon, they never went inside to inspect and explore. And this went on for a full forty days and then the property exploded into flames and was engulfed and destroyed and only then was inspected for the cause of the conflagration. It was found to be randomly sparking electrical outlet malfunctions which started small fires which would ultimately then burn themselves out without much harm to the place; that is until, one of them did.

Sternly he spoke, "Ladies and gentlemen of the jury, from the body of little Cameron came the constant, flashing signals. For forty days and forty nights, it rained the signs and symptoms of a recurrent tracheoesophageal fistula, a TEF. There are no, none whatsoever questions or doubts as to this. It is irrefutable."

And once Richardson and Cleveland had offered their cold gruel of reasons to side with them, they bored in with the chorus of "this is just all about money" platitudes, Kermit returned. He was a rapier unrelenting. He brought down thunder.

"How dare they devalue this child whose family and future were bright with his prospects!? How dare they make cheap estimates as to the worth of this child as to his mother and father and brother? How dare they make themselves the money lenders in the defaced temple of their strategies? Shame! Shame! Shame on them!"

Judge Traxler next charged the jury. "You are the finders of the facts. I am the giver of the law. You are to apply the facts of this case to the law that I give you. Your verdict must be unanimous. We respect your deliberations and we patiently await your decision."

And once the charges had been read to them, and their foreman had been given the verdict form, the jury was taken out and they then went to work.

CHAPTER FORTY

PRESENT DAY

The waiting began.

MRS. ANDREWS ASKED the lawyers what they thought. Eddie replied that they were always hopeful but also guarded in that hope; that in matters like this as we all can see are complicated and trying and we must all keep our expectations measured and managed. He told them, of course, this was all so hard on y'all and the waiting now must surely be the hardest part.

The waiting continued and the afternoon moved along. Everyone found something to occupy themselves with—or they chose to not make the effort. The mood of all was uniformly of desultory exhaustion, fear, worry, despair and a frightful boredom. Newspapers were a preferred resource and sections were shared and spread about. Each side had little spurts of indiscernible whispering and then the lapsing into silence renewed.

There then came a loud knock on the door. It jerked all to lightning attention. A verdict so soon? Judge Traxler swooped in.

"The jury has sent out a question. Madame Bailiff, please bring them in."

The written question was about their deliberative duties. The judge explained the parameters of their work and explained they could not go beyond the facts as presented; that they could not link or connect facts not in evidence. They could not and must not speculate.

They were sent back out to resume their deliberations. Those in the courtroom sagged back into their fitful, restrained restlessness.

About an hour later, there came another knock, just as startling as the first one. The bailiff and Judge Traxler stepped in. But again, there was no decision. It was again a written question. The panel asked if they could read the original lawsuit and all of the defendants' responses.

Cleveland groaned. "Why do they want all that now?" Richardson just made a face.

Kermit thought, *This is good. They're working hard back there, trying to get the whole picture, trying to connect the dots.*

Traxler chose not to bring the jury back to the courtroom. He wrote a response note in return explaining they needed to use their collective memories and recollections and recall, noting that the pleadings, the writings that had been requested were not entered into evidence.

He told the lawyers he also felt to provide such documents would be very prejudicial, considering the plaintiffs had laid out each of their complaints with exacting specificity and the defendants had, as usual, answered only in general denials. They were allowed to respond that way, but to compare and contrast the documents would make the defendants appear to be intentional obfuscators.

There was no dissent but the defense lawyers had amplified their disdain for the panel.

There being no verdict by 5:30, Traxler sent them home with his standard instructions and ordered them to be in their jury room ready to go at 9:30 sharp. They adjourned and all scattered. The Andrews again asked King and Terrell what they thought. The replies were the same. They were told to go on home and get some rest. The waiting weighed on them all but for civilians, it was grinding torture.

The next morning, a new lady bailiff, Mrs. Doris Delmonico was in charge of squiring the jury about. She was droll and quirky in a funny, nice way, had a very Brooklynese accent and immediately reminded all of the actress Selma Diamond from the television show *Night Court.*

She reported to Judge Traxler that her baker's dozen were all in place and chirped that they had sent another note out. Defense counsel began matching eye rolls.

"What could they possibly want now? Do they pay any attention? This jury is acting slow and dumb."

Traxler told them to be quiet. She handed it up. Traxler read it to himself and then informed all that they wanted to hear the testimony, in full, of both Dr. Wayne Taylor and Dr. Malcolm Painter.

Richardson stood to object with Cleveland nodding his agreement, but before Richardson had opened his mouth, Traxler told Richardson to sit down and save his breath, that he was going to allow it, that there was nothing improper about such a request. He said all this appeared to be a jury doing its work with focus and intensity.

He instructed the court reporter to prepare to play her tape recordings of the two witnesses for read back and had the jury brought in to listen to them. It took about forty-five minutes total. They then went back out to continue deliberations.

Later, lunch was brought in and the day dragged along. Kermit went out into hallway to make some phone calls.

Eddie sat with their clients and his stomach churned but he did not let on. It was imperative that he be placid on the surface.

Bailiff Delmonico suddenly came out. "The judge wants to see all the lawyers now!"

Eddie looked around for Kermit. He was not to be seen. Eddie was nervous. He surely wished Kermit was near. But there was no time to search for him. Eddie went back to chambers with the others.

When they were all seated in front of the judge's desk, Bill Traxler said, "They've sent out another note. It has two questions."

Richardson could not restrain himself. He voice was loud with grumpy, whiney frustration, his face red with elevating blood pressure and disgust. He blurted, "Oh for God's sake! What now!? These people are unbelievable! This is just stupid! What stupid question are they asking now?"

Cleveland, always happy to singsong alongside his boss, shook his head up and down like a bobblehead doll on steroids. "Yes, yes, yes, that's right! That's right!"

Eddie Terrell just wondered what the note said and wished fervently Kermit would come through the door right away. But no such succor was forthcoming.

Traxler eyed the two defense lawyers and then said to Bailiff Delmonico, "You've seen these two questions, Bailiff. Do you think they are stupid?"

"No, Your Honor. I don't think they're so stupid. No, sir, not at all."

"Well, why don't you go ahead and read them to us? Yes, please do that." He handed her the note.

She cleared her throat, squared her shoulders, held the paper with two hands close to her face and in her finest, most not at all Tar Heel lilt but in her best New Yawk Williamsburg Dyker Heights dees dems dose spicy, the words came clear and well formed from her mouth.

"Number One. May we award the plaintiffs more money than they have asked for?"

"Number Two. May we please have a calculator?"

There was complete and total silence in the room. Eddie felt as though a lightning bolt had seared into the center of his brain and body and was permanently lodged there, sparking and shocking and lifting him. He was lightheaded floating.

Richardson and Cleveland slumped in their seats. Their color was not good.

Judge Traxler said, "You sure you don't want to make a call now? It appears y'all are in some serious trouble."

As before, they declined again in quiet, unsteady voices.

"As you wish. Bailiff Delmonico, please bring me a calculator that works."

She vanished and returned quickly with a big gray one with red keys and a wall cord.

Traxler plugged it in and performed some quick computations to make sure it was an accurate thing. He then turned it to Richardson and Boston and instructed them to make as many calculations as were necessary for them to be satisfied that it worked as it was supposed to. As they began that affirmatory effort, Traxler growled at them. "I don't want to hear y'all say later that the jury had been given by this Court a faulty or deceptive calculator."

"It seems fine." The two looked resigned, as though they needed the proverbial cigarette and a blindfold.

"Then bring them into the courtroom."

Traxler explained to the jury panel that they would have to depend on their individual and collective memories as to what the plaintiffs asked for in money damages. He handed the foreman the calculator and told them to go back and continue with their work. He also told him he would quickly be sending verdict forms back and explained those to the group as well.

Eddie whispered to the Andrews that it appeared they were going to get a verdict in their favor but no one was sure what the amount might be. He advised them to continue to be still.

The defense crowd was huddling and milling around and could be heard telling their crowd the same with the added reassurance that they did not think it would be much because it was just a young kid; hell, not even a kid, just a baby.

Kermit returned and Eddie filled him in. Kermit cocked an eyebrow and in the style of Sherlock Holmes spoke.

"Well, isn't this interesting? Let us now just sit and wait some more."

Another hour or so passed. The anticipation was heavy and grinding. Then came another loud knock on the door.

"All rise."

"Please be seated. I am told that we have a verdict. Would the bailiffs please bring the jury out?"

They single-filed into their seats, the foreman clutching the verdict form. Eddie and Kermit and all watched them closely, trying to read them to see if they could tell what was getting ready to happen. All faces were poker.

"Please give me the verdict form."

It was handed to Judge Traxler. He read it in two stages. Eddie studied him. Traxler's eyes read the first question, which was the one as to whether there was negligence or not. A "no" would collapse it all and there would be no need for Traxler to read further. Traxler's eyes moved down to the second question which was if you find there was negligence, then what amount of monetary damages would be awarded the plaintiffs. As Traxler read, his eyes widened.

Eddie's hands were slightly shaking. He held them tightly in his lap, under the counsel table. He would not look at Mr. and Mrs. Andrews. He would not look at Kermit. He kept watching Judge Traxler.

Judge Traxler read over the verdict form again. "Alright. Madame Clerk. Please publish the verdict."

The clerk stood up and took the sheet of paper. The foreman and all the jurors stood as well.

"Number One. We the jury find for the plaintiffs."

"Number Two. We the jury award to the plaintiffs the sum of one million two hundred and fifty thousand dollars."

"This is our unanimous verdict and all of our signatures are on this verdict sheet."

The court reporter gasped audibly and the full silence of the courtroom enveloped them again for a few moments.

And then there it was. The joy and the disappointment were set loose. There were the smiles and tears and frowns and grimaces but all tried to stay restrained. It was mostly a losing effort. Eddie grinned at Kermit and Kermit grinned at Eddie. The Andrews were quietly shaking hands with their lawyers and mouthing, "Thank you. Thank you. Thank you."

Judge Traxler asked all to be seated. "Mr. Richardson. Mr. Cleveland. Do you wish to poll the jury?"

"No, Your Honor."

"Very well." Traxler released the jury with his and the Court's thanks and as the jurors walked out and past the plaintiffs' counsel table, they each paused to shake hands or say a kind word. No such acts of kindness or respect were visited on the defense side. They were studiously ignored. It was obvious the defense had laid a very big egg, really more like a very big turd in their punchbowl.

Judge Traxler told all the lawyers that he would entertain any post-trial motions within the next ten days. He suggested this could be done with a brief telephone conference call, signaling to the defense that he would provide no post trial assist. His clerk would assist with the scheduling.

He thanked everyone for their good and hard work and went to his chambers. He was seen smiling and shaking his head in wonderment as he went out the door.

Richardson rumbled over to the plaintiffs' table. Always the most affable of sorts, he muttered bitterly, "Congratulations, but of course, you know we are going to appeal this thing. That is nothing but a runaway jury."

Kermit just smiled at him. "That's nice and we will see, won't we?" Kermit winked at Don which made Don's face tighten.

Eddie followed on. "Don, you really do have bad manners. Remarkable. I expect your sainted momma, wherever she might be, would be appalled by you. I'd wager she'd take you down a few more notches. You're a bully and a damn bad one at that. Now go away. Get on away from us! We won. You lost. Now, deal with it."

Eddie gave Don a hard look that read, "Don't fuck with me. You'll come to regret it."

Don backed and turned away and Kermit thought Eddie's invocation of Don's mother somehow resonated with him. Mommy issues can undo even the biggest of assholes.

Mikey and all had watched the exchange with restrained amusement but their delight was so obvious in their eyes and faces. Narcy watched them grimly, his lips pursing in and out in involuntary resentment. He stared baldly, eyes narrowed at Mikey.

They all began to pack up. Even the Andrews had expended their reservoir of hugs and handshakes.

The defense filed morosely out. But then, Dr. Narcy came back down the aisle. He looked the assembled plaintiffs' group over, laying obviously burning eyes on Mikey, caught by her beauty and by his anger and resentment. He was in high dudgeon.

"Young lady, your husband is a trashy horse's ass. How could a grown woman like you countenance with such a reckless fool?"

"Oh, I think he's pretty smart and we have the papers with big numbers on them to prove that. And just by the way...."

She dangled her ringless left hand and fluttered it at Narcy.

"We're not married. We live in sin and have for a very long time, and guess what? We like it. It's fun!"

Narcy's face contorted in moralistic, sour disgust. He pivoted to Eddie and looked him over. Eddie stood mute, blank.

"You know, Terrell, you ought to try out for the Little Theatre over there in Winston-Salem. You'd be great. You are some kind of actor." Narcy's tone was snide and stretched out in contempt.

"Why thank you, Doctor, but that's such a small stage. But the good news is Broadway's calling me! Now run along with your playmate Donnie boy!" And Eddie laughed as did the others and Narcy stalked away in a snarling huff, slamming the courtroom doors as he exited.

Kermit's smile of amusement was high wattage. "Now, please let me be the leader of our troop now for just a moment. Let us all exhale and enjoy their collective agitation and of course, our wonderful victory. We have confused and befuddled them and from my vantage point, we have soundly thrashed them. We have just experienced a great event and an even greater moment here just a few minutes ago. We all know we still have a ways to go here, but it looked to be a pretty clean trial to me. Working on responding to their appeal will be our next effort, but for now, let us stand down and enjoy this.

"I want to suggest that even as I speak, our collective adrenaline is now rapidly burning off. I know I am exhausted and I expect we all are. John and Susan, you both have been magnificent in the face of some very powerful forces and we are grateful to have you as our clients. Yes, we need to, we want to celebrate and indeed we will, but first, let us all take our leaves and go carefully on back to our homes.

"In true candor, this has been an inexplicable pleasure, but I now feel the need to go someplace quiet, sit down, and have a large glass of Champagne."

They all laughed again and hugged some more and shook hands some more and then carefully packed their things up and left the building and it was then done, all done. They held the high ground.

CHAPTER FORTY-ONE

AFTERMATH – IT'S NOT FAR NOW

Present Day

THE EVENING AFTER the afternoon of reward, Eddie and all his people joined Kermit at Graylyn for that glass of Champagne. Alph called LeeAnn and she joined them. LeeAnn and Cas sat next to one another and put their heads together. They had in a short time become close and liked one another. Cas felt liberated by Alph and LeeAnn's assignations. She wasn't quite sure why but she was. Alph adored them both and the paramour and the mentee adored him.

Cocktails and dinner followed. It was not a raucous affair though good humor abounded. It was a few hours of thoughtful observation and good conversation with delicious food and clever toasts. It was a fine first denouement.

Kermit came to the office the next day before returning to Columbia and he and Eddie briefly conferred as to their next steps.

Regaining some semblance of "normalcy" after a big trial is always difficult and the path back to the regularity of the office's many files and many cases and many problems and many people is always an erratic one. The excitements of those past days still burned and popped. They would go fast and then they would go slow. Their hills and valleys, the moments of energy and lassitude ebbed and flowed. But they got after it and force fed one another their work and thinking and assignments, and the track was cleared. Eddie had a renewed sense that things were going to be just fine.

A week later, Judge Traxler's clerk coordinated a conference call with all the lawyers. It was perfunctory.

"Mr. Richardson. Mr. Cleveland. I have reviewed your submissions. All motions for a new trial and any other accompanying motions are denied. Plaintiffs are to draw up the appropriate orders. Any questions?"

There were none. Traxler thanked them for their participation and rang off the line.

There was no subsequent small talk among counsel. There was no collegiality. The rupture was long since complete.

Notices of appeal were soon thereafter filed by the defense.

Fabian Fahtly delivered his insured's check for half a million and accompanying releases. He and Eddie visited for a few minutes.

"Thank God I got us out of that clusterfuck!"

"Yes, that turned out to be the wise thing to do."

"I know lots of folks think I'm a pompous ass but at least I'm pleasant. That Don Richardson! Jesus! Now there's a true asshole!"

"Yes, I think you are onto something there."

"Eddie, do you think there will be any negotiation as to settlement while their appeal is pending?"

"Fabian, I pretty much doubt it. But I think we are duty-bound to explore such possibility so we will, I guess, try."

"Hmmmm...yes, of course. Well, I must be going. Oh, by the way, if what looks like a good med mal or serious tort comes my way, might you be so kind as to look it over?"

"We'd be happy to. And thank you for coming by with the necessary paperwork. I appreciate it."

Eddie held the door and the fellow left. It was late afternoon. As he watched his new friend amble to his car, the germ of an idea began to form in Eddie's mind. He went to Alph's office where Cas was being regaled with war stories. He shut the door.

"Let's talk. I've got an idea."

Eddie laid it out and asked what they thought. They liked it. Eddie then went to his office and called Kermit and then the Andrews and explained to them what he was thinking and asked for their permission to make the effort. They all discussed it and the green light was lit.

After the verdict, word spread rapidly around the courthouses in Guilford County and Forsyth County and around law offices all across the Piedmont. The case was written up in the *Winston-Salem Journal* and passed down the line to *The State* in Columbia. Eddie and Kermit were asked to be interviewed but declined as an appeal was pending. All defense counsel had no comment.

The publicity was enormous. The volume of calls and inquiries and entreaties to the two lawyers' offices ramped up and there was no time to revel in the light of weeks' ago glory.

Patty and Polly and Mikey picked up their games and told Eddie and Alph and Cas that the deluge was here and that, despite the immense satisfaction of their big win, there was no time for lollygagging. They were behind on a lot of matters and it was time to hook up their proverbial bush hogs and get to clearing their underbrush.

Eddie dictated a letter and asked Patty to prepare it in five originals. He reviewed them and signed them and asked that it be sent by FedEx overnight express. He liked sending significant items that way. A FedEx mailer always caught one's eye and attention much more convincingly than an ordinary envelope.

It was sent to Don Richardson, Donnie Cleveland, and Rosen Derrick, the senior adjuster for Narcy's and Ostroff's medical malpractice liability carrier, the Patient Fund For Compensation (PF2C). Extra copies were enclosed for forwarding to the doctors. It was the prudent thing to do. Eddie had, in the past and on more than one occasion, been aware that Defense Counsel would keep their clients in the dark for some extra time in situations like this in order to gin up more fees. It was always the fees, the hourly fees that were the summit of their work. The Andrews and Kermit were copied as well.

The letter read as follows:

Re: Andrews vs. Narcy and Ostroff/Case # CVS 1604/Guilford County, N.C./Hon. William Traxler presiding

Dear So and So:

I trust this communication finds you well.

We offer the following proposal. It will stand good for only one week/seven days from the date of this letter.

The Andrews were awarded by the jury a few weeks ago the sum of 1.25 million dollars.

Appeals have now been filed by the defense. Post-judgment interest in this jurisdiction is annually computed and compounded at twelve (12) percent. Generally speaking, and as you well know, a full appellate run to both Court of Appeals and Supreme Court usually takes in excess of two years.

Counsel for defense will now, as they pursue these appeals, along with their assigned associates, paralegals, and legal assistants, begin to generate more and more hourly fees. We all know that such is just, as they say, "the nature of the beast." And you know the best you can gain from a successful appeal is just another trial with those attendant, piled on new fees and expenses and also, the second presentation of your case with, as might be said, "its warts and all."

We are now offering to accept in full settlement and compromise of this matter with dismissals with prejudice the sum of one million dollars. A cashier's check in that sum along with all necessary settlement documents, including dismissals with prejudice, must be received and executed within forty-five (45) days.

Think of the time and expense that you could collectively avoid. This obviously is a very significant discount and by accepting this proposal, all uncertainty and chance would be immediately removed from the equation.

Please understand that this proposal is not made out of weakness but rather comes from our confidence. We believe an objective review of the proceedings will signal that it was a clean trial, presided over by one of the most respected Superior Court judges in the state. If the verdict is upheld, which we believe is most probable, a simple computation illustrates that in addition to all incurred legal fees, the final judgment would approach 1.7 million dollars. As is often said, "you do the math."

Lastly, I would note that as you all know, our good fortune over the years has helped this firm (and this certainly applies to Mr. Kermit King's as well) amass plenty of wealth and thus if you will, ammunition for any coming battles. We can stay the course, whatever such might be. It is, as well, helpful that Mr. Andrews has a fine job that supports his family comfortably and also, that the Defendant Hospital settled out in the middle of trial for $500,000.

And too, I would think that Drs. Ostroff and Narcy would prefer to see this difficult matter put behind them. Currently, it all must be quite a distraction to them, and even if they were to get a new trial, it would also take them away from their professional work for another great block of time, thus costing them much money as well. Please note we have provided herein duplicate, signed originals of this letter of proposal so they may provide their input as well.

We look to hear from you promptly. We promise you this is the only time we will make this proposal. The figure is non-negotiable.

We thank you for your attention.

Respectfully submitted,
s/Eddie V. F. Terrell

Alph and Cas and Mikey and Patty and Polly looked it over.
"What do y'all think?"
"What the hell. Looks good. Fire away."
And they did.

CHAPTER FORTY-TWO

THE DEFENSE CRACKS, THEN SPLINTERS

Present Day

A FEW DAYS LATER, Eddie got a call from an angry Don Richardson.

"Terrell, you son of a bitch. Now you want to take the bread out of my mouth?"

Eddie could see Don's fat, red face. "Hello, Don. Nice to hear from you. Hope you and yours are well. And don't be talking bad about my aged momma; I'll get her over here to box your ears!"

"Fuck you! There isn't a chance in hell I'm going to go along with this!"

"Ah well, I see. That's unfortunate, but isn't it true that it really is not your call to make? You can only advise but the final decision rests with Derrick. I think that's right. You work for the insurance company. They don't work for you."

"You know Dr. Narcy ain't gonna go along with this!" Don spluttered.

"Come on, Don. Calm down. This is just business. It's just about saving a pile of money now. Cutting your losses. And as far as Narcy goes, his input to the insurance company carries all the weight of but the smallest of feathers. Less than negligible. So, think it over. Be a team player. Help the carrier to continue to like and respect and need your, shall we say, dynamic services. It would not do, would it, to get on their bad side right now, would it?"

"Oh, to hell with you! Goddamn, it was just a little kid."

"Yes, Don, it was just a lovely young child robbed of his life, his future."

Richardson slammed his phone down. Eddie smiled. They really did have the Prince of Darkness by the short hairs. No matter how it all ended up, they had gotten into his fat, arrogant head, and was truly a victory.

A while later, Patty came in and told Eddie that Donnie Cleveland wanted to drop by. Eddie said, "By all means, tell him to drop by soon," and that, "time was a wasting."

An hour later, Patty brought Cleveland into Eddie's office.

"Hey, Donnie. Thanks for coming by. What's up?"

Cleveland smiled and let out a chuckle. "Oh, come on, Eddie. You know what's up. I'm not going to beat around the bush. I'm not here hat in hand but I am going to recommend that the PF2C make the deal. Dr. Ostroff wants this thing over and in truth, so do I. Working with Don is like wrestling a slobbering bear with extraordinary bad breath. It's been exhausting. You whipped us fair and square. "

"Donnie, I appreciate your coming and telling me that. And, I agree with your assessment of your case co-counsel. I don't think I need to say anything else. I hope you are going to pass your thoughts and recommendation on to Derrick soon."

"Yes. I'm meeting with him in Charlotte this afternoon. I expect you'll hear from him soon."

Their meeting was ended. After Cleveland left, Eddie felt bad that he had mind-mocked him so often. But he quickly got over that. The trend line was a good one. It was time to wait a little bit more.

The next morning Rosen Derrick called and told Eddie, in obvious good humor, that despite his forever and eternally ingrained reservations about ever settling cases, there was a time and place for exceptions, that this was one of those times and they would accept the deal and settle the case exactly on the terms presented.

"Eddie, you laid out an irresistibly complete case to get this thing finished. I compliment you. At this point, it's a business decision, just about the money"

"Thank you, Rosen. We got lucky. Your crowd got unlucky. So, who is going to do the paper work?"

"Interesting you should ask. Donnie Cleveland's office will do it all. Don

Richardson called me mad as hell, demanding we not settle. I explained to him that all the other participants, including a quick canvass of our advisory board, felt otherwise, and since it was our ultimate call, the case was going to be resolved. He didn't calm down. He didn't say, 'I see.' He didn't accept reality. He told me, well, he yelled at me, that he was sick of being our puppet, that he wasn't going to work for us anymore and that he was sending over his final billing statements and all of his open files, which are many, no later than tomorrow. He said he was out. Seems he fired us. How about that?"

Derrick was almost giddy. There was no dismay. It was obvious that the emerging scenario pleased him.

"Damn, talk about cutting your nose off to spite your face. That must be a pretty good stream of income to kick to the curb like that…"

"Eddie, you're so right. Just between you and me, I'm not sorry about this, not one bit. Don's been, over time, a fine warhorse but also been getting pretty big, really too big for his britches so for us, it's good riddance. He can go peddle his ill temper and impatience and imperial ways someplace else now. A guy like him and his skill set can easily be replaced. As the fellow somewhere out there said, 'The graveyards are full of indispensable men.'"

"Well, how about that. Damn. That's pretty surprising."

"It sure is, but I'm looking at it as a gift. Now, we'll get all this in gear and get it done. But remember this. The next times out and I emphasize 'next times' plural, we are not going to go so soft on you. You know that I'm sure."

"Yes, I do, but you know as well that we will try our damndest to help y'all see the light from time to time."

"I have no doubt. I gotta go. I will talk to you soon."

The case was over, truly over, and the word was passed all about and there was great happiness and relief. The call to Kermit was especially sweet and the two lawyers reveled in the surfeit of happy war stories they had now successfully put in their storehouses. And too, the fees earned were not too shabby either.

Three weeks later, Eddie took Alph and Cas with him to meet with Donnie Cleveland and Rosen Derrick to finalize all matters. Eddie thought it was a good thing to let Cas meet Derrick and to see the whole thing through soup to nuts style and also, chances were better than good that one of these days, Cas was going to be dealing with Derrick and folks like him one on one so it was all part of taking her training wheels off.

Alph came along just for the happy ride. The last years had been one great big amusement park and he rolled around in it in unbridled joy and happiness. They were gathered in Cleveland's office. Once the check was received and the sign-offs were made, Cleveland asked Derrick, "You want to tell them or should I?"

The Andrews' lawyers looked quizzically at Cleveland.

Derrick laughed. "You tell them. Go ahead. I think it's therapeutic for you to deliver this news. After all, Don was pretty much your tormentor, your personal pain in the ass, wasn't he...?"

"I think all will find this to be very interesting." Donnie Cleveland took a deep breath. "As you know, Don threw a major league tantrum with Rosen here, broke all the china, and told everyone to basically go to hell."

"Yes, that seems to be the case. And, I am sensing a Paul Harvey moment here. Pray, do continue."

"Here's the rest of the story. This is from the horses' mouths on the inside so I think it is legit. Don went back to his office and remember, this is his firm, his name is the lead senior partner's on the door, he is the big kahuna and the founder. He called all of his senior people in, went into a monologue which quickly turned into a raging rant, cussed everything from A to Z out and told them he had told one of their biggest and most lucrative, long-time clients to basically go fuck itself, that he had been used and wronged and he was done with being, he said, his words, 'their serf, their peon.' He then summarily dismissed them with a wave of his royal hand."

"Oh, what a picture this makes and why do I think we aren't quite done here...?" Eddie looked happily mischievous.

Alph said, "What a jerk. In my old shop, full of seasoned defense lawyers, we would have tossed him out on his ear."

Cas was just sponging it all up. She was in the belly of the beast now.

Donnie looked at Alph and paused. "Bingo! The next morning the firm's management committee walked into Don's office, shut the door and told him they were sick of his big shot bully boy act, told him that either he was going to leave and go hang his shingle someplace else or they and most of the others, including support staff, were going to bolt to calmer pastures. It was given as an immediate ultimatum. There would be no redemption allowed, no anger management classes offered. It was either him or them.

They left him to his thoughts and an hour later, he walked out. He fired the carrier. His firm fired him. Lots of poetic justice here, don't you think?"

"Good God! Yes! That's a great story with a flourish to the finish! I guess we'll see him around after a while, but I wonder what he can put together now that's worth a damn. He's older. He's toxic. He's kinda cooked, don't you think?"

Rosen Derrick grinned and said flatly, "A lesson to be learned. A rule. Don't shit in your own mess kit."

It was both a blessing and a benediction. They all left it at that.

CHAPTER FORTY-THREE

A NEW WORRY?

A Few Weeks Later

THE RHYTHMS OF the office were coming on back as neglected lamps will flicker and flicker and then burn brightly. The pace was good and steady. The pipeline of good work, good cases was full. They were all happy, working well and effectively together. They were a six-horse hitch, the stage coach carrying, rushing the gold to Virginia City. Eddie was at peace, albeit it was at a loping gallop.

All sorts of people would come in and out of the offices, clients and lawyers and helpers and too, their regular delivery people and service technicians. It was a busy space. Most folks liked to be there, on the inside, even those that came bearing their troubles.

One afternoon, Mikey came in from meeting some friends for lunch and went into Eddie's office.

"Hey, sweetie. What's up? How was lunch?"

"Eddie, a weird thing just happened."

"What? What weird thing?" He eyed her. She was noticeably distracted.

"Eddie, as I was getting out of my car, I looked toward Cherry Street and I swear, there was that nasty Dr. Narcy cruising past our office. He was going slow and eyeing our place."

"You sure?"

"Well. Pretty sure. Yes, yes, I think I'm sure."

There was the pause for silence, for thinking.

"Hmmmm. Okay. Well, yes, if it was him and I promise you I don't doubt you…well, he's an asshole, but I don't think it's anything more than him just out driving around. A coincidence."

"Eddie, he came around twice. What's he doing over here anyway, away from Greensboro? It bothers me."

"Did he come around again?"

"No, he did not come back. I waited and watched."

"Guess he's just got a burr up his ass. People have been known to do this sort of thing after they get hit with something. They want to come look and see where the people that have hammered him hang their hats. Let's just pay good attention and be watchful out there. I'm not trying to minimize you but I just don't think there is much to this."

He rose from his chair and came around and gave her a big, reassuring hug. "It's ok. I got you."

He could feel her tension ease. She kissed his neck. She sighed. "Okay. I'm holding you to it. I've got work to do." And out she went.

Eddie looked out the window. She had always been foxhole tough, his stalwart. Surely that asshole couldn't be that stupid. He and Mikey had been together a long time now. They loved and adored one another. They were, as is said, aging together nicely. The idea that someone could be troubling her was troubling to him. He did not like the sensation but there were some lowering clouds and there was no horizon to see.

He went out and let everyone know who Mikey had seen, said if it was him, then probably a no big deal, but "let's all pay attention out there, please."

They all paid attention. Their gazes were not rapt.

CHAPTER FORTY-FOUR

A REAL WORRY

A Few Days Later...

SOME DAYS PASSED and the hypervigilance of the earlier moment settled down and back to the basic, general agitation of a busy litigation law office. They were very busy and it was engrossing and exciting. If idle hands were the playthings of the devil, then Lucifer must have been bored to death.

They were bending to a trifecta of cases in the big front legal assistants' room involving the all too often disastrous effects of alcohol.

Eddie and Patty were going over MAIT (Major Accident Investigation Team) reports of a gruesome hit and run from down near Lake Norman. It had been a party for a bride-to-be and her bridesmaids. They were walking back to their shared rental house a few minutes after midnight and were on a path well off the edge of the roadway walking home from a night of celebratory but mild partying when a speeding car swerved and screeched out of a side street, ran off the edge of the road, hit two of the young ladies, corrected, gunned it and turned left and was gone. One girl was killed and the other suffered both broken legs, a shattered pelvis and many other life-threatening injuries. She ultimately survived. The driver and his car were found the next morning, hidden in a house out in the country.

Polly and Mikey had been putting together a complaint and written interrogatories that would soon be served on a physician's practice and its four principal doctors. The medical group had been out on the lake next to the Belews Creek Power Station up in Stokes County above Winston-Salem.

Their twenty-seven-foot custom-built Manitou party barge was powered by twin Mercury 500 horsepower V-12s—those being much more fitting for an ocean-going, deep sea fishing boat. The registered owner of the boat was listed as what turned out to be the physicians' partnership LLC, "The Stoke It Group."

At 2 a.m. on the clear night in question, under a full moon, the boat, named "Stoke It and Stroke It," at an estimated speed of greater than twenty knots, sliced through a two-man canoe being calmly paddled across the lake's placid waters by two teenage hikers and campers from Mississippi. One was thrown clear. The other's body did not rise to the surface of the lake for six days. The case had been referred to Eddie by good friends from Jackson, lawyers he had worked with many times in the past down that way.

Law enforcement files contained large, color photographs of the contents of a huge cooler from the boat which, to put it mildly, contained prodigious amounts of liquor and beer, handles and bottles and cans crammed into it cheek to jowl. There was an accompanying inventory list and Mikey had just been sent shopping to physically replicate the cooler's contents. The assemblage of such would make a powerful statement during depositions, and if need be, at trial. They all felt that the possibility of trial was remote.

Cas and Alph were preparing deposition questions for Cas to use when she questioned the managers and bartenders who had been on the noon to eight shift at an Applebee's just on the northern outskirts of Winston-Salem, well up University Parkway. She was flying further and further away from the nest each week.

A Forsyth County volunteer fire captain had been rushing to a rural fire call, emergency lights and sirens fully enabled, when a late model Cadillac sedan suddenly jerk-crossed the double yellow line and hit him head on. Had he not been in a big, sturdy Ford dually 350 Super Duty with a massive bully bar, he would have been killed. Instead, he was "just" almost killed and was forced up under the steering wheel and dashboard. His legs were crushed. His skull was fractured. He suffered five broken vertebrae and many other injuries.

The investigation revealed that the female driver and her significant other, who had been following her in his own vehicle, were both convenience store clerks who had gone off shift late that morning and had gone into Applebee's and started drinking wine and shots. Their bar ticket was lengthy and her pulled BAC later read out at .28. The video surveillance tapes could not be found; suspicious of course-lost, hidden or destroyed? And when the crash occurred, the fellow following just kept on going.

For about an hour, there was negligible conversation in the room, only murmurs along with the sound of papers rustling and pages turning. Sometimes someone would get up and go get a book or a drink or for Patty, go out to the porch and take a smoke break.

Mikey came back in. Eddie, not looking up, asked, "Hey, babe. Did you get the stuff? Don't you need some help bringing it in?"

She was silent and then hotly blurted, "No, I didn't get the stuff. I was trying to and then, guess what? That doctor asshole showed up again." She sat heavily next to Eddie.

Alph, startled, threw his arms up in the air and swept one of his beloved cups and saucers off the table where it all shattered when it hit the floor. All work stopped. Patty, hearing what was going on, rushed back inside. They all turned to Mikey.

"Oh, shit! Tell me what happened. Oh, I'm so sorry!" Eddie also thought to himself that Alph losing some of his china was a bad signal, a bad sign. He could feel the black clouds rolling back in. He felt sick to his stomach.

"Eddie, I'm scared. The son of a bitch is stalking me! How do we stop it? I'm really scared now!"

"Yes, you are right. I understand. We will figure something out." He reached for her hand. She pulled away. Eddie understood.

CHAPTER FORTY-FIVE

THUS, A PLAN

THEY ALL SAT in silence for a minute or so. Mikey, a bit calmer but still hot, asked again. "So, what are we going to do? I can't stand this shit! Can we call the cops, call the district attorney, call that damn, fat fuck of his lawyer Don Richardson? Sue this bastard?" She was spitting the words out but her surging emotions were burning down and she put her face in her hands and began to weep. Eddie felt helpless.

Alph, trying pour some oil on the troubled waters, searched for salutary clues. "Mikey, I am so sorry and troubled about all this. We all are. We are, I promise, going to help find a way to make this stop. Can you describe for us what exactly happened, if you can? Please, if you could, I think it would help."

Mikey sat up, nodded yes, wiped her eyes and exhaled. She was reassembling her courage.

"Let's see. Here we go. I went out to the ABC store on Country Club. I had a long list and asked a clerk to help me get it together. He got us a small shopping cart and we started going down the aisles. It's a good-sized place and they're stacked pretty high as y'all know so you can't see over the tops plus all the walls are top to bottom full. There are five aisles I think so it's a long push and pick, back and forth as we go. The clerk could not have been nicer. He was very careful to make sure we were getting the right stuff, the right sizes and amounts. He said to me, 'Lady, this is gonna be some kind of party you're going to be having.'

"I explained to him that it was not for a party. It was for an illustrative exhibit in a wrongful death case where a young man from Mississippi got run down by a boat full of doctors who had all this juice on board. The clerk obviously thought I was speaking Greek and only replied with a sad, 'Oh...' and shook his head. We kept going and the cart was filling up.

"We came around a corner to go down the vodka and tequila and gin aisle, the white liquor aisle, and I looked up and there he was, fat, just standing there staring at me. I remember he had on a baseball cap and a ratty rain coat. I froze. I couldn't move. He kept looking at me, really more like looking through me."

Alph asked quietly, "Mikey, did he say anything? Did he touch you? Did he try to touch you?"

"No, no, he didn't touch me or try to touch me. He was too far away at the end of the aisle. He didn't seem to make any move like that. He was not physically threatening. He was...well...emotionally threatening." Mikey knew that she needed to be accurate. "But he did speak to me."

"What did he say?"

"It made my blood run cold. He said in a low voice, like a growl, 'Now, you know. Now, you know. Now, you will know.' That was it."

"What happened next? Then what?"

"I looked away. I couldn't look at him. He was ugly and gross and scary. The nice clerk asked me if I was all right, if I knew that person, what was going on. He saw instantly that I was scared. I told him that that guy was stalking me, that he was a doctor who had just lost a big case, big money to my husband's—sorry, Eddie, I didn't know quite how to put it—law firm. We looked back up and Narcy was gone. The clerk said, 'I'm going to get my manager.' I told him it was too late. Her asked me if I was okay. I told him yes and no. He nodded. He asked if I wanted to finish my list, finish my shopping. I told him 'no, I'm pretty shook up right now.' I apologized for him having to put everything back up on the shelves. He said, 'No, ma'am, not a problem.' I asked him his name. It was Evans Renkins. I figured we might need it later on. He asked me if I wanted to sit down for a little bit, said that they'd put me in their office, asked me if I wanted a drink of water. I did giggle at that. I'm sure I sounded like a nervous fool. I told him that it was funny—a drink of plain old H2O in a place like this. He nodded and said, 'Yes, ma'am.' I told him I just wanted to get back here to our office. He asked me if I was okay to drive and I told him I thought I was. He walked me to my car. We looked around carefully to see if that bastard was anywhere around. No sign of him. Young Mr. Renkens waited and watched me until I drove out of the parking lot. I made sure I drove the speed limit and came straight back here. That's it."

Alph asked, "How you doing now?"

"Not so good." She began to leak tears again. Polly got her some tissues and patted her back. Cas was horrified. Patty was mad.

Eddie said, "Yes, that son of a bitch is stalking you. Damn! We need to lawyer this out and figure out how we're going to deal with it."

"Yes, I understand." Mikey was calm.

"So here are the options. One, do nothing now and watch and wait and see what happens next. That is unacceptable to me."

There was no objection.

"Two, go see the district attorney or call the cops."

Alph offered, "No, we haven't got enough meat on the bone yet. We know what's going on, but the powers that be need lots more ammunition and we are nowhere close on that yet."

"Three. Sue him and file for a restraining order."

Patty was sharp-tongued. "Fuck that. It takes way too long and they'll argue it's all a bunch of nothing and that Eddie and Mikey just hate Narcy and want to fuck with him. It could go on for months."

"Four, call his lawyer Don Richardson and tell him to get Narcy away from you for good or we will press charges and/or file a lawsuit."

Cas weighed in. "Please, if I may, how would that do any good? Richardson hates our guts and has just been publicly humiliated and the case is over. Formally, Don isn't even Narcy's counsel any longer. Why would he care or want to care...? I just don't see it."

Eddie nodded slowly, thoughtfully, taking it all in. "You know, I've got a dear friend, an old fraternity brother from Chapel Hill, one of my very few, all-time, long time best friends from New Iberia, Louisiana, at the Shadows on the Teche, who has witchcraft and voodoo coming out of his ears and ass. Despite the fact that he has killed it in the oil business over in Houston and is an investment guru, he ain't lost his old touch and contacts. His mother was a first lady of the Episcopal Church down there and also an honest to God white witch, a good witch who cast spells and made potions to combat and thwart evil doers. He comes by this particular skill set legitimately. Any takers?"

They looked at him as though he had suddenly arisen through a plume of sulfur and fire. He chuckled. "Okay, maybe later on that one...he once told me he had a gal that could give ovarian cancer to a man."

Mikey looked at him imploringly. "Eddie, now stop that. I know who you are talking about. Yes, he's amazing, but I'm not interested right now in long distance amazing. What can we do? You know Narcy is going to do something again. And it sure looks like I'm the bait, the bait for you." She shivered.

"Yes, that's most likely. But it appears that so far he picks his spots and that good amounts of time run between them. So we are going to do something. Yes, we are."

"What? What are we going to do?"

Eddie did not respond to Mikey. Instead he asked all to get back to work as best they could. He quietly but firmly admonished them to stay steady, to hold the line. He told Mikey he would be back with her in just a minute. He asked Polly to come back to his office. When the door was closed, he told Polly that this was just between him and her, that it was not to be revealed to anyone and that he would appreciate it if she would privately go to the small conference room across the way and call Narcy's hospital and get his home address. Polly cocked an eyebrow and asked, "Okay on the secret. And, Eddie, why?"

"Easy, Polly. We're going to send him some flowers on behalf of the grateful family of one of his well-treated patients. Thank you for getting this done. Now, please bring me that little bit of information once you have it. And ask Patty to come in and see me, please."

Patty rolled in. "So, what's the plan?" There was a slight Cheshire Cat smirk on her face. She knew her Mr. Terrell pretty good.

"This is on only a 'need to know' basis and you don't need to know. I'll let you know once and if I think it's prudent, okay?"

"Oh, Jesus. Here we go again. Got it. What you need from me?"

"Please call Curt Minor and Big Rise and tell them I'd like to meet at his drink house at 9 in the morning, to bring Kenny with them and also, please rummage through our cash box and bring me ten grand in old money in a paper bag. Tell them I'd appreciate it if they'd give this a heavy priority. I need this."

"Oh, shit! Are you gonna have Narcy popped?!"

"Certainly not. Just gonna get him some flowers."

Patty jeered, "Yeah, enough to drape his fucking big box coffin...Jesus...I'll get it done right away. I'll call you when the meet is set."

Eddie walked out with Patty, got Mikey, and they left for the day.

Once they had departed, Cas leaned over to Alph and Polly. "What do y'all think is going on?"

"Something that we all hope works," whispered Polly.

Alph added, "My money is on Eddie. Dear God, whip that horse home."

"When will we know what's going on?"

"Just between you and me, I hope never."

Patty had her back turned from them and was speaking very softly into the phone. They could not hear what she was saying. They all knew it was not for them to hear, whatever it was. They went back to work. Well, they tried to.

CHAPTER FORTY-SIX

EXECUTION

CHINESE TAKEOUT, REASONABLY greasy, really pretty good. That's the ticket.

"What you want? Come on, now. A little food and drink will help. You've had a shock. Let me help a little. You need some sustenance. It'll help you sleep. Please." He implored on the verge of begging.

Mikey thought on it for a few seconds, made a crinkle face, and then relented reluctantly.

"Alright. Alright. How about some egg rolls? Just a couple for me. No hot mustard, just sweet sauce. And I'll try to eat a little plain fried rice but you gotta help me eat it, okay? I just don't know how far I can get with this and you know I may puke it all up no matter what, sooner rather than later."

"I'm with you. I'll get some of the same. Really not too hungry either but a good drink or two will help, I think."

They pulled into a local, trustworthy joint on Peters Creek Parkway which had been there long enough to earn a reputation of No Four Pot cuisine (No dog, cat, rat or squirrel). Eddie ran in and ordered and paid and got back to car quickly. He knew he was babysitting Mikey and himself too.

Enough minutes later, a young Asian boy with shining, well-brushed blue-black hair underneath an impeccable, crisp, white pressman's paper hat and long white apron and white hospital pants and white T-shirt brought a white paper bag to the car.

Eddie gave his young, long-time buddy QinShi a twenty and clasped hands in front of his face in reverence and thanks and headed home.

Lynn Dee Drive on the little lake in the little trees was small and innocuous and inconsequential to the eye but it was their sanctuary.

Eddie cracked some white for her, gave her a full pour and noted gratefully she was at least thirsty. He gave himself a stiff complimentary bourbon and they sat and mostly did not speak and only with desultory effort, picked at their food. She asked for more wine and went to the bathroom. Eddie took that opportunity to retrieve from his bedside drawer a handy 1-milligram Ativan (better living through chemistry) and dropped the little tablet in her glass and swished it dissolved with his finger. She returned and swallowed vigorously. Soon, she was yawning and ready to crash. He gently took her to bed, tucked her in and rubbed her back until she snored. And then, he went back to their kitchen and had three more big busters. Later, after pleasantly tight, he went on to their bed and laid in and rested his hand on her hip, squeezed and washed away.

But before halfway into his brown water nightcaps, Patty called. It was a rifle-shot, four-word exchange. "Hey—9—Thanks—Night." The click did not count.

Eddie thought to himself, *Damn, boy, you are getting way long in the tooth for this kind of high stakes shit. Is this it? Can this be it? Lord, I hope so. Too many adventures!* His mind wandered back into the comfort of his softening, spreading medulla oblongata-like Silly Putty he played with as a kid but now so much better. He took another big pull and mulled everything he could come up with which was becoming a narrowing box canyon. He didn't mind. Tomorrow was coming and his ability to retrieve and comprehend and work it and move it was still there and would be anew. He was older and getting older still but he could go and he would. She counted on him. They counted on him. He counted on him. End of story. He fell asleep quickly. And then he got trampled and flayed.

That night, the dreams of the troubled and the drunk kicked his lame, cracked back door open and stomped on in. It was basically the hell game of Whac-A-Mole. It hard surged and hard sucked back; to describe any of it as ebb and flow was soft and pantywaist and weak. There was no comfort here in this litany of bad and worse options.

She had left him. She was gone. It was horrible. He twisted, tossed, contorted in his shallow, uncomfortable mind. She had run hellbent from the liquor store, run from that hideous, leering son of a bitch into the parking lot, shrieking, hysterical, lost in a paralyzing, limping fear. Eddie saw her but could not reach her. A car hit her. She folded over in slow motion. Her head cracked the asphalt. The car was not going fast but fast enough. Blood came out of her ears. Her face and arms turned an eerie, ghostly white. The driver jumped out and rushed to her. "You came out so fast. I am so sorry! I am so sorry! Oh, my God!!" The words came out in slow motion as through cotton. Eddie closed his eyes as tight as he might though his eyes were already closed and yet they were horrified wide open. The wail of EMS marked it was on its way.

They took Mikey to Wake Forest, sirens shrill screaming to the ER, off Interstate 40, down the Cloverdale Exit, past the Shell station to the left and up the rise where the scary, big red letters read blinking ER ER ER, to the great Level One Trauma Center. Eddie knew this. He was a medical malpractice guy. But there was no sense of hope. He was helpless and so was the girl he loved.

Eddie watched from above. He might as well have been in a vet's office. Useless except he was not allowed to offer his comfort. Dogs with euthanasia coming were allowed better. Though he did not have a dog any longer, he understood and was used to it. He had been for decades a spectator to the obscenity of horrible injury, of stripping death. There was an assembly, a clot of busying doctors hovering all over her. Dignity was being tossed out the window. Mikey was stripped, ripped and cut naked as the gurney rolled, no Victoria's Secrets here, as they and the mob looked for contusions and swellings and the warning signs of things that go big bump in the night. Her pubis and breasts might as well have been her knee caps: offensively bothersome but it was all quick and things were going so fast.

They rolled her in as if it was the last fourth turn of the World 600, coming on bumping, shoving, sliding, slamming, three abreast, speeding, efficiently. No check in, that would get done later, no need now, this was an urgent matter. They took her vitals, took her blood, poked away at her, rolled her over for a good look at her back, thumped her, listened to her, brought a portable X-ray machine in, both sides now, studied on her, checked her pupils over and over again with their pen lights and peered at the canals of her ears, hooked her up, ordered the administration of stimulants and medicines, a cascade of color coded lines of this and that flowing. They studied her vital signs while the machines in the psychedelic constant colors of an Etch A Sketch sublimely beeped and rang and buzzed, and the lines and graphs were above normal but they did not move much, only wavered and shook within tight ranges so they caucused about her and moved her, all dangling hooked up, to the ICU, and so, she went up three floors on the big, wide silver elevator and was taken by this gaggle of doctors into a smaller, more electronic room and was there looked over again with the thoroughness of a full body proctology exam and then, once the mechanics were done and only a nurse with Eve Arden glasses and a severe mien was left with her, she was still, very sublime and quiet, a quiet, lovely smile on her lips. She was comatose. He had lost her forever. He bit his lower lip until it bled. They told him it was no longer touch and go. They told him it was a significant traumatic brain injury. They told him only time would tell. They told him he could go; that they would let him know.

He felt she had become a shadow. He had become less.

And in his abject, groveling, terrified sorrowing, there then came a roulette wheel of things to consider, for after all she was gone.

He saw that he was so lonely. Friends, such as they were, offered suggestions for prospects for relief and for blind dates, for lunch and drinks and dinner. He sat in bars and approached strangers. He called old flames and lamely explained his absence and his present. He paid a dating service to arrange rendezvous with unsatisfactory, cloying candidates for assignations. He was repeatedly offered by many sympathetic mercy fucks to relieve his libido. He consulted with a life coach. He thought of just swearing women off. And all these choices and options spun about as a great wheel of fortune, none of which he wanted. He hated Pat Sajak and Vanna White. He wanted them to take their smug, ultra-tanned ways and getting longer teeth and leave but they would not until he woke up and that seemed to be a long way off. They kept spinning the damn wheel with their fake smiles and false interest. Despicable and cruel. He was in a trap. And then, he wasn't.

He, startled, woke up, shook the long train ride of nightmare away, though its messaging was imprinted on him. He sat up. Mikey was still there and he touched her leg softly and kissed her cheek. She did not stir. She purred in her sleep. Eddie slipped out of bed, showered and dressed. He dressed as Terrell the trial lawyer. He left her a note that she was to stay at home until he returned. He had a nine o'clock meeting and should be home by ten. She could call him whenever she wanted but she was to stay at home.

He drove to the office. Patty was already at her desk. No one else was there. She looked him over and handed him a thick, brown paper sack as she smoked. She also handed him a small piece of paper with an address on it that Polly had provided. He thanked her and asked her to thank Polly. It was very quiet in the office.

"It's close enough to nine. Go over to his place at East 17th now. They'll all be there. Whatever the fuck it is, good luck."

He drove into East Winston and parked at the front of the place. He went up the wooden steps and they were all there in the front room.

There were happy and curious greetings. They were glad to see one another but they also knew there was a task at close hand. Eddie cut to the chase quickly. He handed Curt the bag and the slip of paper.

"Thanks...I think." Curt smiled wanly. "Tell us about this."

"That's payment for the job I need done. If it's not enough, let me know. You know I play square."

Curt nodded. Rise and Kenny watched closely.

"So, what's the job?"

Eddie explained. There were no questions. The meeting ended in ten minutes. Curt would call Eddie once the job was complete.

Eddie went home and sat with Mikey. She asked what was going on. Eddie replied a terse "Later." They watched a lot of television and ate junk food and talked of everything but the day. Eddie was exhausted from his night's turning in the barrel of loss. Mikey was refreshed after a good night's sleep. Later in the day, they went and got takeout from the Diamond Back. It was a vacuous time on the surface, but they both knew it was not. They played their roles. Mikey knew she was on the verge of being avenged.

Curt asked Kenny and Rise to come along. They stayed in the car while Curt visited a hardware store and a cooking supply store and a Dollar Tree. Curt explained the plan in pieces as he came back from each place. They went back to Rise's and watched TV and drank a few beers and smoked a little dope. The time passed. They were mellow and cocked ready too. As dusk came on, they moved.

They drove east on Interstate 40 and took the airport exit, then wheeled north. They winded about past Oak Ridge Academy, a small military school, and went up into the sparse neighborhoods behind it. They found Narcy's place. It was a nice enough little white cottage surrounded by shrubbery that had long ago longed for pruning. It sat back in a grove of hardwood trees. The nearest streetlight was a block down the street.

They parked in the shadows and watched and waited. It wouldn't take long. They had been told that Narcy was fat, slow and consumed with himself and thus distracted and oblivious. They had been told too that his eternal sidekick, the sycophant troll named Pirright, aka The Abacus, would probably be in the vicinity.

As dusk came on, a car pulled into Narcy's driveway next to the cottage. The troll got out, carrying two bottles of something and went without knocking through the door on the side porch.

The stakeout knew that time had to pass for the imbibing to proceed to effect. They discussed how they would next proceed.

Ninety minutes later, they, all wearing black clothing and shoes, put on their black balaclavas and thin black cotton gloves. They slipped from the car and warily approached the side door of the cottage. They carried no guns.

They stood to the side in the bushes. Kenny tossed a handful of rattling, fallen pecans at the door. They waited. Soon enough, the Abacus, the eternal errand boy, opened the door and peered out. The bright porch light lessened his range of view. Kenny power snatched him outside and cuffed his mouth with his large paw. Abacus squirmed but made only quiet grunts of resistance. His mouth was wrapped in tight duct tape and his wrists and ankles were zip tied. His eyes bulged in fear. He was pulled into the shrubbery and flipped over onto his stomach. His whimpers were virtually soundless. A swift kick to his ribs silenced those imprecations. No words were spoken. No words were ever spoken. Kenny stood over him with a firm, light foot on his back. Rise and Curt flanked the concrete slab of the side porch.

They waited. Dr. Seamus Narcy soon enough came to the door, called for Robert and receiving no response, stepped out onto the porch, looking about and again called for his minion. As he searched and called, they took him hard down onto the gravel driveway. Rise pinned his arms and Curt taped his mouth. Rise sat on him. He struggled but his obesity outweighed his desire. They zip tied his ankles and too, zip tied his left hand to his belt at the small of his back. They left his right hand free.

Curt then wrestled a thin black mitten onto Narcy's right hand and pulled his arm straight out beyond Narcy's trunk. Rise held him close. Curt pulled a stainless steel meat pounder from his pants pocket and struck hard at Narcy's hand repeatedly. The sound of the blows were those of dry, thin chicken bones cracking and shattering. Narcy moaned softly. Curt kept hitting. Curt then stopped hitting.

They knifed the zip ties off Narcy and Abacus. They pulled the mitten off Narcy's right hand. It revealed a bloody, broken pulp. Both men lay still in their shock and pain. Curt put the meat pounder back in his pocket. The assailants moved to their car and drove away.

And thus did Dr. Seamus Narcy find his last true calling. He became a surgical consultant and nothing more.

CHAPTER FORTY-SEVEN

GOTTA KEEP MOVING

BACK IN WINSTON, Curt called Eddie. Again, the communication was brief and terse and kindly.

"It's done. All good."

"Thanks. You need anything?"

"No, we got plenty. Thanks."

"Come see me in a month or so. Just wander in."

"I will. Appreciate the business. Glad we could help."

"Thank you."

Eddie went to Mikey and told her she was safe now. Mikey knew she need not ask how this state of affairs had come to pass. She thanked him. She hugged him and thanked him some more and he hugged her and kissed her and was still so taken with her.

"Eddie, there will always be something, won't there?"

"Probably."

She nodded.

"Well, should we go out for dinner? It's late but I expect we can find some place."

"Yes, let's."

And again, their allegedly normal life and all its lights came back on.

EPILOGUE

A FEW DAYS AFTER **Dr. Narcy** was neutered, Eddie went with Mikey to the liquor and grocery stores and they gathered up all of the stuff, the booze and beer that had been listed by law enforcement as being onboard the doctors' party barge when it slashed through the little canoe and drowned the young man from Mississippi. The boaters were coming from a bar and party spot on the far south edge of the lake named 'The Party Cabin' but was universally known by all as 'The Lake Loose'. Eddie loved the name for obvious reasons.

At the liquor store out on Country Club, Mikey sought out Evans Renkins and introduced Eddie to him. Eddie thanked him for his kind help and told him it had been a tough time for Mikey.

Renkins asked, "How are things going now? Y'all alright?"

"Oh yes. Yes, it is now. All quiet on the western front, as they say." Eddie winked at Evans Renkins. Renkins nodded. No need for any more conversation than that.

They made their substantial purchases which filled all of three booze boxes and with Renkins help, hauled them out to be loaded in Eddie's car.

Renkins mused. "I recall the situation now. This young lady told me what it was about. Good luck with it. From where I'm sizing it, I believe those docs have a very big problem."

Eddie grinned and agreed with him and thanked him again and the couple drove away.

A few months later, the case settled in a voluntary, pre-discovery initiating mediation for 1.25 million dollars.

The bachelorette and bride-to-be fiasco was filed and served on the bar as a wrongful death and dram shop action. The hit and run driver, who was a well-known 'celebrity' bartender employee was jailed, charged with vehicular hit and run homicide and other serious, top grade felonies and even just initial and cursory investigation revealed a lengthy record of drug and alcohol-related charges attached to his loose-lived life's efforts.

As discovery proceeded, it came to light that the owners of the bar had destroyed the security camera tapes of the evening in question and that the jailed driver had been observed by numerous witnesses at the bar taking numerous shots while on shift and also dancing manically by himself. One of the bar's owners admitted that they were planning on firing the bartender because he often kept coming to work drunk or stoned.

There was a 3 million dollar liability policy in place. Eddie demanded all of it.

At mediation, six weeks before trial, defense counsel offered half of the policy and then threw out the anchor. The carrier had brought a senior adjuster in from Chicago. The guy was a purposeful, obdurate horses ass. The mediator was frustrated and, in private, gave Eddie the green light to rip the big city boy a new one.

When they all gathered for the formality of conclusion, Eddie thanked them all for their time, cussed the adjuster out up one side and down the other and told them he would see them in the courthouse. Alph giggled and warned the defense, "Oh Hell boys, all you've done is kicked at a hornet's nest." The mediator laughed and laughed. He'd done his best but just got totally stonewalled. And too, he'd gotten to watch Eddie torch the asshole.

As was his habit, Eddie always went a week before trial to Joseph A. Banks and bought a new, dark suit. And so he did. And after it had been fitted and alterations had begun, his cell rang. It was the lead defense counsel on the line. The fellow said there were two more depositions the insurance company wanted taken. Eddie, not at all surprised by this, said "Sure. Line 'em up."

There was a pause and then the defense lawyer laughed and said, "Eddie. I'm just kidding. You can have the full policy. The 3 million is yours. The case is over. You win. Aren't you pleased?"

Eddie said nothing and then grumbled. "Wish you'd called yesterday."

"Why just yesterday?"

"...Cause I just spent $400 bucks this afternoon buying a new suit for trial..."

The Applebee's case, another dram shop matter, was clear cut. Defendant managers and employees when deposed, threw in the towel early and often and happily too with the approval of a cooperative defense counsel. They were not mendacious and noted many, many deviations from proper and safe alcohol service.

Cas was thorough and precise and Alph was thrilled for her and for their firm. Cas had the 'it', the comfortable manner and ways of a seasoned trial lawyer. The employees answered her questions straightforwardly and with no evasion or ducking.

Their client had been badly injured and his injuries were seriously and permanently debilitating. Their client's attending trauma surgeon from Wake Forest, during his deposition, was meticulous and complete in laying out the extent and scope of his patient's injuries and their permanence. That he was tall, movie star handsome and articulate in the most normal and comprehensive of ways made for a compelling presentation of trauma medicine.

When Eddie read over her deposition transcripts from the case, he could easily see that Alph's tutelage combined with Cas' innate talents were creating a rising star. And when he read the deposition of the trauma surgeon, he could not help but think of Dr. R. Adams Cowley and the marvelous, (one of Eddie's most favored books) SHOCK TRAUMA by Franklin and Doelp. Cowley was considered to be 'the Father of Trauma Medicine' in the country and was a pioneer across the field.

(Many say that Paddy Chayefsky's film 'The Hospital' starring George C. Scott as Dr. Herb Bock is modeled after the often mercurial and erratic Cowley)

Once discovery was completed, it was agreed by all that a high-low arrangement was in order. It was decided that the case should be arbitrated and the ranges were set at 2 and 6 million dollars. Liability was to be admitted. The arbitrator did not know the figures. After presentations and his deliberations, the arbitrator awarded 3.75 Million.

And of course, the cases kept coming in the door. And the wheels kept turning.

Dr. Narcy was never seen nor heard from again.

And Eddie and Mikey stayed the course.

A NOTE FROM
THE AUTHOR

Dear Readers,

If you have gotten this far, to this little page, then you know that Kermit King and I were mightily successful with our efforts in the case named as CAMERON. It is a true depiction of an actual case and trial. Of course, most names have been changed but the work leading up to the trial and the action of the trial itself are absolutely faithful to the facts. And too, much of the aftermath is true as well.

It was a crowning achievement and accomplished in spite of very daunting odds. We, in truth, kicked their ass.

And I wanted to write about it because it was exciting and dramatic and also to pay tribute to my dear friend and mentor, Kermit King. I wanted to let him read and see how remarkable he was 'in action'.

I write this little end piece in mid-January of 2023. I am hopeful that SLIM AND NONE, the third book in the Eddie Terrell Trilogy, will be brought out into the public domain soon. I turned the final manuscript over to the editors on February 8th, 2022. Covid has slowed us a bit but we are re-energizing quickly.

On March 19th of 2022, Kermit, after a fall, died. I along with a legion of friends and family and admirers were and are heartbroken. I think of him

every day, always in appreciation. He was my great mentor, my great teacher.

I have always thought that he had the biggest and best brain of any trial lawyer I have ever encountered in my 45 years of trial practice. And since that is my fervent belief, I also believe that some way, somehow, Kermit will find the path to the story of CAMERON and his magnificent role in its unfolding.

Kermit was the Best.

www.ingramcontent.com/pod-product-compliance
Lightning Source LLC
Chambersburg PA
CBHW061630190726
48289CB00006B/1545

9 781732 906648